Firefight

Also by Chris Ryan

Non-fiction
The One That Got Away
Chris Ryan's SAS Fitness Book
Chris Ryan's Ultimate Survival Guide

Fiction
Stand By, Stand By
Zero Option
The Kremlin Device
Tenth Man Down
The Hit List
The Watchman
Land of Fire
Greed
The Increment
Blackout
Ultimate Weapon
Strike Back

In the Alpha Force Series
Survival
Rat-Catcher
Desert Pursuit
Hostage
Red Centre
Hunted
Black Gold
Blood Money
Fault Line
Untouchable

In the Code Red Series
Flash Flood
Wildfire
Outbreak

CHRIS RYAN
Firefight

CENTURY · LONDON

Published by Century 2008

2 4 6 8 10 9 7 5 3 1

First published in Great Britain in 2008 by
Century
Random House, 20 Vauxhall Bridge Road,
London SW1V 2SA

www.randomhouse.co.uk

Addresses for companies within The Random House Group Limited can be found at:
www.randomhouse.co.uk

The Random House Group Limited Reg. No. 954009

A CIP catalogue record for this book
is available from the British Library

ISBN 9781846053290 (Hardback edition)
ISBN 9781846053306 (Trade paperback edition)

The Random House Group Limited supports The Forest Stewardship
Council (FSC), the leading international forest certification organisation. All our
titles that are printed on Greenpeace approved FSC certified paper carry the FSC logo. Our
paper procurement policy can be found at www.rbooks.co.uk/environment

Typeset in Bembo by Palimpsest Book Production Limited, Grangemouth, Stirlingshire
Printed in the UK by CPI Mackays, Chatham ME5 8TD

ACKNOWLEDGEMENTS

To my agent Barbara Levy, editor Mark Booth, Charlotte Haycock, Charlotte Bush and the rest of the team at Century

'I do not wish to kill or be killed, but I can foresee circumstances in which both these things would be by me unavoidable.'

– *A Plea for Captain John Brown*, Henry David Thoreau

PROLOGUE

Rome, Italy. Mid-December. 17.00 hours.
Rain fell in the darkness outside the Moschea di Roma, Rome's only mosque; but despite the cold drizzle outside, inside Abdul-Qahhar felt warm. There were many men here for evening prayer, filling the magnificent interior of the mosque with the heat of their bodies and the comforting sounds of their chants as they knelt towards Mecca. And as prayers came to an end, they stood up and shook hands with one another, smiles on their faces as they chatted with exquisite politeness under the huge, ornate, white dome of the mosque.

'I invite you to join us for tea,' said the man with whom Abdul-Qahhar had enjoyed a number of conversations in the past couple of weeks.

'Thank you,' Abdul-Qahhar replied. 'But tonight I think I will just go home. *Allahu Akbar.*'

The man shrugged his shoulders, but in a friendly manner. '*Allahu Akbar,*' he replied in the traditional way, before smiling and turning to another group of friends who had congregated nearby.

Abdul-Qahhar had not been in Rome long. When he arrived he was just another foreign student at the university and barely knew anybody; but the first thing he did was hunt out the mosque, and soon he had been embraced by the arms of that community. Like-minded people in a strange land.

1

Prayer was important to Abdul-Qahhar. It refreshed him. So much so that he found he did not mind the rain as he stepped out of the mosque and down the steps. It was not far to his little bedsit, which he had chosen because it was so close to the mosque, and he arrived there quickly – wet, but not disconsolate. He put his key to the door of the apartment block, but as he did so it opened anyway, as the elderly lady who lived two floors below him exited.

'*Buona sera*,' he said with a smile, doing his best to pronounce the unfamiliar words in an understandable way.

The old lady stared aggressively at him, then brushed past, mumbling to herself. She had never been friendly, at least not to him. It was common enough for people to be like that. Abdul-Qahhar might be wearing fashionable Italian jeans, but no amount of denim could hide the colour of his skin, and there were many people, especially in these difficult times, who saw no more than that. It made some of his fellow countrymen angry, but Abdul-Qahhar wasn't an angry kind of person. Be polite to everyone, that was his motto. Be polite to everyone, and they will soon learn that they have nothing to fear from you.

'*Buon Natale*,' he called after her. 'Happy Christmas.' Of course, Christmas meant nothing to him, but he understood its importance, especially to the inhabitants of Rome, living as they were in the shadow of the Vatican. As Christmas was just around the corner, he saw no reason to refrain from offering festive greetings to the Italians he encountered in his day-to-day life. Normally they seemed pleasantly surprised.

The old lady did not turn back, however, so Abdul-Qahhar closed the door behind him and climbed the stairs, not bothering to hit the button that illuminated the time-controlled overhead light, because he knew it didn't work. Instead he groped in the darkness, his hand sliding firmly up the wooden banister. On the second floor was the smell of cooking; on the fifth floor he heard the ever-present radio playing Christmas music. Abdul-Qahhar's apartment was on the top floor, and up here it was silent.

The bedsit was sparsely furnished, but his needs were few. A bed, a desk, a bookshelf and a small hob for preparing food. He stripped out of his wet clothes and placed them on the enormous, elderly radiator that heated the entire apartment surprisingly effectively, then went to his meagre closet and pulled out some dry jeans and a T-shirt. He found it strange wearing these Western clothes instead of the more comfortable dishdash, but he could not wear the all-in-one Arabic garment in the streets of Rome, or any other Western city for that matter, and he knew he had to get used to a different style of dress. He fixed himself something to eat, then sat cross-legged on his bed and immersed himself in his battered, treasured copy of the Koran. He should really be studying, but sometimes he hankered after the nannying effect the holy book had on him, and this was one of those times.

As his eyes scanned from right to left and he absorbed the poetry of the text, Abdul-Qahhar lost track of time. When finally he looked at the small clock on his bedside table, he was amazed to see that it was nearly midnight. Regretfully, he closed the book, placed it on his little book-shelf, and went to the sink to fetch himself a glass of water.

He stopped. There was a noise from somewhere. From outside. But he was on the top of the building, eight floors up. It must have been just a bird, or perhaps the rain. Walking to the window he pulled back the frayed curtains, but saw nothing other than the rooftop of the opposite apartment block and the clouds scudding in front of the silvery crescent moon. He drew the curtain again and put the noise from his mind. Sometimes the pipes could make strange sounds in these old buildings, sounds that could be creepy in the middle of the night. That was it. The pipes. He returned to the sink, turned on the tap, filled his glass and sipped it thoughtfully.

Abdul-Qahhar was halfway back to his bed when there was another noise. He turned his head quickly towards the door. It seemed to have come from outside, in the corridor, and this time round there was no mistaking it: it was no bird; it wasn't the rain; it didn't sound like the pipes. It sounded to him like there was someone there, outside his apartment.

The blood ran cold in his veins.

'*Chi è?*' he called. And then, because he was unsure of his Italian, he lapsed into English, a language with which he was more confident and which was more widely understood than his native Arabic. 'Who's there?'

There was a pause, a silence. And then, with the sudden force of a thunderclap, they came at him from two sides.

The door burst open and Abdul-Qahhar just had time to see three men, dressed in black and wearing dark balaclavas, burst in before the window shattered and another two landed only feet away from him. All five men brandished ugly-looking weaponry and the guns were pointed his way.

'Hit the floor!' one of them shouted in a muffled American accent. 'Hit the fucking floor. *Now!*'

Abdul-Qahhar felt a harsh blow on the back of his knee and collapsed, jelly-legged, to the floor.

'Hands behind your back,' the American voice instructed as the barrel of a gun was placed against his head. He did as he was told, and as his wrists were roughly handcuffed with what felt like strips of plastic, a warm, moist sensation spread through the cloth of his jeans.

'He's pissed himself,' a terse voice said – an English voice this time, one of the men who had come through the window. There was no distaste in the way he said it, just a cold, clinical tone of observation. Certainly he didn't sound surprised.

4

'Hood him,' the American instructed and instantly a piece of course material was forced over Abdul-Qahhar's head, then tied uncomfortably round his neck; he could breathe, but only just.

Too scared to speak, he was manhandled to his feet and pushed forward, through the door of his flat and down the steps. None of the men said a word as he was rushed down the seemingly endless flight of stairs and out into the pouring rain. Above the patter of the raindrops on the ground, he heard another noise. It was the engine of a vehicle, and it was being revved. Abdul-Qahhar heard the sound of doors opening, and without ceremony he was bundled into the back and pushed over. He shouted out in Arabic as his head hit the metal floor.

'Shut the fuck up!' a voice said, as the doors slammed shut and the vehicle jolted into movement.

The urine-soaked patch of his jeans was cold and clammy now; but his head was hot as he took deep breaths in an attempt both to calm himself down and swallow big gulps of precious oxygen. In his mind he saw the guns of his abductors, and could still feel that patch on his head where the barrel of the rifle had been pressed. He closed his eyes in the darkness of his hood and started to mutter the prayers that he had recited in the mosque only a short time ago. '*Allahu Akbar min kulli shay. Allahu Akbar min kulli shay.*' But in the middle of his private chant, he spluttered as a heavily booted foot kicked him hard in the stomach.

'Quiet!' a voice barked and Abdul-Qahhar did as he was told. Perhaps soon, he thought to himself, he would wake up; perhaps soon he would find himself on his bed, having nodded off over the Koran; perhaps soon the nightmare would end.

In the darkness, time had no meaning. Abdul-Qahhar could not have said how long it was before the vehicle came to a halt and he was manhandled out of the rear

5

doors. Outside the rain had stopped, but it seemed to be incredibly windy and there was a loud mechanical noise that he could not quite place.

'Take his hood off!' a voice shouted. The material was untied and the hood pulled roughly from his head. Abdul-Qahhar scrunched his eyes up painfully as a bright light shone directly in his face. As he gradually opened his eyes, however, he saw what was making the noise and the wind: an enormous helicopter, preparing for take-off.

One of the balaclava'd men approached him with his gun. 'We can do this one of two ways,' he screamed above the noise of the helicopter. 'You come quietly and get on the chopper without a struggle; or we do it the painful way.'

Abdul-Qahhar felt his body start to shake. 'Please,' he begged, 'I have a great fear of flying. Please, there is a terrible mistake. I don't know who you are, or what you think I've done, but there really has been the most terrible mis –.'

He was cut short as the butt of a rifle struck him hard in the pit of his stomach. He bent double in pain, but as he did so he was dragged towards the helicopter. The rotating blades sounded louder, an enormous, ear-filling whine, and the force of the wind almost threatened to blow him over. As a renewed surge of panic overcame him, he started to struggle. 'Please!' he yelled. 'There has been a mistake!' And almost as though he had lost control of his own actions, he made to run away from the group of armed figures who were escorting him to the chopper.

He didn't get far. One of his captors grabbed him hard by the throat; another forced the hood over his head again. 'No!' Abdul-Qahhar shouted. 'Not that! Please, I will come with you!' But even as he spoke, the hood was tied around his neck once more and he felt himself being dragged closer to the helicopter.

He was on a ramp now and the noise of the rotors

seemed to fill all his senses. It was too much: his fear of flying seemed to pulse through every vein, and with a great and terrified roar he made one last, desperate attempt to break free from his captors.

It was a vain move. Instantly he felt the sickening crunch of hard metal against his head. A moment of dizziness, of nausea, before he fell hard to the ground, mercifully un-conscious, at least for a little while.

When he awoke, the hood had been removed from his head. His skull was pounding and he felt sick. He had no way of knowing how long he had been out cold, but he could tell that they were airborne and he found himself unable to move through terror. He tried to speak, but the words would not come out of his mouth, which was sand-paper-dry. As he looked up, he saw the five men still there with him, only now they had taken off their balaclavas. Through the gloom and his fear, however, he found it impossible to tell one face from the other.

After a while, the popping in his ears and a slight lurch in his stomach told him that they were losing altitude. 'What is happening?' he croaked.

But nobody answered – they just kept their weapons trained on him.

Minutes later they landed. 'Welcome to Poland,' a gruff voice said.

'Poland?' he gasped. 'What do you mean? I promise you, this is a mistake.'

Nobody answered. Instead, Abdul-Qahhar was manhan-dled to his feet and roughly escorted off the chopper. There was snow outside. The cold air hit his lungs like an elec-tric shock, and the rotors of the chopper whipped up the powdery snow into a blizzard that chapped his face harshly and blinded him. His captors seemed to know where they were going, however. They pulled him away from the chopper and towards a large mound of earth, covered in thick snow, but with a concrete opening in the side. There was a door, which was open and out of which came a flood of yellow light. Abdul-Qahhar was pushed through that opening, down a flight of steps and along a long, dimly lit underground corridor.

The room to which he was taken was icy cold and contained nothing other than a hard metal chair firmly bolted to the ground and a large tinted window in one of the grey concrete walls. Abdul-Qahhar's handcuffs were removed, then he was thrown into the chair; a new set of sturdier cuffs strapped his arms down, before his legs were also fastened to his chair. Without a word, his captors left the room; he heard them lock the door behind him.

'Let me go!' he shouted. 'Please! Let me go! I'm just a student. You've got the wrong person.' He felt a tear ooze down his face as his voice echoed off the concrete walls. No one answered his call.

It was freezing, and soon his teeth were chattering and his limbs shaking.

'Help me!' he shouted. And then, more feebly, in a voice that no one would have heard, even if they were listening: 'Help me. I'm so cold. Please, help me.'

Time passed. Minutes, hours, he didn't know. Abdul-Qahhar had never realised he could be so cold; all he could do was try to master it, to persuade himself that everything was going to be all right. 'You have done nothing wrong,' he repeated to himself. 'Believe you have done nothing wrong and they will believe it too. *It is a mistake.*

'*I have done nothing wrong.*

'*It is a mistake.*'

He felt himself falling asleep, as though his body were shutting down.

'*I have done nothing wrong.*

'*It is a mistake.*'

8

The door burst open and two men entered. Abdul-Qahhar was relieved to see they were not carrying guns, but his relief was short-lived as one of them approached him, lifted his head by the chin and struck him hard across the face.

'You have information we need,' the man said. He had a thick mop of blonde hair and his accent was English. 'You are going to tell us everything.'

'I promise you,' Abdul-Qahhar begged, 'I do not know what you mean.'

The Englishman sneered at him and stepped aside to allow the second man to approach. He had a shiny, shaved head and a thin, aquiline nose and when he spoke it was with an American accent. 'You realise,' he said, in little more than a whisper, 'that you are not on US or British soil. The usual laws guaranteeing the safety of interrogated prisoners do not apply here.'

'Please –,' Abdul-Qahhar breathed.

The American stepped back and turned around so that he was facing away from the prisoner. 'I'm going to tell you one thing before we start,' he announced, a bit louder now. 'Not a threat, just a statement of fact.' He turned back to look at him. His face was serious and one eyebrow was raised. 'If you don't tell me what I want to know, I promise you, you're gonna think Guantánamo is a fucking vacation camp.'

Abdul-Qahhar stared fearfully back at him. 'Guantánamo?' he whispered. 'I'm not a terrorist.'

His interrogators didn't even blink. 'We'll be back when you're ready to speak,' the American said, and the two of them walked briskly out.

'I'm not a terrorist!' Abdul-Qahhar shouted after them. 'You just think that because of the colour of my skin. *I'm not a terrorist!*'

Yet again, his voice echoed around the empty concrete room. Abdul-Qahhar saw his breath billowing in the icy air, and he allowed his head to fall on to his chest, his body trembling even more violently than before.

He was awoken from his cold-induced stupor by water, a bucket of the stuff being thrown over him. His body temperature was so low that he couldn't tell how hot it really was, but to him it felt boiling. He screamed. Then he felt cold again.

The two men were back. They were standing in front of him.

'Please,' he shivered. 'Don't hurt me. *Please.*'

'You have information that we need,' the American insisted.

'I do not know what you are talking about. I promise you, I do not know. If I knew, I would tell you.'

'Does the name Faisal Ahmed mean anything to you?'

Abdul-Qahhar blinked. Now more than ever he needed to sound convincing.

'I have never heard that name in my entire life. I swear to you.' His wet clothes stuck to his skin.

The two men glanced at each other and something seemed to pass between them. Then the American looked over at the tinted dark window and nodded. 'Bring them in,' he called.

Moments later, the door opened again. Two more men walked in, both wearing blue overcoats. One of them was pushing a steel trolley, the other had a shiny metal drip stand. They stopped just by Abdul-Qahhar's chair, then both of them pulled on a pair of surgical gloves and wrapped cloth masks around their faces.

One of the masked men spoke. 'You sure you don't want to take him to the waterboarding room?'

'No need,' the American replied. 'We'll have this guy talking in no time.'

Abdul-Qahhar started to shake more violently as he

watched one of them hand a plastic bag full of colourless liquid to the drip stand. It was the second man, however, who spoke to him.

'I'm going to insert a needle for the drip,' he said, his voice muffled slightly by the mask. 'It will hurt less if you do not struggle.'

Abdul-Qahhar felt his eyes bulging as the medic approached with a small needle. He started banging his restrained arms up and down against the chair, but it made no difference to the medic. He placed one gloved hand on the prisoner's arm and slowly slid the needle into one of the plump veins halfway up. Abdul-Qahhar gasped. The medic attached a long plastic tube to the pouch of liquid suspended from the drip stand, then turned and undid a small screw-top cap at the end of the needle hanging limply from Abdul-Qahhar's arm. A jet of blood spurted momentarily on to the concrete floor, but the medic soon had the drip tube attached. He turned to the interrogators. 'It's ready,' he said.

The American nodded, then looked blankly at Abdul-Qahhar. 'SP-17,' he said cryptically. 'Developed by the KGB. The most effective truth serum we have at our disposal. Of course, if you still refuse to talk, then we have other means of extracting the information we want.'

He paused, as though waiting for that to sink in, then bent over and placed his face only inches away from his captive. 'It's up to you what method you choose, but let me tell you: by the time we've finished with you, you're gonna be singing like a fucking canary.'

Abdul-Qahhar closed his eyes.

It is a mistake.

I have done nothing wrong.

I *have* to believe that.

'Please,' he whispered. 'I have nothing to hide. If you would only tell me what this is all about, maybe I could be of some assistance to you—'

But the American had already stepped away and nodded at the medic, who turned a valve on the drip tube. Abdul-Qahhar felt something cold rush into the vein in his arm.

There was silence in the room. Abdul-Qahhar, feeling his teeth chattering again, clenched them together to stop it happening. After a minute or so, however, he released them. It suddenly seemed as though the room was not so cold. There was warmth, or maybe it was just him. The light didn't seem so harsh; it was softer, warmer. He glanced at the needle in his arm, then smiled as he understood what was happening. It was the drugs. The drugs were making him feel better. Maybe, he thought to himself, this was what Westerners felt like when they drank alcohol.

'I'm going to ask you again,' the interrogator's voice said. 'Does the name Faisal Ahmed mean anything to you?'

'It means nothing,' he replied, drowsily.

The American turned to the medic. 'Increase the dose,' he instructed. The medic turned the valve once more and again they waited. The warmth increased, and the wooziness.

He heard the American's voice. 'You have information about a terrorist strike.'

Abdul-Qahhar shook his head.

A pause. Lights seemed to dance around the room.

'You have information about a terrorist strike,' the American repeated, relentlessly.

Again he shook his head. He felt comfortable for the first time in hours.

A minute passed.

'You have information about a terrorist strike. You can tell me about it now or you can tell me about it later. One way or another, though, you *will* tell me about it.'

And all of a sudden, Abdul-Qahhar smiled. There seemed to be no reason to hide it any more. No reason to pretend – to himself or anyone else – that he did not know what they were talking about. They were not going to hurt him.

'I'm going to ask you one more time. Does the name Faisal Ahmed mean anything to you?'

Of course it meant something to him. Faisal Ahmed – the men at the mosque had barely spoken of anyone else. Faisal Ahmed, the warrior, they had called him.

Slowly, Abdul-Qahhar nodded his head.

The two men looked at each other and the American stepped back. Abdul-Qahhar noticed how the light seemed to reflect off his bald head. It transfixed him and he was only woken from his brief reverie when the Englishman spoke.

'Good,' he said. 'Well done, Abdul-Qahhar. You're doing the right thing. Now listen to me carefully. We know he's planning something big. All you have to do is tell me when and where. As soon as we have that information, you can go home.'

Abdul-Qahhar felt his head nodding. 'I would like to go home,' he said drowsily.

'Then tell me,' the Englishman insisted. 'When and where?'

He had a pleasant face, this man. When he smiled, there were creases on his cheek. Perhaps, once he had told them all he knew, they would let Abdul-Qahhar sleep.

And so he spoke in a clear voice, or as clear a voice as he could manage, like an eager child wanting to impress a teacher.

'Three weeks,' he announced. 'Three weeks. London.'

ONE

They were in the toy department. A long line of children snaked around the whole floor, waiting patiently. His daughter Anna looked longingly at the sign. 'Visit Father Christmas in his grotto,' *it read in bright, festive colours.* 'A present for every child.'

'Can I go and see Father Christmas, Daddy?' Anna asked. 'Please?'

She tugged on his hand and looked up at him with those wide, appealing eyes. In other children, an expression like that could be put on, but not with Anna. She was six years old and wore her emotions plainly on her face. She was desperate to see Father Christmas and she so rarely asked for things. She was not brash or confident. It meant she was picked on at school sometimes, but she seemed to deal with it in her kind, sad little way.

He looked at the line of children. It would take an hour to reach Father Christmas, maybe more. A quick glance at his watch told him they didn't have time — the train back down to Hereford left in forty minutes, and they still had to struggle across London through the Saturday afternoon Christmas shoppers. He glanced at his wife, who shook her head imperceptibly.

He bent down to look at her face to face. 'I'm sorry, sweetheart,' he said. 'We haven't got enough time. Another day, hey?'

Anna's lip wobbled and she gazed at the floor. He knew what she was thinking, at least he thought he did. You always say that, Daddy. You always say you haven't got enough time. You always say another day.

But she didn't say anything. Obedient. Good as gold. Like always.

15

'Come on, love,' he said, doing his best to sound bright. He took her little hand in his and together the family of three wove their way through the crowds. Anna kept looking back and gazing at the line of luckier children, and each time she did he experienced that little surge of guilt that only a parent can feel.

He put his hand on Laura's shoulder. 'You go on,' he told her. 'I'll meet you downstairs, by the entrance.'

His wife looked at him with a mixture of suspicion and amusement. 'What are you doing, Will?'

He avoided the question. 'I'll meet you downstairs,' he said, before lightly touching Anna's hair. 'Stay close to Mum,' he warned.

Still smiling, Laura led Anna off down the ornate escalators. He watched her disappear before turning back into the toy department.

He knew what he wanted. Anna's eyes had lingered over an enormous fluffy dog, as soft as snow with a big brown ribbon. It was expensive – even Anna could tell that, he thought. Certainly it was too expensive to be bought on a whim with a Regiment salary, but what the hell – he spent half his life in the most far-flung shit holes of the world. Why shouldn't he treat his little girl now and then? He grabbed the toy and headed to a till.

As he handed over his credit card he heard the explosion.

There was a momentary silence all around him, and then everyone started to panic. The line of children dissolved into a mass of worried faces, and from the corner of his eye he saw two security guards rushing towards the escalators. He dropped the cuddly toy and didn't bother to grab his card back from the cashier. Instead, he ran through the crowds, ignoring the shouts of the couple of people he pushed out of the way with his impressive bulk. He reached the escalator before the panicked crowds could swarm towards it, and charged down several steps at a time, his heart thumping.

The pungent department store smell of perfume hit him as he charged for the exit, his eyes darting around, trying to get a glimpse of his wife and daughter. But he couldn't see them; all he saw were frightened faces. And as he grew closer to the doors, he saw other things too, things that would have turned the stomach

16

of a civilian, but which barely penetrated his emotional shell. He saw a woman with a chunk of shrapnel embedded in her cheek. Her body was shaking with shock, and a woman next to her was screaming at the sight. He saw a man whose white shirt was soaked red and who fell to the ground as he passed.

But he didn't see his family. Not until he reached the door.

They were lying on the floor, Laura's body draped over Anna, as though she were trying to shield her from something. And around them, seeping outwards, was a pool of blood.

He had seen hundreds of dead bodies in his time. Hundreds of mutilated corpses. He had seen children gasp their last breath, women garrotted. He had seen men die as a result of his own bullets.

But never anything like this. The scene sliced through him like a cold knife.

'NO!' he roared as he launched himself towards them.

A security guard stepped in his way. 'Stay away, sir,' the man instructed, but nothing was going to stop him. He punched the guard squarely in the jaw, then threw himself down to his family. He felt his trousers soak through with their blood and he touched his trembling hands first to his daughter's neck, then to his wife's.

Nothing. No pulse. Their faces had the deathly pallor that he recognised so well.

'Wake up!' he shouted. 'Wake up!' His brain refused to process the information that it had been so clearly given. He refused to accept that they were dead. He grabbed his daughter's face in his hands and bent down to give her the kiss of life. As he did so, he felt himself being grabbed from behind. The colleagues of the guard he had floored – three of them – were on him, pulling him back. He tried to struggle, but somehow he felt as though his strength had been sapped, so he allowed himself to be pulled away.

The air was filled with screams and with the jolly sound of Christmas music being piped around the store. And then there was shouting. A man's voice, hoarse and desperate. He realised it was his own.

'My family!' he bellowed. 'It's my family! Let me see them. YOU HAVE TO LET ME HELP MY FAMILY! . . .'

'YOU HAVE TO LET ME HELP MY FAMILY!'

Will Jackson awoke with a start, surprised by the sound of his own voice. Sweat poured from his body, but he was cold. He looked around, expecting to see his wife and daughter there, then the brutal reality hit him, as it had done every morning for the past two years. His wife and daughter were not there. They were lying in a churchyard on the outskirts of Hereford. They were cold and dead.

What he saw instead was a small apartment. After the bombing, he had moved out of the military accommodation he shared with his family and given up everything that went with it – though there was no way he would have been able to face staying in that place without them even if he had carried on in the Regiment. Instead he had moved into this one-bedroom ex-council flat several floors up that had little to recommend it other than cheapness and the fact it was close to the churchyard.

It was a bland place, with none of those little things that turn a house into a home, none of the softening touches that a woman's hand can bring. In fact, no woman had been in this place since he moved in – not for any reason – and it showed. Dirty washing-up was piled in the sink, clothes were scattered over the floor, and by the door there was a collection of empty bottles that he knocked over with a curse at least twice a day. There was an empty bottle by the sofa on which he had crashed, too. He drank vodka from time to time to numb the pain, but there was a down side. The more he drank, the more vivid were his dreams. Night after night he was forced to relive with crystal clarity the horror of that Christmas shopping trip two years ago; night after night his family were brutally taken from him yet again.

He pushed himself to his feet and immediately regretted it as a wave of alcohol-induced nausea surged through him. He retched, then ran to the bathroom where he vomited a thin, putrid liquid into the toilet, before resting his back against the bath, head in hands as he waited for the cracking pain in his skull to go away.

Two years. They said the pain would go away and he had believed them. Christ, he'd lost enough people over the years – friends, colleagues – so many that he'd lost count. But they were different. Soldiers always know that death is a possibility. He'd killed enough enemy targets in Afghanistan, Iraq, Sudan and Pakistan to accept that there would always be casualties on both sides. But a mother and her daughter. In London. At Christmas. *That* you didn't expect. And the pain couldn't be healed with a Regiment funeral and a few beers in the mess afterwards.

Will stood up uncertainly and looked at himself in the mirror. He hadn't shaved for three weeks, or was it four? A long time, anyway. Longer than he would ever have considered when he was in the military. With trembling hands he splashed some water on his face, squirted a blob of shaving gel on his palm and rubbed it into his whiskers, before picking up a razor. He tested the blade against his thumb, but it was blunt and rusty, so with a disdainful sigh he threw it back into the sink and washed the gel out of his beard. Shaving could wait another day, he thought.

Maybe a run would sort him out. He ran a lot and worked out too. Exercise was one of the few things that kept him sane and at times he took it to excess, as though by making his body feel the pain, the anguish in his mind wouldn't seem so all-encompassing. But the hangover was bad today. Tomorrow, perhaps. He'd work out tomorrow.

Stripping down, he washed, then walked back naked to the main room, where he scrabbled around for a relatively fresh pair of jeans and a T-shirt, before making himself a cup of strong, black coffee – the only thing that he could ever say with any confidence he would have in his cupboards. He gulped it down, relishing the burning sensation it gave as it sloshed down his gullet, then put the cup with the rest of the washing-up, grabbed his leather jacket and left the flat.

It was misty out, and cold. Biting cold. But it cleared Will's head as he strode the familiar route to the churchyard, his hands firmly pressed into the pockets of his jeans. He couldn't see that far ahead of him on account of the mist, and the yellow light of the street lamps cast a ghostly glow over the pavement as he walked through the early morning half-light. There were few people out at this hour – it couldn't have been much past 6.30, though Will seldom wore a watch these days, so he couldn't check – and he preferred it when the streets were empty. It was a surprise, therefore, when he became aware of the car.

He heard it first, the low rumble of the engine a little distance behind him. He didn't know what made him look over his shoulder – perhaps it was the fact that, despite being lost in his own thoughts, he had the feeling the engine noise had been in his consciousness for a good couple of minutes. He stopped and squinted his eyes slightly. The car's headlamps cast ghostly beams towards him and it looked as if it was black – though everything seemed monochrome in this light. The car was moving at a snail's pace, but as Will stared at it, it sped up and drove past. His eyes hadn't deceived him, he noticed. It was indeed black – not just the paintwork, but also the windows. He watched it as it drove to the end of the street and out of sight.

He blinked, then looked around. There was no one else in the street, at least nobody he could see through the mist, and he was instantly suspicious of the car. It had driven off as soon as he had clocked it. But who the hell would be following him at this time of day? At *any* time of day?

Then he smiled and shook his head. For fuck's sake, Will, he told himself. I know old habits die hard, but you're a pensioned-off squaddie. Enough of the paranoia. Blacked-out windows? It was probably just a bunch of slappers on their way home after a hen night. He sniffed and continued on his way.

The rusting metal gate to the churchyard creaked as he pushed it open and the noise seemed unusually loud in the silence. It pleased him that the mist was so thick – this, along with the earliness of the hour, would keep people away and he'd have the place to himself. Will weaved his way through the familiar tombstones until he came upon the one he was looking for. When his wife and child had first been buried, the grave they shared had been at the end of a row. Now, though, as more plots had been used up, the row had been completed and a new one started. Will didn't like that. He didn't like the idea that their grave was just one of many. But people will always carry on dying, he told himself. Even him, one day.

Will stood in front of the grave, his breath billowing in clouds from his mouth and nostrils, and let the silence surround him. He found himself shivering from the cold, but that didn't matter – just being here in their presence soothed him. Noticing a patch of lichen growing on the stone, he stepped forward and rubbed it off, before taking a few paces back and reading the inscription as he had done so many times before.

LAURA AND ANNA JACKSON
TAKEN FROM US BUT ALWAYS WITH US

He had never been good with words and had struggled over that simple epitaph for weeks. But in the end he was convinced it said what it was supposed to. Will stared at it, reading it over and over. He lost track of time.

It was a sudden sound that snapped him out of his reverie. Behind the gravestone was a high hedge and the noise seemed to come from that direction. He looked up sharply, but saw nothing. His eyes narrowed, however. No matter how bad his hangover, it couldn't mask all his instincts and Will Jackson knew, without knowing quite how, that he was being watched.

'Who's there?' he called.

Silence.

'I know you're there,' he said. It was probably just some wino, hanging around the churchyard with a bottle because he knew the police were more likely to be concentrating on the down-and-outs in the city centre. But Will didn't like the idea of people loitering by his family's grave. If no one else was going to move them on, he would.

'You might as well come out,' he insisted. 'Don't make me come and get you.'

Still nothing.

He sized up the hedgerow. It was too high to vault, but there was a gap just a few metres along. If he ran there he would be able to catch his peeping Tom before he had a chance to run away. He made as if to leave, then turned and sprinted through the hedge, fully prepared to make chase.

The man behind the hedge, however, didn't run. And he wasn't a wino, either. He wore a suit, was well turned out and he stared at Will with an expressionless gaze.

'What the –?' Will started to say, before striding towards the man. He suddenly felt overcome by an irrational anger. How dare this bastard spy on him, now of all times? How dare he intrude on his moment of grief? The man just looked back, his eyebrow arched in a superior manner, and all Will's anger and frustrations seemed to bubble to the surface. Something about the aura of arrogance that emanated from this guy made him seethe. He launched himself at him.

The man didn't move. He didn't need to, because before Will could get his hands on him, he heard a click.

It came from behind and it made him freeze. He recognised it, of course – the sound of a safety catch being flicked off – and almost instinctively he raised his hands, before turning slowly around to see another man, also suited, and clutching what looked at a brief glance to be a 9mm Glock. 'Get on the floor, Jackson,' he said harshly. 'You know the routine. Do it, now.'

Will's lip curled, but slowly he put his hands behind his head, fell to his knees, then lay prostrate on the ground. The dewy grass was wet against his cheek. 'What the hell's going on?' he growled.

'You'll find out soon enough,' the man with the gun replied.

As he spoke, he walked past Will towards his colleague. Will didn't hesitate – his arm lashed out and grabbed the man's feet, pulling him to the ground. In an instant, Will was on him. He punched him sharply in the pit of his stomach, then grabbed his gun hand and knocked it against a sharp piece of flinty stone that was lying on the grass. The man shouted in pain, then released the gun. Will grabbed it and jumped to his feet, keeping the weapon pointed directly at the head of his assailant.

'Right,' he said tersely. 'We'll try again. What's going on?'

The two suited men glanced nervously at each other, but they didn't reply.

'*I said: what's going on?*' Will shouted.

'It's all right, Will,' a voice said from behind him. It was calm, well-spoken. Will spun round to see a third man standing about ten metres away. He wore a heavy, black, woollen overcoat and a pair of square spectacles with clear frames. His hair was dark and lustrous, though he was clearly older than his lack of grey hair suggested. He was smiling. 'It's all right,' he repeated. 'They're with me.'

Will found that his breathing was heavy and trembling. He pointed his handgun at the new arrival.

'Really? And who the fuck,' he asked, spitting the words out, 'are you?'

TWO

The man in the overcoat ignored Will's question.

'I'm delighted to see that your skills haven't completely deserted you,' he commented. 'It costs Her Majesty's government a lot of money to train up our special forces. It would be a desperate shame if all that money and effort went out of the window the moment they go back to civvy street.'

Will kept his gun trained on the man, who did not seem unduly worried. Instead, he looked over at his colleague lying on the floor. 'You can get up now,' he said.

'Stay on the fucking ground!' Will barked. 'You get up when I say so and not before.' He strode towards the figure in the overcoat, his arm stretched out until the gun was firmly against the man's forehead. 'I'm going to ask you one more time,' he whispered. 'Who are you?'

The man remained perfectly still. 'Lowther Pankhurst,' he replied. '*Sir* Lowther Pankhurst if you want to be strictly accurate. You can just call me Sir.'

'In case you hadn't noticed,' Will replied, his voice shaking with anger, 'I've got a gun to your head. I'll call you anything I like.'

Pankhurst sighed. 'You really don't know who I am, do you, Will?'

'Should I?'

'Two years ago I believe my name would have been passingly familiar to you, yes. I'm the Director General of MI5. Offhand, I'm not entirely sure how many laws you're breaking holding that gun to my head, but I imagine it's enough to keep you behind bars for the rest of your life. I think now would be a good time to put it down, don't you?'

Will looked him in the eye and Pankhurst stared back confidently. He showed no signs that he was lying, but Will didn't move. 'I don't believe you,' he said. 'What would the head of Five be doing here with a couple of inept spooks?'

'Inept?' Pankhurst replied, surprise in his voice. 'Oh, they're not inept. They're good, actually. Just not as good as you.' He sniffed. 'Even if you *have* been drinking.' He raised his voice. 'Would you be so good as to show Mr Jackson some identification?' he called in the direction of the two suited men.

They approached, each holding an ID card of some description. Will barely looked at them. 'OK, fine, pleased to meet you,' he said sarcastically as he lowered the gun. 'Now what the hell do you want?'

Pankhurst made a display of brushing down the lapels of his coat with his fingertips. 'In answer to your previous question,' he said, without looking at Will, 'I'm here in person as a matter of courtesy.'

Will scoffed. 'What are you talking about? Bill and Ben over there just put a gun to me. I'm afraid your idea of courtesy and mine are a bit different.'

'The alternative,' Pankhurst replied with a smile, 'was to send a team in to get you in the middle of the night and bring you back to London under duress. I think that would really have set us off on the wrong foot, don't you?'

'What are you talking about?'

Pankhurst looked at the two spooks and gestured at them to move out of earshot. 'Shall we walk, Will?' he suggested. Without waiting for an answer, he headed back into the graveyard. Will followed.

'I've read your file,' Pankhurst said. 'You've been through a lot. You have my sympathy.'

'I don't want your sympathy,' he replied.

'No. I don't imagine you do. But you have it neverthe-less. Nobody should have to go through what you've been through.'

Will clenched his jaw as they continued to walk among the graves. 'You didn't come all the way down here to tell me how sorry you are.'

'No,' Pankhurst said flatly. 'I didn't. I came down here to ask for your help.'

Will's eyes flickered sideways towards him. Pankhurst was looking straight ahead. Cool. Emotionless.

'Sorry, mate.' Will was damned if he was going to call this guy 'sir'. 'I've done my bit for queen and country. You're barking up the wrong tree.'

They walked on in silence.

'The thing about working for queen and country,' Pankhurst said quietly, 'is that it's *we* who decide when you've finished. Not officially, of course, but we have our methods.'

Will stopped. 'Are you threatening me?'

Pankhurst turned to look at him and smiled. 'Of course not, Will. I wouldn't do that to a colleague. I'm just making you aware of certain practicalities.' His face became serious. 'We really do need your help, Will. And not just us. The lives of thousands of people might just rely on you making the right decision. You're right, I could have sent anyone down here to talk to you and no doubt you would have sent them packing. This is more important than that, so I wanted to come and speak to you in person.'

'Why me?' Will asked. 'What the hell can I do? I've been out of the game for two years now.'

Pankhurst's nose twitched. 'You work out or go running almost every day,' he noted. 'You drink heavily a couple of times a week. Not much different from being at Credenhill, I'd say.'

Will's eyes narrowed.

'Oh, we've been keeping an eye on you, Will. And actually there are certain reasons why you're ideal for what we have in mind. It's complicated and I can't explain here. I'd like to invite you to come back up with me to London. Now.'

Will looked around. The spooks were following at a discreet distance and a few members of the public had started to wander around the graveyard.

'It doesn't sound to me like I have much choice,' he remarked.

Pankhurst's smile grew broader. 'No,' he replied, conversationally. 'You don't.'

★

Will's request to head home and pick up a few things was denied and once the gun had been politely but firmly removed from him by one of the spooks, he was escorted to the waiting car. Its windows were blacked out and its interior plush, but Will felt uncomfortable as he sat in the back next to Pankhurst, while the spooks sat up front. Barely a word was exchanged as they sped up the motorway towards London.

As they travelled, Will gazed through the darkened window at the scenery speeding by. He had not left Hereford for two years – he felt as if there were an invisible bond tying him to that lonely gravestone, as though moving too far from it was a betrayal of sorts. Driving towards London, the place where they had died, seemed wrong. Funny, he thought to himself, how he could spend half his life in theatres of war in the most godforsaken parts of the world, yet a simple trip to London could put him on edge.

Then he looked around him. The director of MI5 was sitting next to him; two spooks were up front. He had to remind himself that actually, this was anything but a simple trip to London. What could they possibly want with him?

All he knew how to do was fight and there must be a hundred other people – highly trained and still in service – who could do that as well as him. No matter how hard he thought about it, he simply couldn't work out Pankhurst's game plan.

It took two hours to get to the outskirts of London, and another hour to struggle through the traffic to Thames House, MI5's headquarters on Millbank. Once they arrived, Pankhurst escorted Will to an office at the top of a building in an out of the way corner. An efficient-looking secretary was waiting outside the office to greet them and she gave Will what he thought was a slightly disapproving look. Probably used to men in suits, he thought to himself.

'Coffee?' Pankhurst asked.

'Yeah,' Will replied. 'Black.'

Pankhurst nodded at the secretary who walked briskly away to fetch the drink. When she returned, Pankhurst addressed her. 'Let Mr Priestley know we're ready for him, would you?' he asked, before ushering Will into the office.

It was comfortable inside – all oak panels and deep carpet. A window looked out over the Thames. Pankhurst took his place behind a large desk on which sat a black PC and indicated that Will should take a seat in a comfortable armchair opposite.

'So are you going to tell me what this is all about?' Will asked.

'Presently,' Pankhurst said, calmly. 'We have to wait for one more.'

Will found that he was digging his nails into the palm of his hand. A couple of hours ago, he thought to himself, I was puking my guts out. He still hadn't quite shaken off his queasiness and suddenly he wanted more than anything to be back home. As soon as he'd listened to what these people had to say, he'd tell them to piss off, then get the hell back to Hereford.

His thoughts were interrupted by a knock on the door. 'Come!' Pankhurst called.

The door opened and the secretary appeared. 'Mr Priestley,' she announced before stepping aside to let another man in.

Pankhurst stood up; Will stayed where he was. 'Donald Priestley, Will Jackson,' the director introduced them. Will looked up to see a silver-haired man who must have been comfortably in his sixties. He had smiling, appealing eyes and tanned skin and did not seem at all put out that Will had declined to stand up to greet him.

'Call me Don,' he said warmly in an American accent, stretching his hand out so that he could shake it. 'I've heard a lot about you, Will.'

Will's eyes flickered over to Pankhurst, who looked on with an unreadable expression in his face. 'I wish I could say the same about you,' he replied, reluctantly shaking the older man's hand.

'Mr Priestley is with the CIA,' Pankhurst informed him. 'He's their highest-ranking representative in London.'

'I'm very pleased for him,' Will replied. 'Now, do either of you want to tell me what this is all about?' He slurped dramatically from his coffee, eyeing them both over the rim of his cup.

Pankhurst cleared his throat, then walked back behind his desk and opened a drawer. He pulled out a file from which he took a colour A4 photographic print. He handed it to Priestley, who in turn gave it to Will. It was a picture of a prefabricated warehouse – or at least the remains of a warehouse. Half of one side seemed to have been destroyed, either by a collision or some sort of explosion. The scene looked vaguely familiar.

'Isn't this –?'

'Royal Mail warehouse,' Pankhurst supplied. 'You probably saw it on the news. There was an explosion there about six months ago. Caused by a substance called TATP, though you probably know more about that than I do.'

Will nodded. 'Triacetone triperoxide,' he said, automatically. 'Cheap, easy to get hold of. Dangerous, though. It's highly unstable – put a foot wrong and you'll blow your way back to Allah.' His brow furrowed as the image of the churchyard appeared in his mind's eye. 'Or whoever.'

'Terrorist cells are using it more and more,' Pankhurst agreed. 'It's easy to keep tabs on people buying huge quantities of fertiliser for bomb-making, but this stuff you don't need so much of, so they can stay under the radar. Crude, but effective. You can see for yourself.'

Will looked back at the photo. 'How many dead?' he asked curtly.

Pankhurst and Priestley glanced at each other. 'None,' the MI5 man said. 'The explosion was carried out at midnight when the place was deserted.'

He handed Will another picture. This one was of a burned-out estate car smashed into the side of a building. 'Glasgow airport,' he said. 'Couple of years ago. No doubt you heard about it. I could show you more if you like.' He waved the sheaf of pictures at him. 'But it's all much of a muchness.'

Will handed the two photos back to the director. 'You didn't just invite me here to look through your photo album,' he noted. Priestley smiled at this waspish comment. From elsewhere in the file, Pankhurst pulled out a third photograph and gave it to Will.

It was a black-and-white image of a Middle Eastern man. He wore a close-cropped beard and his hair was shoulder-length. He gazed unsmilingly out of the photograph, his brown eyes giving nothing away. It was a calm picture of a calm man. This was no grainy surveillance photo; it was a close-up, taken against a white wall. He knew that his picture was being taken.

Will looked up enquiringly. 'Who's this?' he asked Pankhurst.

Again the two older men glanced at each other. 'I'm sure I don't need to remind you, Will,' Pankhurst said after a briefly awkward moment, 'that you have signed the Official Secrets Act.'

Will laughed scornfully. 'And who do you think *I'm* likely to leak official secrets to?' he asked. 'The shit-kickers in my local?'

His sarcasm did not seem to penetrate Pankhurst. 'Just so as we're clear,' he said. 'This man's name is Faisal Ahmed. He was born in Afghanistan in 1969.'

Will nodded. 'And you think he's behind these bombings?'

Pankhurst smiled, but without humour. 'Oh,' he said. 'We know he's behind the bombings. That's not our biggest problem.'

There was a silence as Will waited for Pankhurst to elaborate, but it was Priestley who spoke next.

'Our problem, Will,' he drawled, 'is that he used to work for us.'

THREE

Pankhurst sat back in his chair, scanning Will's face for signs of interest. Will was careful to give him none.

'Perhaps I should take over, Lowther,' Priestley said, and Pankhurst nodded his agreement.

The CIA man walked to the window and looked out over London for a moment as though collecting his thoughts. Then he turned round and addressed the room. 'Some of what I have to say will be familiar to you already, Will, but please bear with me.'

Will shrugged.

'Faisal Ahmed, as Lowther has already said, was born in 1969 in a village just south of Kandahar in Afghanistan. His parents grew tobacco. They weren't wealthy, but they weren't especially poor either. They got by – quiet people, not political. Just typical, hardworking Afghans. Their village, though, was home to a number of Afghan mujahideen, fighters opposed to the Afghan government. When the government invited Soviet forces into their country to deal with the mujahideen in 1979, Ahmed was ten years old. He watched as the Sovicts entered his village in order to hunt out mujahideen supporters. They were – how can I put it – indiscriminate in their investigation techniques. Ahmed and his older sister watched soldiers raping his mother. They then shot her in front of his father, telling him that unless he confessed to being a member of the mujahideen, they would kill him too. He refused and the soldiers carried out their threat, leaving Ahmed and his sister to fend for themselves.'

Silence fell on the room as Priestley's words sank in.

'The Soviet–Afghan war lasted, as you know, for nine years. The policy of the American government at that time – under President Carter and President Reagan – was to support the mujahideen. Reagan even went so far as to publicly refer to them as freedom fighters. We funded them, both with money and armaments, and we encouraged them to bring about regime change in that country.

'Ahmed's experiences of the Russians engendered a fairly predictable response. Days after his parents' death, he hunted out the leaders of the local mujahideen faction and told them he wanted to become one of their number. His youth was not an obstacle; in fact, it was a positive advantage.' Priestley gave a small smile. 'Groups like this like to get them young, I've noticed. So, aged ten, Ahmed was given a Kalashnikov; by the time he was twelve, he was picking off Soviet soldiers with a rare skill. He learned how to use hand grenades and other explosives. He learned how to arm and defuse land mines. He became part of the sorry military apparatus of that unfortunate country.

'The CIA, of course, were involved in what was going on in Afghanistan. The US, you see, wasn't funding the mujahideen without wanting anything in return. A weakening of the Soviet armed forces was one of those things; but it was clear to anyone with half a brain that the region would be unstable for some time to come. My predecessors understood the importance of having our own eyes in Afghanistan; but, of course, it's difficult for a Westerner to operate effectively over there without attracting suspicion.

'So we started to cherry-pick a few of the mujahideen who were most interesting to us. We wanted them young, so that we could bring them round to our way of thinking. That wouldn't have been too difficult, of course – strange as it sounds, the Americans were considered allies of the mujahideen back in the Eighties, not enemies. Most of all, we wanted people that displayed an aptitude for the kind of work that would be expected of them. Faisal Ahmed ticked all the boxes.

'In 1985 our agents in Afghanistan approached him. He was sixteen years old at the time and by all accounts filled with a brutal hatred of all things Russian.'

'I don't blame him,' Will interjected, getting caught up in the story despite himself.

'Nor do I, Will,' Priestley agreed. 'But this Afghan teenager killed more Soviet soldiers before his sixteenth birthday than most special forces kill in an entire career. He seemed driven to avenge his parents' death on an almost daily basis and he was very, very good at it. The CIA made him an offer. He was told he could leave Afghanistan and come to America for five years. We would train him – channel his raw aggression and undeniable talent, and pay him. The sort of money we were talking about would have made him a wealthy man in Afghanistan. When he was twenty-one, we would return him, fully trained, to his own country. We would continue to pay him and he would be free to fight for his country in whatever way he saw fit. The only proviso was that he would agree to pass intelligence on to us about what was happening on the ground, within Afghan factions that we had no hope of infiltrating in any other way.'

'So what you're trying to tell me,' Will said, 'is that you manipulated a sixteen-year-old boy into being a spy.'

For a moment Priestley didn't respond. He stared at Will, his blue eyes wide and his face surprisingly open and honest. 'Yes,' he said finally. 'I guess that is what I'm trying to tell you. Ahmed was shown pictures of the Empire State Building and the White House. He was told he would be able to visit Los Angeles and Florida. We manipulated him; we played to his youth. It's not really something to be proud of, but you know as well as I do, Will, that pride is a luxury we are sometimes not allowed. And it would be wrong of me to suggest that Ahmed's reasons for coming to America were entirely patriotic. He was a young man being offered a chance to see the world. He accepted keenly.

'There was only one thing that could potentially cause problems. If the sixteen-year-old Faisal Ahmed had disappeared, only to reappear five years later, it would have caused suspicions. We needed, therefore, to stage his death so that he could be reinserted into the region under a new identity. Clearly, nobody in Afghanistan could know about this. Ahmed, however, was firm on one point: he would not keep his plans a secret from his sister, Latifa. She had looked after him when their parents died and she was, in many ways, the only thing he had left in the world. It would destroy her, he insisted, if she believed that her brother, her last remaining relative, had died.

'Rightly or wrongly, the CIA agreed to his condition, so Latifa Ahmed was the only person apart from his handlers who knew what was about to happen. Ahmed made the plan himself. He captured a Russian soldier, took him back to his village and killed him with his bare hands. A gun would have been easier, but it was important that no bullet was found in the soldier's body. He stripped off the Russian's uniform, replaced it with some of his own clothes, then put the corpse in the driving seat of his own car. He then constructed an explosive device, placed it under the vehicle and, under cover of night, detonated it.

'Immediately after that, he disappeared. The soldier's body was too mutilated to be recognisable and everyone assumed it was Ahmed. Latifa herself led the mourning at his funeral, but by the time his burial ritual was over, the boy was on a plane to the US.

'His military transport landed him in a deserted part of

the Midwest, where he was given four American passports, each with a different identity.'

'What the hell did he need four different identities for?' Will asked.

'What he needed,' replied Priestley, 'was the ability to switch identities at ease. During his five-year training period, he memorised more than fifty different identities, each with their own personal history. It took him six months to learn good English and a year to learn everything our special forces could possibly teach him about surveillance and espionage techniques. He was already good with a gun, but by the time the CIA had finished with him, he was a world-class marksman. He underwent gruelling torture sessions and by the end of his training he could withstand pretty much anything we threw at him. We taught him about bomb-making, escape and evasion. He became expert in intelligence techniques. In every area of warfare, espionage and counter-intelligence, he learned everything that we could teach him, soaking it all up like a sponge. He became, quite simply, the best of the best.

'I held a much more junior position in the CIA at the time, but I had the opportunity to meet Faisal Ahmed when he was in the US. I also met several other Middle Eastern operatives who were undergoing the same treatment. None of them had anything approaching the same kind of aptitude as Ahmed. He struck me as being markedly more intelligent than the others, but also completely determined. I don't mind admitting that I found him pretty scary.'

Priestley paused, poured himself a glass of water from the jug on the cabinet and took a thoughtful sip, all the while keeping his eyes on Will. It made Will a bit edgy and he looked down at the picture of Ahmed that was still in his hands. Determined, Priestley had said. He certainly looked that, if you could tell anything from a photo. Scary? Well, maybe, if you were easily scared. Will wasn't.

'While we were training Ahmed,' Priestley started up again, 'the situation in Afghanistan changed. In 1989 the Russians withdrew. What followed was close to anarchy – mujahideen factions all across the country started fighting each other under the command of their various warlords. We may imagine that Ahmed watched what was happening in his country from afar with increasing horror. At the same time, of course, he was becoming Westernised. He grew to believe that the American way of life had much to recommend it and while he was keen to return to his home country, he seemed to have a genuine loyalty towards the authorities who were training him. I don't deny that the fact he was being well paid probably helped, but from our perspective, by the time the twenty-one-year-old Faisal Ahmed was ready to be introduced back into Afghanistan, we knew that he was as near as we would ever get to the perfect spy.

'He did not disappoint us. As soon as he returned to his home country, he went about insinuating himself into the ranks of a group of mujahideen that was being heavily funded by a Saudi Arabian benefactor. His name was Osama bin Laden.'

Will's eyes widened and he couldn't help notice that Priestley seemed pleased that this last nugget of information had finally elicited some kind of response from him.

'Of course,' Priestley continued, 'back then Bin Laden was not the bête noir he is today. Al-Qaeda was yet to be formed, although he had led a group called Maktab al-Khidamat, which channelled money into the mujahideen for the Afghan war. The CIA were interested in Bin Laden anyway, because even though we were kind of on the same side back then, his anti-American stance was no secret.

'In the early 1990s the Taliban started to emerge as a powerful force in the country, then al-Qaeda. Ahmed was effectively Westernised by then; certainly he had no sympathy for the Taliban or al-Qaeda. He was able to infiltrate the higher echelons of both those groups – he even met Bin Laden a couple of times in the mid-Nineties – and even when American policy towards the mujahideen changed, he remained loyal to us. He was an intelligent guy and I guess he saw what was happening, saw that the Taliban could only ever be bad news for his country.'

'And, of course, you were still paying him,' Will observed flatly.

Priestley nodded. 'We were, as you so rightly point out, still paying him,' he agreed. 'And we got our money's worth, Will. You don't need to know the details, but let me tell you – the kind of information that was fed to us by Faisal Ahmed during the late 1990s was pure gold dust. Information of al-Qaeda plots, details of their rank and file, their structure. If it weren't for him, we'd have been in the dark. I don't think it's an exaggeration to say that his information directly saved thousands of lives. Thousands, Will. And you know what? If he'd still been with al-Qaeda at the time, there's a very good chance that 9/11 would never have happened. That's how important he was to us.'

'So what went wrong?' Will asked.

Priestley shrugged a little sadly. 'His cover was blown.'

'Who by?'

Priestley and Pankhurst glanced at each other. 'We don't really know, Will,' the American admitted. 'But it seems likely that it was someone in our own ranks.'

'You're telling me that al-Qaeda infiltrated the CIA?'

'No security service is impregnable, Will,' Priestley said quietly. 'We've shown that by infiltrating enough ourselves. You'd be surprised if I told you some of the places where we have agents.' He smiled. 'Which I'm not going to do, of course. Anyway, Ahmed was taken over the border into Pakistan, to an al-Qaeda training facility. He was tortured for three days – brutal torture, Will, sickening torture. Physical and mental. The skin on his back was flayed and allowed to go septic. He was beaten and branded. But as far as we know, he didn't crack. And at the end of it, more dead than alive, he managed to escape. He fled west into Iran, from where he managed to make it to the United Arab Emirates. Ten weeks of escape and evasion, horribly wounded. It was something else.'

Will nodded.

'It was in the UAE that he contacted us and we picked him up. For someone who had been through such a lot, he was still remarkably calm and focused. We offered him safe passage to the US, but he declined.'

'I'm not surprised,' Will commented.

'Why's that, Will?'

'Because governments aren't exactly famous for treating their ex-soldiers well,' he said. 'And with everything he knew, he could easily have become a potential liability to the US. He was probably scared that someone would come up to him in a dark alley and put a bullet in him.'

Priestley smiled.

'I don't think he was afraid of that, Will. Despite what you might think, the US government *would* have looked after him. We're not as bad as some people make us out to be, you know. No, that wasn't the reason. The reason was that we couldn't tell him who it was that blew his cover. He knew that coming back into the US under CIA protection would be a death warrant. And so he decided to go to the UK – somewhere he could be anonymous. Somewhere he could be safe.'

'Don't give me that,' Will sneered. 'I bet you stopped paying him once he was no use to you.'

'We didn't have to continue paying him, Will,' Priestley continued, 'because our British counterparts took over that job.' He glanced over in Pankhurst's direction.

The director had been sitting in his chair, fingers pressed

together, and a look of concentration on his face as Priestley's story had unfolded. Now, though, he stood up, walked to the front of his desk and perched on the edge. 'Faisal Ahmed,' he explained, 'was a unique asset for us. We were very grateful to the CIA for allowing us to make use of him.'

'He wanted to carry on working?' Will asked. 'After everything he'd been through?'

Pankhurst looked Will straight in the eye. 'What else could he do, Will?' the director asked. 'He was intelligent enough to know that if a military man stops his career before the time is right, he risks wasting away into nothing.'

Will looked down awkwardly as Pankhurst continued.

'Ahmed was a stranger in a strange land. He had been a fighter from the age of ten, a trained spy from the age of sixteen. Now he was in his early thirties. I hardly think he could have been expected to go and work in a supermarket, do you? We gave him work to do. We made him feel useful. On his arrival in England he was given a new identity and a place to live in an area of London known to be a hotbed of fundamentalism. It wasn't long before he had infiltrated a number of terrorist cells and was using his considerable skills to tip us off about their activities. Faisal Ahmed warned us about any number of potential terrorist strikes all over the country and we were able to prevent them. He worked with us for three years and in that time I estimate that he put a stop to ten major terrorist operations.

'But then, in 2003, he went dark. Vanished completely.'

Pankhurst stood up and walked over to the window. 'It's pretty hard to vanish in this country when MI5 really want to find you, Will. But as you've heard, Ahmed was well trained.'

'Maybe he left the country,' Will suggested.

'That's just what we thought, at first. Until intelligence started coming in that a person matching his description was involved in masterminding a series of low-level terrorist strikes like the ones I just showed you.'

'The Glasgow Airport bombing?'

'Among others. The intelligence was sound and we know Ahmed was involved. We even discovered where he had been staying on a couple of occasions – bedsits, usually, on the outskirts of satellite towns around the UK, the sort of places anyone could merge into the background with ease. But every time we closed in on him, he had always disappeared. At first we cursed our bad luck, and of course the excellent training the CIA had given him.' He smiled somewhat ruefully at Priestley, who affected a look of false modesty. 'But soon it became clear that there was more to it than that. Ahmed was being tipped off and it could only be by someone in the security services.'

'Five's got a mole, you mean?' Will asked directly.

'Yes, Will,' Pankhurst said calmly. 'Five's got a mole. Like Don says, it's hardly a great surprise – we expect this sort of thing from time to time. But it means we are extremely compromised in our search for Ahmed.'

'Why do you think he went dark?' Will asked.

'We don't know,' Pankhurst admitted. 'Not for sure. But we can hazard a guess. The last contact we had was in February 2003, about three weeks before the invasion of Iraq. You don't have to be a political scientist to know how unpopular that little move was, even among ordinary white Britons and Americans. But obviously it was also very unpopular among moderate Muslims in both countries. We can only surmise that Ahmed objected to the invasion on some ideological level and that caused him to change his allegiance.'

'He's a strangely principled man,' Priestley interjected, 'and if you think about it, it makes a certain amount of sense. When the US invaded Afghanistan after 9/11, there were sound reasons for doing it, not least that the Taliban were most likely giving Bin Laden refuge. But Iraq? That was political, cynical – at least, that's what plenty of people thought.'

'Anyway,' Pankhurst continued, 'whatever the reason, the first terrorist attack that we know Ahmed was involved in occurred about two months after the invasion of Baghdad and they've been going on ever since. With a few exceptions, nobody has been hurt in any of his attacks – it's almost as though they've been warning shots, as if he's letting us know that he's still around and that he's –' Pankhurst seemed to be struggling to find the word.

'Pissed,' Priestley supplied helpfully in his American drawl.

'Quite,' Pankhurst muttered. 'Recently, however, there has been a development.'

'What sort of development?' Will asked.

Pankhurst sniffed. 'A significant one,' he said flatly. 'We've been picking up a lot of intelligence chatter about Ahmed – nothing concrete, but it was clear something was in the offing.' He narrowed his eyes. 'You are aware, I suppose, of the existence of what certain people have taken to calling "black camps"?'

'Yeah,' Will said slowly. He had heard the rumours of course – that there were places outside the legal jurisdiction of America and Britain where suspects were taken to be interrogated in ways that were illegal in more civilised countries. Places they could be tortured without there being any comeback. Places you didn't want to end up.

'Well, we got lucky with one of our leads. A joint British and American operation apprehended a young Pakistani student in Rome three days ago. He was taken to a black camp and –' again Pankhurst seemed to search for the right word, '– persuaded to reveal everything he knew about, well, everything. He informed us that Faisal Ahmed is planning a terrorist strike against London some time in the next three weeks. Something major. We bled our informant dry, but that was all he could tell us. We don't know where it's going to happen and we don't know when. All we know is, it *will* happen.'

Pankhurst's stark prediction seemed to echo around the room. The two men stared at Will for a while without saying anything.

'Well, I don't know what you think I can do about it,' he said in an attempt to break the uncomfortable silence.

The two men remained expressionless. The American turned again to look out of the window. 'I was in New York on 9/11, Will,' he said quietly. 'I've never seen such horror. I've never seen fear like that in anybody's eyes. But you know what? Compared to Faisal Ahmed, the men who plotted and carried out that attack were amateurs. Ahmed's the best there is – if he wanted a major strike on London, he has the capability to make it the most horrific act of violence we've ever seen.'

'Fine,' Will replied. 'I still don't see where I come in.' He was getting impatient now and wanted to leave. His eyes flickered over to the door and he wondered what would happen if he just walked out.

'You come in, Will,' Pankhurst said quietly, 'because you've been out of service for the last two years.'

Will blinked. 'What are you talking about? That makes no sense at all.'

'I told you, Will. We have a mole. We don't know who it is and we don't know where it is. Most importantly, we don't know how far their influence extends. You, however –' Pankhurst gave him a thin smile. 'As far as we can tell, you've had no contact with the military or with the authorities since you retired two years ago. We've been watching you for a while, Will, and it seems your longest conversations have been with the gentleman round the corner who runs the off-licence.'

Instantly Will stood up. 'For fuck's sake,' he muttered. 'I don't have to listen to this shit.'

He made for the door.

'I apologise, Will,' Pankhurst announced. 'That was uncalled for. Please, sit down and hear me out.'

Will stopped in his tracks. He found that he was shaking, but at least his brain hadn't turned to jelly. He knew Pankhurst was going to finish saying what he had to say – if Will walked out before that happened, chances were that he'd only be dragged in again, and probably a lot less politely than last time. A frown wrinkled on his forehead as he turned and sat down again.

'Thank you, Will,' Pankhurst said quietly, and for a moment Will thought he sounded genuinely grateful. 'The truth is, we need you. We need someone clean and we need someone we think might just be a match for Ahmed and for the operation we have in mind. We don't have many options, Will. We don't have *any* options, apart from you.'

'I'll level with you, Will,' Priestley continued. 'I wanted to put one of our boys on this job. But then Lowther showed me your file and even I've got to admit it's impressive. You've fought your way out of some pretty nasty corners.'

'Yeah, well that was a long time ago. If you've read my file closely enough, you'll see that I've got more reason to hate terrorists than most. But there's nothing I can do about it. Not now. I've been out of it for too long.'

'I don't think that's true, Will,' Pankhurst said. 'I saw the way you dealt with my people this morning.'

Will shrugged. 'Whatever,' he said. 'I'm not interested. You can find someone else and that's my last word. Now if there's nothing else, I'd like to go.'

'Actually,' Pankhurst said a bit too quickly, 'there is something else.' He exchanged a worried glance with his CIA counterpart, then took a deep breath. 'There's one other thing I haven't told you.'

Will's eyes narrowed. 'What?' he demanded.

'I mentioned that Ahmed's bombing campaign had practically no casualties, that they were like warning shots.'

'Yeah?'

'There was one exception. Two exceptions, actually.' The director looked piercingly at him and as he spoke Will felt a sickness in his stomach and a hot surge of adrenaline. Pankhurst took another A4 photograph from the sheaf and held it lightly in his fingertips. 'It was two years ago,' he said, his voice flat. 'A bomb outside a department store in Knightsbridge. Two casualties, both female, a mother and daughter.'

He handed the photograph to Will. Drawn to it like a bystander to an accident, he looked at the image. He knew it well, of course. It had haunted his dreams for months on end. He recognised the curve of the woman's back as she wrapped herself around her dead child. He recognised the way the little girl's long, honey hair was spattered over her bloodstained face.

His hand started to shake even more.

'I'm sorry to have to tell you this way,' Pankhurst continued, relentlessly. 'But you need to know. Faisal Ahmed killed your family, Will. And now you're the only one who can do anything about it.'

FOUR

The room seemed to spin.

Will was barely aware of the other two men as they stood there, watching him intently, checking to see what his reaction would be. The photo in his hand seemed to fill all his senses, to bring back all the grief like a sharp shard of glass slicing right through him. He found that he was biting on his lower lip, so hard that he could taste the hot, metallic flavour of his own blood, and without a word he stood up. The picture fell to the floor as he did so, but Will didn't bother to pick it up. He had no need of a photographic reminder of that scene. It was etched on his brain and would be until the day he died.

'You bastards,' he whispered.

The two men remained silent.

'*You fucking bastards!*' he shouted. 'Why didn't I know about this before?'

'It wasn't necessary, Will,' Pankhurst replied calmly.

'*I'll decide what's fucking necessary!*' he yelled. 'They were *my* family. Not a couple of pawns in your fucking game.' His body was shaking now and he felt violent. He wanted to hit them, to make them feel his pain; but something stopped him, paralysed him. He looked from one to the other and their blank gazes infuriated him even more. In the end, he simply turned and left the office, slamming the door. Neither Pankhurst nor Priestley tried to stop him.

His blood running hot in his veins, Will half-walked,

half-ran through the corridors of Thames House. He didn't wait for a lift to get to the ground floor; instead he used the stairs, taking in several steps at a time. It felt better that way, as though he were putting distance between himself and the information he had just learned. People turned to look at him as he tore past them and at the exit two security guards stood in his way, clearly suspicious of him. He barged through them and out into the streets.

It was cold out. Icy cold. Will drew several deep, shaky breaths and relished the feeling of the freezing air piercing his lungs like an icicle. He looked around him, then hurried down the road and randomly round a corner, soon finding himself lost in the area around the back of Millbank. He knew what he was looking for and it wasn't long before he found one.

As he entered the Morpeth Arms, a warm fug of air hit him; but the sensation gave him no comfort like it once did. He was in here for a reason. He approached the deserted bar and beckoned the bored-looking barmaid. 'Vodka,' he told her. 'Double. No ice.'

The first drink warmed him up slightly, but it didn't calm him. Nor did the second. Only when he had downed three large vodkas in quick succession did he even begin to feel remotely soothed after the shock he had just received; and it was only after the fourth, handed to him by a now slightly alarmed looking barmaid, that his hands stopped shaking.

It was all too much to process. In the past hour he had been forced to relive his family's murder; he had looked upon the face of their killer; and he had been handed the opportunity to seek retribution.

But retribution wasn't what he wanted. It wasn't what he needed. He needed oblivion.

He ordered himself a pint and set about trying to forget.

★

Don Priestley looked at the Director General of MI5. 'That was a shitty thing to have to do, Lowther,' he said.

Pankhurst shrugged, as if what had just occurred had barely affected him. 'Nothing like as bad as what will happen if we don't get our hands on Ahmed. We can't have another 9/11, Don. London won't tolerate it. I won't let it happen.'

'You really think this guy is our best bet?'

'I've done my homework, Don. I've spoken to people, asked around. When Will Jackson was in the SAS, he had a reputation. He was the soldier everyone wanted. You've seen the missions he's led – Iraq, Sudan, crucially Afghanistan. You've heard of Gray Fox?'

'Yeah, thanks, Lowther. I've heard of Gray Fox.' Of course he had. Formerly known as the US Army Intelligence Support Activity unit, Gray Fox was headed up by Delta Force, but worked closely with the Seals, the SBS and the SAS. And he'd read about Jackson's exploits with the unit in Iraq. According to his file, they'd received intelligence that a group of six suicide bombers were planning a hit in Baghdad. Jackson had led a surveillance team, dressed up in Arab gear, that had followed all six bombers back to a house in the Iraqi capital and all the information they had pointed to the likelihood that they would be strapping up and getting ready to leave within the hour. Raiding the house would have been a dangerous option, because all it would have taken was one flick of a switch and both the bombers and the Gray Fox team would have gone up like a bonfire. Yet they couldn't risk letting them back out into the capital.

Jackson's solution had been high-risk. He and his team had staked out the place, posting Regiment snipers all around the house. If a single sniper had been compromised – a distinct possibility in that hostile territory where, if just one Iraqi passer-by had suspected something, the alarm would have been raised – the bombers would have known they were there. Moreover, the shooters had to hold their nerve until all six bombers were out of the house and in their sights.

Against the odds, Jackson's team had managed it, killing all six men at the same time before they could warn each other or go out and do their bloody work. They'd made a little piece of SAS history that day. Priestley had heard that even Delta Force had a grudging respect for the success of the operation and that was like praise from Caesar.

But that was in the past and from what he had seen, Will Jackson wasn't the same any more. 'Lowther,' Priestley said. 'I agree that back in the day he was the man. But now? He's a mess. Has he got any fight left in him? Christ, I don't blame the guy. Look what's happened to him. But you can't put someone like that into the field of war. If you can't trust any of your guys, why don't I just get Washington to send Delta Force in?'

Pankhurst's lips went thin. 'You'll excuse me for pointing out, I hope, Don, that the last time Delta Force and the SAS were on active service in Afghanistan, it was the British special forces who fared rather better.'

Priestley fell silent.

'Will Jackson was in Afghanistan in the summer of 2002,' Pankhurst continued, implacably. 'He led a four-man unit behind enemy lines and reconnoitred there for two weeks, sending regular updates on al-Qaeda positions. The day he was called back to base, the unit was spotted by two scouts, who shot and badly wounded one of the unit. Will Jackson hunted them down before they could report back, killed them, hid their bodies where they wouldn't be found, then single-handedly carried his wounded colleague back to base in the midsummer heat. You might think he's a mess, but he's skilled, well-trained, resourceful and – most importantly – he has a reason to find Faisal Ahmed.'

Pankhurst let that sink in before continuing.

'He reacted to the news about his family much as we

thought he would. I'll concede I didn't expect him to walk out, but I've had psychometric reports done by three of our top analysts. He'll come round. He wants to find Ahmed just as much as we do; he just doesn't know it yet. If I'm wrong, you can bring in your people. You'll have my full support. But I'm not wrong, Don. You'll see.'

Priestley looked unconvinced. 'I sure hope so, Lowther,' he said with a sigh. 'I sure hope so.'

★

The afternoon passed in a blur of booze and self-loathing. Will swallowed pint after pint, but the more he drank, the more the images from the morning flashed before his eyes. His wife and daughter, cold, dead. Faisal Ahmed, his unfeeling eyes staring confidently out. Part of Will wanted to hunt the guy down, to look him in the face, then put a bullet in his head. But another part of him – the greater part – wanted to run away back to Hereford. Back to the graveyard, where he could weep and be alone with his grief.

The pub started to fill up. He was on his fifth pint – or was it his sixth? – when he noticed the woman who had taken the bar stool next to him. She wore a smart grey business suit, had a drink in front of her and was toying nervously with a cigarette.

'Bloody smoking ban,' she smiled at him.

Will grunted and took another sip from his pint.

'Just been stood-up,' she said, before adding, rather quickly, 'Not by a boyfriend. I was meant to be interviewing someone. I'm a journalist.'

'Right,' Will replied, a bit ungraciously.

She smiled at him again. A pretty smile. 'I'm Catherine, by the way,' she blurted out. 'Kate. My friends call me Kate.' Her hair, Will noticed, was cut into an attractive brown bob and it flickered appealingly over her cheek as she put her

51

head to one side. Nice, but his instinct was to keep himself to himself. It was almost inbuilt in him to be immediately suspicious of anyone talking to him without a reason.

'Look,' he said, 'I don't want to sound rude, but I've had a bit of a weird day and I don't really feel like shooting the shit.' He gulped at his drink.

'Weird day?' Kate gabbled. 'Tell me about it. I woke up this morning, and −' She faltered. 'It's no good,' she said. 'I've got to have a cigarette. Fancy one?'

Will looked at the packet of fags on the bar. He hadn't smoked for years, but all of a sudden he found he had a craving for it. 'Yeah, all right,' he murmured.

A small smile of satisfaction flickered over Kate's face and it didn't go unnoticed by Will. She put her coat on and he escorted her to the door.

They stood outside in silence, tobacco fumes billowing from their nostrils in great clouds. Kate stamped her feet against the cold and she finished her cigarette long before Will. They were just turning to go inside when there was a shout. The alcohol had made him woozy, and Will didn't catch what it was, but he certainly understood its implication. Before he knew it, three men in their twenties − brash young city types, clearly drunk, still wearing their suits, but with their ties loosened as much as their tongues − were jostling around Kate, laughing lewdly. All the confidence Kate had shown in the pub seemed to disappear, and she shrank away.

Will acted almost instinctively. He stepped in front of Kate, putting his bulk between her and the three men.

'Leave her alone, lads,' he told them.

The men looked at her and laughed. 'Who are you?' one of them goaded him. 'Her pimp?' The three of them creased with laughter once more, just as the repressed anger Will had been feeling all afternoon welled up in him.

The man who had insulted him didn't even see Will's fist as it flew through the air with such speed and force. But he knew when he had been hit. His cheek cracked and his nose exploded in a shower of blood. He hit the ground with a thump.

'Jesus, you fucking psycho!' one of his friends exclaimed as they bent down to see if he was OK. 'What the hell did you do that for?'

Will looked at the smear of blood on his fist, disgusted with himself for having lost his temper so easily. It was the drink, he told himself. He wanted, more than anything, to be away from this place, but he couldn't leave the girl.

Will kneeled down and grabbed the man who was looking after his friend by the scruff of the neck. 'Take your mate,' he whispered threateningly, 'and fuck off out of it.'

The man gave him a hateful look, but he nodded his head, picked up his friend, who was still bleeding profusely from the nose, and the three of them hurried away.

My God, Will thought to himself. Has it come to this? Roughing up drunken yuppies on the streets of London. The ex-SAS man felt sick with himself and all of a sudden the alcohol-induced wooziness returned. He turned to Kate, who had a shocked expression on her face. 'I'm sorry,' he said. 'I'd better go.' He plunged his hands into his pockets and walked down the street. If he got the right train, he could be back in Hereford in a couple of hours.

'Wait!' Kate called. She fell in beside him, having to trot in order to keep up. 'Look, er . . . thanks. For back there, I mean.'

Will shrugged as he walked, then pulled out his hand and looked indifferently at the other man's blood on his skin.

'Oh my God!' Kate said. 'Are you all right? Are you hurt?'

'I'm fine.'

'No you're not,' she said decisively. 'Come on, you've got to get cleaned up.' She tugged on his sleeve to slow him down, then lifted her hand and hailed a black cab that was passing. How it happened, Will didn't know – his mind was still scrambled by the events of the day – but before he knew it, he was being hustled into the back by this woman he barely knew and twenty minutes later he was walking up a narrow flight of stairs to her flat in North London.

It was warm and comfortable. Will waited in Kate's pristine kitchen – such a far cry from his own – while she found him dry towels and a dressing gown, before showing him to the bathroom. He mumbled a few embarrassed words of thanks, then closed the door, stripped off his dirty clothes and turned on the shower. The water was hot and it felt good as it seared his skin, washing away the blood and the grime and the effects of the alcohol he had drunk. He closed his eyes and allowed everything to wash over him. Seemingly from nowhere, the words Pankhurst had spoken flashed through his mind: 'If a military man stops his career before the time is right, he risks wasting away into nothing.' Was that what was happening to him? Was he becoming a shadow of his former self? Was the old Will Jackson dead? He found himself frowning at the thought. What would his wife have said? 'Get yourself together, Will. Stop feeling sorry for yourself.' He could almost hear her voice.

'You all right in there?' Kate shouted from behind the door.

He turned off the shower. 'Fine,' he said, before climbing out, throwing on the towelling dressing gown and roughly drying his hair. The mirror was steamed up, so he wiped his hand over it to get a look at himself. Why was he doing that? he wondered to himself as he ruffled his dark hair into position. He glanced down at the clothes on the floor. Should he put them back on? Imperceptibly he shook his head. Will knew where this was leading.

I shouldn't be here, he told himself. It isn't right. But then he thought of his own flat in Hereford. Bland. Unwelcoming. He had gone to the pub to forget his troubles, but who would blame him if he tried to find oblivion in the arms of this woman who seemed to be making her intentions perfectly clear.

It had been a long time. A very long time. He took a deep breath and caught a glance of himself in the mirror once more.

When Will finally stepped out of the bathroom and looked down the corridor, Kate was waiting for him, framed in the doorway to her bedroom. She had changed clothes: gone was the business suit, replaced by a pair of tightly fitting jeans and a sapphire blue top that accentuated the curve of her hips and her breasts. She leaned nonchalantly against the edge of the doorframe, a mischievous smile playing on her lips.

Will took a step forward. That unfamiliar trembling of anticipation washed over him and suddenly it was all he could do not to run towards her. 'Do you pick up a lot of hooligans in bars?' he asked lightly.

Kate arched one of her eyebrows. 'Are you a hooligan, Will?'

'When I want to be.'

'Well, I might start bringing home a few more, if they all look like you.'

'They don't,' Will replied. 'Mostly they look like that bloke with the broken nose.'

'Ah,' Kate replied, and Will thought he heard a slight tremble in her voice. 'In that case, I think I'll stick with you.' She turned and stepped into her bedroom.

It was dark outside by now and Kate had dimmed the lights. She stood at the end of the bed, her smiling eyes looking widely up at him as he walked in. Will approached and put one arm round her, against the small of her back. She needed no encouragement to press herself against him and as he felt the warmth of her body and the hotness of her breath against his, a world of stress and worry seemed to fall from his shoulders.

They kissed – tentatively at first, but with increasing passion. Will's free hand slid up her top and she took in a deep gulp of pleasure as his fingertips brushed her breasts. She pulled on his dressing-gown cord, then lightly placed her hand on his chest muscles, before taking a step back and removing her top in one deft movement.

Will approached her again, then pulled her roughly towards him, feeling that long-forgotten thrill surge through his body. She looked up at him with undisguised longing in her face and their lips met again. The kiss was more passionate this time, more serious, and Kate moaned with pleasure as their lips met, digging her well-manicured nails firmly into his skin. Will pushed her on to the bed. She gazed up at him, then closed her eyes with an expectant smile as he lowered himself eagerly on to her body.

★

The basement of his safe house was illuminated only by a single light bulb hanging from the ceiling. Below it was a large, square, wooden table at which he sat, the constituent parts of a disassembled Heckler & Koch MP5 sub-machine gun spread out in front of him. A small, oil-filled radiator on one side of the room emitted a surprising amount of warmth, so despite the cold outside he wore nothing but a pair of jeans and a vest that displayed the contours of his biceps. His beard was neatly trimmed and his dark skin shone in the lamplight.

On the corner of the table was a television. The sound was muted, but the images showed the British Prime Minister and the American President shaking hands and smiling for the cameras. Ahmed's lip curled and he reached over to switch off the set. There were some things he couldn't bear to watch. Instead, he went back to his work.

In one hand he held a rag doused with cleaning solvent

from the small pot by his side and he meticulously, thoughtfully, rubbed away at the grey metal of the barrel. He liked the smell of the cleaning solvent. There was something comforting about it. Warming. Even before the Americans had trained him, when he was just a boy, the importance of cleaning your weapon had been impressed upon him by his mujahideen instructors. Indeed, he had barely been a teenager the day he first saw the horrific results a poorly kept weapon could have on the user. They had been firing guns in the wasteland on the edge of his village – just target practice. An older man had been laughing, bragging about what a good shot he was. He took aim at a pebble placed on a rock some twenty metres in the distance and fired. The gun exploded in his face, shredding his skin so that he appeared like a piece of meat. His howls echoed far and wide as, blinded, he was taken back to the village. The women had attempted to care for him, but the wound soon became septic and he had died only a few days later. A miserable, painful death.

The men had said that it was because he had not cleaned his gun. Even as a boy, Ahmed doubted that – it was probably a faulty, cheaply made weapon – but he knew then that he would never take the risk. At that young age he had decided on two things: never brag about how good a shot you are, and always clean your gun.

Back then, in Afghanistan, they had used something different – a thick oil that stuck to your fingers and stained your already dirty clothes. He had liked that smell too, just as he had enjoyed stripping down the weapons – mostly AK-47s in those days, taken from dead Soviet soldiers or supplied by the Americans.

He stopped for a moment and sneered. He really had thought the Americans were their friends back then, when they gave them money and ammunition. But not now. No, now the Americans had shown their true colours; shown exactly what the life of a Muslim was worth to them. He snorted heavily to himself and continued to clean the gun barrel.

No one would ever find him here, of that he was certain. The first thing he had done when he arrived in England was establish a number of safe houses – places he, and only he, knew about. He would never tell anyone where these safe houses were, no matter how close they were to him or how much he trusted them. That was the rule: these were places where he could disappear utterly, for weeks, even months at a time. They were chosen at random, so that nobody could second-guess where he would be staying; and they were always rented under false names – names that could never be tracked back to Faisal Ahmed.

The gun barrel was clean. He held it up to the light and looked through it. The shiny curve of its interior pleased him. Ahmed placed it back down on the table, picked up another piece and continued to polish and clean another of the satisfying metallic components.

When the cleaning process was finished, he clunked all the pieces together in order, grunting in satisfaction when the last one slotted in. He caressed the gun momentarily, as if caressing a woman, then scraped his chair back, picked up the MP5 and carried it to the side of the room. Along each wall were rows upon rows of metal shelving, firmly bolted together. The shelves were packed from floor to ceiling. Boxes of Semtex, G60 stun grenades, lined up neatly like toy soldiers. A couple of bulky Claymore mines with their long reels of detonating cord. There was an abundance of guns, too: a C8 carbine and grenade launcher, a Remington 870 with RIP tear-gas rounds and a selection of handguns. Faisal Ahmed knew that no amount of weaponry, ammunition or explosives were a substitute for his own clear thinking and tactical awareness; but the time would come when he would need firepower and it was good to know that everything was in place.

He put the MP5 where it belonged on the shelf, then turned his attention elsewhere. There was a sleeping bag and a rolled-up foam mattress. He unfurled them on the floor. Then he checked that the door to the basement was locked, before taking a small handgun from the shelf. He slotted a loaded magazine into it, rested it by his makeshift bed and turned off the light. In the darkness he clambered into the sleeping bag, but it was a long time before he fell asleep.

Sleep never comes easily, he found, when you know that someone wants to kill you.

★

The first time they made love it had been frenzied and quick. Kate had continued to dig her sharp fingernails into his back, noisily and vigorously responding to his enthusiasm. When it was over, they didn't speak a word: they simply lay there, her arm draped over his chest, her leg hooked over his. How long they lay like that, Will couldn't have said; but after a while he felt her hand moving gently over his torso and she was snuggling up meaningfully to him. It felt good. He rolled her over and pinned her down by her arms; Kate closed her eyes and groaned in anticipation as he kissed her.

It lasted longer the second time, but was no less passionate. When they had finished, they both fell into a deep, satisfied sleep.

It was still dark when Will awoke suddenly. He glanced over at the clock by the bedside. Half-past four. He laid back and stared into the blackness. His throat was dry and he would have liked to get up and find a glass of water; but he didn't want to wake the slumbering form next to him. So instead he remained still, with only the darkness and his thoughts for company.

Was it wrong, what he had just done? It felt strange, being with a woman other than his wife. Had he been sober, had he been thinking straight, perhaps he wouldn't have done it the first time. But as he lay there, he found that he didn't feel bad. He didn't feel he had betrayed anyone.

Betrayal. That one word brought to his mind the image of Faisal Ahmed. You can tell a lot from a photo, he thought to himself. An awful lot. Ahmed was a good-looking man. His eyes were calm. He seemed at peace with himself. At peace with what he had done.

And then Will thought of the churchyard. The cold, lonely grave where, thanks to that man, his family lay dead.

In the darkness, something became clear to him: wasting the rest of his life was no way to honour his family. Their death was only worth mourning if life was worth living. Strange how it had taken a night in bed with someone he barely knew for him to realise that.

Strange, too, how something else was perfectly clear to him now. The two men at Thames House, unwittingly, had offered him a lifeline. A way out of his bland existence. They might want Faisal Ahmed dead for the best of reasons, but in this moment of honesty Will knew one thing: he wanted him dead so that he could avenge his family. Avenge them, and move on.

As quietly as he could, he slipped out of bed. Kate stirred, but did not wake, as he groped his way out of the bedroom and into the bathroom, where he turned the dimmer light on low. His clothes were still on the floor; they felt dirty and greasy as he dragged them on. He was just pulling the belt buckle tight when the door opened. Kate stood in the doorway, naked and dishevelled. She eyed him seriously.

'Are you going?' she asked.

'I have to,' Will replied. 'I'm sorry.'

Kate inclined her head. 'I won't see you again, will I?'

Will hesitated. 'Probably not,' he answered, honestly. 'It's best this way, I promise.'

'Another woman?'

Will smiled affectionately. 'No, Kate,' he said, 'not another woman. Just something I have to do.' He stepped forward and kissed her on the cheek. 'You take care, Kate,' he said kindly. 'And be careful who you take home from the pub next time. They're not all like me, you know.'

'I wouldn't know,' Kate told him. 'That's the first time I've done it. The last, probably.'

And with a half-smile, she watched as without any further word of farewell, Will descended the steps and let himself out of the flat.

It was freezing outside and Will had a raging hunger. It took him twenty minutes to find a café that was open. An inviting yellow light spilled out on to the street from the misted-up shop windows and inside it was already nearly full of workers guzzling down hot drinks and plates of fried food. Will ordered the works and sat on his own, gulping down mouthfuls of sweet tea and ignoring the tabloids strewn over his table. When the food came, he devoured it, then ordered more tea and prepared to sit it out until nine o'clock.

At quarter-past, he was striding up to the front entrance of Thames House. A security guard instantly stopped him and Will realised he must look a state in his dirty clothes; but that didn't prevent him saying what he had to say.

'I'm here to see Pankhurst,' he announced flatly. 'My name's Will Jackson. I imagine he's expecting me.'

Within minutes he was being ushered up to the same office as yesterday.

Pankhurst was by himself now, sitting behind his big wooden desk. His suit was immaculate and not a hair was out of place. He did not look at all surprised as Will was shown in and once they were alone he indicated that Will should take a seat.

'I'll stand,' he told the Director General.

'As you wish. I take it you've given some thought to our discussion of yesterday.'

Will looked at him with intense dislike. He had only known this man for twenty-four hours, but already he loathed him. Loathed his self-satisfied demeanour. Loathed the way he had manipulated him. Loathed the fact that they had the same aim now. Different motives, but the same aim. Like it or not, Will Jackson and Lowther Pankhurst were on the same side.

'What is it you want me to do?' he asked.

FIVE

Pankhurst pressed his fingertips together. 'It's complicated, Will,' he said. 'Why don't you sit down, let me order you some coffee.'

Reluctantly, Will took a seat. 'Forget about the coffee,' he said. 'Just talk.'

Pankhurst nodded his head. 'We need to find Ahmed, and we need to find him quickly. But we're stabbing in the dark. Truth is, we haven't got a clue where he is. Don Priestley's a yank through and through, always exaggerating the Americans' capacity to do things; but he wasn't exaggerating about Ahmed. They did a *very* good job with him. If he doesn't want to be found . . .'

'You must have people looking.'

'Of course we have, Will. We've got a *lot* of people looking. But it won't do any good. We don't even know if he's in the country.'

'Then how the hell — ?'

Pankhurst raised his hand in the air to silence Will's outburst. The director stood up, moved round to the other side of the desk and perched on the edge, just in front of Will. 'You don't like me, Will,' he said suddenly. 'That's OK, you're in the majority. My job means that I have to do some pretty unlikeable things. But we have to work together on this and that means you need to start putting some trust in the fact that I know what I'm talking about. Are we agreed?'

Will held his gaze and for a moment the two men simply stared at each other.

'We're agreed,' he conceded finally.

'Good.' Pankhurst returned to his seat and continued as if that little confrontation had never happened. 'As I say, we have a lot of people looking for him, but I don't hold out much hope that he'll be found. But we have another lead and that's what I want you to follow up.'

'What's the lead?'

'His sister. Latifa Ahmed.'

Will blinked. 'You think she'll know where he is?'

'It's possible,' Pankhurst replied. 'At least, she's our best shot. It seems that Ahmed was always very close to her. Don Priestley told you yesterday that she was the only person in Afghanistan who knew the truth when Ahmed staged his own death. What he didn't tell you was that they kept in occasional but regular contact while he was in the US.'

'How?'

'Letters, mostly,' Pankhurst said. 'Ahmed would pretend to be a distant cousin living in Kabul. The letter would be sent to a US contact in the capital, then passed via a long sequence of agents — long enough that it would be nigh-on impossible to trace the source of the letter — before being delivered to her. It would never be more than a few lines and it could take months to arrive. Even so, from what I could glean from Priestley, the CIA were less than wild about letting him do even that.'

'Why did they?'

'Because it was his condition. He refused to help them at all unless he could have some way of letting Latifa know that he was OK. The CIA had to give in. Then, when he was reinserted into Afghanistan in 1990, he found his own ways to keep in touch with her.'

Pankhurst paused for a moment. 'Tell me, Will,' he

continued, 'how much do you know about the Taliban and the way they treated the women of Afghanistan?'

Will shrugged. 'Bits and pieces,' he said.

'Right. Well let me give you some idea of the conditions under which Latifa Ahmed was forced to live when the Taliban came to power in 1996. She was forced to wear the burka, of course; she was banned from proper medical care if she was ill; she was looked upon as a third-class citizen. But in actual fact, Latifa had it a lot better than most women in Afghanistan at the time. Ahmed saw to that. He had infiltrated the highest echelons of al-Qaeda by then and had influence among the Taliban authorities. Of course, no one knew she was his sister, but he let it be known around the neighbourhood where Latifa lived that if she was interfered with in any way, it would not be tolerated.'

'Sounds dangerous,' Will commented. 'Surely he was worried people would ask questions.'

'It was a risk he ran,' Pankhurst agreed. 'But he meant what he said. In 1998 a member of the Taliban police stopped Latifa in the street. It's unclear what he thought her misdemeanour was, but the punishment he gave her was brutal. Nothing out of the ordinary, you understand, but still brutal. In a busy street she was beaten with a metal stick; her arm was broken and she was left weeping in the gutter. Nobody offered to help, of course, because to do that would have been to risk imprisonment or worse.

'The following day, the policeman was found. His throat had been sliced when he was sitting at his table eating a solitary dinner. Nobody saw the killer go in or out of the house, but rumours travelled fast. Nobody lay a finger on Latifa until Ahmed was outed in Afghanistan in the year 2000.

'When word of his true identity reached al-Qaeda's ears, the rumours that he had been protecting Latifa Ahmed simply confirmed their intelligence. Latifa's luck changed then. She was imprisoned by the Taliban, where we can only assume she experienced the brutality for which that regime is so notorious.'

There was a silence as the two of them considered the kind of horror Latifa would have gone through.

'How do you know all of this?' Will asked after a while.

'When Ahmed arrived in England, we debriefed him thoroughly. At first, all he wanted to do was return to Afghanistan to rescue his sister, but we nipped that in the bud.'

'How?'

Pankhurst's face twitched. 'We told him she was dead.'

'Nice.'

'We do what's necessary, Will. Faisal Ahmed was no good to us dead in a ditch in Afghanistan. We calculated that learning of his sister's death would harden his resolve against the Taliban, make him more likely to help us. The British and American governments had always advocated regime change in the region; if he worked with us, he could be doing his bit to avenge his sister.

'He didn't have to grieve long. British and American troops marched into Afghanistan shortly after 9/11. Latifa Ahmed was discovered in a prison on the outskirts of Kabul and we were able to break the news to a grateful Ahmed that his sister was not dead after all. She wasn't in a good way, though. She weighed a little under six stone and her body was covered in sores. She hadn't eaten for weeks, nor had she been allowed out of the tiny cell in which she had been imprisoned, even to use the lavatory. She was practically swimming in her own excrement.

'From that point on, our intelligence on Latifa gets a bit thin. Faisal Ahmed was already proving his worth to us, so to keep him sweet, we offered to look after Latifa. She was cared for by the security forces out there for a short while – a couple of weeks at the best, until she regained some of her strength – then she disappeared. Our best guess is that after the traumas she underwent at the hand of the Taliban, she hid herself away in a quiet village somewhere – although, as you know, quiet villages are few and far between in Afghanistan. We're fairly sure, from all we know about their relationship, that Ahmed will have kept in touch with his sister somehow. We're equally convinced – and a number of psychiatric reports back this up – that he will have continued to remain in contact with her even after he went dark in 2003.

'As I've said, we rather lost track of Latifa once the Taliban fell. A few days ago, however, word reached us of her whereabouts. When the Taliban were thrown from power, their supporters were scattered around the country. Since then, certain factions have regrouped and gained in strength. It seems that Latifa has been abducted by one of these resurgent factions.

'Why?' Will asked, suspiciously. 'Surely the Taliban have bigger fish to fry at the moment.'

'I don't know,' Pankhurst admitted. 'I don't know why the Taliban do anything. What you've got to remember is that they're a law unto themselves and they have all sorts of warring factions that we don't even know about. I'm sure that most Taliban members couldn't give a fig about Latifa Ahmed. But clearly there's one group that does. If you want to know why, perhaps you can ask her when you see her.'

Will's eyes widened.

'We have an informer in the area who claims he can lead us to her. And that, Will, is where you come in.'

'You want me to go back to Afghanistan?'

'Precisely. You'll meet our contact and your objective will be to extract Latifa Ahmed from wherever she's being held and to bring her back safely to this country for questioning. If she can shed any light on Faisal Ahmed's whereabouts, we have to know. He could strike any minute and, frankly, this is our only lead.'

Will chewed on a fingernail for a moment. 'How reliable is your source?'

Pankhurst shrugged. 'We think he's sound. But we're not following this up because our source is reliable; we're following it up because we don't have any other options. And we don't have the luxury of time: at the moment we've no reason to believe that Faisal Ahmed knows Latifa's location. But he'll find out and we're pretty sure he'll try to free her. We have to get our hands on the woman before that happens.'

Will stood up and walked to the window. He looked out over the Thames to see that a flurry of snow was falling. It would be snowing in Afghanistan, too, not like the last time he was there. It had been high summer then, 35 degrees at the height of the sun, dry and acrid. But the Afghan winters were harsh. There would be deep snow − difficult to move through, easy to be seen in. And Afghanistan − the 'Stan' as the Regiment guys called it − was just as bad now as it was then. Worse, even. All this for a lead that could very well come to nothing.

He turned back to look at Pankhurst. 'How sure are you that Ahmed's planning something?' he asked.

'How sure do I need to be before I act?' the Director General replied, quietly. 'Our intelligence is pretty concrete. The student we apprehended in Rome gave us the basics.'

'Can I talk to him?'

'No,' Pankhurst said quickly. 'No. You can't do that.'

Will nodded, tactfully. He knew what that meant. If the student had been taken to a black camp, chances were he hadn't survived the questioning. Unfortunate for him, convenient for the authorities − they didn't want anyone running around spilling the beans about what they had been through.

'He must have got his intel from somewhere, though,' Will insisted.

Pankhurst nodded. 'He was a regular at the Rome mosque. We've interrogated the people he was friendly with, but they've given us nothing else. Trust me, Will, you won't get anything out of them. Our people are *extremely* persuasive.'

Will fell silent again. The prospect of a return to Afghanistan made him feel sick. But what was the alternative? To go back to the flat in Hereford and pick up his life where he had left off, dividing his time between the graveyard and the pub? How could he, now that he knew the truth about his family's death? How could he, now that he knew their killer was out there somewhere? He stared out of the window over the London skyline. Maybe Ahmed was there, hiding somewhere, waiting to strike. Waiting to kill more innocent people. Waiting to make widows and orphans. Waiting to destroy more lives, just like he had destroyed Will's. How bizarre that Will should have to go all the way back to Afghanistan to find out this man's location. Still, if that was what he had to do . . .

He turned back to Pankhurst. 'I'm not going in alone,' he said firmly. 'I'll need a unit. SAS.'

Pankhurst's nose twitched. 'Out of the question. If I could simply deploy the SAS, I would. You're being brought in precisely because you've been out of play for two years.'

'Cut the bullshit, Pankhurst,' Will snapped. The Director General's face flickered with annoyance. 'You and I both know I'm being brought in because you've gambled that I want Faisal Ahmed dead more than anything in the world.' Will looked around him. 'It's a comfortable office, this,' he said a bit more calmly. 'I'm not used to this sort of luxury. You obviously are. And you've obviously never been on covert ops in the Stan. If you had, you'd know that only an idiot would lay siege to the Taliban in mid-winter. If this were a more straightforward op, you'd be deploying a squadron. I'm asking for three men and if I don't get them, I'm not going.'

Pankhurst fell silent for a moment. When he spoke, it was with the reasonable voice of a skilled negotiator. 'I'm sure we could arrange some NATO troops in Kandahar.'

'I don't want NATO troops,' Will insisted. 'And I don't want fucking Green Berets. I want SAS. I know how they work and I know they're the best. Christ, sir, these guys devote their lives to this kind of work. There's no more chance of there being a mole in Hereford than there is of there being a mole in this room as we speak.'

The Director General took a deep breath. 'All right,' he said, quietly. 'I've asked you to trust me, so I'm going to return the compliment.'

Pankhurst managed to sound almost gracious, but Will knew it was simply that he had the DG over a barrel, so he stopped short of thanking him. 'Don't you have any more precise information about where this woman's being held?' he asked.

'Nothing. Our source is very jumpy – when you meet him, you'll need to win his trust. But we can hazard a guess that you'll be heading south from Kandahar – that's the area where the Taliban insurgency is strongest.'

Will nodded, curtly. He knew how dangerous that part of the world was.

'Listen to me carefully, Will,' Pankhurst continued. 'Your unit are the *only* ones you reveal your objective to and even they cannot know *why* you are extracting Latifa Ahmed. Someone's been tipping this guy off and we don't know how deep their influence goes. I know you've been trained to trust everyone at Hereford, Will, but that's one part of your training that you need to forget. We can't afford to trust *anyone*. Do you understand?'

'Yeah,' he replied. 'I understand.'

'And you're willing to do what it takes to get Latifa Ahmed out of Afghanistan?'

He nodded his head.

'Good,' Pankhurst said. If he felt any sense of satisfaction in Will's acceptance, he didn't show it. 'We can't hang around. We're assuming Ahmed doesn't know Latifa is being tortured, but as soon as he finds out he'll be straight there to extract her. And that woman has a lot of nasty things to look forward to – I don't want the Taliban torturing her to death before we've had the chance to ask her a few questions.'

'Yeah, well my diary's pretty free.'

'I'm sure it is,' Pankhurst replied. 'I'll get in touch with Credenhill now, tell them you'll be there in a couple of hours. In the meantime, I need to give you further instructions . . .'

★

Three and a half thousand miles away, a woman lay on the floor. She did not want to shiver. She did not want to show any sign of weakness, but she could not help it. The snow was thick outside – it had been falling for days now, the flakes piling softly on top of each other, covering the war-scarred ground of her country in a false blanket of purity. As a child, she had loved the coming of the snows. She and her brother would rush out of their small house to play in it the moment they were allowed, their parents watching them fondly from the doorway as they made snowballs and threw showers of powder at each other.

But it had been snowing, too, when the soldiers came; and now, she could not think of the whiteness of the snow without picturing the crimson of their parents' blood as it seeped from their bodies, melting the white powder with its warmth, before mingling into mush. Her childhood delight in the coming of the first snows had ended that day.

The hut in which she was being kept had no floor – just the earth, hardened with the cold, which seemed to leech any of the remaining warmth out of her body as she sat there.

She pulled the thin cloth they had given her to wear tightly around her, but it had been chosen more to cover her body than to keep her warm and it did little good. She even found that she was glad of the burka headdress they had insisted she wear – in that enclosed environment around her head, the heat of her breath at least staved off some of the chill.

She had not eaten for three days; even then the food had been filthy, but she had devoured it simply because she was famished. Every few hours of the day and night, one or two of them would come in. She had learned long ago with these people that it was better to let them do what they had come to do, rather than try to resist. They used thick wooden sticks, mostly, and beat her around the stomach and the back of her legs; she did not dare look at her skin for fear that it would revolt even her, and she had become used to the constant pain and the bruises that grew worse day by day.

One day, a particular man would come in. He was taller than the others and more quietly spoken. His face was scarred – a long scar, starting on his lower lip and finishing somewhere on his left cheek. No hair grew over the scar, which was red and angry, and it gave his face an ugly, gnarled look.

When she had seen that scar, she had known that her life was about to turn unpleasant, because she had been there when it was first inflicted. It had been a while before the Taliban had been overthrown and shortly after they had discovered that her brother – her foolish, reckless, beloved brother – was a double agent. He had come to warn her, to tell her to flee, but the Taliban were close behind. They had burst into her tiny house, knocking down the door – six of them, armed and with wicked, almost hungry gleams in their eyes.

The men were barking harshly in Pashto, shouting at each other to grab Latifa; but they soon fell silent when they saw Faisal Ahmed waiting for them. Her brother had pulled his gun on them. He fired it twice, with a deadly pinpoint accuracy: two Taliban members fell to the ground instantly, their foreheads exploding in a grisly shower of blood and brain; but the others, silent now though still with a terrifying fervour in their eyes, had continued to close in on him.

That was when he drew his knife.

It was a wicked-looking thing, its blade smooth and sharp on one side, hooked and jagged on the other. When he stabbed it into the belly of one of their attackers, the man's entrails came out with it. Latifa had watched as Faisal swung the knife, which still had human gore hanging from it, and slashed another of them across the face. The blade instantly ripped a gash across the man's lower lip and up into his cheek; he had roared in pain and raised his hands to his bloodsoaked face.

Faisal had almost overcome them, but not quite. No doubt if he hadn't come to warn her, he would have been long gone. But he *had* come to warn her and now he would pay the price. They would *both* pay the price for the path he had chosen to take.

That had been nine years ago. The man who held her in captivity now had never made any reference to the day her brother had scarred him so horribly. But they both knew what this was all about. And while he did not hit her or raise his voice to her, she was more scared of him than anyone. He asked her questions. He told her she would die if she did not comply. Despite her state, she had been fully aware of the madness and the thuggery that lay beneath those questions. To stand up to him was perhaps the most difficult thing she had ever done in her difficult life.

There were no windows in the hut, so she had to judge what time it was by the amount of light that peeped through a crack in the wooden walls. It was mid-morning, she guessed. About the time that he usually came. She huddled into one corner, waiting for the sound she so dreaded: her door being unlocked.

It came soon enough and when it did she started shaking through fear as well as cold. She heard the harsh voices first, then the scratchy sound of a key in the lock. Her eyes winced as the door opened, letting in the light, which was blindingly bright from being reflected off the snow. Two men appeared in the doorway, both of them wearing robes, turbans and long beards. One of them carried an AK-47 strapped around his neck – he stood guard outside the door. The second man carried no weapon. He closed the door behind him, then walked towards her. She remained cowering in the corner.

'Get to your feet, woman,' he said softly in Pashto.

She pushed herself up from the ground. Her legs were weak, and it was a strain to remain upright. She found she was glad of the burka – it hid the fear on her face as he looked at her.

'You *shall* tell us where your brother is,' the man insisted quietly. 'Sooner or later, you *shall* tell us. It is the will of Allah.'

She took a deep breath. How close she had been to crumbling on more than one occasion. How close she had come to persuading herself that her brother had brought all this on himself. She did not approve of how he was spending his life. She did not approve at all. But he was her brother. He had looked after her. She loved him. And whenever she found her resolve crumbling, she thought of him as a little boy. So earnest. How could she condemn him to the fate these Taliban monsters no doubt had in store for him?

'I do not know where he is,' she whispered.

The man remained expressionless. 'You are lying, of course,' he said. 'He has been in contact with you. This is not something we suspect; it is something we know. Your pain will not cease until you tell us where he is.'

She stared defiantly at him, though he could not see her expression. They stood there for a moment, face to face in that freezing hut, before he turned and walked out of the room. 'Beat her,' he said to the guard as he left.

She felt her knees buckle at those words, but she did her best to remain standing as the guard entered the hut. He was a huge man – burly and big boned – with a thick-set face and broad, heavy shoulders. He had a look of wild fervour in his eyes as he removed the strap of his gun from round his neck. A look that suggested he would take great pleasure in what he was about to do. Pleasure in carrying out Allah's will.

'Please,' she whispered, but her plea went unheard or at least unnoticed.

The guard made sure that the safety catch of his weapon was switched on. Then he put one hand on the barrel and the other on the handle. He approached her, waving the butt of the gun in her direction.

'Please,' she whispered again. 'Please, don't –'

The butt cracked down hard on the side of her head. She gasped with pain and started to fall; but before she could hit the ground she felt a heavy blow in her stomach as the guard whacked the blunt metal against her skin. It winded her so badly that she could not even make a noise; she just staggered slightly, trying, through her pain, to catch her breath.

And then it began in earnest.

Mostly the guard used the butt of the gun to beat her, though occasionally he used his feet, booted heavily under his dirty white robes. She huddled up into a little ball, like a hedgehog protecting itself, although she had no spikes to shield her from danger – only her damaged and brutalised skin, pulled tight over the bones of her thin body.

'You must tell him what he wants to know,' he would say occasionally. 'It is the only way to make this stop.'

But she said nothing. She even found herself wishing he would use the other end of his gun, to put an end to this. But she knew they would not allow her to die. Not yet. Not while they still had a use for her.

The beating seemed to last for an age – at one point she coughed up what she could only assume was blood into the veil of her burka – and it only finished when the guard himself seemed exhausted. He spat on her prostrate body, then left the hut without a word, locking the door behind him.

The woman did not move. She *could* not move. Freezing though she was, her body was too sore for her even to contemplate huddling up to try and keep warm, so she just lay there, her head spinning, her body pressed against the frozen earth.

She wondered which direction she was facing. Towards Mecca perhaps? Most likely not. She prayed nevertheless. With what strength she had, she whispered the *takbir*: '*Allahu Akbar, Allahu Akbar.*'

Surely God would not be angry with her for facing in the wrong direction.

Surely He did not condone the actions of these men, even if they did it in His name.

Surely He would not condemn her for refusing to say what she knew about her brother, her own flesh and blood, no matter what wicked things he may have done.

Surely He would not leave her to die in this place.

He would send someone to help her. Surely He would.

But who in the world would ever find her here?

★

Will Jackson felt as if he were living in a dream, but he couldn't tell if it was a good dream or a nightmare. Everything just seemed so unreal – Five's sudden appearance in his life;

the night he had spent with Kate; Faisal Ahmed. As he gazed out of the window of the chauffeur-driven car Pankhurst had arranged to take him back out of London, he decided that he wouldn't be at all surprised to wake up and find that he had imagined it all.

He didn't want to wake up, though. He didn't want it to be a dream. For the first time in ages, he felt as if he had a purpose. It was nerve-racking, certainly. Gut-wrenching, even. But somehow it felt right.

Will felt weird as he saw RAF Credenhill, 22 SAS Regiment's Hereford headquarters, approach. He hadn't seen the high fences with huge rolls of wicked-looking barbed wire perched on top of them for two years; he hadn't walked into one of the cavernous hangars that housed each of the Regiment's squadrons; but before that this unfriendly-seeming place had been a home from home. Will had felt comfortable among its training grounds and mess rooms, just like other people feel comfortable in their own gardens. He liked it. Now, though, he didn't relish the idea of walking down its corridors again; he didn't relish the idea of the looks the boys would give him. No doubt rumours had circulated about him since he left the Regiment and tongues would wag even more enthusiastically about his return.

The car pulled up at the main gates. Four soldiers stood guard, each carrying a machine gun and an unsmiling expression. The driver, who had not spoken a word to Will all the way from London, wound down his window. 'Will Jackson for Lieutenant Colonel Elliott,' he told the MOD policeman who came to the car to enquire their business.

The MOD policeman looked to the back of the car and his eyes widened slightly when he saw Will. Will recognised him vaguely – a face from the past that he couldn't put a name to. 'Do you have some identification?' the MOD policeman asked.

Will handed over the MOD pass that Pankhurst had

supplied him with. The MOD policeman took it, stepped back from the car, spoke into a radio handset and within seconds the gates were open and the car was driving through.

Will had been relieved to hear that Half Colonel Steve Elliott was still CO at Credenhill. They went back a long time – indeed it was Elliott who had first selected Will for the ranks of the 1st Royal Tank Regiment when he was a bright-eyed young squaddie. Back then, Will had thought Elliott was little more than a psychopath; but then that was what most potential recruits thought of their commanding officers when they were undergoing SAS training. When Will had been the first to complete the endurance stage of the final phase of his training – a forty-mile hike across the Brecon Beacons with full pack and rifle – he had expected a few words of congratulation. But that wasn't Elliott's style. 'Don't make the mistake of assuming the worst is over, Jackson,' he had informed the exhausted recruit in front of his new colleagues. 'A gentle walk in the hills isn't what you can expect on covert ops.'

'No, sir,' Will had replied immediately.

As time went on, though, Jackson had proved himself to Elliott. More than proved himself, in fact. He had risen through the ranks, and had come to respect and appreciate Elliott's blunt, no-nonsense style of talking. There was no room for bullshit when people's lives depended on you. And after Will's family died, Steve Elliott had been the man who stood by him. 'Don't leave the Regiment, Will,' he had said. 'You'll regret it. Take time out – as much as you like. But don't leave. Don't let the fight go out of you.'

Will had ignored his advice. Now and then in the few months that had followed, Elliott's words had come back to haunt him. But as time passed and a return to the military became less and less feasible, so Will had stopped worrying that his respected commander had been right.

About a year ago, Elliott had dropped him a line, inviting him to get in touch. The invitation had gone unanswered.

The car trundled to a halt in a small car park just in front of the main HQ building.

'Thanks for the lift.'

'Yes, sir,' the chauffeur replied. He stepped out of the car, opened Will's door and stood politely by as he climbed out. Will took a deep breath, nodded to the driver, then strode towards the main building.

A uniformed officer whom Will didn't recognise was at the desk.

'I'm here to see Lieutenant Colonel Elliott,' he said. 'My name's Will Jackson.'

That look again. The soldier clearly recognised his name. Will knew what Regiment gossip was like – he'd lay money on every soldier in the base knowing within the hour that he had arrived.

'I'll tell him you're here,' the soldier replied.

Steve Elliott was a big man – big even compared to the well-built SAS soldiers who surrounded him every day. He wore camouflage trousers and shirt, and Will had to think hard to remember if he had ever seen the man wear anything else. Elliott's nose had been broken in a couple of places and there was an ugly red scar peeping above the top of his shirt and up his neck. No one knew where he had received it, but it was fairly widely known that Elliott had been taken captive and tortured in western Iraq in 1991. Will had never heard him speak of his experience, but then few men ever did talk about things like that. His hair was a steely grey now and his forehead showed the creases of a lifetime's frowning. But Elliott's eyes were smiling as he approached Will and shook his hand.

'How are you, Will?' he asked, warmly.

Will shrugged, his eyes flickering over to the soldier at

the desk, who was watching them with obvious curiosity. 'Is there somewhere we can talk, boss?'

'Of course,' Elliott nodded. 'My office. Come on.'

They walked along the corridor in silence until they came to a door with Elliott's name on it. He held it open. 'Come on in, Will.'

Steve Elliott's office was very familiar to Will. He'd lost count of the number of unofficial debriefs that had taken place here. It was a typical military office – sparse, cold even. On the wall was an old picture of Elliott in the days when he was a squadron leader: his nose wasn't broken then and he looked somehow more innocent, less ravaged by the stress of the job and the passing years. But it was clearly the same man, the same steely resolve in his eyes.

Elliott took a seat behind his desk – a plain table with a telephone and a few papers scattered over it – while Will sat in the seat opposite.

'Can I get you something?' Elliott asked. 'A coffee –'

'Nothing. Thanks,' Will replied. 'Look, boss, I know you tried to get in contact with me a while ago. I'm sorry I –'.

Elliott held up his hand. 'Nothing to apologise for, Will,' he said briskly, and Will nodded in gratitude. 'Christ only knows what you must have been going through,' the commander continued. 'Everyone here was more shocked than I can tell you. You expect to lose people when you're out on ops, but –' His voice trailed off. Will had the impression that Elliott knew he was saying nothing that hadn't gone through Will's own mind a million times.

'Thank you, sir,' he said quietly.

They sat in silence for a moment.

'I'm surprised to see you here,' Elliott said finally.

'Not as surprised as I am to *be* here.'

'Pankhurst told me I'm to give you anything you need and that transport was being arranged to the NATO base in Kandahar. But he didn't tell me much else. Care to elaborate on your away break to the Stan?'

Will looked at his old friend. Elliott was smiling at him, leaning back comfortably in his chair. He looked relaxed, but Will could sense his intrigue, sense that he was desperate to find out what was going on. But as he sat there, Lowther Pankhurst's words rang in his head: *We can't afford to trust anyone.* He might not like the guy, but when the Director General of MI5 tells you to be suspicious, you'd better be suspicious.

'Sorry, boss,' he said calmly. 'I'm afraid I can't tell you that.'

Elliott's eyes narrowed slightly. 'We go back a long way, Will. I'd like to think we're friends. But I have to tell you this: it's a brave soldier who keeps his CO in the dark.'

The veiled threat hung there between them. Elliott clearly did not like the fact that Pankhurst had not told him nearly as much as he would have expected.

'I'm sorry, boss,' Will replied. 'I'm not a soldier. Not any more.'

'But you still think of yourself as one, Will. Why else would you still be calling me "boss"?'

'Old habits die hard, I guess.'

Elliott shrugged. 'Rumours that you're back at Credenhill will be buzzing around already, Will,' he pressed on. 'You're quite a celebrity around here, you know. Even now. If word gets out that you're just a puppet for Five, things could get nasty for you.'

Will couldn't tell from Elliott's demeanour if that was a threat or a warning. Either way, he knew his response had to be the same. 'I won't be around long enough for that to make any difference to me,' he said firmly. 'I'm sorry, boss, but I'm past caring about Credenhill gossip. I'm here to put together a team. I can't tell you what we're doing, not until the operation is over. Probably not even then.'

81

'All right, Will,' Elliott conceded. 'I have my orders from Five. They tell me you need three men.'

Will nodded. 'We'll be going cross-country into southern Afghanistan. It's going to be snowing and if things go as they should we'll have one hostage who won't be in very good shape, so I need at least one person well trained in cold-weather survival. If any of them have had active service in Afghanistan, so much the better. Sharpshooters, well versed in escape and evasion. I need the best, boss.'

Elliott pressed his fingers together and looked at his former employee as though sizing him up.

'All right, Will,' he said finally. 'The lads we've selected will fit the bill. But maybe one day you'll let me know what this is all about.' He picked up the phone on his desk and dialled a short number. 'Let Major Adams know we're ready for him,' he told whoever was at the other end. 'We'll be there in a few minutes.' He replaced the phone on to its cradle.

'Thank you,' Will said, quietly.

Elliott shrugged and an awkward silence fell on the room. Eventually the Half Colonel spoke. 'Listen, Will,' he said. 'I'm not trying to get you to tell me what you're doing, but if you're planning on heading south from Kandahar, you need to be careful. I know you've had experience in Afghanistan; I know you understand how fucked up that place is. But things are different there now. More dangerous, especially in the south. I'm sure you're aware that there are Taliban factions regrouping down there. They're well armed and, frankly, they're desperate. I've lost more men on covert ops in Afghanistan in the last eighteen months than I'd care to count.'

Will listened carefully – he knew Elliott didn't give warnings lightly.

'I've attended enough Regiment funerals this year, Will. Let's not have any more just before Christmas, eh?'

'I don't want funerals any more than you do, boss.'

'No,' Elliott said. 'I know. They said the operation was urgent and that you'd want to get to Afghanistan as soon as possible. When are you planning on leaving?'

Will looked momentarily down to the floor, then fixed Elliott with a determined stare.

'Transport's arranged for tonight,' he said. 'We don't have any time to lose.'

SIX

She had fallen asleep thinking of her brother. Thinking of the last time she had seen him, when his face had been so full of apprehension, his voice so full of urgency. 'You must flee, Latifa,' he had said. 'We must both flee. They have found out about me. It is only a matter of time before they come—'

And now, outside, the sun had set and all was dark, but night and day had no meaning to her in this place; they were just arbitrary markers that punctuated her suffering at regular intervals. She had been asleep for three hours – about the longest she ever managed before she was woken up by the cold or by her aching body. But it was neither of those things that roused her now. It was the sound of the door being unlocked – the sound that haunted her every living moment. She knew that whenever someone came through the door, something unpleasant was about to happen.

She was confused and disorientated in the dark, but gradually she became aware that there were men in the hut with her. Three, maybe four. As she stared around in fear through the veil of her burka, a light appeared at the door. Her eyes squinted with momentary pain as she saw the man with the scarred face in the doorway holding a flaming torch.

'Hold her down,' he said harshly.

Suddenly there were firm hands on her limbs. She

screamed once, but then she found herself unable to make another sound as terror froze her throat. There were definitely four men holding her − she realised that as she was pressed firmly on to the hard earth. She tried to struggle, but the men were too strong.

Looking up she saw the one with the torch standing over her. 'Where is he?' he asked calmly.

'I have told you a thousand times,' she spat, '*I don't know!*' Once more she tried to struggle; once more she was held down.

The man with the torch knelt beside her. He removed the thin shoes she was wearing, then deliberately lowered the burning flame and touched it to the sole of her right foot. She screamed in agony as he held it there for a number of seconds. When he removed it she was whimpering breathlessly, but she screamed a second time when he touched the torch to her other foot.

When he had finished, he spoke a single word to the other men and they released her, but by now she was too agonised and frightened to do anything other than curl up and sob.

Wordlessly, the men filed out of the hut. They closed the door behind them and, of course, locked it before walking away.

★

'You'd better give me the low-down on these guys,' Will told the CO as they walked along the corridors of Credenhill HQ towards the briefing room.

Elliott nodded. 'RWW, all three of them,' he said.

'Good,' Will grunted. RWW − the Revolutionary Warfare Wing, or the Increment to anyone in the know. A secretive group of crack troops, taken from the SAS and the SBS, deployed around the world to train terrorists − or 'freedom fighters,' as the British government preferred to think of them — and carry out hypersensitive, top-secret operations. The Afghan mujahideen, the Khmer Rouge in Cambodia and any number of other bands of guerrilla fighters had been turned into highly effective fighting forces thanks to the skills of the RWW. The Revolutionary Warfare Wing was also used to carrying out politically sensitive operations that would always be officially denied — a roundabout way of saying assassinations. When the head of MI6 had recently gone on the record saying that to his knowledge none of his people had ever carried out an assassination, he'd been telling the truth, because the Increment did their dirty work for them. These guys got deployed all over the world: Iraq, Afghanistan, South America. You name it, if it was a hot spot, the RWW would put in an appearance and its men were among the best the Regiment could provide.

There were other good reasons, though, for drawing his talent from the RWW and he suspected that Pankhurst had specifically asked for them. These soldiers would have undergone the most rigorous vetting of anyone in the British military. Their bank accounts would have been watched; their phones would have been tapped; Will had even heard that there was a policy of entrapment — putting temptation in the way of these guys or trying to trick them into revealing sensitive information to a supposed stranger who was really working for the military. If Pankhurst was worried about a leak, then giving Will a team from the RWW was a neat way of lessening the risk — they were as close to watertight as you could get.

'Frank Anderson's the most experienced,' said Elliott, interrupting Will's thoughts. He recognised the name and a face vaguely popped into his mind. 'Thirty-one years old. Frankly, I don't think he'll be thrilled taking orders from someone who's not currently in the Regiment, but he'll do it.'

'Are you sure?' Will demanded. 'I haven't got time to start breaking people in.'

'If I give him an order, he'll follow it,' Elliott said, confidently. 'And you could do with his experience. He's led a number of expeditions into the mountain regions of Afghanistan, so he knows the country and what you might be up against.'

Will nodded. 'OK. Good.'

'Mark Drew's a bit of a Regiment golden boy. Fucking quiet, fucking fit – endurance levels like I've never seen. Good behind the wheel of a car – not that you'll have much time for sightseeing.'

'Has he been deployed in Afghanistan?'

'No. But several operations in southern Iraq and South America. Trust me, he'll be an asset.'

'And the third one – what did you say his name was?'

'Kennedy. Nathan Kennedy. Popular, bit of a smart-arse. Geordie lad. Got a mouth on him and likes the sound of his own voice, but fucking sharp. He's been in and out of the Congo several times in the last couple of years.'

'The Congo? I didn't know the SAS was there.'

'There's a lot of things you don't know about the SAS, Will,' Elliott said pointedly. 'You've been otherwise engaged, remember? Anyway, Kennedy's very good – at least as good as the other two.'

'Anderson has a family, doesn't he?' Will asked, as nonchalantly as he could. He was hotly aware that two years ago he would never have asked that question. You go in, you do the job and you look after your mates, no matter what their personal situation.

'Does it matter?'

Will sniffed. 'No,' he lied. Truth was, his attitude towards such things had changed. The idea of taking a family man into the field of war was one that he suddenly had diffi-culty with.

'A young daughter. He wouldn't want me to know that I told you that, and he certainly doesn't expect any special treatment because of it. It's a strong team. For my money, there's just one thing about it that doesn't add up.'

Will raised an eyebrow. 'What's that?'

The CO stopped walking. 'You, Will,' he said bluntly. 'You've been out of it for two years. God only knows what your fitness levels are. You've been part of the Regiment for long enough to know that if you don't keep yourself sharp –'

'Don't worry about me, boss. I'll be fine.' Will tried to sound confident, but he knew there was truth in what the Colonel was saying. He'd kept in shape, but there was nothing to guarantee that this would be enough. Christ, he hadn't even held a gun for two years. All the more reason to have a good team around him – he hoped that Anderson, Drew and Kennedy were as good as they sounded.

Elliott led them to a briefing room at the far end of the administrative building, one of several secure areas where operational details were discussed. Will knew that these rooms were padded with a soundproofing material and they had no windows to ensure that there was no line of sight into the room. Elliott nodded at the soldiers standing guard outside as they approached and the doors were immediately held open.

There were four men waiting inside. One was in camou-flage trousers and shirt; the other three wore civvies. They were sitting around a large table, but all stood up as Elliott and Will walked in.

'At ease,' Elliott said, before turning to the man in mili-tary uniform. 'Major Hughes, this is Will Jackson. Will, Major Hughes has been briefed by Five to put your team together.'

Hughes shook Will's hand, before introducing the three men. He was a tall man – taller even than Will – with heavily greased hair combed over in a side parting. He looked almost old-fashioned, like a soldier in a black and white photograph from the First World War. 'Frank Anderson, Mark Drew and Nathan Kennedy.'

Will nodded at each of them in turn. It would have been surprising if he hadn't recognised three members of the Increment by sight and sure enough now that he was in the room with them, their faces were familiar. None of them were clean-shaven and Will understood why: a lot of the Regiment boys had taken to growing beards, as it helped them blend in to those parts of the Middle East where they were regularly deployed. Frank Anderson was broad-shouldered and square-chinned. His hair, clearly balding, was cropped short. No one could say he was a good-looking man. Mark Drew was smaller but just as stocky, with blond hair and flat, blue eyes. Nathan Kennedy was the most severe-looking of the three. His skin was tanned, his eyes brown and he had a gleam in his eyes that would have been cheeky had Will not known that he was a trained killer. Will had a vague recollection of a night a few years back when a few Hereford locals had been riling Kennedy in one of the town's pubs. Nathan Kennedy wasn't the type to let it pass and the civvies – four or five of them – had ended the evening with broken noses. Not exactly a guy with a long fuse, but useful in a fight.

'Can't get enough of the old place, eh, Jackson?' Kennedy asked, laconically. 'What's wrong – not getting enough skirt on civvy street? Thought you'd come and spend a bit of time with some real men, see if the pheromones rub off?'

Drew and Anderson smiled at Kennedy's comment, but Elliott didn't. 'Shut it, Kennedy,' he instructed.

'Right you are, boss,' Kennedy replied with a twinkle. He settled back in his chair and the three of them sat there, evidently reserving judgement on the man who was supposed to lead them into one of the most dangerous places in the world.

Will looked around. The room was fairly empty, with the exception of the table, a few chairs and an overhead projector pointed at a large whiteboard.

'Has this room been swept for bugs?' he asked Elliott.

The CO raised an eyebrow and Will knew why – he clearly wasn't used to being spoken to like that, especially not in front of his men.

'Of course it's been swept, Will. They all are, regularly. You know that.'

'Good,' Will replied. 'I'll need a different room.'

'I beg your pardon?' Elliott replied, his voice dangerously quiet.

'I said, I'll need a different room. I'm sorry, boss. What I have to say to these men is sensitive and I'm afraid I can't brief them in the first room you lead me to.'

Elliott and Will locked gazes and he was aware of the others eyeing each other uncomfortably.

'Are you suggesting somebody at Credenhill has ordered surveillance on this briefing room, Will?'

Will held his head high. He hated having to embarrass his old friend like this, but security was security. 'I'm not suggesting anything, boss. But I'll need a different place to brief them.'

His demand seemed to echo around the room and Elliott appeared unwilling to answer it. 'OK, Will,' he said finally, quietly. 'We'll ignore the fact that your absence from the Regiment has made you forget your manners.' He looked over at the Major. 'Take them to another briefing room,' he ordered.

'Thank you, boss,' Will said.

'All right,' Elliott replied gruffly. 'I'll have someone open up the foreign-weapons armoury for you.'

'And we'll need transport to Brize Norton in about an hour and a half.'

Elliott nodded, then without another word he strode from the room.

Major Hughes silently led the remaining four of them down the corridor to a second briefing room. 'I'm sorry, Major,' Will told him when they arrived. 'I'm going to have to ask you not to come in.'

The Major narrowed his eyes. 'It's not the way we do things around here, Jackson,' he said, waspishly. 'I've put this team together for you. I want to know what they're doing.'

Will looked about, then indicated with a nod of his head that the Major should step aside with him. The moment they were out of earshot, Will spoke quietly. 'My orders come from the Director General of MI5, Major Hughes,' he said. 'You can call him and check or you can do what I say. The end result will be the same – I'm going to brief these men on my own. I'm sorry if that makes you feel insecure, but I don't have time to fuck around avoiding stepping on people's toes. Now do you have a problem with that?'

Hughes looked back at him with unbridled dislike. 'No problem,' he replied.

'Good.' Will turned to the three waiting men. 'Get inside,' he told them. They opened the door and disappeared into the room. Will followed.

This briefing room was much like the other – muffled and windowless. Will shut the door behind him, then turned to address the three SAS men, who stood in a line by the table.

'Right,' he said. 'First things first. There seems to be a bit of resistance to the idea of me giving orders around here.

If any of you have a problem with it, now's the time to pipe up.'

None of the men gave any reaction.

'Good.' He walked up to Anderson – wasn't he the one Elliott thought he might have trouble with? 'You sure, Anderson?'

'The boss says we're to take our orders from you. That's good enough for me.'

Will nodded. 'Right then. Sit down and listen. We're leaving soon and there's a lot to get through.'

The men took their seats and Will started to speak. It felt weird – as if he had never been away – but he fell into it naturally as he repeated the plan he and Pankhurst had devised before he left Thames House.

'At 17.00 hours a C-5 Galaxy military transport plane will land at Brize Norton. It's an American transport, rerouted through the UK for the express purpose of ferrying us to the NATO base outside Kandahar in southern Afghanistan.' He looked at each of them for any sign of surprise or alarm. There was nothing, so he continued. 'Once we reach the base, we're going to be introduced to an Afghan informer. This man knows the whereabouts of an individual who has been abducted by a Taliban faction in the countryside. Our mission is to locate and extract the target and bring this individual back to the UK. Alive.'

'Do we have any idea of the target's current location?' Anderson asked.

'Nothing specific. The source is nervous about who he gives that information to. He'll be coming with us, so we need to be prepared for that.'

'What's the target's name?' Drew asked.

Will's eyes flicked to the door. 'I'll tell you that once we're on our way.'

The men nodded. Will scanned their faces for any flicker

of dissent, ready to stamp on it if he saw it. But there was none.

'OK,' he continued. 'We need to get tooled up. Let's go.'

The foreign-weapons armoury was housed in a small brick building. There were large metal doors at the entrance which were normally locked by chunky padlocks, but as the four of them approached, Will could see that the place had been opened up. They filed quietly inside.

There was something reassuring about the armoury. It smelled comfortingly of gun oil, and metal racks lined the walls, displaying weapons from all around the world, or copies of them. This place housed every armament you'd ever need on a mission, neatly ordered and well maintained. MP5 sub-machine guns, AK-47s, a smattering of MI6s alongside its more modern replacement, the Diemaco C8 carbine, along with a huge number of hand-guns and sniper rifles. There was a large selection of suppressed weaponry and Will knew that much of the equipment in this particular armoury would be non-attributable – no serial numbers, nothing to give anyone a clue as to where it came from or, more importantly, who had been using it. On an officially deniable mission, an attributable firearm was like a fingerprint at a crime scene.

The armourer – no doubt a weapons technician attached to the Regiment from the REME – was waiting for them. His job was to keep track of all the weapons, make sure they were signed out properly and keep them clean and in good working order. What he would never do, however, was ask questions: it wasn't important that he knew *why* the weapons were needed, just that they *were* needed. A couple of years at Credenhill, maybe less, and he'd be on his way, so none of the SAS men felt any sense of comrade-ship with him. He was a gruff, no-nonsense kind of man.

Serious. Responsible. Just what you wanted in the guy whose job it was to make sure your weapon didn't jam at the crucial moment. He nodded a curt greeting at the four-man unit as they walked in, then they went about selecting their weapons.

It was done with a cool detachment, a professionalism borne of respect for the firearms they were taking that could mean the difference between life and death. They selected four suppressed C8s, along with a number of scopes and a 40 mm grenade-launcher attachment. These were duly packed into a heavy-duty protective case for the journey, while Will picked out a Minimi 5.56 mm light machine gun. He hoped they wouldn't have to use it, but if the situation demanded it, this gun had an effective range of 800 metres and was capable of a thousand rounds a minute. Once the Minimi was packed away, they each selected a Sig 226 pistol. Will also took a Sig 230 – smaller, less conspicuous, it could be hidden under civilian clothing without a noticeable bulge. Boxes of armour-piercing ammo were added to the requisition, as well as a stash of fragmentation grenades and phosphorous grenades, then each man carefully signed the forms the armourer gave them.

Once the weapons had been requisitioned, they needed to gather the rest of their equipment. They would wear civilian clothes as far as the NATO base in Kandahar; once there, they would find themselves some local clothes. Once they got out into the countryside, however, they would need cold-weather gear. Into their rucksacks they carefully folded Goretex jackets and pull-on snow suits. As a matter of routine, they each stowed away a Sat phone that would enable them to make encrypted calls from anywhere in the world. Before he had left Thames House, Pankhurst had told Will the Americans had given a promise of air support once he was on the ground. Nice gesture, but Will knew they couldn't rely on it if things turned nasty. Still, it was a comfort to have them, even though Will knew that if it came to the point where he needed air support, it would probably be too late. Finally, they each stowed a set of night-vision goggles. If they conducted their mission under cover of darkness, NV would be invaluable.

By the time they had gathered their equipment together it was gone two o'clock. It would take a couple of hours to get to Brize Norton and as they walked round to the front of the main building they saw a vehicle pull up and wait. It was a standard white minibus – the sort of thing you might expect a scoutmaster to be in charge of – and the driver was dressed in civilian clothes, although Will knew he was Hereford through and through. Steve Elliott was waiting by the minibus, his face unreadable as they approached. He indicated to Will that he should step aside with him.

'I don't like not knowing what my men are doing, Will,' he said, once they were out of earshot. 'I know we're both following orders and I know I don't need to say it, but be careful, OK?'

Will nodded.

'And good luck. I want to see you all back here very soon.'

'You will, boss,' Will replied, quietly. 'You will.' He turned back to his unit, nodded at them and together they climbed into the back of the minibus.

The case of weapons was already waiting for them on the floor, tucked well out of sight of any casual observer, and as they drove out of the heavily guarded gates to RAF Credenhill, they looked for all the world like a bunch of mates going on a trip together.

Inside the bus, the lads chatted calmly. 'You heard about Stevens?' Drew asked no one in particular.

'Aye,' Kennedy replied. 'Out on his fucking ear. Sounds like he went to the bank one time too many.'

Will's face must have registered his confusion. 'Andy Stevens,' Kennedy explained. 'You know him?'

Will shook his head.

'No, you probably wouldn't. Only been with the Regiment a year or so, silly fucker.'

'What'd he do?'

'He was out in Baghdad. Some of the lads were helping transport fucking great palettes of Yankie dollars, which they were sending out there to help rebuild the ragheads' economy. Course, he couldn't resist helping himself, could he? Would've got away with it, too, if some bird at that bank in Hereford hadn't noticed he was coming in every other day to change several thousand dollars.'

'How much did he take?' Will asked.

'No one knows. Enough to get him a fucking court martial, though. Shame – quite liked the lad myself. Bit of a wanker, but if I had a problem keeping the company of wankers, I wouldn't be here, would I?'

The others smiled and the conversation moved on. Will listened to them as they discussed the latest Hereford gossip and the stories they'd heard on the news – anything apart from the job in hand. But when there was a lull in the conversation, Will knew they would be mentally preparing themselves, going through the salient details of the mission in their heads. Anderson, Drew and Kennedy showed no signs of nerves – just a quiet, determined detachment, a confidence that they would be able to get the job done.

Deep down, Will wished he could share in that confidence. Forty-eight hours ago he had been a nobody, just some waster in the pub filling his time with whatever best numbed his grief on that particular day. Now he felt he had a purpose and he started feeling the hot anticipation that always used to surge through him before a mission. It was tempered, though, by an uneasiness, a self-doubt. Steve Elliott had been brutal in his assessment that Will might not be up to the job, yet he hadn't said anything Will didn't feel deep down. But the confidence of the others was reassuring. He tried to put those doubts from his mind and focus on the task ahead.

There was a lull in the conversation. Will turned to Anderson. 'You've got a kid, right?' he said.

Anderson looked surprised that Will should have brought it up. 'Yeah,' he said, warily.

'How old?'

'Nearly three.'

'Looking forward to Christmas, I'll bet.'

Anderson smiled the smile of an indulgent parent. 'Yeah,' he said quietly. 'She is.'

Will nodded and for a moment an image of his own daughter flitted through his head. 'We're going to make sure you're back for her.'

The three other men stared at him in mild astonishment and Will felt a flush of embarrassment rise to his face. What the hell had made him say that? He knew full well that that kind of talk before an operation was strictly out of bounds. These guys didn't even want to entertain the notion of failure and Will knew that Anderson had not even considered the idea that he wouldn't be back home for Christmas. It wasn't that they were blasé, it was just that they knew that full confidence in their own training and ability was their best friend.

Kennedy broke the uncomfortable silence that followed. 'You said you'd give us the name of the target once we left Hereford,' he reminded Will.

Will sniffed. 'Her name is Latifa Ahmed.'

Surprise registered on Kennedy's face. '*Her* name? It's a woman?'

'That's right,' Will said, flatly.

'Easy, tiger,' Drew said to Kennedy with a smile. He looked over at Will. 'Our Nathan's got a bit of a reputation,' he said. 'Pulled pigs in fifteen countries at last count, or was it sixteen?'

'Seventeen, actually,' grinned Kennedy, and Will was relieved that his fuck-up of a moment ago seemed to have been forgotten.

'She'll slow us down,' Anderson noted more soberly. It clearly wasn't a complaint; just an observation.

'Probably,' Will agreed. 'And she's being held captive by Taliban extremists, which means she won't be in the best of health. But from what I know about her, she's pretty tough. And she'll want to get away from that place as much as us.'

'You're under instructions from Five, right?' Drew piped up.

'That's right.'

'So what do they want with her?'

Will couldn't say too much, but he knew that if the unit thought he was keeping too much from them, it might engender bad feeling. 'She has information about a possible terrorist strike against London,' he said evasively, and the three of them seemed to accept that.

'Fucking ragheads,' Kennedy murmured, and the minibus continued to speed down the motorway.

Night started to fall and by the time they reached Brize Norton it was pitch black. Word of their arrival had clearly preceded them and the minibus was allowed to drive straight through and wait at the side of the runway. They arrived just in time to see the lights of the Galaxy emerge through the clouds in the distance. It was an impressive sight as it roared in to land, the engines of this massive transport plane filling the air all around, making it impossible for them to shout at each other, let alone speak. Will had been in enough of these aircraft – and planes like it – in the past, but he was always slightly taken aback by the sheer size of them when seen close up. The Galaxy had a wingspan of almost seventy metres and housed a cargo department nearly forty metres long. As soon as it came to a halt, the engines whirred to a silence and a fleet of refuelling vehicles drove up to it to start replenishing its tanks, while Drew and Kennedy flung open the back doors of the minibus and carried the weapons case out on to the tarmac.

A uniformed man descended from the cockpit of the plane. He walked briskly up to the unit and gave them all a cursory nod. 'You're our passengers, I take it?' he shouted in an American accent.

'That's us,' Will replied. 'How long before we're airborne?'

The pilot looked back over his shoulder. 'As soon as we're refuelled.'

'Do you have any passengers other than crew?'

The pilot shook his head. 'No,' he replied. 'Just cargo. There's seating on the top deck.'

Will nodded, pleased that the pilot hadn't seen fit to ask them who they were or what they were doing. It was often the way in situations like this. Clearly someone had told the yanks not to ask too many questions. Drew and Kennedy picked up the weapons stash once more, and the four of them strode across the tarmac to the steps which led into the aircraft.

The Galaxy had two decks. The steps took them on to the lower one, which was packed full of equipment. Most of it was on enormous pallets, covered with plastic sheeting and held in place by cargo nets. It was impossible to tell what was on those pallets, but Will knew it could be anything from weapons to ammunition to food rations or clothes. At one end of the cargo deck he saw two military vehicles – five-ton trucks, they looked like – and a couple of loadies were milling around them, checking they were secure. At the cockpit end of the cargo deck was a flight of metal stairs. Will and his men headed straight for these and carried their weapons case on to the upper level.

It was deserted. There was seating for perhaps seventy people and the chairs faced towards the rear of the aircraft rather than the front. They all took seats in the front row, but spaced themselves out so that they had a couple of seats on either side of each other, then strapped themselves in.

Around them, the noise of the engines started to get louder. Another man appeared – the flight lieutenant. 'Take-off in two minutes, guys,' he told them, before walking back to take his place up front.

The engines were screaming now and Will felt the aircraft shudder into movement. The lights on the deck dimmed and within a minute the plane was speeding down the runway and was airborne.

Will took a deep breath. He hadn't left British soil for more than two years. It seemed so surreal doing it now under these circumstances.

They stayed strapped in as the aircraft climbed steeply through the clouds; only when it started to level did Will unbuckle his seatbelt. The scream of the engines had subsided a little now, but it was still loud – Will had forgotten how noisy these military transport aircraft could be.

'I'm fucking starving,' he heard Kennedy say from a couple of seats away. The others grunted in agreement. Ahead of them, at the back of the plane, a grey metal microwave oven was fitted into the wall. Next to it was a cold cabinet, which Kennedy opened. He pulled out a cardboard container of frozen army rations, then blitzed it in the microwave. The smell of the starchy food hit Will's nostrils and it occurred to him that he hadn't eaten since his early breakfast in the café near Kate's house. He was hungry, he realised, and when Kennedy had removed his food from the microwave, Will went to get some of his own.

The army rations were plain, but hot and welcome. Will ate three of the little boxes of food – beef stew with dumplings, baked beans with sausage and a chocolate sponge with gloopy chocolate sauce – before his hunger was satisfied and the others also wolfed the rations down enthusiastically.

'We should get some sleep,' he told the others, and they all nodded. They delved into their rucksacks, each taking out a strong string hammock, which they hung from the side of the plane. Anderson came round with a small cardboard box of pills.

'I got these from the med centre before we left,' he announced, handing a tablet to each of them. Will didn't need to ask what it was – taking a sleeping pill was pretty standard procedure before a long flight and these were specially designed to ensure that you got a few hours of well-needed shut-eye, without the risk of waking up feeling drowsy. He put one on his tongue, felt the acrid taste in his mouth and swallowed it. Then, without another word, he climbed into his hammock.

It was strangely comfortable lying there in mid-air and the dirty, mechanical noise of the plane's engines started to become hypnotic. There was a small window by his head and as he lay there he looked out into the blackness, watching the light at the tip of the wing flashing on and off.

If a military man stops his career before the time is right, he risks wasting away into nothing. As drowsiness fell upon him, Will heard Pankhurst's comment echoing in his head. He hated admitting it to himself, but the Director General was right. Will had been wasting away in Hereford, but it had taken this to make him realise it. He realised something else, too. Dangerous though it was, he was looking forward to Afghanistan.

This was what he had been trained to do.

This was what he was *meant* to do.

And it was good to be doing it again.

With those thoughts going round his head and with sound of the aircraft's engines filling his ears, Will Jackson fell into a deep, dreamless sleep.

SEVEN

When he awoke, his ears were popping. The Galaxy was losing height. Will looked at his watch. 2 a.m., UK time. He did a quick calculation – that would make it 6.30 a.m. in Kandahar. Sure enough, as he looked out of the window, he saw that the blackness of the night was giving way to a glimmer of morning light.

Around him the others had already woken and were packing their hammocks back into their rucksacks. No one was speaking – there was no banter, no small talk. Everyone seemed businesslike and efficient. Will hauled himself from his own hammock and started getting his things together.

The flight lieutenant appeared again. 'Ten minutes till landing,' he announced, and the four of them strapped themselves in once more.

Kandahar Airport, Will knew from past experience, was much easier to land at by night. During the hours of sunlight, it tended to merge into the surrounding countryside, whereas when it was dark, the two-mile runway was lit up like a Christmas tree. When he felt the wheels of the Galaxy touch ground, it was a strange sensation. No matter how used you were to flying, there was always a vague sense of relief when the aircraft touched down; but today it was tempered with a heightened sense of anticipation. Up until now there had been a sense of unreality about this whole thing, but the moment he knew he was on Afghan soil, it hit him that

103

there was no turning back. He just had to get on with the job in hand.

Kandahar Airport was a huge, sprawling space. Stuck in the middle of one of the most inhospitable regions of this inhospitable country it was not only a civilian airfield, but home to troops from all over the world. Pankhurst had explained to Will that the NATO-led International Security Assisted Force were based here, but he knew from his own past that it was also home to the RAF's Harrier GR7 detachment as well as the detachments of AH-64 Apache attack helicopters, CH-47 Chinook support helicopters and Lynx utility helicopters. Soldiers from America, Canada, Britain and, of course, Afghanistan worked side by side out of this airport, so it was no surprise, as they walked down on to the tarmac, to see how busy the place was, even at this early hour in the driving snow, which reduced visibility to only a few metres. Voices were shouting above the noise of the aircraft engines; a Harrier screamed down to land on the runway, while all around them were armed troops going about their early-morning business. Everyone's breath steamed in the cold air and as they drove around the airfield, beams of headlamps from all the vehicles flashed blindingly, like mechanical fireflies at night.

It was freezing cold and within seconds of stepping on to the tarmac, snow started to settle thickly on their clothes.

'Will Jackson?' a voice called.

Will looked round to see a figure in RAF uniform standing by a military truck. Its yellow headlamps cut a beam through the half-light and the snow. The four-man unit walked towards him. 'I'm Junior Technician Evans,' he said. 'I've been sent to escort you.' The kid had a shock of ginger hair and green eyes. His face was chapped from the cold, and he barely looked old enough to walk to school by himself, let alone be out here.

Will nodded and they climbed into the truck, Kennedy and Drew bringing the weapons case with them. The vehicle moved off and they were driven along a winding road that skirted the edge of the airfield. It stopped, about a mile later, outside a glum-looking pre-fabricated hut. A couple of trucks were parked outside and from the glow of light coming out of the window, Will could tell it was occupied.

'Who lives here?' he asked the young RAF soldier, gruffly.

'His name is Arthur Rankin, sir,' he replied. 'He's an assistant to the NATO Senior Civilian Representative. He helps coordinate liaisons between the military and the local Afghan population. He's requested that you report to him as soon as you land.'

'Fine,' Will said. He turned to the unit. 'You three wait here. I'll see what he has to say.' He climbed out of the truck and hurried through the snow to knock on the door of the hut.

'Come in,' a voice called, but Will had already opened the door and stepped inside.

It was warm in the hut, thanks to a large electric heater burning at full blast; but warmth was the only comfort the place offered. It was sparsely furnished – at one end was a solitary desk that looked like it came from a school classroom, with a beige computer and a telephone on it. Around the walls were a number of metal filing cabinets and sitting behind the table was an enormously fat man wearing a thick woollen overcoat. Standing at the other end of the room was a tall, skinny man with dark skin, a long scruffy beard and sturdy Afghan clothes. He had a large, hooked nose, deep brown eyes and his hair was bundled into a black turban.

'Shut the bloody door, for crying out loud,' the fat man barked. His voice was posh and it didn't do much to endear him to Will, who closed the door slowly behind him.

'Beastly place,' the man shuddered. 'As hot as hell in the summer, colder than a snowman's bollocks in winter.' He stood up and waddled towards Will. 'Arthur Rankin. Welcome to Afghanistan,' he said, stretching out his hand. 'You must be delighted to be here.'

Will shook his podgy hand without much enthusiasm. 'Not really,' he replied. 'The sooner we can get our business done, the sooner we can leave.' He looked meaningfully over at the bearded man.

'This is Sami,' Rankin said. 'He's your fixer.'

Will nodded curtly at Sami. 'I take it you have details of our contact.'

Rankin rolled his eyes at Will's aggressive demeanour. 'Of course he has the details of your contact,' he said. 'I hardly think he's here for the company or the comfortable surroundings.' He smiled at his own joke. 'I'd like to offer you a seat, but I'm afraid NATO won't stretch to any extra chairs in my delightful office.'

'I'll stand.'

'You'll have to, my friend.'

Will ignored him and turned to the fixer.

'Where do I meet him?'

Sami eyed him warily. 'Kandahar, at eleven o'clock this morning.' His voice was heavily accented, but he obviously spoke English extremely well.

'Where in Kandahar?'

'There is a small café near the bazaar next to the main mosque in the centre of the city. It has no name, but you cannot miss it.'

'I'll say,' Rankin interrupted in his braying voice. 'Ghastly little place, always filled to the rafters with screaming Afghans smoking their revolting tobacco.'

Will did his best to ignore the comment and he could sense that the fixer found Rankin as unpleasant as he did.

'Your contact's name is Ismail,' Sami said, calmly. 'He

has been feeding us good information about what the Taliban in this region have been up to, but he is extremely nervous.'

'I don't blame him,' Rankin snorted. 'If they find out what he's been doing, he'll be in the arms of Allah faster than you can say "Islamic Jihad".'

'Have you met him?' Will asked. He had addressed the question to Sami, but Rankin answered.

'Absolutely not. I try to leave Kandahar Airport as little as possible and there's no way our man would ever come to us here. No, we have agents like Sami on the ground handling him. They pass information on to me and I pass it upwards.' He cast a curious glance at Will. 'I must say,' he observed, 'there hasn't been any intelligence passing through me that I would have thought warranted the arrival of the SAS.'

He looked expectantly at Will, clearly hoping he might enlighten him; but Will remained stony-faced.

Rankin shrugged.

'As I was saying,' Sami continued, 'Ismail is an extremely nervous informant. As he's never met you before, he's insisting on using a double-password.'

'All a bit World War Two to my mind,' said Rankin, 'but if it stops the Taliban waving their cudgels at the little man, I suppose we ought to humour him.'

As each second passed, Will found himself loathing more and more this pompous official who worked in the relative safety of the airport base, yet was so dismissive of the people on the ground risking their lives. 'Why don't you just give me the passwords?' he growled.

'Give them to him, Sami,' Rankin ordered and the fixer handed Will a piece of paper, folded once. Will read the words that had been carefully typed on it and slipped it in his pocket so that he could commit them to memory later. Then he looked back at the smug, fat man opposite him.

'How sure are you of this Ismail's reliability?'

Again Rankin shrugged – he did that a lot, it seemed to Will. 'He's an informant. He's given us good intelligence about the Taliban, but where he gets it from he refuses to tell his handlers. He's reliable, but he's still an informant. He's screwing *someone* over – we just don't think it's us.'

Will nodded, then turned back to Sami. 'What do you think?'

Sami's eyes narrowed. 'My job is not to think about such things,' he replied. 'My job is to stay alive and pass on the information I am given to my superiors.' As he said that word, he hesitated slightly and glanced at Rankin. 'They decide whether to act on it or not.'

'But what's your gut feeling?' Will had only known these two men for a matter of minutes, but already he trusted Sami's instinct much more than Rankin's.

'My instinct,' Sami said, 'is that Ismail is a young man very much out of his depth. The Taliban are not stupid – they will find out soon enough that he is betraying them and when that happens he will be executed. But until then, we would do well to take advantage of the information he is giving us.'

Will assimilated this for a moment while Sami and Rankin watched him carefully. 'I'll need local clothes,' he said, finally. 'And transport.'

Sami inclined his head slightly. 'It has already been attended to. I will be able to come a certain amount of the way with you, but no further. There are barricades on the way into the city, which we will want to avoid, but I know a route that should stop us having to negotiate these. I will get you to within walking distance of the café, but it would go badly for me, you understand, if I were to be seen in the presence of a member of the military.'

Will gave him a nod of thanks, but before either of them

could speak again Rankin gave them both a slightly dismissive wave. 'Speak to the kid who picked you up,' he said. 'He's been told to give you whatever you want. Now if you'll excuse me.'

The fat man turned and put his hands over the electric heater, rubbing them together. Will sneered. He didn't want to be in this guy's presence any longer than was necessary, so he left the hut and hurried back to the truck, Sami following close behind.

★

The clothes Sami had supplied them with were bundled in the back of one of the trucks outside the hut. 'This vehicle is for you,' he told Will as they stood out in the bitter snow. 'It looks old, but in fact it is in very good condition. The paintwork has been scuffed and damaged in order to stop it from standing out. There are not many new vehicles in my country these days.' He kicked one of the tyres. 'These are the only things that might attract attention,' he continued. 'Winter tyres, with a harder tread. But the risk is small, I think. Not many people will know what they are.'

He pulled out a canvas bag, dumped it on to the snowy ground, then climbed into the back of the truck. Once inside, he pulled up a metal panel to reveal a storage area, then grabbed a clinking handful of metal. 'Snow chains,' he said. 'Ismail will not tell me where he is taking you, but it is possible that you may need these. Also there is a –' he seemed to struggle to find the word '– a winch, in case the vehicle comes off the road. The driving conditions south of here are not good. There are also extra tanks of diesel fuel for you.'

'Thank you,' Will said, sincerely. Sami was a typical fixer – no-nonsense, helpful. It angered him that the guy had to put up with an idiot like Rankin. 'You're a lot more help than he was.'

Sami inclined his head. 'I have noticed that a tour of duty in Afghanistan brings out the worst in people,' he observed. 'I do not judge him too harshly. We should ask your driver to take us somewhere where you and your men can change. Kandahar is not far from here, but the road can be slow in this weather.'

'I'll need some local currency,' Will told him.

'I have it here. I suggest I distribute it once you are changed.'

Will nodded and they made their way back to the truck, where brief introductions were made. There was no small talk.

The young RAF soldier drove them to a small hangar which he explained had been requisitioned for the use of British servicemen at the airbase. They attracted some curious looks as, carrying their weapons case, they were led to a private area where they could change their clothes, but they shrugged all that off. Maybe the rumour had gone round that an SAS unit was on site; maybe it hadn't. Whatever the cause of those funny looks, the four of them were too focussed on the job ahead to give them any thought.

The clothes Sami had provided were rough and cheaply made, but they were at least warm. There was no point trying to make themselves look like Afghans, but if they could avoid people thinking they were soldiers it would make what they had to do in central Kandahar more straightforward; and the fact that they all had beards was a help. Once they had picked up the contact, they would be able to change back into their cold-weather gear, which would be more suitable for the journey south. Will donned a pair of thick trousers made from a scratchy, Hessian-type material, a warm woollen jumper and a colourful Afghan hat, the others dressed similarly. They each attached holsters under their clothes – Anderson,

110

Drew and Kennedy had chosen shoulder holsters, but Will had always found a waist holster to be more comfortable. He took the Sig 230 from the weapons case, loaded it, then hid it neatly under his jumper. They carefully stowed grenades and ammunition into their rucksacks, then loaded their Diemacos and slung them across their backs. Once they were ready, Sami took a bundle of afghani, the currency of the country, and handed them around.

By the time they were ready to leave, the snow was falling even more thickly. Junior Technician Evans drove them back to the hut where Sami's truck was waiting, then left them to it as Sami and the unit loaded their things on to the new vehicle, stowing the Minimi and the grenade launchers into the compartment alongside the snow chains, the winch and the spare diesel. Sami looked at the Diemacos slung across their shoulders. 'I would stow those away,' he told them. 'They will only attract attention. You have your handguns, do you not?'

Sami was right. If they wanted to merge into the background, they couldn't walk around the streets of Kandahar with heavy weaponry on display. Will nodded curtly to the others and they stowed their guns as Sami took the driving seat.

It was about fifteen miles from the airport to the town of Kandahar and the snow was falling heavily. Occasionally a rocky mound would rise up out of the earth, but apart from these solitary hills, the immediate area was flat and featureless. The roads were nearly deserted – whether that was because of the snow or because people were keeping off the road in this dangerous part of the world, it was impossible to say. Now and then Will noticed an ordinary Afghan by the side of the road, struggling on foot through the snow; it didn't escape his notice how many of them had elderly AK-47s strapped across their backs.

When they heard the truck approaching, they always stopped and watched, unsmiling, as it passed. This was hostile territory.

Sami drove slowly and carefully. It took more than an hour. As they travelled, Will gave the unit their orders. 'I'll be going in alone,' he said. 'If the four of us barge into this café, we're going to attract attention and if our contact is as jumpy as that idiot back at the airfield says, we can't risk scaring him off.'

'We should cover you,' Anderson suggested. 'Take up positions outside the café, in case anything goes wrong.'

Will thought for a moment. In a situation like this it was all too easy to get cocky, to assume that because this was the relatively straightforward part of the operation, nothing could go wrong. It would be a mistake and Anderson was right to suggest that Will needed a bit of back-up.

He pointed at Anderson and Kennedy. 'You two,' he said, 'follow me at a distance. Keep it subtle – I don't want our guy taking fright.' He looked at Drew. 'You,' he said, 'stay with the truck. Once I've made contact, that will be the RV point.'

The three men nodded their agreement as the vehicle trundled towards Kandahar. Will pulled the slip of paper Sami had given him from his pocket and committed the double password to memory.

– *Do you have the time?*
– *My watch runs slow these days.*
– *I know a good watchmaker in Kabul.*
– *Kabul is a long journey in the winter.*

Once he was sure he had firmly remembered the words, he spoke to Sami.

'Tell me more about this Ismail character. If he's going to be coming with us, I want to know who we're dealing with.'

112

'Very well,' Sami replied, politely. 'I will tell you what I know. He is about twenty-eight years of age and his parents were imprisoned by the Taliban when he was about seventeen. My understanding is that a *sarinda* – an Afghan musical instrument – was found in their house, which was considered sinful by the regime. They both died in prison. Ismail, I would say, is a very clever young man, but nervous at the best of times. After his parents were imprisoned, he followed the Taliban's rules to the letter, as most people did, so that he would not be destined for the same fate. He took a wife, whom I have never met, and I believe they have a young son.'

'How did you manage to recruit him?'

Sami shrugged. 'In the usual way,' he replied. 'A mixture of gentle persuasion and money. The people here are very poor – they will do many things for a few extra dollars and Ismail has a family to keep. I imagine he caught the eye of the Taliban insurgents because he is a very devout man and now they believe he acts as one of their –' Sami seemed to struggle for the word. 'Sneaks,' he settled on, finally. 'But his devotion does not, happily, extend to the kind of extremism they espouse. I truly believe he thinks that informing on them is a holy act, no matter how scared it might make him feel; the money is just an added bonus. He has been very useful, too. So useful that I do not think all of the information he supplies is acted upon, simply in order to maintain his cover.' Sami glanced over his shoulder at Will. 'Someone in your government must want this woman he knows about very badly. They have instructed that we pay him a great deal of money to lead you to wherever it is that she is being held.'

Will's eyes flickered towards the other three, but they did not seem to have raised an eyebrow at what Sami had said; and Sami was evidently too discreet to question Will any further.

'Ismail's English is serviceable, but not perfect,' the fixer continued, 'and he is not a physically strong man. I would advise that you do not expect him to fight or to endure extreme environments in the same way that you have become used to.'

'Sounds a fucking liability to me,' Drew complained.

'Maybe,' Will said, 'but without him we don't have an objective. He comes with us, liability or not.'

They drove on in silence.

As they hit the outskirts of the town, the roads became less treacherous as more vehicles appeared. Among the elderly and run-down civilian cars, Will saw a number of military trucks bearing the UN logo, which told of the heavy military presence in this part of the world. Normally this would make their job more secure, but for the moment, Will didn't want anyone to link them to NATO, the UN or the British or American army. What they were doing was under the radar and he wanted to keep it that way. Sami took them off the main road as soon as he could and continued their journey through a series of intricate, winding streets, not ideal for a large vehicle, but they were at least clear of the various security forces that would be barricading other entrances to the city.

The further they travelled into the centre, the more people there were. Large numbers of Afghans – some in traditional dress, others wearing more Westernised clothes – went about their daily business, shuffling up and down the snowy streets, moving quickly because of the snow. Some of them carried wicker baskets of food; others were empty-handed. No one paid any attention to their truck as it trundled past; in fact, nobody seemed to pay attention to anything.

Surprisingly frequently Will caught sight of two or three soldiers in camouflage uniform and carrying what looked to him like excessively heavy weaponry for patrolling the streets. There weren't many cars on the road and those that were had clouds of greasy diesel smoke billowing from their exhausts; they looked rickety in the extreme. Walking was clearly a far more common method of getting around, so several people walked in the road, all but ignoring the beeps from the horns of those who were trying to drive. At one point the unit stopped outside what could only be described as a shack, from which the appetising aroma of meat being grilled over hot coals wafted towards them. A customer bought a kebab, but Will noticed that the shopkeeper refused to hand it over until he had the money firmly in his hand.

Further along, they passed what looked to Will like a former administrative building. It was ramshackle now, its windows blown out and one side reduced to a pile of rubble – a monument to some violent incident in the not too distant past.

'We don't want to be dropped off too near the café, but it needs to be in sight,' he told Sami as they passed an impressive-looking mosque, its golden dome heavy with snow and people swarming outside.

'I know a suitable place,' Sami replied. 'It's not far now.'

The street where they stopped was thin but straight – Will noted with approval that they had a good line of sight at either end and they could see directly on to a bustling square. Anderson and Kennedy took their Sig 226s from the weapons cache – the slightly larger firearm was fine for them as they wouldn't be getting up close and personal with the contact, at least not yet.

'Is that the bazaar up ahead?' Will asked Sami.

The fixer nodded his head. 'The café is one of the doors you can see on the other side of the square.'

'Give us thirty minutes,' Will told Drew, tersely. 'If we haven't returned, come and get us.'

'Roger that,' Drew murmured. If he was upset at not being on the front line, he didn't show it.

'Remember,' Sami continued, 'Ismail is nervous. If you do not recite the double password *exactly* correctly, he will take fright and it will take weeks to regain his trust. Do not mention my name to him – he will only deny knowledge.' He turned to Drew. 'You can remember the route out?'

Drew nodded his head.

'Good,' Sami replied. 'Ismail will not want to risk being seen with me, not in public. I have to go now.' He opened the car door. 'Good luck.'

He climbed down from the car, walked nonchalantly to the end of the deserted street and disappeared around the corner. 'That's the last we'll see of him,' Anderson muttered.

'He's a good fixer,' Will said. 'He's thought of everything. OK, let's go. Remember, not too close.' He opened up the back of the truck and jumped out.

Kandahar had a certain smell to it, he noticed as he headed down the street. The smell of rotting rubbish, of food cooking, of sewers; and the blanket of snow that had fallen over the city could not hide the unpleasantness of it. As he walked, snowflakes settled on his clothes and he reached the end of the street with a light dusting already covering him. He knew that by now Anderson and Kennedy would have exited the vehicle, but he didn't look behind to check – it wasn't necessary, and he didn't want to draw attention to his trail.

To his right, he saw a large makeshift wall across the road, constructed of what looked like bags of concrete. Armed men were questioning anyone who wanted to drive through, as well as a fair number of ordinary Afghan pedestrians. Will was pleased Sami had directed them round that and he turned left to follow the rough pavement that surrounded the main square.

The square itself was lined with bombed-out buildings, but the centre, separated from the buildings by the road that was still almost empty of cars, was crowded: a huge market place was laid out and despite the relentless snow, crowds of Afghan women, some dressed in warm robes, others completely covered by the burka, gathered round talking in little groups. Stallholders stood guard over stalls that held small amounts of sorry-looking produce and the whole thing was covered by a large canopy that looked almost precarious under its heavy blanket of snow.

There was a sudden roar as a plane flew overhead. Will looked up and recognised a Harrier patrol aircraft, but nobody else, it seemed, paid it any attention. Clearly these people, inhabitants of a war-ravaged country for so long, had seen so many air patrols that they had ceased to be a curiosity.

Will gave himself a moment to get his bearings. The north side of the square, Sami had said. He glanced in that direction, over the top of the heads of the women in the bazaar; there seemed to be a crowded area on the other side, so he started walking round the edge of the square to see if that might be his place.

He had only gone a few paces, however, when his path was blocked. Two men – burly with dark rings under their eyes – blocked his way. They both carried ancient AK-47s. Neither of them was in military uniform. Just a couple of thugs, Will realised, intuitively. One of them spoke harshly to him in a language he didn't understand – Pashto, no doubt – but the tone of his voice made it clear he was demanding something.

The muscles around Will's eyes tensed up slightly and he felt his right hand brush instinctively to his waist where the Sig was concealed. The last thing he wanted now was a fight. He felt sure his contact would be looking out for him, but if there was a scene, he might be frightened off. Moreover, a gunfight would undoubtedly attract the attention of the heavily armed troops dotted around.

The man spoke again, more aggressively this time. Without looking, Will knew that Anderson and Kennedy would have their hands firmly round their gun handles now, ready to react with swift, brutal force if anything went wrong.

And it looked to Will as if that was just what was about to happen.

From behind him, he heard a familiar sound – the metallic click of a safety catch being removed. The men looked behind Will with an expression of distaste; he turned round to see two armed soldiers brandishing their weapons. One of them pointed his gun at the Afghans, then jabbed the barrel to the side to indicate that they should move on. The Afghans hesitated, but after a moment they did as they were told, walking down the street away from Will, but still casting a threatening gaze over their shoulder as they went.

'You shouldn't be walking around here by yourself,' one of the soldiers said in an American accent. 'What are you doing in Kandahar?'

Will had to think quickly. 'Private security,' he said with brash confidence. Beyond the soldiers he clocked his colleagues. Anderson was on the side of the road, his hand under his woollen overcoat; Kennedy had taken up position in the centre of the square. Both of them, Will could tell in an instant, were ready to react.

'Are you armed?'

He nodded.

'OK. Well we advise that you see to your business and get back to an area of safety as soon as possible.'

Will suppressed a sigh of relief. 'I intend to,' he said.

With a nod, the two soldiers walked away. Will saw his colleagues' arms fall to their side as the tension of the

118

situation diffused, but he didn't make eye contact with them. He just turned and continued on his way.

As he reached the north side of the square it became clear to him where the meeting point was, just as Sami had described it. The café had large glass windows at the front, but these had been taped over with some kind of thick gaffer tape to prevent them from shattering, then covered with large sheets of metal mesh, which made it difficult to see inside. The door was open, however, and the snow on the ground around it had melted from the warmth emanating from within. From several metres away Will could hear the noise of voices and smell the thick, sweet tobacco that pervaded the air.

He glanced at his watch. Five to eleven. Stepping up to the doorway, he looked inside.

It was dimly lit and crowded. There were no women, just men, all sitting at rickety wooden tables or congregated around a bar area where a harassed-looking barman provided coffee in tiny white cups. As Will stepped inside, there were a few suspicious glances in his direction, but before long everyone found themselves drawn back into their animated conversations, allowing Will to sidle up to the bar – the only place where there seemed to be any room. He pointed at one of the small cups of coffee, then handed over one of Sami's notes when he was presented with his drink.

He stood there against the bar for five minutes, maybe ten – long enough, certainly, for the coffee he didn't really want to go cold. When he looked at his watch it was five past eleven. It made him uneasy that nobody had made contact yet. Perhaps he was being too surreptitious. He turned round and faced out to the centre of the room, so that his white skin would be on better display. As soon as he did that, he heard a voice next to him.

119

'Do you have the time?'

Do you have the time? The first phrase of the double password. Will turned his head slowly to see who was speaking. The man was short and fat, his face clean-shaven. Hadn't Sami said that Ismail was a devout Muslim? Wouldn't he be wearing a beard? But that was the opening line, so he responded, word for word, in the way he was supposed to.

'My watch runs slow these days.'

The man nodded. 'My friend is a good watchmaker in Kabul.'

Will stopped. He knew the correct response – *Kabul is a long journey in the winter* – but the man's words had not been correct. '*I know* a good watchmaker in Kabul.' That was the wording, and this guy had got it wrong. Alarm bells started to sound. If Ismail had been rumbled by the Taliban, he might well have given them the wrong password; and Will had been suspicious of this man the minute he set eyes on him.

There was only one option. He had to walk away. Immediately.

Will stepped from the bar and headed briskly to the door. No one seemed to pay any attention to him leaving, but he could tell that the man he had just spoken to was following him. For the second time in ten minutes he felt his hand moving towards the gun strapped around his waist. He upped his pace and stepped out from the warm, smoky interior of the café on to the chilly, snow-laden street.

The first thing he did was scan for Anderson and Kennedy. He saw them immediately – Kennedy still in the square but facing on to the café, Anderson about fifteen metres to his left, standing in the street. In front of Will, parked just outside the café, was a small car. Its engine was turning over and, unusually given the weather, the window was wound down. The man from the café brushed past Will and spoke

120

to the driver, a lanky, bearded individual with a white turban. It was a quick conversation, conducted in Pashto, and from the way the man kept looking at Will, he could tell that it concerned him.

On the periphery of his vision, he could sense Anderson and Kennedy closing in.

The man from the café stepped aside and the driver from the car put his head out. 'Will Jackson?' he said hesitantly.

Will narrowed his eyes, but didn't answer.

'You must get in the car. Now.'

Will hesitated. Anderson and Kennedy were only metres away now. He only had to say the word and both these men would be looking down the barrel of a gun. But then he looked at the driver: his face was nervous, his eyes wide, but he didn't look as though he was trying to pull a fast one. He just looked scared.

He looked up at his colleagues and briefly shook his head. They stopped in their tracks. Will strode to the car, opened the back door and climbed in. It was cramped inside, and the heaters were blowing full blast. He pulled his Sig from under his jumper and deftly put it to the man's head. Immediately the driver started to shake.

'Drive,' Will told him. 'Now.'

With shaking hands, the driver tried to put the car in gear, but he seemed too nervous and the engine crunched loudly as he failed to manage it.

'*I said drive!*' Will barked. The driver tried again, this time managing to knock the car into gear.

'Go round the square,' Will instructed, and the car moved off at a stuttering pace.

'Please, do not shoot me!' the driver begged.

'Then do exactly what I tell you,' Will replied. 'What's your name?'

'My name?' He sounded surprised. 'My name is Ismail. You were meant to be meeting me, yes?'

'I'm asking the questions. What was that pantomime back there in aid of?'

'What is pantomime, please?'

'*Just tell me what was going on,*' Will growled.

Ismail breathed deeply. 'It was to make sure you were the right person. Passwords are not foolproof. If the Taliban suspected me and learned what the passwords were, they might pretend to go along with the mistake to get proof, then abduct me. Only the right person would walk away if they heard the wrong password.'

Will found that he, too, was breathing heavily, in anger; but there was a curious logic to what the terrified Afghan in the front seat had said. He lowered his gun. 'Stop the car,' he ordered.

Ismail pulled over on the side of the street.

'Turn off the engine and hand me the keys. Then get out.'

The trembling Afghan did as he was told. Will stepped out of the car, too. He slipped the Sig back into its holster, but kept his hand firmly around the handle under his jumper. 'If I see anyone following us, I'll shoot you right here,' he said, quietly, so that none of the passers-by would hear.

'No one is following us,' Ismail assured him. 'I promise you.'

'You'd better be right.' Will looked around. Sure enough, Ismail's parked car was the only one in the street. 'OK, walk. And just in case you're thinking of running, you might like to know that we're being covered by two men who can shoot a bullet through a coin at fifty metres. Understand?'

Ismail turned to look at him. Although his eyes were still frightened, there was an open honesty in his face. 'You do not perhaps understand how I have risked my life to do this,' he said, quietly, 'and the life of my family. Every second

I spend with you, I risk our lives even further. If I wanted to run away, I would have done it long ago.'

Will stared at him and felt the stirrings of a grudging respect. But respect or no respect, he had to cover himself and his unit.

He nodded in the direction they needed to go.

'Walk,' he told Ismail, curtly. 'Now.'

EIGHT

Once they had RV'd back at the truck, Drew took the wheel, Kennedy sitting beside him. Ismail was bundled roughly into the back by Will and Anderson.

'You sure this is the right guy?' Anderson asked, once they were all inside.

Ismail looked anxiously at Will, knowing that his safety was hanging on the words of the man he had so clearly just pissed off.

Will stared coldly back at him. 'Yeah,' he said, finally. 'I'm sure.'

'Looks like a fucking Fundie Jundie to me,' Kennedy muttered from the front.

'Shut up, Kennedy,' Will snapped. 'Ignore him,' he told Ismail. 'For now, at least.'

Having perfectly memorised the route Sami had taken into Kandahar, Drew retraced it as the others sat silently in the back. Anderson and Kennedy eyed Ismail with distrust; Ismail, in turn, looked as though he was wondering what the hell he had got himself into, stuck in a vehicle with these dangerous men.

Will was certainly angry with the frightened Afghan, but he couldn't quite pinpoint why. The guy was only being careful, after all. Maybe he just didn't like the fact that Ismail had pulled the wool over his eyes. In situations like this, you want to be control and for a few moments back there, Will hadn't been. It had given him a bad feeling.

124

Once they reached the outskirts of the city, Will spoke. 'OK, Ismail,' he said. 'You'd better start talking. Where are we going and how long will it take us to get there?'

Ismail's eyes flickered anxiously to each of the SAS men in turn before he answered. 'The village where the woman you are searching for is being held is a day's drive from here. The main road south will take you most of the way, but the snow will have blocked off the smaller road that leads to the village itself. You will have to make your way there on foot.'

'Lovely,' Kennedy murmured. 'A walk through the snow in the dark. Maybe we can attack the Taliban with snow-balls.'

'I'll fucking attack you if you don't shut it,' Anderson growled, 'and not with snowballs.'

'I'd rather engage the Taliban under cover of night anyway,' Will said. He wasn't worried by the sniping between them – it often happened when adrenaline was running high. As long as they could rely on each other in battle, that was what counted.

He turned back to Ismail. 'Are you sure you'll be able to lead us there?'

'Positive,' Ismail said, confidently. 'It is the village where I was born. That is the reason I know what is going on there.'

'What's the main road south like?' Anderson asked.

Ismail raised an eyebrow. 'Like all roads in Afghanistan,' he said, simply. 'It is very dangerous. There will not be many cars, not in this weather. But wc may encounter roadblocks. Some of them will be military, others will have been set up by bandits who will want to take all the money we have. And if we don't give it to them, they will try to take it by force.'

The SAS men maintained a grim silence. Will knew exactly what they were thinking.

11.35. They had been driving for perhaps half an hour and the last remnants of the urban sprawl of Kandahar had finally dissolved into nothing, when Will instructed Drew to pull over. 'What is wrong?' Ismail asked.

'Nothing's wrong,' Will told him. 'We need to get our weapons ready. If we come across trouble, we don't want to be scrabbling around looking for guns.'

'But I thought you had your gun,' he said. 'You pointed it at me.' He sounded so concerned about this, that the others could not resist a smile.

'We've brought some back-up,' Will told him, opening the compartment in the floor of the truck to reveal the weapons cache. Ismail's eyes widened slightly as the Diemacos came out and he fell silent – though from that moment on, Will kept noticing that Ismail would glance anxiously at the guns from time to time. Each time he did so, Anderson looked at him with a certain distaste.

'You do not like me, I think,' Ismail said.

Anderson looked away.

'You do not trust me, perhaps.'

'You're an informant,' Anderson growled. 'You're double-crossing someone. I just hope it isn't us.'

Ismail smiled a patient smile. 'I think perhaps you do not know how life is in Afghanistan.'

'Bollocks to that,' Anderson replied, vigorously. 'I spent six months this year in the Stan and three months the year before that. I've had every Taliban fucker in this godfor-saken country throw everything they've got at me and I've lost count of the number of mates who've had their brains blown out of the back of their heads. So don't tell me I don't know anything about Afghanistan, my friend.'

An uncomfortable silence followed Anderson's outburst – a silence only broken when Ismail spoke. His voice was measured, reasonable.

'I did not mean,' he said, calmly, 'that you know nothing

of Afghanistan as a theatre of war. Your ability in that field is beyond question and I thank you for the sacrifices you have made on my country's behalf. I meant that perhaps you do not know what life is like for we ordinary citizens. I despise the Taliban as much as you – they killed my parents, after all. But I would not be running the risk I run simply out of revenge. We are a poor country and many people struggle even to buy food. I do what I do so that I am able to feed my young son – your British government pays me enough for the information to make it worthwhile. Tell me, my friend, do you have children?'

Anderson nodded, curtly.

'And is there anything you would not do to put food in their mouths?'

Ismail's direct question was not met with an answer. Instead, Anderson redirected his gaze out of the window. The young Afghan did not press the issue, but it was clear to all of them that he had given Anderson something to think about.

The snow started to fall more thickly, dancing in the beams of the headlights and flying towards the car like a million tiny bullets. Drew was forced to reduce his speed to little more than a crawl as he peered through the windscreen, his face screwed up in concentration as he negotiated his way through the blizzard. The area south of Kandahar was not mountainous, like other parts of Afghanistan; but there was a steady upwards incline as they drove up out of the geographical bowl in which the city was situated. It was difficult to see clearly through the blizzard, but when Will did manage to get a view of the landscape, he saw it was a gently undulating terrain. There were a few trees, but they were sparse. More striking were the remnants of Afghanistan's past battles that lay abandoned by the side of the road. He counted the hulking shells of Russian T-55 tanks, anything of any use already stripped out of them.

There were burned out armoured cars, discarded oil drums – the debris of a country that had been at war for as long as it could remember.

Every now and then they felt the wheels spin ineffectually on the icy road and towards mid–afternoon, despite Drew's skill behind the wheel, they felt themselves skidding towards the side of the road. They jolted around inside the truck as Drew calmly drove into the skid and brought the vehicle to a halt. It was clear that the going was getting tough, so they attached the snow chains that Sami had provided. They drove off again and the chains crunched noisily under them, but the truck held the road much better.

As the afternoon wore on, the snow stopped falling and they were able to see around them a bit more clearly. When they stopped to replenish the truck with diesel from one of the tanks that Sami had supplied, the others stood guard around the vehicle, pointing their guns up into the hills, which they all knew from experience of this treacherous country could be hiding unknown dangers.

Everywhere was covered in a blanket of fresh snow and Will felt as if they were the only people for miles around in that spectacular winter landscape. As if to shatter the illusion, Ismail spoke.

'The Taliban are very strong in this region,' he said, quietly. 'It feels like there is nobody around, but there are many villages around here, cut off by the snow. When the Taliban were thrown from power, they took refuge in places like this. They are not afraid to kill the villagers to get what they want, so now they run these places with the same reign of terror as they ran all of Afghanistan only a few years ago. I myself have seen them hang the body of a father in front of his children. I pray my own son does not have to witness such a thing.'

He stared out of the window into the landscape beyond, leaving the unit to imagine that grizzly scene. Will found it turned his stomach, but something deep inside him refused to be entirely horrified by what Ismail had described. At least parents were *supposed* to die before their children. He looked over at Anderson, who was staring thoughtfully at the floor. Was he thinking about his own kids? Will wondered. Was he wondering if he would be eating Christmas lunch with them in just over a week's time? Despite the snow all around, Christmas seemed a million miles away in this benighted country.

And with the thought of Christmas, the image of Laura and Anna, his family, lying dead on the floor of that department store so many thousands of miles away, flashed into his head. In a brief surge that lasted only a few seconds, he relived all the pain that had been with him ever since. Somewhere, he thought to himself, out in the bleak, uninviting landscape around him, was the key to his revenge. He found himself gritting his teeth, almost looking forward to the business ahead.

'Road block.' Drew said the words calmly, but Will instantly shook off his reverie as the truck came to a halt. On either side of them was a hilly mound with low bushes covered in snow. He leaned over and looked through the windscreen. Sure enough, a couple of hundred metres down the road, they saw a large vehicle parked to one side. Two men were standing in the middle of the road just next to it. From this distance it was impossible to see if they were armed, but Will felt sure they would be.

'ISAF?' he asked, tersely.

'I think it is unlikely,' Ismail replied. 'There are too few of them and I am not aware of any NATO bases in this region.'

'It's an ambush,' Anderson said, quietly. 'Look. Footprints.'

He pointed up into the hillock along one side of the road, a scant fifteen metres away. Just as Anderson had said, there was a trail of prints in the snow leading up to a little line of bushes, small enough to go unnoticed, but large enough to hide a man. Will looked to see if he could find anyone there. At first, he saw nothing; but as he squinted his eyes, something moved. It was only a tiny movement, but enough to shake a little shower of snow from one of the bushes on to the ground beneath. He looked more carefully. Sure enough, he could make out the outline of a man's head. He even thought he could see the black metal of a gun barrel pointing out through the bush.

'There's someone there,' he announced.

'Both sides,' Kennedy said. 'I've clocked one on our right too. Looks like someone's preparing for a surprise party – and I bet they've forgotten to bring any cake.'

They needed to move quickly and decisively. 'Drive up,' Will said, calmly. 'When they come to the window, nail them.' He looked at Anderson. 'We'll de-bus as soon as that happens. Fragmentation grenades at the ambushers, then take them out.'

Ismail started breathing heavily. 'You're going to kill them?'

'Not if they kill us first,' Will stated, flatly.

'But what if –?'

'Shut up, Ismail,' he ordered. 'They haven't set up this ambush for fun. They have the advantage and if we don't take the fight to them, we'll be corpses on the side of the road within a minute.'

Ismail fell silent.

'Their main target's going to be our vehicle, so we need to get the hell out of here. When I say the word, me and Anderson are going to jump out the back and hit the ambushers with grenades. When we do that, jump out and take cover at the side of the road. We'll take it from there. Can you do that, Ismail?'

The frightened Afghan nodded mutely.

In the front, Drew and Kennedy had taken the Sigs from their holsters and laid them on their laps. Will readied his weapon, while Anderson fished two fragmentation grenades from his rucksack and handed one over.

'Let's try and finish this with the same number of holes in our bodies as when we started,' Kennedy drawled.

No one laughed.

'Go!' Will told Drew.

The truck moved slowly forwards. Ismail's heavy breathing became more panicked as they approached the roadblock, but Will tried to put that sound from his mind as he concentrated on the matter in hand. His awareness had become crystalline and precise; a strange sense of calm had descended over him. The calm before the storm.

The roadblock was ten metres away now and the truck slowed down while the two men approached the front windows, one on either side. Will shifted to the back of the truck, ready to jump out as soon as he heard the crack of the weapons, but he managed to steal a glance at the two of them. There was no way these men were soldiers: they were walking with a louche, arrogant gait and one of them had his weapon – an AK-47 – resting over his right shoulder. They wore warm, heavy Afghan clothing, and their bearded faces were locked in an unpleasant sneer. One of them, as he approached, seemed to look over to where the ambushers were hidden; he nodded, imperceptibly.

The man who had approached the driver's window tapped on the glass, indicating to Drew that he should wind it down.

This was it. In a matter of seconds it would be over.

Drew and Kennedy wound down their windows. Immediately the man on Drew's side started to speak, his voice an incomprehensible babble of harsh, guttural Pashto.

He didn't get the chance to say much.

Almost as one, Drew and Kennedy raised their guns, pointed them directly at the faces of the two men, and fired. Will heard them thump to the ground. 'Now!' he hissed and instantly he and Anderson opened the back doors of the truck and jumped out. They pulled the pins from their fragmentation grenades and hurled them in the direction of the two ambushers, before jumping to the low bushes at the side of the road to get some natural cover. Ismail followed, scampering away from the truck with his arms held protectively over his head and Will was aware of Drew and Kennedy de-bussing too.

He and Anderson engaged their rifles and pointed them in the direction of their targets. The grenades exploded with a deafening crack and seconds later the two men staggered from the bushes where they were hiding. Even from a distance, Will could see that his man was horrifically wounded from the shrapnel in his face. He mercilessly aimed the Diemaco at the guy's head and fired a single shot. The ambusher fell backwards into the bushes, blood from his head spraying over the virgin snow.

Will heard the crack of Anderson's rifle and turned just in time to see the second ambusher collapse to the ground.

And then, all around them was silence. The sort of silence you only experience when there are dead people about.

Silence or not, they needed to check that their targets were indeed dead – leaving a wounded hostile behind you was a sure way to end up with a bullet in the back.

Will strode towards the man he'd nailed. As he did so, he heard two bangs as Drew and Kennedy administered head shots from their pistols to the fallen enemy.

It was the third bang that they didn't expect.

Will felt the shock of a high-calibre bullet whiz past him. It slammed into the open door at the back of the truck, instantly destroying the metal as though somebody had crumpled a piece of paper in their hand.

'Hit the ground!' Will yelled and the five of them dived into the thick, powdery snow.

'Where is he?' he heard Anderson yell and Will scoured

the hillside to see where this surprise enemy fire was coming from.

Suddenly, from his right, there came a barrage of muffled fire. It was Kennedy. He let off five silent shots from his suppressed Diemaco and somewhere up the hill there was a yell of pain. A figure tumbled forwards from behind a mound of snow.

One final shot from Kennedy was all it took to dispatch him.

Silence again.

Will was breathing heavily, hardly noticing the chill of the snow. They lay there for a good minute, carefully scanning the hillside as they searched for any more hidden ambushes.

Nothing.

'Get back to the truck!' Will called. They pushed themselves up and stepped backwards to the vehicle, firing the occasional shot to give them cover. From the corner of his eye, Will was aware of the corpse collapsed by the passenger door. His head had been completely shot open, the warm blood still oozing from his shattered skull melting the snow around him. Good, Will thought to himself. That was one ambusher they didn't have to worry about. They'd have to leave the guys that Will and Anderson had nailed. There could be other ambushers up there and they couldn't risk examining the bodies. They just had to get out of there as quickly as possible.

He was just by the truck, a couple of metres from Drew, when he heard a voice. From behind the ambushers' vehicle another Afghan had appeared. His hands were stretched in the air in a gesture of surrender and he walked nervously towards them.

Instinctively, Drew had raised his firearm and had it aimed firmly at the surrendering enemy. The Afghan stopped and a tense silence descended. Drew looked over at Will, his eyes questioning.

He was waiting for an order and Will only had a split second in which to give it.

He looked at the Afghan. Then he looked back at Drew and nodded.

Instantly, Drew pulled the trigger. The Afghan crumpled to the ground. 'Get in the truck, everyone,' Will instructed.

They all took their places – all except Ismail, who insisted on sitting on the floor of the vehicle. 'Are they gone?' he whimpered.

'Stay down!' Will told him in a tone of voice that he knew would do nothing for Ismail's state of mind – but he didn't have time to mollycoddle anyone now. The door on his side of the truck had been all but destroyed. He pulled the other one shut as Drew moved the vehicle away. They would just have to drive with the back blown open.

As the truck speeded up, he pointed his rifle out the back; passing the ambushers' vehicle, he aimed precisely and then shot into two of the tyres. They blasted into a mass of shredded rubber. Will felt a surge of grim satisfaction – if any of those bastards were nearby, they wouldn't be following very easily, if at all.

Ismail was hyperventilating now, looking up at Will and Anderson with a strange mixture of awe and fear. Will felt a surge of momentary sympathy – they might be used to situations like this, but Ismail sure as hell wasn't.

'You can get up now,' he told the shivering Afghan.

Ismail pushed himself up almost reluctantly and took a seat on one of the benches along the side of the truck. His eyes darted around from man to man, then widened when Kennedy looked at them over his shoulder: his face was spattered with the blood of the man he had shot at close range.

'You all right?' Kennedy grunted.

Ismail nodded.

'You did well,' Will told him.

'I did nothing,' Ismail replied. 'I am not—' he struggled to find the right word, '– I am not suitable for this kind of situation.'

'Well you'd better get used to it,' Will told him, bluntly, 'because chances are it's going to get harder than that.'

He stared at Ismail, who did his best to stare back. But after a while the Afghan lowered his gaze back down to the floor.

No one said anything and the truck trundled on down the icy road.

★

A dusty red light from a small fire illuminated the hut, but only just. Seated in a wooden chair by the fire was a tall, bearded man. His face was scarred, from the lower lip up to his cheek, and no hair grew where the ancient wound had marked his face.

Two other bearded men stood a little distance away from him. One of them spoke. 'We should just kill her now, Jamal,' he said. 'It is clear that the woman will not tell us what we want to know.'

Jamal stroked his scarred lip with a long, slender finger. He remembered the day the wound had been inflicted. His slight sneer flickered across his damaged lips as he recalled the face of the man who did it. 'I do not agree,' he said, quietly.

'What more can we do?'

Jamal's eyes narrowed. 'Many things,' he whispered. He gazed silently into the fire, as though contemplating the embers.

'Is it so important, Jamal?' the other man asked. 'Is it so important that we find this brother of hers? It is becoming a struggle to keep her alive. It would be much easier if we killed her now.'

'Important?' Jamal asked. 'Yes, it is important.' He looked at each of the men in turn. 'The Taliban are the true students of the Koran. We *will* be returned to power in Afghanistan. God will see to it. But what will people think when they discover that this man who betrayed us at the highest level has been allowed to go free? What will that do to our authority?'

'But he may not even be in this country.'

At this, Jamal looked angry. 'Do you not think that we have influence that extends further than Afghanistan? Do you not think that we have people willing to do God's work in America, the Great Satan? Do you not think that we have brothers in Washington and London and all over the West? Believe me, if that woman knows where he is, she will tell me, and in the name of Allah I will have him hunted down and killed.' He looked meaningfully at the two of them. 'Or perhaps the name of Allah is not as important to you as it is to me.'

The two men shifted uneasily. 'Of course it is, Jamal,' one of them replied. 'But is it necessary for so many of us to guard her day and night? She is too weak even to stand up, let alone try to escape.'

Jamal continued to stroke his scar. 'It is very necessary,' he stated. 'We are not the only people who wish to learn the whereabouts of Faisal Ahmed, of that you may be sure. It is not a matter of *if* they try and rescue her; it is a matter of *when*.'

'But who would be so foolish? We are heavily armed, and with all this snow —'

'It is not our weapons or the snow that will bring us victory,' Jamal insisted. 'We fight in the name of Allah. To die in his name will be glorious. Who in this room does not crave *shihada*, martyrdom?'

Jamal's face shone as a silence fell on the room and the irrefutable truth of his statement sunk in.

'I suggest you go back to your positions,' he said, after a while. '*Allahu Akbar.*'

136

The two men bowed slightly. '*Allahu Akbar*,' they said, before turning to leave.

★

'We need to stop here.'

Will checked his watch: 18.30 hours. Ismail had not spoken in the two hours since the ambush and even the SAS men had been quiet. They all sensed, Will knew, that they had been lucky. The people in this part of the world were well armed and life was cheap. If the hidden ambusher had been a bit more precise with his shooting, there would have been some British corpses lying back there in the snow with their Afghan attackers.

Will stared out of the window. It was twilight and the landscape looked no different to him than any they had passed for ages. 'You sure?' he asked Ismail.

'Positive,' their informant nodded. 'The village is about two kilometres east of here.'

'OK,' Will called to Drew. 'We need to find somewhere to stow the vehicle.'

Finding a suitable place was difficult – the region did not offer any natural cover and in the end they were forced simply to leave the truck by the side of the road. As Drew turned the engine off, Will was struck once again by the ominous silence all around.

'We should scran up before we go,' Kennedy said. They all delved into their rucksacks and pulled out army rations: silver-foil packs containing high-energy food. Will threw one over to Ismail, who tore it open suspiciously and picked without enthusiasm at the beef and dumplings inside.

'Eat it up,' Will told him. 'It's fucking freezing out there – you need the energy.' He squeezed the cold food from his own ration pack into his mouth. Beans, he realised as it went down, though these things all tasted pretty much the same. Hardly gourmet stuff, but it was welcome and it wasn't exactly as if Will was used to dining in the finest restaurants. Sami had supplied some bottled water in the truck, which they drank from. They wouldn't be taking it with them, though – it was unnecessary weight and with the snow all around they'd be fine.

When they had finished eating, they started getting their clothes ready. The Afghan garments that Sami had given them were discarded, to be replaced by Goretex jackets over which were pulled their thick, all-in-one snowsuits. Will handed a spare snowsuit from his pack to Ismail, who seemed uncomfortable with it, but pulled it on nevertheless – now that the engine of the truck had stopped running the temperature inside was rapidly dropping thanks to the fact that the back door had been obliterated in the ambush.

Over their snowsuits they attached military vests covered with pouches in which they stowed grenades and ammunition – all of them ignored Ismail's frightened, wide-eyed stare at the extent of their firepower. Once they were dressed, it was almost fully dark outside. Will pulled a GPS unit from his pack and recorded their current location; the others did the same. Then he stowed it away and addressed his men.

'Two kilometres,' he said. 'In this weather, we should be able to cover that in an hour.' He glanced at Ismail. 'Maybe an hour and a half. It's 19.25 now. We'll have good night cover when we hit them.'

'Do we have any idea where the target is being held?' Anderson asked Ismail.

Ismail shook his head. 'I do not know,' he admitted. 'But it is not a big place and from what I understand they are guarding her heavily.'

'OK,' Will continued. 'We'll be heading east into the village. When we get there, we'll pair off: me and Anderson, Drew and Kennedy. Ismail, once you've led us there, you stay where we put you and we'll pick you up on our way out. If we get separated, RV back at the truck. And listen to me carefully, everyone: I don't care what happens or how many ragheads you have to nail, she comes out alive.'

There was a serious kind of silence from the men before Will spoke again.

'All right,' he told them. 'Let's go.'

They slung their weapons over their shoulders and debussed in silence.

The snow was thick – a good couple of feet, which made the going slow; but a bright moon lit the way, casting shadows on the white ground. It meant that for now they did not need their night-vision goggles. The snowsuits and the exercise kept them warm, Ismail was less of a hindrance than Will thought he would be and it was not long before they saw lights in the distance. Minutes later they were in range of the village.

Ahead of them – thirty metres, Will estimated – they saw a low concrete building. A bright light shone from the roof out into the snow. Will jabbed his finger to the left to indicate to everyone that they should head in that direction to avoid being floodlit, but as he did so, the light failed. The unit were left temporarily blinded as their night vision adjusted to the sudden darkness.

'The village gets its electricity from a generator,' Ismail whispered. 'But it can only supply electricity for a few hours a day. They have switched it off now.' He pointed in the direction of the building in front of them. 'That is where the generator is kept.'

'We'll head there,' Will replied. 'It's a good place to leave you.'

They moved towards the generator building. As they approached, Drew and Kennedy crept around each side, guns at the ready, to check no one was standing guard. As soon as the place was clear they signalled for the others to approach.

The snow in front of the entrance to the generator was well trodden, but now that the electricity had been turned off for the night it was unlikely anyone would come back here, so it would be safe for Ismail. It was difficult to make out in the heavy snow, but the village ahead of them looked much as Ismail had described it – not too big, maybe 200 buildings crudely created from some kind of breeze block. The roofs were covered in snow and there was, of course, nothing in the way of street lighting.

'Ahead of you is the main square,' Ismail told the unit as he pointed away from the building. 'Most of the dwelling places are along the west and the south sides of it and I think it unlikely that anyone will be held prisoner in that area. On the far side are some other buildings – a school-room and various run-down shacks. I think you will find that a more profitable place to start searching.'

Will nodded. 'Get inside,' he told Ismail, 'and stay out of sight.'

'You will come and find me?'

'When we've done what we need to do, yes.'

Ismail bit his lip. 'And how long will that be, do you think?'

Will glanced towards the village. 'As long as it takes,' he replied. 'But if we're not back in half an hour, you can assume something's gone wrong.'

'And what do I do then?'

'Fucking run for it,' Kennedy said, tersely. 'And hope the X-rays don't feel like chasing.'

Ismail looked at the SAS man as though he could not work out if he was joking or not. 'What are X-rays?' he asked, his simple question betraying the total innocence that marked him out as being totally unsuitable for this situation.

'Enemy combatants,' Will said, quietly. 'But don't worry about it. We'll have them covered.' He gave the scared

Afghan what he hoped was a reassuring smile, then handed him his Sig 230. 'In case you need it,' he said. 'Good luck, Ismail.'

Ismail took a deep breath. 'Thank you,' he replied, before slipping quietly inside the generator room, leaving the four-man unit outside.

'Thank God we've ditched him,' Kennedy muttered, and it was true. Will might feel sorry for the guy, but it was a relief to be on their own. They had needed Ismail to get them this far, but from now on a man who gibbered at the sight of a firearm was only going to be a hindrance. Silently, they removed their NV goggles from their packs and placed them over their heads. Will blinked as his eyes adjusted to the sudden, green-tinted clarity. Ahead of them was a cluster of single-storey dwellings; from most of these places he could see smoke curling from the chimneys – clearly the inhabitants of the village had fires in their humble houses to keep away the chill. It suggested to Will that not many people would be about.

A sudden howl filled the air – a dog, probably, scavenging around the village. The sound seemed to echo over the snow-covered plains. Will hoped for the dog's sake that it didn't come across any of them. They wouldn't be able to risk it alerting anyone else to their presence, so their only option would be to put a bullet in its head. The dog howled again. It was eerie, like this whole fucking place. The sooner they could get out of here, the better.

He nodded at Drew and Kennedy, who took the lead, skirting around the back of the crude, box-like dwellings, while Will and Anderson aimed their Diemacos forward, ready to take out anyone who caught sight of them. But so far they had seen no one. There was nobody outside. There was nothing to suggest their arrival had been clocked.

Drew and Kennedy stopped, pressed their backs against the wall of one of the buildings, then gave Will and Anderson

141

the cover they needed to advance. They continued in this way, silently, for a couple of minutes until the dwelling places started to thin out. Up to their left, fifty metres away, they could see the larger buildings Ismail had mentioned. There was movement here, men standing outside carrying guns. Overt security. It looked hopeful.

'We should attack from both sides,' Anderson breathed.

Will addressed Drew and Kennedy. His voice was tense. 'You two, stay here. We'll skirt round to the other side. Once we're there, take them out.'

'Roger that,' Kennedy replied.

Will and Anderson waited until they were sure the guards were not looking their way, then ran to the back of the large building, confident in the knowledge that if anyone saw them, Drew or Kennedy would nail them in seconds – and at fifty metres they would be sure of hitting their targets. Once there, they peered around the other side. There was a large concrete building with a corrugated iron roof on the north side of the village. Standing outside it, rifles in hand and surveying the surrounding countryside, were two men. In front of them was a metal bin, flames flickering from the top. The snow around it had melted. They did not seem to want to stray far from the warmth of that fire and Will didn't blame them.

It was instantly clear to both SAS men that they would have to take these guys out if they wanted to alert Drew and Kennedy to their presence here and a cursory nod between them was all it took to establish that this was what they were going to do.

They raised their rifles, got the targets in their sights and fired. Their suppressed weapons let out two almost silent shots as they doubled-tapped each of their targets. Two head-shots: they fell immediately.

Will didn't even see them hit the ground. Once they were neutralised, his attention had to be elsewhere. He edged round the corner of the building and looked back towards the area where they had left Drew and Kennedy. His NV illuminated all the dwellings they had sneaked behind, he could see the snow-covered square in the middle of the village and the two guards in front of the main building were in plain view.

But he couldn't see the two SAS men.

He gave it thirty seconds. Still no sign.

'Shit,' he whispered. 'Where the fuck are they?'

As he spoke, Will turned round to look at Anderson. He was facing Will, the butt of his weapon still dug firmly into his shoulder, ready to take on anything that came at him. What he wasn't ready for, however, was what came from behind.

The instant Will saw the three Taliban fighters approaching from behind the building, he raised his gun to fire.

Anderson inclined his head slightly – it must have looked to him as though Will was aiming the weapon in his direction. The surprise was not allowed to register for long, however, because within a split second the sound of gunshot filled the air and Anderson hit the ground, a bullet lodged firmly in the back of his skull.

'*Anderson!*' Will roared. The situation had gone noisy now and there was no need for silence. His stomach was turning over as he realised that his partner had just been nailed. Sheer rage descended on him and on instinct he started pumping bullets into the Taliban who had just killed Anderson. Two of them fell, then a third. For a moment all thoughts of the mission left Will's mind – he just wanted to kill these people.

But suddenly they were swarming around him – four of them, maybe five, all armed, all pointing their guns directly at him. His weapon was knocked from his hands and landed with a clatter next to Anderson's still-warm body.

Instantly they were upon him, smashing the NV goggles

from his face, beating him with their guns and then, when he was on the ground, kicking him brutally in the stomach and the head until he was helpless with the pain. Finally, he felt himself being dragged to his feet and pulled out towards the central square.

Drew and Kennedy were there too, captured, their hands bound behind their backs and their NV goggles ripped from their faces. They looked stunned. And well they might. It had all happened so quickly and none of this made any kind of sense. They had approached in darkness; they had kept out of sight; the mission had barely even begun and nobody in the village could have known that they were coming.

Nobody, Will realised with a sickening lurch in his stomach, except one person.

As he was pushed roughly towards Drew and Kennedy, his eyes scoured the groups of bearded Taliban extremists who had congregated to witness the capture of the SAS unit. He knew who he was looking for and he saw him soon enough.

Ismail was standing on the corner of the square, flanked by two Taliban men, both considerably taller than him. One of them had a deep scar on his lower lip. Ismail hadn't been roughed up; he hadn't been bound. As Will's eyes met his, he gazed at him expressionlessly.

Then, unable to keep up that stare for long, the young Afghan's eyes fell to the ground. He turned and wandered off, alone, through the door of a small hut in the shadows beyond.

NINE

The brutality that their Taliban captors inflicted on them happened in a blur. Hugely outnumbering the SAS men, they seemed to take pleasure in kicking and beating them to a pulp. One of them struck Will so hard on the forehead with the butt of his gun that blood streamed down over his eyes, stinging them and blinding him. Only when the three of them were bruised and battered almost beyond recognition did they hear a man bark a single word that they didn't recognise. Immediately the beating stopped.

Held at gunpoint, their hands were tied behind their backs with lengths of roughly made rope.

'It was that fucking informant,' Kennedy gasped under his breath as they were being tied up. 'He sold us down the fucking river.'

'I know,' Will said, quietly. He glanced over to the corner of the square to see if Ismail had reappeared, but there was no sign of him. For now they had other things to worry about. Their Taliban captors began talking harshly to them in Pashto, jabbing them with guns and pushing them in the direction of one of the buildings they had been trying to storm. The three of them were marched through the main door and into a dark room. Their packs were taken from them and the door was locked from the outside.

The moment they were alone, curses started to fly around the room – most of them from Kennedy and most of them aimed at Ismail. 'Little raghead bastard!' he fumed. 'All that bullshit about his wife and kid. Anderson was right about the fucker all along.' The fact that his face was cut and his body was bruised seemed to worry Kennedy far less than Ismail's treachery. Will, too, was less concerned about the physical injuries that had been inflicted on him, choosing instead to feel his way around the dark room, searching for a way out.

As soon as Anderson's name was mentioned, however, they all fell silent. What a great Christmas present for his family back home this was going to be. They wouldn't even have a body to bury – just a plaque somewhere in St Martin's, Hereford, and a few kind words from someone in authority. Will tried to put from his mind the thought that must have been going through the heads of Drew and Kennedy too – that unless they experienced a sudden and remarkable change in their fortunes, that plaque in St Martin's would be joined by three more.

The door opened and they were blinded by the light of a couple of torches shining in on them. A man walked in, his body silhouetted in the doorway. Will could tell that he was aiming a gun in their direction.

This is it, he thought to himself. Strangely, he found he didn't much mind the idea of his impending death. All he felt was a vague sense of remorse that he would not be laid to rest alongside his wife and daughter.

The man spoke. Slowly and in deeply accented English, he addressed the SAS soldiers.

'You were foolish to come here.'

No one replied.

'Your friend is dead,' he continued. 'At first light, his body will be dragged to the outskirts of the village. The wild animals will be glad of it. The rest of you have until dawn to consider the grave insult you have inflicted on Islam in coming to this place. Then you will be executed and you will join your friend.'

Without another word, the man stepped backwards into the darkness and the door was firmly locked once more.

'Happy fucking Christmas to you, too,' Kennedy said, under his breath. But there was no mirth in his voice.

Their room was windowless and pitch black. In the darkness, Will edged towards the door. Standing with his back towards it, he gave it a rap with his bound hands. It sounded solid. There was no way they'd be able to break that door down, not in these conditions.

It was freezing cold, too, although their snowsuits offered them some protection. The cold wasn't their biggest worry, though. The chilling words of their Taliban captor rang in Will's head.

They were stuck in this place.

There was no way out – not even for men of their ability.

All they could do was wait until sunrise and the horrors that it would bring.

★

Her feet were ravaged by the branding she had received earlier. She would have had difficulty standing up, even if she had wanted to. Instead, she remained huddled on the cold, hard ground, foetus-like.

She was beyond hunger now. Her stomach, which for days had shrieked at her to satisfy it with food, had withdrawn into a dull ache that seemed always to be there. Her exhaustion caused her to exist in a semi-drowsy state, somewhere between sleep and wakefulness, a half-coma from which she was only roused when they came in to question her or to inflict more brutality upon her person.

But suddenly, from outside, a noise caused her bruised eyelids to flicker open. A gunshot rang out through the air, the harsh bang sending a shock through her as if she herself had been shot.

And then there was a voice: '*Anderson!*'

The woman blinked. The name meant nothing to her, but the voice that shouted it did.

It was English.

She had not heard any foreigners in this village. It was full of ordinary Afghans and the brutal Taliban insurgents. No British or American troops, as far as she could tell, had come this way. Not in this weather.

Until now.

A tiny flame of hope sparked up within her and like a small candle in a dark room it seemed to bring warmth and light.

But as quickly as she was filled with hope, it drained back out of her again as she heard the harsh voices of her captors.

'Bind his hands,' someone said in Pashto. 'And imprison them in the schoolroom. We will deal with them at first light.'

There was a scuffling, then the banging of a door. The woman felt sick. Then she felt numb. Then she closed her eyes once more and for the first time since she had arrived in this hellish place, she wept. And as the tears finally came, she felt for all the world as though they would never, ever stop.

★

When death comes, it is best that it comes quickly.

Ever since he had started in the Regiment, Will had been of this point of view. And when his family had died, he had comforted himself in some small way that at least they had known nothing about it. At least the end had come quickly.

The end had come quickly for Anderson, too. A bullet in the back of the head. If you were going to buy it on an op, that was the best way to go. No torture. No anticipation. It wouldn't be much consolation for Anderson's family, but it was true. In a weird kind of way Will wished he had been in Anderson's shoes. At least he wouldn't have to go through this. The waiting. Waiting for the inevitable.

In the darkness, it was impossible to tell how much time passed – three hours, Will guessed, maybe four – but once they had established that there was no way they could undo the ropes binding each other's wrists, the three SAS men were silent for a good deal of it. A deep, impenetrable silence, broken only by the occasional sound of the Taliban guards talking outside their building. Will wondered if the same things were going through the heads of Drew and Kennedy as were occupying him. The dog that they had heard on the other side of the village barked a couple of times, but then all was still. Midnight? One o'clock? Their captors had taken their watches and time meant nothing. None of them could tell whether it was passing quickly or slowly.

It was strange to think that Latifa Ahmed, the one person who could lead Will to his family's killer, might be no more than a stone's throw away. Strange and unspeakably frustrating. There were moments when it was all he could do to stop himself from roaring with anger; at other times he felt hopeless, helpless.

And then, as he closed his eyes in the darkness, in his mind's eye he saw the photograph of Faisal Ahmed that the Director General of MI5 had shown him only yesterday. Ahmed's calm eyes seemed to stare out at him. Will had never met this man and Ahmed probably didn't even know that Will existed; yet their lives were inextricably linked. Ahmed had taken everything from Will; and now, because of him, Will was going to lose his life, while Ahmed would be free to conduct his acts of terrorism on London. And yet, Will had come here to rescue the one person in the world Ahmed seemed to have feelings for.

His thoughts were interrupted by the opening of the door. He looked in that direction, but all he saw were the silhouettes of their Taliban captors. Three of them, maybe four. It was difficult to make out in this light. Surely they hadn't come for them already; surely there were a few more hours of night-time yet. He got to his feet, just as the Taliban threw something into the room. It flew past Will's head and bounced against the back wall, hitting the ground with a dull thud. They threw something else in — heavier this time — and it fell just in front of the door, which they closed without saying a word. Will heard them lock it.

'What the fuck—?' Kennedy started to say.

Will had already turned and was on his knees in the darkness, trying to find the object they threw in. His hands felt blindly until they came across something. It was icy cold and damp in patches. It was only when he felt the short-cropped hair that he realised what it was.

'Jesus!' he spat. 'It's a fucking head!'

'Anderson,' Drew replied almost immediately. 'It's his body here.'

'The fuckers cut his head off, just to put the shits up us,' Kennedy raged. Will heard him stand up and kick the solid wall violently.

There was a silence as they absorbed what had happened. The Taliban were giving them a message: *this is what you can look forward to.* Will felt his jaw clenching. He was fucked if he was going to give them the chance. But they were without weapons and there was no way out of this room.

'I've got an idea,' Drew said in a soft voice.

'What?'

'Anderson. He carries a buckle knife. They might not have seen it.'

Will felt a surge of hope. Buckle knives, which slid inside the protective leather of your belt, were difficult to notice if you didn't know they were there. If Anderson had one on him, they might be in with a chance.

Instantly the three of them headed towards where the body lay. In the darkness, Will could already sense that Drew was on the ground with his back to Anderson's headless corpse, unzipping his bloodied snowsuit and feeling for his belt. 'Bingo,' he said after a minute.

'You got it?'

'Yeah, I've got it.'

Drew stood back to back with Kennedy first, so that their tied hands were next to each other. Slowly, he started slicing through his colleague's ropes. 'Mind my fucking wrists!' Kennedy complained more than once; but minutes later he was free and it was easy then for him to cut the ropes from Drew's wrists, then Will's. Once they were free, Will sensed a new determination in them. They had nothing to lose. Will was fucked if he was going to give in to these Taliban scum without a fight.

'How many guards do you think we have outside?' he asked.

A pause. 'Don't know,' Drew said, quietly. 'A couple, maybe. They're not going to be expecting much from us, so it'll be light.'

'That's what I thought. Reckon we can take them, if we can get them into the room in the first place?'

'Don't like our chances much,' Kennedy said. 'But I don't fancy hanging around waiting for them to give us the fucking Marie Antoinette treatment.'

'Me neither.'

Will ran through his idea a couple of times – it was straightforward, but they needed to be sure they were fully familiar with it, because if this went wrong, the Taliban outside wouldn't wait until morning to shoot them. They'd do it there and then.

'Bit risky,' Drew observed when he had heard what Will had in mind.

'Fancy waiting till dawn?'

'Not really,' Drew replied, calmly.

When the impromptu briefing was over, they put the plan into action.

Kennedy took Anderson's corpse and, standing in the middle of the room, held it in front of him so that it acted as a shield should the guards get a chance to shoot. In his hand, he clutched the buckle knife. Will and Drew stood on either side of the entrance. When everyone was in position, Will started scratching on the inside of the door, trying to make it sound as if he was tampering with the lock. It was better than making an obvious fuss, he had decided; this way their guards would be more likely to investigate.

Sure enough, after only a moment of worrying away at the door, he heard voices outside, then the noise of a key in the lock. He stepped aside, feeling his blood suddenly pumping heavily through his veins.

If this was going to work, they'd have to move quickly.

A Taliban guard appeared at the door and shone his torch directly into the room. Immediately Kennedy was illuminated. The guard shouted something in Pashto and strode towards them. His gun was in his arms, but it was not raised. That, Will realised, would be his mistake.

It all happened in seconds. A second guard entered and they made their move. Silently Will and Drew stepped behind the two guards and each wrapped a single strong arm around their necks. Will squeezed as tightly as he could, feeling his biceps bulge against his victim's flesh. With his other hand he grabbed the guard's gun and moved it away so that he couldn't shoot randomly. A strangled sound came from his throat and from that of Drew's man. Kennedy dropped Anderson's body, which fell heavily to the floor, then approached the now captive Taliban. Using the knife, he started stabbing them in the eyes with a kind of frenzy. Each time the knife went in it made a sucking sound and he gave it a little twist. Blood was everywhere and for a few brief seconds Will felt the limbs of his man flailing uncontrollably. He squeezed tighter.

Then, suddenly, his man fell still.

Will let the Taliban guard fall and about twenty seconds later, Drew did the same.

The Taliban guard's torch had dropped to the floor and was shining away from them. It illuminated the shattered remnants of Anderson's head.

'Make sure they're not going to wake up on us,' Will breathed.

'My fucking pleasure,' growled Kennedy.

He bent down to the ground next to the Taliban guard that Will had floored and without hesitation he plunged the knife deep into the neck of the fallen man. With a swift, silent, lethal efficiency, he moved over to the other guard and repeated the operation.

By this time, Drew had picked up the torch and was shining it on the two corpses. Will grabbed their Kalashnikovs and gave them to Drew and Kennedy. For himself, he took the knife, still sticky with the warm blood of the Taliban guards, from Kennedy, then took the key that one of the guards was still gripping. He unstrapped Anderson's belt and put it on himself, then resheathed the knife. He also took his dead comrade's watch: 00.57. They'd been in there for hours. Patting one of the guards down, he found an extra torch.

'Torch off,' he told Drew, who extinguished the light, plunging them back into sudden darkness. They crept out of the room, which now resembled a bloodbath, and locked the door behind them.

The main square of the village was deserted. At some point during their incarceration it had started to snow again and the flakes had begun to cover up the footprints that both they and the Taliban had made. The moon was still high in the sky, brightly illuminating the village. Good thing too, Will thought to himself. Their weapons and packs had been taken and they only had two antique-looking Kalashnikovs between them. Time was of the essence. Someone could come to relieve the guards they had killed at any moment. The instant they realised what had happened, the whole village would be lit up like a Christmas tree and the Taliban would be crawling all over the place. There was no time to locate their own guns – it was more important to find their target and get the hell out of there before it all went tits up for a second time. And if they happened to come across Ismail while they were looking, Will was sure they'd find time to avenge Anderson's death.

Still, he felt naked without a gun. What was more, one shot from an AK-47 would wake the whole place up. He'd feel much more comfortable with a suppressed weapon. On a whim, he looked over to where Anderson had fallen. Remnants of the poor bastard were still there, the snow spattered with brain matter, bits of skull and hair fragments. But Will paid no attention to that: he was just relieved to see that the Taliban, foolishly, had left the man's gun propped up against the wall. He grabbed it, then turned and went back to the others.

'Split up,' he breathed. 'You two search the buildings here; I'll take the north side. RV back here in fifteen minutes.'

Drew and Kennedy nodded and, cat-like, went about their work. Will felt much more comfortable now that he had the Diemaco in his fist and he ran silently up to the north side of the village, doing his best to conceal himself in the shadows that the moon cast on the frozen ground; where that was not possible, he just moved quickly.

Up ahead there was a large, low, concrete building, not unlike the one in which they had just been imprisoned. It seemed different to the small dwelling places that were dotted around and had a military truck parked outside – though a layer of snow over the vehicle suggested it hadn't been moved for at least a couple of days. After all, Will thought to himself, where would anyone drive to from here? The building had several metal doors evenly spaced around it, each firmly locked with heavy iron padlocks. At one end there was what looked like a wooden shack and beyond that the undulating snow stretched off into the darkness.

Will examined the locks. If he had the equipment, he could pick them in a trice, but God only knows where their Taliban captors had stashed their packs. For a brief moment he considered using the Diemaco to shoot the locks off; but even though the suppressed weapon would make little noise, the sound of the bullet against the metal would alert anyone nearby to his presence. No, he was going to have to think of another way in.

He skirted around the back of the building to see if there was any other entrance. Nothing. But as he was there, he heard a noise.

Quickly he turned, his back to the wall, pointing the Diemaco out into the dark, snowy countryside beyond.

Silence.

Perhaps it was an animal. The dog he had heard earlier. Then again, perhaps not.

He held his breath and kept his eyes peeled.

That sound again. It was coming from somewhere to his left. Will pointed the Diemaco in that direction. He was holding his breath, his finger poised a hair's breadth from the trigger.

He listened carefully. Suddenly the noise came again.

Will blinked. He realised now what it was. It was the sound of someone sobbing. A woman. And it was coming from the wooden hut at the end of the building.

Carefully he edged his way along the concrete wall to the hut; as he did so, the sound of the sobbing grew fractionally louder. Checking there was no one around to see him, he put his ear against the hut's wooden wall. There was no mistaking it. Someone was crying inside. He edged around to the front – the door to the hut was padlocked like all the others. There was no way in.

He had to think quickly. The likelihood was that this was Latifa Ahmed, but he couldn't be sure. And he couldn't risk making a noise breaking into the hut and alerting anyone to his presence.

After a moment's thought he crept round to the back of the hut.

It was a reasonably well-constructed hut, but it was still little more than planks of timber nailed on to a wooden frame. Will ran his hand along the planks until he found one that seemed looser than the others. That would do. He pulled out Anderson's buckle knife, then levered it into the groove running along the edge of the plank, just where it was nailed into the frame. With a forceful yank, he levered it away.

The timber creaked and immediately the crying inside stopped. Will dug the knife in deeper and levered it once more. Now there was enough room for him to get both hands around the plank. He pulled hard. As he had hoped it would, the wood came away from the frame.

Once the first timber plank was loose it was simpler to pull away the second and the third, which gave him enough space to get inside the hut. He pulled the torch he had taken from the dead Taliban guard from the pocket of his snowsuit. Shining it along the barrel of his Diemaco, he looked inside.

What he saw sickened him.

A woman sat on the ground. The veil of her burka was beside her and she stared into the bright light of the torch with a look of the most abject fear and desperation. Her face, Will realised after staring at it for a moment, was blue and puffy with bruises – so much so that she seemed to be having difficulty opening her eyes. Her black hair was matted and dishevelled and her feet, which were bare below her thin robes, were swollen and seemed to glisten painfully in the light of the torch – sores, Will deduced, weeping from some unspeakable torture. Her whole body was shaking violently, though whether that was through cold or through fear he couldn't tell. A mixture of both, probably.

Will moved the light away from the woman and shined it around the rest of the hut. It was empty. The only thing the beam of the torch illuminated was a small pile of excrement in the corner.

He moved the gun and the torch back on to the woman's face and as he did so a curious cocktail of emotions overcame him. He was nauseated that anyone could do such things to a woman and filled with a burning need to bring some sort of retribution on her tormentors. But at the same time, he couldn't forget who she was: Faisal Ahmed's sister. The sister of the man who had killed his family. Will was glad that his face was hidden behind the bright light of the torch – it meant that she would be unable to see the harshness in his expression.

He needed to be sure it was her and that meant frightening her even more than she was already. But it was necessary – a mistake here would be catastrophic. He edged into the hut and approached. Shining the torch down on her, he rested the gun barrel on her head.

'What's your name?' he whispered. The woman he wanted, Pankhurst had told him, spoke some English, so if it was the right person, she would understand the question.

Her body started trembling even more violently and she looked up at him with wide, frightened eyes.

'*What's your name?*' Will hissed, insistently.

Again, silence.

157

'Tell me now,' he told her, 'otherwise I'll kill you.'

The woman took a deep breath and finally she spoke. Her voice was desperately frail, a thin, cracked, weak sound.

'My name,' she said, 'is Latifa Ahmed. And if you kill me now, you would be doing me a great service.'

TEN

'Get to your feet.'

Latifa's frightened eyes looked up at him. 'I cannot,' she said.

'What do you mean, you can't?' Will demanded. But even as he spoke, he directed his torch back towards the woman's feet. The bright white light illuminated the weeping sores.

'They burned my skin,' Latifa said in pitiful explanation. 'They brought fire and burned my skin.'

'Jesus,' Will whispered. The woman was a mess. But there was no time for sympathy. He strode towards her, letting the Diemaco hang from its strap.

'Did Faisal send you?'

The question wrongfooted Will for a moment, and he hesitated. 'Yes,' he lied, finally, knowing that this was one way to get her on side. He despised himself for doing it. 'Your brother sent me.' He put his hands under her armpits and roughly pulled her up.

Latifa's body was impossibly bony and she was as light as a child. The moment her feet touched the ground, however, she opened her mouth to scream. The sound never left her throat – Will's hand was there before she could make a noise and he held it firmly over her lips while her body adjusted to what was clearly an agonising pain. Her breath came in short, sharp bursts and tears came to her eyes.

'Listen to me,' Will hissed. 'I'm going to get you out of

here, but you have to do as I say. If you *don't* do what I say, they'll kill all of us. Do you understand?'

Latifa, her eyes wide with fright and hate, nodded.

'Good. I know you're in pain, but you're going to have to deal with it. Can you do that?'

Latifa moved a hand up to his and pulled it firmly from her mouth. 'Yes,' she said, a hint of steel entering her frail voice. 'I can do that.'

Will nodded. He couldn't help feeling a twinge of respect for this woman; it was an uncomfortable sensation, given how much he wanted to loathe her for what her brother had done. As if to conquer his confused emotions, he tugged her arm forcefully. 'Come on,' he whispered.

They squeezed through the back of the hut and out into the snow. Latifa walked barefoot and painfully and the expression on her face spoke of the agony she was experiencing. Will kept his Diemaco raised, the torch switched off to avoid anyone spotting them from a distance. It seemed to take an age to get back to the RV point, but Latifa was treading gingerly and Will knew that short of carrying her, there was no way he could speed her up.

By the time they reached the RV point, Latifa's whole body was shaking with cold, pain and fear. Drew and Kennedy were waiting for them, hiding in the shadows with their guns pointing outwards. 'Fuck me,' Kennedy breathed when Will and Latifa joined them. 'Is that her?'

'Yeah,' Will stated, flatly. 'That's her.'

'Christ,' he whispered. For once Kennedy was lost for words.

Latifa's shivering was getting worse. 'She's not going to make it at this rate,' Will muttered. 'She's going to freeze.' He lowered his weapon and started removing his snowsuit. As soon as it was off, he felt his body temperature drop, but it was more important that Latifa had some warmth –

Will was in much better shape to withstand the cold than she was.

'Put this on,' he told her.

The woman stared back at him uncomprehendingly.

'*Put it on!*' he repeated, before abruptly forcing her limbs into the snowsuit. Only when she was more suitably dressed did Drew speak.

'She's not in any kind of state to make it back to the truck,' he observed, quietly.

He was right. Creeping around the village was one thing, but it was a couple of hours' hard walk through the snow back to where they had left the vehicle. Even if they managed to raise her body temperature, she wasn't going to make it.

'You'll have to carry her,' Will told them. 'Between the two of you. One person carry her, the other provide cover from the rear.'

'What about you?' Kennedy asked.

Will glanced around him, remembering Anderson's body in the schoolroom.

'I'm going to deal with Ismail,' he said, calmly.

'Don't be a fucking idiot,' Kennedy snapped. 'Look, Anderson was a friend and I'm sorry he's dead. But we're lucky we're not all in two pieces like him and we haven't got the time for revenge killings. We all leave together. Now.'

Will's face stiffened. Kennedy was right, of course. With Anderson down, all they had to think about was the mission: their priority was to get Latifa the hell out of here and that was what they should be doing. But somehow Will couldn't quite see it that way; and besides, there was another reason for putting a bullet in Ismail's skull.

'They'll find out that we've gone before long,' he said. 'When they do, they'll want to follow us. Ismail knows where we're headed. I need to stop him from telling them.'

Kennedy looked unconvinced. 'He's probably told them

already. We need to expect a surprise party when we get to the truck.'

'But if he hasn't,' Will replied, 'we don't want them following us. I need to deal with it.'

Kennedy shrugged his shoulders. 'It's your fucking skin,' he said, before turning to Latifa. 'Can you get on my back?' he asked.

Latifa just stared at him.

'Fuck it,' Kennedy murmured, picking her up in his arms. 'Don't think I'm carrying her all the way.'

A flicker of a smile passed across Drew's face. ''Course not,' he murmured. 'Listen, we entered the village from the west, so I don't think we should leave that way. Let's head north, then skirt round to the west.' He looked out into the barren snowscape beyond the village. 'That way,' he pointed.

Kennedy grunted in agreement.

'How long do you need here?' Drew asked Will.

Will shrugged. 'Twenty minutes max,' he said.

'Right. We'll wait at the truck for half an hour. If you haven't shown by then, we're leaving.'

'Roger that,' Will nodded, then watched as the two SAS men and the shivering woman disappeared into the darkness.

The hut into which Will had seen Ismail disappear was at the opposite corner of the main square, but he couldn't risk heading straight there – he would be too exposed, easily picked off by anyone with a weapon. So he crept around the edge, keeping to the shadows and treading as softly as he could. He felt strangely naked without his snow-suit. Light. Already the chill had started to penetrate to his skin, but he did his best to put that from his mind. Keep moving, he told himself. Keep moving and you'll be OK.

His footsteps crunched in the snowy ground, but other than that there was no sound as he approached the hut he had seen Ismail enter. It was built on top of a concrete foundation block perhaps half a metre high and it had posts at regular intervals around it, which held the flat roof up. There was a wooden door on one side, but a quick recce around the building told him that there were no windows or any other mode of entry. He stood by the door for a moment, holding his breath as he strained his ears to hear any sound from within.

Nothing.

Will stepped to one side of the door, put his back against the wall, then used the barrel of his Diemaco to rap on the wood. Tap-tap-tap. Quietly, but loud enough for anyone inside to hear.

Still nothing.

He tapped again. This time there was a shuffling inside, then silence.

Will waited. He couldn't risk barging in – it would make too much noise and he would be an instant target in the doorway. No, he'd have to wait for anyone inside to come to him and if that didn't happen, he'd have to abort.

His breath steamed in the cold air as he continued to press himself against the wall.

More shuffling. Someone was approaching the door. He could sense they were just on the other side now and he thought he could hear a faint click – the sound of a weapon being readied.

The door opened.

It all happened in a couple of seconds. As the door edged open, Will saw a handgun appear in the crack. Instantaneously he brought the barrel of his own gun down fiercely on to the hand; there was a whimper of pain and the gun fell to the ground. Will barged in, pushing the figure roughly to the floor, and kicking the door shut behind him.

What little light there was inside the hut came from a small, smoky lamp with a flickering yellow flame. It sat on a wooden table; elsewhere there were a couple of stools and a yellowing mattress rolled out in one corner. And on the floor, staring up at Will with a look of such abject fear as the SAS man had never seen in his life, was Ismail.

Will raised the Diemaco and aimed it directly at the head of the terrified Afghan.

'The man those bastards killed had a family,' he whispered. 'Thanks to you, someone's father won't be coming home.'

Ismail shuffled on his back away from him, but Will kept the gun aimed steadily at his head.

'I had no choice,' Ismail whispered. 'I promise you, I had no choice!'

'Don't give me that shit. Of course you had a choice. Them or us. It's very simple.'

Ismail closed his eyes, clearly preparing himself for the end to come. 'They found out two days ago that I was informing against them,' he stuttered. 'They abducted my wife and my little boy. They said they would kill them if I did not do as they said.' He opened his eyes again. 'They were serious,' he said with a sudden and simple conviction.

Will felt his lip curling. 'I don't believe you,' he growled, though in his heart he knew that Ismail's words had the desperate ring of truth.

Ismail was shaking now and his skin was sweating despite the cold. 'How did you break out?' he asked.

Will remained silent.

'It doesn't matter,' Ismail whispered. 'If you escape, they will kill me anyway, and my family. But not before torturing me first to see if I know where you have gone. My family is as good as dead. Perhaps it is best that you end it all for me now.' He closed his eyes again and took a deep breath.

Will's finger hesitated on the trigger. Whether Ismail was telling the truth or not, he was a liability to the safety of their mission. He should plug him now. Silence him. Make sure he could not tell the Taliban where to look for them.

164

But something stopped him. Silently he cursed himself. Two years ago he wouldn't have given this a second thought; if Drew or Kennedy were in his position now, Ismail would already be dead.

'Did you tell them?' he asked, quietly. 'Where the truck is, I mean.'

Ismail looked up at him. 'No. Not yet. But they asked me if I knew where it was. I will do my best not to take them,' he replied. 'But I am not a strong man. I am not like you and your friends. I cannot guarantee that I will be able to withstand their tortures. You must either kill me or leave quickly before they realise you have gone.'

The Afghan's ultimatum hung in the air. He continued to shiver, his whole body consumed with trembling.

'You're coming with me,' Will stated, firmly.

An uneasy smile came on to Ismail's frightened face, and he shook his head. 'I cannot,' he whispered. 'If I do that it would be like pulling the trigger on my family myself. You do not perhaps understand quite what the Taliban are capable of.'

'I've got a pretty fucking good idea,' Will murmured, almost to himself. He thought for a moment before speaking again. 'Get up against the wall,' he said, quietly. His Diemaco was still pointing directly at Ismail's head.

For a moment Ismail didn't move. But then he nodded his head fearfully and shuffled backwards.

Once he was pressed against the wall, Will stepped back. He opened the door with one hand. 'Stay there,' he told Ismail, before turning and stepping outside.

The Sig handgun that he had given the Afghan and which only a minute earlier he had knocked from his hands was still lying in the snow. He bent down, picked it up and stepped back inside. Ismail was still huddled against the wall. Will placed the gun on the table.

'If you're not going to come with me, then you're on

your own. Use this to defend yourself when they come for you.'

Ismail looked nervously at the gun. 'I am not a fighter,' he whispered.

'I didn't say you were, Ismail. Just do what you have to do.'

The two man stared at each other.

'You must go,' the Afghan said finally. 'They will soon find out you are gone and if they catch you—'

Will nodded, curtly. Then, without saying another word, he left the hut, leaving the frightened Afghan shaking in the semi-darkness.

★

Ismail stared at the gun.

Soon, he knew, his wife and little son would be facing the barrel of some such weapon and it would be the last thing they saw on earth. It was all he could do not to retch at the thought of it. These Taliban, he knew what they were like. He had lived through their regime. They were merciless. There was no way they would believe Ismail that he had not released the SAS men. No way at all. They would kill his family in front of him, not because they were involved in any way; just to make Ismail himself feel the pain.

A coldness ran through him as a possibility suggested itself. Perhaps there was a way to save them after all. Perhaps there was a way out of this, for his wife and child if not for him. If Ismail himself was not around to witness his family's death, there would be no reason for the Taliban to kill them.

It was like a game of chess. And as his father had taught him so many years ago when they played during the summer outside the cafés of Kandahar, in chess you must sometimes make sacrifices in order to win.

Big sacrifices.

Ismail realised that his body was shaking as he approached the table and touched the handgun before picking it up and feeling its weight.

What he was about to do was *haram*, forbidden. A line from the Koran flashed through his mind: *Whoever takes his life with a piece of iron will be punished with the same piece of iron in the hell fire.*

The piece of iron he held in his hand was cold. He prayed silently that Allah would look with forgiveness on what he was about to do.

And then, the whispered words of the *takbir* repeating on his lips, he put the cold metal to his head and closed his eyes.

★

It was probably a mistake — Will knew that as he left the hut. But if Ismail had been telling the truth, he was as much a victim of the Taliban as Anderson or Latifa. He didn't deserve a bullet in the head for that, even if it was going to make their escape more risky. But Drew and Kennedy had a good head start and Will himself would be out of the village within minutes.

But his train of thought was shattered by a sudden bang.

A single gunshot.

He flung himself against the nearest wall, looking for the source of the fire; but intuitively he knew where it had come from. Poor bastard.

The gunshot, he knew, would attract attention. He had to get the hell out of there, and fast.

Will upped his pace, skirting around the main square. The others had left from the north, near the units where they had been held. Will wasn't going to do that — if anyone had been roused by the gunshot, the first thing they would do would be to check on the SAS men. That area would be swarming with Taliban within minutes. Instead he headed west, back the way they came, darting down the dark streets where the huts of the ordinary Afghan villagers were to be found. Behind him, in the distance, he heard shouts. Thirty metres away, maybe forty. Too fucking close, in any case. The dog he had heard earlier began barking; this time, though, it was joined by two or three others. It sounded like bedlam back there. Clearly their escape had been discovered.

His breath steamed heavily in front of him and as he ran along the snowy streets he became aware of voices all around. He stopped for a moment, listening carefully. They were to his left and right, but not straight ahead. Will continued to run.

Ahead of him he could see the generator building where they had left Ismail earlier that evening. He sprinted towards it, then hid behind the back wall, which faced out on to the snowy landscape beyond. But as he held his breath and listened, he could hear people approaching the generator. It sounded like two voices.

Will's eyes narrowed slightly as he gripped his Diemaco.

He edged to the corner of the outbuilding, listening carefully. They were near, but he was sure they hadn't seen him – they were just searching here on the off-chance. That gave him the element of surprise. He pressed the Diemaco hard into his shoulder, then swung round the corner of the building.

He nailed the first of them before the guy even knew he was there, the suppressed weapon firing a silent shot that hit him straight in the face. He collapsed like a stone to the ground. But in the split second Will took to aim his weapon at the second man, his Taliban pursuer managed to raise his AK-47. Will released a lethal headshot that brought the man to the ground, but not before his target had managed to release a single burst of fire from his own weapon. It missed Will by several metres, but the sound of gunshot seemed to echo all round the surrounding countryside.

'Shit,' Will whispered to himself. Everyone would have heard that and when they found the two Taliban corpses lying in the snow, they would know which way he had escaped.

There was no time to hide the bodies. It was now just a matter of who was quickest. He checked his watch: 01.35. The others had a twenty-minute start. He *had* to catch up with them.

Will ran to the back of the generator building and plunged into the snowy countryside beyond.

Distance was what he needed – distance between himself and the Taliban. They would be making chase any minute. They would be on foot. The snow was too deep for any kind of vehicle, so it would all come down to how much distance he could put between them. With a pang he realised that they could well be using the NV goggles they had taken from the SAS team earlier in the evening: it spurred him on to move even faster through the snow.

'*Don't look back*,' he whispered to himself. The temptation to do so was immense, but it would only slow him down. They'd be on his trail any minute – there was nothing he could do about his footprints in the snow and the Taliban would just have to follow them.

He pushed on into the darkness, cursing his decision to go back for Ismail. Clouds scudded against the silver moon: occasionally the way ahead would be lit surprisingly brightly as the moonlight reflected off the snow; but mostly it was pitch black. Will had to rely on his in-built sense of direction and hope he was going the right way. At one stage, the moon peeped out from behind the fast-moving clouds and illuminated the way ahead. There were footprints – two sets. Drew and Kennedy, it had to be. He was on the right path.

He should be catching them up soon. Will would be moving faster as they would be slowed down by Latifa

Ahmed. Christ, he thought to himself. It was going to be a relief. Three men's firepower would make him feel a lot more confident than just his.

He continued to pound the snow-covered earth, his lungs swallowing great mouthfuls of freezing air as he ran.

At first he didn't hear it; his heavy breath was too loud in his ears. But eventually the sound was unmistakable. It was not so much a bark as a yelp. It sounded thin and desperate.

Dogs. And they were close.

How close, Will couldn't say. He allowed himself a moment to stop and listen. The wide open space around him meant that it was difficult to tell which direction the sound of the dogs was coming from. One moment it would be coming from the east, behind him; the next minute, it seemed to come from the north or the south.

'Shit,' he muttered. He started running again. The dogs would be faster than their masters, but also faster than Will. And somehow he doubted that all they were after was a pat on the head and a juicy bone.

As he ran, he prepped the Diemaco. The minute the dogs came into view, there really was only going to be one option.

The barking grew louder. It was frenzied and Will tried to work out how many animals he could hear. Three? Maybe four? It was impossible to tell: the noise of their yelps seemed to merge into one great howl of fury. The more of them there were, the more difficult this was going to be. He would have to wait until they were close enough to see, but they would be fast-moving, unpredictable targets. He'd need to take them all out before they got close enough to attack.

Will stopped to give himself time to prepare. He turned round, hit the ground and lay on his front, ignoring the uncomfortable sensation of cold snow seeping through his clothes. He pressed the butt of his Diemaco hard into his shoulder, then surveyed the darkness, waiting for the first sign of the animals he could hear so clearly, but could not yet see.

The horrific noise of their barking grew even more frantic. It was as if they sensed they were close.

They emerged like ghosts from the darkness, silhouettes that seemed to dart around without coming any closer. Will knew they *were* coming closer, however. It was just a trick of the light. As if called to attention by that one thought, the moon suddenly emerged from behind the clouds and the ground was illuminated before him like a floodlit football pitch.

He only had a few seconds to take it all in. There were five of them, running as a pack. One dog strayed a few metres away from the others, but immediately rejoined them. It got too close to another of the animals, however, and was snipped and snarled at by its pack mate. It was obvious that they were hunting like this out of necessity, not unity. They were lean and vicious-looking, as if they had not been fed for many days; even from a distance Will could see a wildness in their eyes that chilled him.

These were mad dogs. They were hungry and they had caught the scent of food.

They were about thirty metres away and had not yet seen Will pressed down in the snow. That soon changed, however. As soon as they caught sight of their quarry, their snarling and yelping became hysterical. Their pace quickened as they bolted towards him. Twenty metres. Fifteen.

One of the dogs was out in front. The leader of the pack. It took all Will's self-control not to rush the shot. Fifteen metres was close range, but the target was moving unpredictably. He kept the gun trained accurately at the head of the beast and only when he was sure he was on target did he squeeze the trigger.

The bullet entered the dog's skull with a deadly silence.

As soon as it was hit, the dog raised up in the air. The animal's forward momentum, combined with the power of the bullet, caused it to flip a somersault on to its back, spraying blood from its exploding head across the surrounding snow and all over the rest of the pack. The remaining four dogs halted. They looked back at the fallen animal and, as if they had suddenly forgotten about Will, they turned on its corpse. Easy meat. As one, they started to rip into the flesh of their dead pack mate.

'That's right,' Will whispered as he watched the horrific scene with a crashing sense of relief. 'Get stuck in.'

He started to aim at a second dog. They might have been distracted, but he wasn't going to leave any of them alive. His eyes narrowed and he squeezed the trigger.

Click.

'*Fuck*,' Will whispered. The weapon had jammed. He tried to fire it again, then a third time, but no luck. It was as good as useless.

Gingerly, he started to push himself up. The dogs were thankfully distracted, but as he got to his feet, a fight broke out among them. Two of the animals, more dominant than the others, started to snap at their mates, warning them off from helping themselves. The two losers whimpered slightly, but they clearly understood the pecking order. Low growls rumbled in their throats; one of them allowed its tongue to loll lazily from the corner of its drooling mouth; and they turned to look at Will, who had no firepower now with which to stop them.

Then they fell silent.

Will swung the Diemaco over his head just as the two of them, in unison, started to bound towards him. Gripping the barrel of the gun firmly, he prepared to fight off these snarling animals using his weapon as a bludgeon. But their teeth were sharp and they were desperate. He knew his chances were slim.

It all happened in what seemed like a fraction of a second. The dog in front leapt at him, just as Will raised the gun over his shoulder like an axeman preparing to chop wood. The beast was so close he could smell it and he knew in that instant that without a working gun, he would be no match for the animals.

But just as he was beginning to swing the Diemaco, there was a loud bang from behind him and the dog fell to the ground, its head blown away. Will felt the animal's blood spatter over his face as, from behind him, a weapon cracked repeatedly through the night air, despatching the remaining three animals with pinpoint accuracy.

Will turned to see a familiar figure lower his Kalashnikov.

'Jesus Christ,' he breathed at Kennedy. 'Leave it a bit later next time, will you?'

Kennedy grinned. 'Didn't really think you'd need my help against a few Snoopies.'

'Fucking weapon jammed,' Will spat. 'I'll have something to say to the armourer when we get back home.'

'Yeah, speaking of which—' Kennedy peered into the darkness beyond the carnage of the dead dogs. 'They probably heard the sound of this fucking AK back in Hereford.'

'The Taliban won't be far behind,' Will agreed. 'How far ahead are Drew and the girl?'

'About a hundred metres. I only came back because I heard the sound of the dogs – figured they probably hadn't been let out just for a bit of fresh air and a run around. Did you find Ismail?'

Will nodded.

'You plug him?'

Will sniffed and looked back towards the village. 'He's dead,' he said, quietly. 'But it doesn't matter. We've still left a trail.'

'OK,' Kennedy said briskly. 'I don't think it's far to the truck now. Let's get moving.'

'Roger that,' Will said with relief and the two men started running through the snow, leaving the scene of their sudden and violent butchery behind them.

It only took a couple of minutes for them to catch up with Drew and Latifa. Drew was carrying her, but still moving surprisingly quickly. Will did his best not to look at the woman's face. Drew himself seemed neither surprised nor pleased to see them; he just spoke as if they'd never been away.

'I've found the tracks we made on the way in,' he stated. 'We're going in the right direction.'

'We need to up the pace,' Will told him. 'There's Taliban following. They're not waiting for us at the truck, but they won't be far behind.'

Drew nodded and silently they hurried on through the darkness.

It took about ten minutes to get to the truck. Snow had fallen, leaving a thick blanket over the chassis and drifting heavily against one side; it had even entered through the hole at the back where the rear door had been ripped off. Drew deposited Latifa in the back of the truck, where she sat gazing expressionlessly into space; then he stood back with the rest of them. 'We're going to have to dig it out,' he said.

Immediately they went to work on their hands and knees, shifting armfuls of snow out of the way so that the vehicle could move freely. Now that he had stopped running and without his snow suit, Will started to feel the cold all the more; his hands and feet were numb and he put more energy into digging to try and keep warm.

Soon they had dug the car out. Drew handed his Kalashnikov to Will, then took the wheel once more. Kennedy sat beside him in the front, his own gun pointing out of the passenger window back the way they'd come. Drew turned the ignition and their ears were filled with the thin, reedy sound of the engine trying, unsuccessfully, to turn over.

No one spoke. Drew tried again; again the engine coughed and spluttered before dissolving away into nothing. 'Battery must be cold,' he muttered. 'It's below freezing out there.'

'Well you'd better get it moving, quickly,' Kennedy said, his voice suddenly tense, even a little high-pitched. 'X-rays approaching.'

Will turned his head quickly. Sure enough, in the distance, highlighted by the silvery light of the moon, he could just make out figures coming towards them. Impossible to tell how many. But enough. A hundred metres away – and counting.

'How long till we get started?' he asked Drew, tersely.

'Impossible to say,' Drew replied. 'Could be a few minutes.'

Even before Drew had finished talking, Will was opening up the weapons stash. The Minimi 5.56 mm light machine gun was there waiting for him. 'Cover me while I set it up,' he told Kennedy.

Kennedy nodded. 'I'm counting about twenty of the fuckers!' he shouted. As Will pulled an ammunition belt out of the weapons stash, he started firing single shots from his Kalashnikov. It wouldn't be enough to overcome the number of enemy that were approaching, but it would slow them down and give Will time to set up the machine gun. Clutching the weaponry, he jumped down from the back of the truck and crawled along the ground, while Kennedy continued to fire off an occasional shot from his AK.

There was a trench on the side of the road. Will rolled into it, then opened up the V-shaped bipod at the end of the gun's barrel before feeding the small ammo belt into the chamber.

Behind him, the truck's engine coughed, them fell silent again.

Will heaved the machine gun over the edge of the trench.

It sank slightly in the snow, but he could feel the bipod hitting firm ground. His eyes squinted involuntarily as he aimed the weapon in the direction of the enemy. And then he fired.

The harsh chugging of the weaponry filled the air and the gun shook as the ammo belt rattled through it. A spray of gunfire showered into the approaching enemy and Will watched with satisfaction as about half of them fell to the ground like grass bending in the wind.

But that still left at least ten and they were approaching relentlessly.

He held fire. Behind him, the engine of the truck had roared into life. Drew was expertly massaging the throttle to warm the engine without letting it stall and Will heard Kennedy shouting at him. '*Get back in the truck! I'll cover you!*' A shot from the Kalashnikov rang through the air.

Will pulled the machine gun towards him and crawled back to the truck. As soon as he climbed into the vehicle, he felt it lurch backwards as Drew reversed around in a tight turning circle, so that they were pointing the right way again. 'It's like a fucking zombie movie out there!' Kennedy yelled. The snow chains crunched noisily into the powder, but they did their job well. The truck held to the road and in an instant they were moving.

But there was still gunfire and it wasn't coming from Kennedy, who was facing the wrong side of the road now. With a roar, Will smashed the butt of the machine gun through one of the windows at the back of the truck, then turned the weapon around and started firing indiscriminately in the direction of the not-yet-dead enemy.

Latifa shrank back; she might even have screamed, Will wasn't sure. His whole body shook with the force of the weapon as, in this last, desperate burst of gunfire, he struggled to make sure that they were not scuppered by a stray enemy bullet bursting into one of their tyres – or one of their heads.

Whether he hit anyone he didn't know; but eventually, Drew turned a corner and they found themselves out of the range of the enemy.

Will eased his finger off the trigger, silencing the noise of gunfire. He was breathing heavily, panting almost. They all were – even Latifa, whose face was an undisguised picture of stress and panic.

The truck trundled along, as fast as Drew could safely make it travel. Back on the road – they hoped – to some kind of safety.

ELEVEN

'We should cuff her.'

Kennedy was glancing over his shoulder at Latifa, who sat huddled in the back, opposite Will. Her body was shaking and Will worried that she was too frail to make it to Kandahar. He put that thought from his mind: the woman was no good to him dead. Slowly she glanced at the SAS man in the passenger seat and looked silently at Kennedy for a full ten seconds before speaking. 'Where is it you think that I am wanting to escape to?' she asked in faltering English.

'I don't know and I don't care,' Kennedy replied, brutally. 'But we've already made the mistake of trusting a stranger once today and we're coming back one man down.' He threw a set of Plasticuffs to Will, who caught them in one hand.

Latifa turned her attention to him. It was only now that Will took in her features, though he was aware that she must have looked a lot different before the Taliban got their hands on her. Her skin was dark, of course, and she had long black hair, matted and greasy, that seemed to cling to the side of her face. She might have been pretty once, but any prettiness had long been beaten out of her.

And she stank. Jesus, she stank. A fetid, pungent smell that filled the whole car.

'You think I wish to return to those animals?' she asked. There was no anger in her voice; she just sounded slightly bemused. Thinking back to the horrific state in which he had found her and the sight of the wounds on her feet, Will didn't blame her.

'No,' he said, gruffly. 'I don't think you'll be going back to them. But I don't know for sure that you'll want to stay with us.' He grabbed her wrists a little more roughly than he intended to, then strapped the Plasticuffs around them.

Latifa accepted being bound without a struggle. It was almost as if this were part of the natural order of things. 'Do you know my brother?' she asked.

Will looked sharply at her. She was gazing directly at him.

The truck trundled over an especially uneven bit of road. He waited for it to level out before he answered.

'No,' he said, doing his best to keep his voice level. 'But I know of him.'

'You said he sent you to rescue me.'

Will could feel Kennedy's gaze on him, but he ignored it. 'Something like that,' he told Latifa evasively.

'Ah,' Latifa nodded. 'Something like that.' She smiled sadly, then looked out of the back of the truck. Somehow, Will could tell that she knew he was lying.

He changed the subject. 'We'll get you medical help when we reach our destination.'

'And where is our destination?' Latifa asked, softly. Her voice had a sing-song quality; close your eyes, Will thought, and you wouldn't know the pain she was in.

'You'll find out.'

She turned to look at him again and Will found her piercing eyes made him feel quite uncomfortable. 'Yes,' she said. 'I will find out.' And then, almost to herself, 'We all find out our destination, sooner or later.'

The journey back to Kandahar air base was an uncomfortable one. The air was bitingly cold and now that some of the adrenaline that had been pumping through him had subsided, Will's body began to ache from the beating their Taliban captors had given them. All the way along their bumpy route back, he clutched the Minimi firmly. It seemed large and ungainly in the enclosed space of the truck, and the cold metal bit harshly into the chapped skin on his hands. But he didn't let go. He wanted to be prepared for any ambushes like the one they had encountered on the way. They'd had the element of surprise back then; now, though, with the back door of the truck blown away, the glass smashed in and the occupants all looking like they'd gone a few rounds with a grizzly, they would alert the attention of anyone they passed.

But they met no one, other than the frozen corpses of the men who had tried to attack them on the way in. They looked a lot less dangerous with their brains spread out around them, a dusting of white snow over their dark skin. Seeing their dead bodies lying there, however, Will could not help thinking of Anderson. He didn't want to imagine what the Taliban had done to his body. The chances of it having been buried with respect were slim. Will glanced over at Drew and Kennedy. Somehow, from their heavy silence, he knew they were having similar thoughts.

Will was roused from his reverie by a shout. It was Latifa. A change seemed to have come over her. There was a blankness in her face that he had not noticed the last time he looked and a low groan was escaping her lips. She started talking in Pashto, her voice guttural and anguished. She raised her bound fists as though trying to brush something away, then cried out again. Jesus, she looked half-dead. More than half. He had to stop himself from telling Drew to drive faster, but he knew that the woman didn't have a lot of time left. If they didn't get to a medic soon, she'd be a goner.

'Delirious,' Kennedy observed from his seat in the front.

Will touched his hand to her forehead. 'She's burning up.

It's hardly surprising – they fucked her up pretty badly back there. Her feet are a mess.'

'Well it's still a good couple of hours back to the base. I hope she makes it – if septicaemia sets in out here, she's a goner.'

Will's eyes narrowed. For some reason caring for this woman went against every urge in his body, but he knew what he had to do. He lay the Minimi down beside him, then leaned over Latifa, hoping to persuade her to lie down on the floor of the truck. But as soon as he touched her, she started writhing and screaming – a long, desperate scream that ended with a single word.

'*Faisal!*'

And then, as if woken from a dream, she seemed to see Will. She looked around her, as though seeing her surroundings for the first time.

'Where are we?' she asked.

The utterance of Faisal Ahmed's name on this woman's lips had shocked Will and it was a moment before he answered.

'We're on our way to Kandahar Airport,' he told her gruffly. Then, moved by the fear that was still etched on her face, he added, 'You're safe. We're going to get you some medical treatment. Do you think you can make it?'

Latifa took a deep breath and nodded her head, resolutely. Then she closed her eyes and allowed her body to shake in rhythm with the jerky movements of the truck.

The sky grew imperceptibly lighter as the sun began to rise over southern Afghanistan. A new sun for a new day. Better than the last, Will hoped.

Gradually the road became busier. As the risk of roadside attacks declined, Will found himself becoming more worried about Latifa. That blank look in her face had returned. Occasionally she would gaze around her as if she had no idea where she was; now and then she would shout

out, though more weakly than before, but Will felt useless to do anything. They needed to get to the airbase, and fast. He felt a huge sense of relief when they started to approach it.

It was strangely comforting to see the bleak, sprawling mass of concrete ahead of them, to sense the bustle of activity as they drove in. And Will found himself somehow soothed by the mechanical drone of a plane overhead.

'Nothing like coming in under the radar,' Kennedy said, sarcastically. Will looked around him: the sight of their battered truck was attracting curious attention from many of the troops of different nationalities they passed.

'Half these guys probably never even leave the base,' Drew grunted from behind the wheel. Tiredness showed in his voice and Will wasn't surprised. On top of everything else, it had been a long, difficult drive.

They pulled up outside the hangar where they had prepared themselves the previous day and started to unload what remained of their weaponry, so that they would be able to get Latifa out of the back. As they were doing so, the Junior Technician who had helped them yesterday – Evans, did he say his name was? – approached. He had a slightly awed expression on his face as he looked at the state of the men and their vehicle. 'Do you need anything, sir?' he asked quietly.

Will looked at the kid with a sense of irritation that he quickly checked. He was only doing his job. 'Tell Rankin I need to see him now,' he replied, gruffly.

Evans nodded, then disappeared to deliver the message.

Once the weaponry was unloaded, Will turned his attention to Latifa. Her face was sweating and for a dark-skinned woman she was alarmingly pale. Her eyes seemed to roll in her head.

'Latifa,' he called.

She didn't seem to hear him.

'*Latifa!*' More forcefully this time.

She turned her head and gazed at him. It was impossible to tell whether she was taking in anything he was saying.

'You need to get down,' he told her. 'Can you do that? Can you walk?'

For a moment there was no response, but then, excruciatingly slowly, Latifa started to push herself towards the back of the truck. Painfully, she manoeuvred herself into position, then climbed down on to the slush-covered tarmac. She winced as her wounded feet touched the floor and an expression of agony flashed across her face; but then she took a couple of difficult steps towards the hangar.

'Here,' Will said gruffly, unable to watch this woman's discomfort, no matter who she was. 'I'll carry you.'

Latifa's face winced again, as if she were unwilling to accept such a humiliating offer of help. But she was too weak to turn it down, so Will lifted her light, bony body and carried her inside. Even through the thick snowsuit, he could tell that she was burning hot and he could feel her limbs trembling.

The area of the hangar that they had been allocated was sparse, but there was one chair that was a little larger and more comfortable than the others scattered around. Will placed Latifa in it. 'Take the snowsuit off,' he instructed.

'Easy, tiger,' Kennedy murmured.

'Shut up, Kennedy,' Will told him, before turning back to Latifa. 'Get it off, now,' he repeated. 'I'm not messing about.'

Latifa's eyes rolled again as, weakly, she held up her thin wrists, still bound together by the Plasticuffs. Will nodded, then searched around the room until he found something suitable to release them – a pair of sharp scissors made short work of the plastic bands. 'Just don't do anything stupid.'

Latifa's head lolled, but she managed to curl her upper lip into an expression of contempt. 'I am in the middle of a military base and I cannot walk,' she croaked. 'I hardly think that I am a match for you brave men with your guns.'

She started to undress.

It should have been easy for her to wriggle her thin body out of the snowsuit intended for Will's larger frame, but she was weak and it took her a long time. It was only once she had removed it that Will was reminded of how badly she stank and now that she was in the light, he could see how ragged and dirty her robes were.

But it was her feet he was most concerned about. Out in the field, there had been nothing they could do, but now they were back at the airbase it was essential that she received some kind of medical attention. The wounds were bad and it looked to Will as if they were infected. If they turned septic, she could die and the whole mission would have been for nothing.

He got to his knees and gently took her right foot in his hand.

'Jesus,' he heard Kennedy whisper from behind him.

Latifa's feet were disgusting. They were swollen and puffy – perhaps twice their usual size – but it was not this that made them such an alarming sight. They were covered in enormous welts and scars which oozed a mixture of viscous white liquid and barely coagulating blood – as though her feet were weeping some vile, putrid poison.

'She needs a medic,' Will murmured. 'An antibiotic jab at the very least and something to get her fever down. Otherwise she'll be away with the fairies when we get back, if she even makes it.' As he spoke, Junior Technician Evans reappeared. 'Well?' he asked him curtly. 'Is Rankin ready for me?'

The young soldier seemed nervous. 'No, sir,' he said, meekly. 'He asked me to tell you that he may have time later in the day.'

Will exhaled heavily. 'Wait here,' he told the other two SAS men. 'Make sure she doesn't move.'

'Fat fucking chance,' Kennedy murmured as Will stormed out of the hangar.

He didn't bother with the truck; he just strode straight across the airbase in the direction of Rankin's Portakabin. For some reason it filled him with fury that he had to ask for help from this jumped-up pen-pusher; but if help was going to be given, it was damn well going to be given on Will's terms. Bollocks to rank and etiquette – Will was no longer army, so the usual rules didn't apply.

He didn't bother to knock and burst in through the door. There were two young RAF officers in there, standing in front of Rankin's table, apparently receiving a dressing-down. Rankin stopped in mid-flow the moment he saw Will enter. 'You'll have to wait outside,' he bellowed, clearly not recognising Will even from yesterday.

Will strode quietly into the room. 'Get out,' he said, cursorily, to the two men standing at Rankin's desk.

The men glanced at Rankin a bit nervously. He was fuming. But as he looked at Will, his eyes narrowed with sudden recognition as he twigged who he was. He nodded at the two men and they hurried out.

'How dare you come barging in here –' Rankin started to say, but Will interrupted him.

'I need a medic and I need us on the first plane out of here to Brize Norton.'

Rankin shook his head and smiled a patronising smile, as if Will's request was quite impossible. 'You seem to think you can just swan in here and command all our resources –' he blustered, but Will had no patience for any of this. He strode round to Rankin's side of the desk, grabbed him by the neck and pulled him to his feet. Rankin's comfortable chair toppled over as Will pulled the man's face towards his.

'Your contact,' he hissed, 'was dirty. One of my men has been beheaded in some shit-hole Afghan village, and I've half a mind to do the same thing to you so that you know what it feels like. The rest of my team are lucky to be alive and if I don't get a medic immediately the whole mission will go tits up anyway. Get your pampered arse in gear and do what I tell you, otherwise I'll see to it that you're moved somewhere that'll make you think Kandahar Airport is the fucking Ritz. Got it?'

Rankin's face was red and flustered as Will threw him against the wall. He looked at the SAS man with thinly veiled loathing. 'Whatever you say,' Rankin agreed in a strained voice. 'I'll have a medic there immediately.'

'Good.'

'But –' he said forcefully, his patrician accent making him sound like an enraged public schoolboy '– make no mistake about it, Jackson. I *will* be speaking to your superiors about your behaviour.'

It was all Will could do to keep from laughing. 'My superiors?' he snorted. 'I don't *have* any superiors.'

And with a sneer at the ridiculous man behind the desk, he turned and left.

★

Barely ten minutes later what remained of the SAS team were standing around Latifa Ahmed. An airbase medic had brought a stretcher bed to the hangar and as they watched he was inserting a needle into each of Latifa's arms. The woman herself was asleep on the stretcher – through tiredness or illness, Will couldn't tell which.

The medic wore the uniform of the US air force and was characteristically no-nonsense. 'Intravenous antibiotic drip,' he said to nobody in particular as he attached the tube of a drip bag to the needle on her right arm. 'It's

186

strong stuff, but it could take twenty-four hours before you begin to see any improvement.'

'That's too long,' Will said. 'We have to be on a transport back to the UK today.'

The medic shrugged. 'You've got to do what you've got to do,' he said. If he wanted to know why this SAS man had to get home with a tortured Afghan woman in such a hurry, he knew better than to ask. He started attaching a second drip bag to her other arm. 'This should reduce her fever, make it easier to travel.'

'Will it wake her, make her able to speak?'

'Could do. To be honest, pal, she's lucky to be with us. Where the hell did you find her?'

'South of here,' Will replied, evasively.

The medic nodded. 'Fucking Afghans,' he said. 'I've removed plenty of shrapnel that they've put in our boys over the last couple of years, but you think they'd give each other a break.' He bent down and pulled a pair of tongs and a clean swab from his supplies case. 'Especially the women,' he murmured. He stepped to the end of the bed and started dabbing the swab on Latifa's feet. Gobbets of sticky fluid came away from her flesh and within seconds the swab was soaked. The medic disposed of it in a waste sack, then armed himself with a fresh one.

It took twenty minutes of skilful doctoring before the medic was satisfied that Latifa's feet were clean enough to be bandaged. 'The bandages will need to be replaced daily,' the medic said as he packed up. 'But if you're taking her back to the UK, I guess that's going to be another guy's job, not mine.' His eyes flickered back towards the patient and for a moment his no-nonsense attitude seemed to disappear. 'I don't know how she got those wounds, but this woman's been through hell. Make sure she's well looked after.'

Will turned away. He knew what was awaiting Latifa

Ahmed back in England and he knew he couldn't make that promise.

'Thanks for patching her up,' was the only reply he could manage.

There was a plane leaving for Brize Norton that evening, which gave them the whole day at the airbase. Drew and Kennedy went to find some hot food for them all, coming back with plates of stodgy, carb-heavy army rations – some kind of stew that was bland, filling and more welcome than almost anything Will had ever eaten. They wolfed it down, then Drew and Kennedy curled up in a corner of the room to get some desperately needed shut-eye.

Will himself, however, couldn't sleep, despite the fact that exhaustion seemed to have seeped into his veins. Instead, he hovered around the stretcher bed where Latifa lay. For some reason, he didn't want her to leave his sight. This trembling bag of bones whom they had rescued at such a high cost was precious to him now. She held the key to something he realised – now he was one step closer – that he wanted desperately.

Revenge.

And if he didn't get revenge, it would destroy him.

It was mid-afternoon and Will was still sitting by Latifa's bedside listening to her heavy breathing when he became aware of Drew standing behind him. Kennedy was still asleep.

Will couldn't work Drew out. During the whole mission, the guy had hardly spoken – not like Kennedy who never missed a chance to spout some sarky comment or other. Drew was solid, dependable. You got the impression that he was always watching. Always listening. Kennedy was a good soldier, but Drew understood things more deeply.

'You not going to get some kip?' he asked Will.

Will shook his head. 'On the plane, maybe.'

Drew shrugged, as if to say, *It's your decision.* 'So, do you think us humble foot soldiers will ever find out exactly what it is the powers that be want with this woman?' he asked, looking meaningfully at Will. 'Or are you going to keep that under your hat?'

Will looked away. 'She might have some information,' he said, hoping that would bring an end to the conversation. But it didn't. Drew's eyes seemed to burn into him.

'It's personal, isn't it?' Drew asked, quietly.

Will shifted uneasily in his seat. 'What do you mean?'

Drew sniffed. 'Don't get me wrong,' he said. 'You're a good soldier. But there's a lot of good soldiers in the Regiment. Why bring you in if you're not involved in some other way? And I've seen the way you are with her – you don't know whether to pity the woman or hate her. There's more going on here than any of us know. Kennedy and I weren't happy about it at first. It was Anderson who talked us round.'

Drew's words seemed to pierce Will like bullets. It was horrible, losing someone on a mission; but he hadn't really known Anderson. Imagine what the other two must be feeling. 'I'm sorry about your friend,' he said, humbly.

'Don't be,' said Drew. 'He knew the risks. We all did. It could have been any of us – it just happened to be him. And if it wasn't for you, we'd never have got out of that fucking prison and this woman would be dead by now.' He paused. 'Whoever she is.'

Will fell silent.

'I know you probably can't tell us everything,' Drew continued. 'But that's OK. You know the code, though. You *can* trust us – me and Kennedy, I mean – despite what happened back there. You *have* to trust us. Just like Anderson trusted you. Just like we *all* trusted you.'

As he spoke, a voice spoke in Will's mind. It was Pankhurst, the man who had sent him out here in the first place. '*I know you've been trained to trust everyone at Hereford, Will, but that's one part of your training that you need to forget. We can't afford to trust anyone.*'

189

Will blinked. He didn't know what to say to the earnest SAS man standing in front of him. Instead he looked over at Kennedy. 'You'd better wake him,' he said. 'We'll be leaving soon.'

Drew paused for a moment, then nodded, He walked over to where Kennedy was lying and gave him a gentle kick in the ribs.

'Not now, sweetheart,' the drowsy SAS man mumbled. 'I've got a headache.'

★

It was dark when they wheeled Latifa's stretcher bed out of the hangar towards the runway. The return journey wasn't to be in the Galaxy, but in a British C-17 Globemaster, and as they wheeled the woman across the busy tarmac, they could see empty pallets being loaded into the back, along with a few military vehicles that were being transported, for whatever reason, back to Brize Norton. There were quite a few strange looks from the loaders as they wheeled Latifa up a ramp and into the belly of the rumbling transport aircraft.

As on the way out, there were no other troops being ferried on this journey – it was solely for equipment – and the Globemaster had a smaller crew than the Galaxy. Just three, all told, plus the SAS team and Latifa. Will was relieved. Fewer people meant fewer questions and he wasn't in the mood for shooting the shit with curious squaddies wanting to pick his brains about the Regiment. He just wanted to get home.

Latifa's fever was beginning to subside, just like the medic had said it would. As she was wheeled into place in the Globemaster she even opened her eyes, looked around in brief confusion, then closed them again.

The stretcher was strapped in place against one of the walls of the plane before the three SAS men took their seats. Minutes later they felt the rush of G-force as the aircraft took to the sky.

'And amen to that,' Kennedy said, as they felt the plane turn sharply in the air to get them on course for England. 'Hope I don't have to pay a return visit to the Stan for a long time to come.'

They might have been sleeping all day, but it was a long, boring flight home and Drew and Kennedy obviously felt they still had some recuperating to do, so they each swallowed a sleeping tablet and within half an hour they were flat out. Will, though, had other plans. Once his companions were asleep, he unbuckled himself and walked over to Latifa's stretcher bed. Her eyes were open now and her head was turned so that she could gaze out of one of the little windows into the inky night sky. It was a moment before she realised Will had approached.

'I have never left Afghanistan before,' she croaked, weakly. But if she was scared she didn't show it.

'Do you feel any better?' he asked.

She shrugged. 'I feel as if I am not going to die anytime soon. So I suppose I feel better, yes.'

'You speak good English,' Will observed.

Latifa turned her head to look out of the window again. 'There was a time in my country, before the Taliban, when women were allowed to educate themselves.'

'They say things are getting better.'

She snorted, weakly. 'Look at me,' she said. 'You think this is progress?'

There wasn't much Will could say to that.

'We'll be in England in a few hours.'

'I see,' Latifa replied. 'And then what?'

'And then we need to ask you a few questions.'

'Ah,' she said, softly. 'More questions. The Taliban asked me many questions.' She looked piercingly at Will. 'This is about Faisal, is it not?'

Will took a deep intake of breath. 'It's about Faisal Ahmed, yes.'

'You do not like it when I speak his name,' Fatima noticed with an intuition that rather unnerved him.

He shrugged and Latifa closed her eyes. 'What is it that my brother has done?'

'What makes you think he's done anything?'

'Because I know him almost better than I know myself. He is a man of action. And because I know that no government would risk the lives of their soldiers to come and rescue me from the hands of the Taliban if it were not for the fact that he is in some kind of trouble.' She opened her eyes again. 'You saved my life, yet I do not even know your name.'

'Will,' he told her. 'Will Jackson.'

'Well, Will Jackson,' Latifa continued, 'let me tell you this. I do not approve of the path my brother has taken. Even when we were children I used to beg him to pick up his schoolbooks instead of his guns. At first I used to pray that it was just a boyish phase, but it was not. Even when he was small, he never had any doubt of the difference between right and wrong. But what he did not understand – what he still does not understand, I think – is that what is right for one person is wrong for another.'

Latifa spoke carefully. Slowly. As though each word was an effort. Somehow it gave the effect of making her speech sound even more meaningful. And as she spoke, Will felt a surge of hope. This woman loved her brother, but she didn't necessarily like what he did. If she knew what was going on, maybe she would be inclined to help them.

'You need to listen to me carefully, Latifa,' he said. 'Your brother is planning something. An act of terrorism. We don't know what and we don't know when. We just know it's going to be big. You're our only chance of finding him. We know he keeps in touch with you. We know that if anyone can lead us to him, it's you.'

Latifa smiled a little sadly. 'You want me to lead you to my brother when he does not want to be found?'

'That's right.'

She fell silent for a moment. 'It is exactly what the Taliban wanted,' she said, finally. 'At least, it is exactly what the men holding me wanted. One of them, I think, had a personal argument with him. They too believed that my brother had been in contact with me. That is why they were torturing me – so that I would give him up. But I never did.'

Will narrowed his eyes. 'Thousands of people, Latifa,' he said, somewhat impatiently. 'Thousands of people could die if your brother goes through with his terrorist strike.'

'So you tell me,' Latifa replied. 'But I do not believe it. My brother is many things, but he is not a terrorist.'

'We have proof, Latifa.'

'You may show me all the proof you wish, Will Jackson. I will still not believe it.'

Will took a deep breath in an effort to control a sudden wave of anger. 'It seems to me,' he said, curtly, 'that perhaps you don't know your brother as well as you think. Faisal Ahmed *is* a terrorist. I have better reason to know than most.'

'How so?' the woman on the bed asked, weakly.

Will fought the urge to spit it out. Latifa's denial of her brother's true nature angered him. He turned away. Fuck it. For all he cared Pankhurst could torture the truth out of her when they got back – one way or another, she *would* give them any information she had.

But as he approached his seat he stopped. Something made him spin round and stride back up to her. Before he knew it, the words were tumbling out of his mouth. 'I know,' he hissed at her, 'because Faisal Ahmed planted the bomb that killed my family. A mother and a daughter. So don't try and tell me that bastard was whiter than white, because I've seen the evidence and I'm not fucking buying it!'

His outburst seemed to echo around the cabin.

He and Latifa stared at each other and something seemed to crackle between them. Will heard himself breathing heavily, trying to calm himself with great gulps of air.

Finally Latifa spoke. 'I am sorry for the death of your family,' she said, meekly. 'When I was young I saw my mother and father murdered in front of me. I know something of how you feel. Faisal too, he saw −'

'Forget the excuses,' Will snapped. 'Do you know where your brother is or not?'

Latifa stared at him, but her lips remained firmly shut.

'Fine,' Will retorted to her meaningful silence. 'In case you're interested, it's not just the British government who want to find your brother. It's the CIA too and they're not exactly well known for being shy and retiring about stuff like this. Trust me − you won't like the way they get people to tell them the things they want to know. But it's your choice.'

'You are right,' Latifa said, firmly. 'It *is* my own choice. Your family meant everything to you, I can see that. So perhaps you will understand why it is that I cannot betray my brother, no matter what it is that he has done.'

Will felt his lips thinning.

'You have come a long way to rescue me,' Latifa said, 'and for that I am more grateful than I can tell you. But you have seen what the Taliban did to me; you have seen the wicked things they inflicted upon my body. Now you, too, are threatening to try and extract the same information out of me. It makes you no better than them.'

She winced, as though a sudden bolt of pain had run through her and Will noticed that she shifted her bandaged feet. She breathed heavily for a moment before speaking again.

'And what is it, I wonder,' she asked, her voice a curious mixture of bemusement and contempt, 'that makes you think that if the Taliban cannot torture Faisal's whereabouts out of me, with their viciousness and their lack of regard for human life or suffering, the British or the Americans can?'

Will looked at her face. Despite her weakness, despite her fever, despite everything that she had gone through, it carried an expression of indomitable determination. In that instant, he knew that the Afghan woman lying before him was not messing around.

No matter what he had done, she would sooner die than betray her brother. Faisal Ahmed could kill thousands – millions – and still she would keep her own counsel.

If she knew where he was, she would never, ever tell them.

'I think I would like to sleep now,' she whispered; and as she spoke, her eyes closed.

Will stood there for a minute, not knowing what to do or what to say. Then he kicked his heels around, found a sleeping tablet and swallowed it hungrily.

It was a long flight back to Brize Norton and the last thing he wanted was to be awake with the thoughts that were now swimming around in his confused and angry head.

TWELVE

Will awoke suddenly.

His body was aching, but his mind was instantly aware. There was a change in the sound of the engines, a more high-pitched whine that suggested they were losing altitude. He looked around him. Latifa was asleep, but Drew and Kennedy had woken and were looking out of the window.

'Something's up,' Kennedy said.

'What do you mean?'

'Look at the time.'

Will glanced at his watch. Three in the morning, Afghanistan time. They should have landed at Brize Norton hours ago.

'Care to tell us what's going on?' Drew asked Will, pointedly.

'Fucked if I know,' Will muttered. He turned around and headed up to the flight deck, where he banged on the door of the cockpit. 'What's going on?' he shouted. 'Where the hell are we?'

The door clicked open and the flight lieutenant of the plane appeared. 'Change of course,' he told Will.

'What the hell do you mean?' Will asked him, completely confused.

'We got our orders a few hours ago. We've been redirected.'

'Where to?'

'Poland.'

Will blinked. 'Poland? What the hell are we doing in Poland?'

'We were hoping you could tell us,' the flight lieutenant said, pointedly. 'I think it's more likely something to do with your cargo than ours, don't you?'

Will swore under his breath, then strode back to be with the others.

'Any info?' Kennedy asked, tersely.

Will told them the news and both SAS men looked baffled. 'What are we doing landing in Poland?' Drew asked.

'I don't know,' Will replied, quietly, but in truth he had an idea. He remembered his conversation with Lowther Pankhurst and Don Priestley, about how they had extracted the information about Faisal Ahmed in the first place. He glanced over at Latifa, still slumbering.

Sleep well, he thought to himself. It won't last for long.

They strapped themselves in and prepared for landing.

As soon as the aircraft came to a halt, Will was up. A flight of steps had been moved to the side of the plane and he bounded down them into the icy night air. The snow here was thicker than it had been in the Stan and it was blowing a blizzard – the plane had been lucky to land at all. The airfield was not busy, but there were a couple of other planes parked up and a small convoy of military trucks were waiting on the tarmac. Grim-faced soldiers, all heavily armed, were milling around; and standing by one of the trucks was a solitary figure. He wore a heavy black coat and held a black umbrella, though it didn't do much good as the snow was drifting sideways against his clothes. He looked quite out of place against all the military men in their camouflage fatigues.

It was only when Will was a good deal closer that he realised who it was.

'Good morning, Will,' Lowther Pankhurst said, as blandly

as if he were greeting someone in the office on a Monday morning. He turned to a couple of soldiers standing nearby. 'Get the woman down,' he ordered.

'Yes, sir,' the soldiers repeated in unison. Will detected their American accents.

'What the hell's going on?' he asked Pankhurst, angrily. 'What are you doing here? What are any of us doing here?'

'Please, Will,' Pankhurst said, mildly. 'Calm down.'

'*Don't tell me to calm down!*' he raged. 'I've just been through hell to get this woman. I want to know what you're doing with her. Why weren't we warned about this?'

'We're going to ask her a few questions. That was always the plan, wasn't it?'

'In Poland?'

'Yes, Will. In Poland.'

'Why?'

'I think you know why, Will.'

Pankhurst was right. In the last thirty seconds he had confirmed all his suspicions. 'Black camp?' he asked.

Pankhurst's face twitched slightly. 'Really, Will, it's not a term I'm particularly comfortable with. But yes, there are certain resources available to us here that are not available to us back home. It's one of Don Priestley's little operations and he's kindly given us access. It really is amazing how skilful they are here.'

Will felt sick. Despite everything he knew about Latifa Ahmed, he had seen what the Taliban had done to her. He had seen what she had gone through. Talk about out of the frying pan and into the fucking fire.

'You're wasting your time,' he told Pankhurst, quietly.

'I beg your pardon?'

'I said you're wasting your time.'

'I sincerely hope not, Will,' Pankhurst said, pointedly. 'I understand you're one man down. It would be a terrible tragedy if nothing came of your mission.'

'You're lucky we're not four men down.'

'We're *all* lucky you're not four men down, Will. Ahmed could strike at any moment – the intelligence chatter has gone off the scale. You did well to find the woman and bring her back safely. But you needn't worry about it any more. We'll be taking care of things from here on in.'

Pankhurst turned his back on Will.

'She won't talk,' the SAS man called after the Director General. 'I've already interrogated her. I think she knows something about Ahmed's location, but I'm telling you, there's no way on God's earth that you'll make her give him up!'

Pankhurst stopped, paused a moment, then turned back to look at Will. 'I think, perhaps, you underestimate just how persuasive these people can be.'

Will sneered at him. 'Actually,' he said, 'I don't think I do. I think *you* underestimate just how much Latifa Ahmed has been through. The Taliban wanted Ahmed's location, too, and they did things to that woman that you couldn't even imagine.'

A mock frown furrowed Pankhurst's brow. 'I do hope, Will, that you haven't become too emotionally involved in this mission.'

'Don't give me that crap, Pankhurst. I'm here *because* I'm emotionally involved. When I found Latifa Ahmed, she wasn't much more than a few hours from being dead. Push her too hard and you'll kill her yourself and anything she knows will die with her.'

But as he spoke, he noticed that Pankhurst was looking beyond him. Will turned back to see Latifa's stretcher bed being carried off the plane. In a moment of madness he started to calculate his chances of taking down the men who were carrying her. But of course, it would be idiotic; even if he managed it, what would he do then? Besides, he had his orders. And wasn't he meant to despise Latifa Ahmed anyway?

'You can travel with me, if you like, Will,' Pankhurst interrupted his thoughts, quietly. 'Or you can travel with your
unit. Either way, I wouldn't recommend staying here. It's
terribly cold and we really don't know how long this is
going to take.'

★

The convoy trundled slowly through the snow and the
gloom. Latifa had been loaded into a separate truck along
with a couple of guys who said they were medics but
who, Will knew, would soon be involved in something
that they surely never expected when they underwent their
medical training. Will had absolutely no idea where they
were and began to lose his bearings as the truck wove its
way down a series of winding lanes. There were no houses,
no signs of life. This truly was the middle of nowhere.

He had chosen to travel with Drew and Kennedy, but
was beginning to wish he hadn't. Clearly they didn't believe
Will when he said he'd had no idea that they were going
to be re-routed, and they were making their displeasure
felt by a stern silence that was, Will couldn't help thinking,
more suited to a couple of teenage girls than two burly
Regiment soldiers. He felt he owed them an explanation.

'They're taking her to a black camp,' he said, darkly. 'They
want to torture information out of her. They can't do it in
England, so they have these places—'

'Yeah, thanks Einstein,' Kennedy interrupted. 'We know
what a black camp is.'

'I didn't know about this,' Will reiterated.

'Whatever,' Kennedy said, flatly. 'They'd better go easy on
her, though. She's been pretty well fucked-up. Slap her on
the arse and she'll probably drop dead.'

'Yeah, maybe,' Will replied. He wasn't too sure.

After about an hour of driving, they came to a halt and

de-bussed. Will looked around. There was not much here – just a small hillock, covered with thick snow, in the side of which was a concrete door. Yellow light flooded from it. The truck carrying Latifa opened up and the SAS men watched as the woman they had rescued was stretchered down and carried through the door.

Pankhurst had joined the team and he ushered them in with a sweeping gesture as though they were about to enter a decent restaurant. 'Shall we?'

They found themselves filing down a flight of steps and along a dim underground corridor. As they walked, Will peered over at Latifa's bed. She seemed drowsy, but aware. Their eyes met and in that moment he felt her fear. She could tell what was coming – of that he could be sure.

Nobody spoke as the sound of their footsteps echoed down the corridor.

Suddenly the soldiers pushing Latifa's stretcher bed came to a halt. There were two doors – they opened one of them, took her in and shut the door behind them. Will, Pankhurst, Drew and Kennedy were left in the corridor. Pankhurst turned to Drew and Kennedy. 'You two,' he said, 'there's a room down there on the left. You can wait for us there.'

They looked at each other a bit uneasily, but even Kennedy seemed reluctant to offer one of his usual sarcastic ripostes. They stepped aside and followed their instructions, while Pankhurst spoke to Will. 'I want you in on this, Will,' he said, quietly.

'Why?' asked Will, sickened at the thought of what he was about to witness. Shooting a Taliban guard in the head was one thing; watching his own side torture a defenceless woman was quite another and he wasn't sure he wanted to get involved.

'Because,' Pankhurst said slowly, not taking his eyes from Will's, 'if she gives us Ahmed's location, I think it's a good idea that you hear it directly. You'll want to go after him yourself, won't you?'

Will felt his lips curl. Yet again, Pankhurst was manipulating him; yet again, the Director General had read him well.

'All right,' he muttered. 'Let's get it over with.' They walked through the adjoining door.

The room in which Will found himself had three concrete walls. The fourth wall was a huge sheet of glass looking on to the next room and he could tell from the dark sheen that it was one-way. A small loudspeaker was embedded into one of the concrete walls, through which they could hear everything that was going on. Will watched what was happening in silence.

Latifa had been wheeled into the room by the soldiers, who swiftly left. Waiting for her were two other men, both in white coats. One of them – a red-haired man with round spectacles and a grim expression – gave Latifa a cursory examination. He looked at her bandaged feet. Even from here Will could tell that blood from the wounds had started to saturate them, but the man – presumably a doctor of some kind – did not seem to think it was worthwhile replacing them. Using his thumb he pulled down her lower eyelid, before talking to his colleague.

'She needs an adrenaline shot,' he said in an American drawl. 'Otherwise it's not going to have the same effect.'

His colleague, whose grey hair was thinning, nodded. Behind him was a white cabinet from which he removed a glass vial filled with a clear liquid and a hypodermic needle. He filled the needle in a matter of seconds, while the red-haired man started to roll up the sleeve of Latifa's robe to find a suitable place for the injection.

'Jesus,' he muttered as he saw the mottled bruising that went all the way up her thin arm. He went around to the opposite side of the stretcher bed and tried the other arm. This was also bruised, but not so badly, and he located a suitable patch of skin. The other man passed him the injection and he clinically punctured the skin with it.

The effect was immediate. Latifa's breathing rate increased and her eyes shot wide open. The two men took a step backwards and observed her in a slightly detached manner, as Latifa tried to raise herself on her elbows. Then they looked at each other. 'She's ready,' the red-haired man stated. 'They can come in.'

His colleague left the room and returned less than a minute later with two other men. One of them had a thick mop of blonde hair and was carrying a large leather bag; the other had a shiny, shaved head and a thin, aquiline nose.

'Strap her down,' he said to the blonde-haired man in an American accent. His colleague delved into the bag and pulled out several sturdy leather straps.

'Don't you dare touch me!' Latifa hissed as he approached, but the man didn't pay attention. He pushed her back down on to the bed and, ignoring her pathetic struggles, shifted her a bit further up so that her head was dangling over the edge of the bed. Then he wound the straps around her body and under the stretcher several times before buckling each one tightly. There was no way she could move.

The shiny-headed man turned to the two medics in white coats. 'You can leave now,' he told them; they quickly left the room.

Will glanced to his side at Pankhurst. The Director General of MI5 was standing bolt upright, his jaw clenched. 'What are they going to do to her?' Will asked.

'It's very quick,' Pankhurst replied, quietly. 'Most people break in about ten seconds. Fifteen at the most. She won't suffer for long.'

Will narrowed his eyes. There was nothing in the room

that looked to him anything like an implement of torture. As Pankhurst was speaking, the two men had wheeled Latifa's bed to the far end of the room, where a short length of rubber hose was attached to a tap in the wall.

'You know what we want?' the American asked Latifa.

It clearly took a great effort for Latifa to stop her head from lolling back over the edge of the bed, but she managed it. 'I will not tell you anything,' she whispered.

The American nodded. From the leather bag he pulled a rectangular cardboard tube and with surprise Will realised it was an ordinary carton of kitchen cling film. The man tore off a short length, held it tightly at each end, then approached Latifa's head. As he did so, the blonde-haired man took the rubber hose in one hand and turned the tap on. Water escaped over the white tiled floor and down a small outlet clearly put there for this very purpose.

'Waterboarding,' Will whispered to himself.

'As I say,' Pankhurst replied, 'an extremely effective technique.'

It was with a brutal swiftness that the cling film was pulled tightly over Latifa's face. Her mouth was wide open and as she tried to breathe it caused the cling film to make a tight, concave indentation in her mouth. The American man pulled the back of her hair so that her head was pointing down to the floor, then his colleague directed the flow of the water over her face.

One second.

Two seconds.

Three seconds.

Latifa's body started to jerk as she struggled against the straps that were tying her firmly down. She couldn't scream because of the cling film, but the quiet sound of the water splashing over her face and on to the door was enough to send a shudder of revulsion down Will's spine.

Four seconds.

Five seconds.

'They'll kill her!' Will said urgently.

'No they won't,' Pankhurst replied. 'They know what they're doing.'

Six seconds.

Seven seconds.

The American had to struggle to keep her head down.

Eight seconds.

Nine seconds.

Ten seconds.

'Stop!' the American said. His blonde-haired colleague pulled the water away and the cling film was ripped from Latifa's face. A deathly gasp escaped her throat as she took a desperate intake of breath, then another. The American allowed her to get her breath back before he spoke.

'Where is Faisal Ahmed?' he asked, directly.

'She won't tell him,' Will murmured.

Sure enough, Latifa refused to speak; but her rattling breath filled Will's ears.

The American's face twitched slightly. This was not, Will deduced, what he had expected; and Pankhurst also suddenly looked uncomfortable. The American ripped off a fresh, dry piece of cling film, nodded at his accomplice, and the process started once more.

'Christ,' Will whispered. Torturing defenceless women. This wasn't what he'd signed up for.

It lasted a little longer this time – perhaps fifteen seconds, though it seemed to Will like a hell of a lot more. When the cling film was finally ripped from her face again, her breathing was even more panicked, but at the same time weaker. Will's face was screwed up with distaste. 'She can't take much more of this,' he told Pankhurst.

'That's kind of the idea,' he snapped back.

The American spoke again. 'Where is Faisal Ahmed?'

Latifa's choking breaths came in short, sharp bursts. For about thirty seconds they were the only sound in the room; but finally she spoke. Her voice was quiet, trembling and hoarse; but her words left no room for doubt.

'You may do what you like to me,' she whispered. 'I will never tell you.'

The American inclined his head. Will had the impression that he was vaguely impressed with Latifa's resistance. With a sense of relentlessness, he ripped himself a third piece of cling film.

As he did so, Latifa's head swung to the left and she looked at the glass; even though he knew she couldn't see through it, Will felt she was staring directly at him.

'Please,' she breathed. '*Please—*'

'He can't keep doing this!' Will burst out. It was a struggle for him not to rush into the room and stop it from happening. 'It'll kill her!'

Pankhurst didn't reply.

A third bout of waterboarding began. Latifa continued to struggle against the ropes that were binding her, but her movements were much weaker now. Barely noticeable.

'*It'll kill her!*' Will shouted in sudden frustration.

'If she doesn't tell us what we want to know,' Pankhurst hissed, his usually calm demeanour suddenly absent, 'then it doesn't matter.' His words were severe, but even Pankhurst had a look of doubt in his face now.

Will blinked. A surge of anger flickered through him. This wasn't right. It didn't matter *who* Latifa's brother was. *This wasn't right.*

'Fuck it,' he murmured to himself. In a flash, he burst out of the door and into the room where the waterboarding was happening. He crossed it in three swift strides, grabbed the shiny-headed American by the throat and hurled him out of the way, before punching the blonde-haired man holding the hose so hard that he crumpled immediately to the floor. Instantly he ripped the cling film from Latifa's face.

The American came at him. Will allowed him to approach before almost casually kneeing him in the groin. He collapsed with a groan of agony as Will started unbuckling Latifa's straps. She was still gasping, painfully – Will gently put his hand behind her head to support it, then lifted her up into a sitting position. The noises she was making sounded like they should have come from an animal. But at least she was alive.

And then Pankhurst was there, framed by the doorway, his face a thundercloud. 'What the hell do you think you're playing at, Jackson?' he demanded.

Will stood in the middle of the room, breathing deeply, shakily. What *was* he playing at? He knew the stakes. He knew why they were doing this. But that didn't make it right. There had to be another way.

'Get out of the room,' Pankhurst continued. 'Let these men carry on with their work.'

The two torturers had started to get to their feet, but they were eyeing Will nervously, not knowing what he was likely to do next. Will sensed Latifa rolling on to her front, then huddling up on top of the stretcher bed into a little ball, her arms clutching her head as a choking, weeping sound escaped her throat.

Tentatively, the bald-headed American stepped towards the bed.

'Leave her alone,' Will growled. 'Touch her and I'll kill you.'

'*I'm giving you an order, Jackson!*' Pankhurst barked. '*Get out of that room, now. Get out of that room or you can kiss goodbye to your chance of going after the man who butchered your wife and child!*'

Even as the Director General spoke, Will felt something

snap inside. In two giant strides he stepped to the doorway where Pankhurst was standing and grabbed the man by the neck, lifting him from the ground and pushing him up against the far wall of the corridor. When he spoke, it was little more than a whisper; but his voice carried with it all the hate he could muster.

'If you ever – *ever* – mention my family again, I swear I'll break your neck.'

Pankhurst's face started to redden as Will tightened his grip. 'Put me down,' he croaked, but somehow that just made Will want to squeeze tighter.

And then they were there, men with guns. 'Get to the floor!' a voice shouted. 'Get to the floor or we'll shoot!'

As if he were flicking a fly, Will hurled Pankhurst to the ground, where he fell in a heap. And just as the Director General was getting to his feet, Will lay on the floor. He was aware of Pankhurst standing over him.

'You've blown it, Jackson,' he spat.

From inside the room, Will could hear the sound of Latifa's desperate racking sobs.

'You're the one who's blown it, Pankhurst,' he hissed.

'What do you mean?'

He was going to have to talk fast. Talk fast to save Latifa Ahmed's life and talk fast to stop the whole operation from going tits up.

'Can't you tell she's never going to reveal his location? And even if she does, what do you do when you get there, find he's gone and realise that you've waterboarded your only lead to death – or to the point of insanity?'

There was a pause.

'Get to your feet,' Pankhurst instructed, curtly.

Will did so, holding his hands in the air so that the three soldiers whose weapons were trained on him didn't think he was about to make any sudden moves. His eyes flickered into the room – Latifa was still curled up into a ball, but at least the two torturers had kept their distance. For now.

'Think about it,' Will continued. 'From everything you've told me about Faisal Ahmed, he'll do anything for his sister. If she won't lead us to him, it's obvious what we have to do: let him know we've got her and get her to bring him to us.'

Pankhurst was looking at Will with an expression of great dislike; still, he didn't speak for a moment and Will sensed that he had got the Director General's attention. They stared at each other, the only sound being that of Latifa's desperate sobs.

Finally, Pankhurst spoke, but not to Will. He addressed one of the soldiers who was still holding the SAS man at gunpoint.

'His team are in the holding room down the corridor,' the Director General said. 'Take him there and stand guard outside. If any of them try to leave, shoot them.'

The soldiers glanced at each other a little nervously. But they had their orders. 'Let's go,' said one of them to Will. 'Hands on your head.'

For a moment Will didn't move; he just fixed Pankhurst with a harsh glare. Then he felt the barrel of a gun poking him and he started to walk down the corridor. 'You're making a mistake,' he called back to Pankhurst; but the older man didn't answer.

The room in which Drew and Kennedy were waiting was surprisingly comfortable, with a couple of low-level sofas, a coffee table and even a kettle for making hot drinks. The two of them were sprawled on the sofas, which seemed dwarfed by their massive frames; but they sat up sharply when they saw that Will was being held at gunpoint.

'You heard the man,' the soldier told Will. 'No heroics.' And with that he shut the door on the three of them.

'What the f –?' Kennedy started to say.

'They're waterboarding her,' Will interrupted, angrily. 'I stepped in.' He strode around the room, systematically looking for another way out; but there was none.

'Christ,' Kennedy replied. 'She's probably beginning to wish she was back with her caring, sharing Taliban.'

Drew, however, kept quiet; but he stared at Will with a look that was heavy with meaning. Will stopped pacing and from nowhere the words Drew had said to him back in the Stan resounded in his head: '*You can trust us . . . You have to trust us. Just like Anderson trusted you. Just like we all trusted you.*'

More than ever, those words rang true. These men had followed him into battle. They'd risked their lives under his command. Pankhurst might think that nobody could be trusted, but one thing was immediately clear to Will: Drew and Kennedy had proved themselves. He owed it to them to tell them what was going on; then he was going to ask them to do one last thing. Help him escape and take Latifa with them. Together they would lure Faisal Ahmed far more effectively than these moronic spooks and their cack-handed techniques.

But just as he was about to speak, the door opened and Pankhurst strode into the room. His brow was furrowed and the fury of a couple of minutes ago had not left his face.

'How would you do it?' the MI5 man asked, shortly.

Will's eyes narrowed as his mind started rushing through the logistics of his hastily put-together plan.

'We take her back to the UK,' he said, finally. 'Leak it that she's been detained on terror charges and put under house arrest. Blanket coverage – TV, radio, internet chat rooms, the works. If Faisal Ahmed's as good as you say, he'll try and extricate her.'

'If Faisal Ahmed's as good as I say,' Pankhurst retorted with a hint of sarcasm, 'he'll succeed.'

As Pankhurst spoke, however, Will became aware that

Drew and Kennedy had stood up and were now flanking him on either side. It helped: any lack of confidence he might have felt was suddenly bolstered.

'No he won't,' Will replied, calmly.

'How can you be so sure?'

'Because there will be three of us and only one of him.'

A silence followed, as Pankhurst seemed to be weighing up his options. 'Ahmed will know it's a trap.'

'Of course he will,' Will countered. 'But think about it. He was willing to risk being discovered by al-Qaeda just to make sure his sister was well treated. Everything we know about him suggests that he'll do whatever it takes to rescue her.'

Again Pankhurst fell silent.

'You won't break her,' Will insisted, quietly. 'You know that. She'd rather die.'

A tense hush filled the room. Everyone knew that a woman's life depended on what was said next.

'London's beginning to resemble Ulster twenty years ago,' Pankhurst announced without taking his eyes off Will. 'We've shut down the major terminals, main artery roads are closed, we've got unmarked cars in every other street. All leave's been suspended from the Met and there's armed police at every underground station. The population of the capital is in a frenzy – they know something's around the corner and they're right.' He stopped a moment to let that sink in. 'If this goes wrong,' he continued, 'you know what will happen. You know the stakes.'

Will nodded. 'It won't go wrong,' he said.

He looked to either side of him, where Drew and Kennedy were standing up straight, exuding confidence and menace. Their silent support made him feel a great deal more sure of himself.

'It *won't* go wrong.'

★

211

Latifa Ahmed remained on the stretcher bed, huddled on her front, her legs bent under her and her head in her arms. She had not opened her eyes since they had taken the soldier, Will Jackson, away, but she could tell that the two men who had been interrogating her were still in the room. It wasn't over yet: they were just waiting for the go-ahead from the man in the black coat.

Her body was shaking uncontrollably and though her lungs had been replenished with precious air, her abdomen ached as if she had been beaten.

They had different ways of torturing people, these Westerners with their white coats and syringes. But deep down, she had fully realised in the last few minutes, they were no better than her Taliban torturers. The sensation of what had just occurred, the feeling of drowning, of knowing that death was almost upon you, was as terrifying as anything she had undergone in Afghanistan.

'Get out.'

The voice made her open her eyes and for an instant she stopped sobbing and looked up. It was Jackson and he was talking to the two men who had been interrogating her.

'I said, get out.'

The bald man, the one who had put the film over her face, looked as if he might argue, but then he clearly thought better of it and pushed past Jackson out into the corridor. The other man followed.

And then Jackson was there by her. He looked stern. Tired, but stern. Something in his face reminded her of Faisal. What was it? Determination, perhaps. Strength.

'We're taking you back to the UK,' he said, firmly.

Latifa gave a weak smile.

'For more torture?' she asked.

His lip curled slightly. 'No,' he said. 'No more torture.'

An enormous wave of relief crashed over her. If anyone

else had said this to her, she wouldn't have believed them: she would have just thought it was part of the torture. But there was something genuine about this man. She didn't think he would lie to her.

'Thank you,' she said, simply. 'For everything. You are a good man.'

Jackson's face remained stern. 'Don't be too grateful,' he said, flatly. 'You're coming with us for a reason.'

'And what is that?'

'To lure Faisal Ahmed out of hiding.'

Latifa closed her eyes as a strange sense of numbness passed over her. She coughed, painfully. 'You wish to use me as—' She struggled for the word. 'As bait?'

Jackson's face remained stony as she gazed up at him.

'You and my brother,' she said weakly. 'You are both soldiers. You both fight for what you think is right.'

'Perhaps,' Jackson replied. 'But we have very different ideas of how to go about it. Of what is acceptable.' He bent down slightly so that his face was closer to hers. 'Don't get too hung up on what a good man I am, Miss Ahmed,' he whispered. 'I *am* going to catch your brother. And when I do, I won't hesitate to do what has to be done.'

She could hear his breathing. Slow. Controlled. He meant what he said.

'And what is it,' she asked, steadfastly holding his gaze, 'that has to be done?'

The question hung in the air.

'They say,' she continued, 'that my brother is a great fighter. One of the best. You understand, I suppose, that if he believes you have been mistreating me, he *will* kill you.'

She looked up at him, as earnestly as she could.

'Not if I kill him first,' Jackson said, gruffly. She felt her stomach tighten as he turned and walked out of the room.

Latifa Ahmed watched him go with a sickening sense of apprehension. Then, once more, she fell back on to the stretcher bed and waited for the soldiers to wheel her out to the plane.

THIRTEEN

London. Later that day.

'I sure hope you know what you're doing, Lowther.'

Don Priestley sat in Pankhurst's comfortable office. It was four o'clock in the afternoon, and the C-17 Globemaster had only touched down at Brize Norton at 08.30 that morning. Pankhurst was tired, ratty and – though he would never have admitted it to his American counterpart – not at *all* sure that he knew what he was doing.

'I was there, Don,' he replied, impatiently. He rubbed his forehead with his fingers as the memory of Latifa Ahmed's cling-filmed mouth passed through his mind. He'd put a brave face on it in front of Jackson, but just the experience of watching it had been traumatic enough. The image wouldn't leave him. 'I watched the interrogation. Jackson was right – they weren't going to break her.'

Priestley raised an eyebrow. 'Maybe they would have had a better chance if your guy hadn't kicked them in the *cojones.*' He waved a piece of paper in the Director General's direction. 'They made their report already.'

Pankhurst sighed heavily in frustration. It was certainly true that Jackson's heroics hadn't helped matters; but then, maybe, if he hadn't intervened . . .

'They did it three times, Don. I've seen the same statistics as you. Even the most hardened terror suspects fold in a matter of seconds using your clever little technique.'

'It's not *my* technique, Lowther,' Priestley replied, seemingly a little abashed. 'The Japanese have been doing it for years. All I'm saying is, are you sure this Jackson character is the right guy to take it from here?'

'I wish he weren't. I don't like him. He's insubordinate and a loose cannon. But we've got to be pragmatic. Jackson and his team just whisked that woman away from under the noses of the Taliban. That's no mean feat. And he still wants Ahmed's head on a plate even more than we do.'

'I don't know about that,' Priestley murmured. 'You've seen the latest intel.'

'Enough to know it's close.' He stood up and looked out of his window. '*Shit,*' he swore suddenly and Priestley looked surprised to see an expletive leave Pankhurst's lips. 'Sometimes I think every man Jack on the streets knows more about Faisal Ahmed than we do. We've got chatter coming in from all sorts of unexpected quarters – just last night we took two Muslim teenagers into custody. They both admitted they knew the name Faisal Ahmed, that he was planning something. But that's *all* they knew.'

'You couldn't probe a little further?' Priestley asked, delicately.

'No,' Pankhurst insisted. 'Not with their lawyers sitting next to them. And we'd be airlifting planes full of them to Poland if we did it your way.'

'Like I say,' Priestley complained. 'It's not *my* way.'

'Whatever you say. All I know is I'm hearing the same rumours from everywhere. He's planning something soon, but no one knows where or when.'

'Where are they keeping the sister?'

'At the moment she's in protective custody in Paddington. News of her "arrest" should hit the wires in an hour so, then she's being moved to a safe house in the North Downs. Jackson's prepping it at the moment.' Pankhurst passed his hand over his eyes. 'I don't know when that man ever sleeps.

Anyway, it's a location Ahmed knows – we used it to debrief him when he first arrived in the UK. Jackson thought that if we used a familiar site it would make it more likely that he would try a rescue attempt.'

Priestley looked dubious. 'It would also make it more likely that Ahmed succeeds. And actually having the woman there, on site, seems like madness to me. This is pretty high-risk, Lowther, if you don't mind me saying so.'

Pankhurst shrugged. 'Jackson's convinced that if Ahmed has any suspicion that his sister isn't really there, he'll abort. He says it's what he would do.'

'Can't you at least have some proper back-up? A cordon around the area – men nearby ready to go in if Ahmed does show his face?'

'How can I, Don? Five's compromised. If I mobilise everyone, I risk giving Ahmed a direct feed into everything that's going on.'

Priestley's eyes narrowed and he looked as if he was about to say something. In the end he seemed to decide against it, but he didn't look happy.

Pankhurst noticed that look. 'If you have a better plan, Don, I'm all ears.'

But Priestley, for all his criticism, clearly didn't. 'They've been instructed, I hope, to shoot to kill. If they give Ahmed a second's leeway—'

'Of course, Don. They're professionals. They know what to do.'

'Good,' the American nodded. 'You have a shortlist of Ahmed's possible targets in London?' he asked, though it sounded more like a statement of fact than a question.

'Of course – the usual suspects. Thames Barrier, Buckingham Palace, the London Eye, any of the bridges. Our people still think the Tube is his most likely target. Security levels have been raised, but you can't stop and search everybody that uses the Underground. God only

217

knows how many casualties there'll be if he puts his mind to it down there – not to mention the fact that London will grind to a halt for months.'

There was a pause.

'Cities bounce back,' Priestley said, quietly. 'Look at New York.'

Pankhurst blinked. 'You won't be offended, I hope, if I fail to see much comfort in that notion.'

'Of course not, Lowther,' Priestley replied, his voice soft, reasonable. 'Of course not. But you know that if my country can do anything to help. Anything at all.'

Pankhurst turned around. He regretted having snapped at Priestley – they were on the same side, after all. 'Thank you, Don,' he replied. 'I understand your President has already made the same offer to the Prime Minister.'

'And if Will Jackson needs any back-up whatsoever – men, equipment. I'm sure he's well prepared, but the offer's there.'

Pankhurst rolled his eyes. 'You know what these SAS boys are like,' he said. 'They'd rather accept help from St Trinian's than Delta Force. Question of pride, I think.'

Priestley looked confused. 'St Trinian's?' he asked. 'Who are they?'

Pankhurst smiled tiredly. 'Never mind, Don,' he said. 'Never mind.'

★

Will looked up at the imposing building in front of him. About twenty miles south of London, nestled in the chalky North Downs of Surrey, two miles from the quaint market town of Dorking, Maple Hall was a large, deserted country house. Will had specified to Pankhurst on the flight back from Poland exactly what it was he wanted. Ideally, it should be somewhere Ahmed knew, because that would bolster his confidence, make it more likely he would try and spring Latifa. It needed to be somewhere fairly large, so that their Afghan terrorist would feel he had options when it came to devising an approach route. But there also needed to be space around the building, so that the SAS team could keep up a high level of surveillance. When Faisal Ahmed approached, they wanted to know about it.

From his satellite phone on board the plane, Pankhurst had come up trumps. Maple Hall was just right.

The spook who had driven Will and Kennedy there from Brize Norton had told him something about its history. During the Second World War it had been a regional centre of operations. After the war, it had become a barracks of sorts, a place for soldiers and special forces on training exercises in this part of the world. For the last fifteen years, however, it had been pretty much out of service, one of a number of MOD buildings that were kept on simply so that the Government had somewhere private and out of the way, should they ever need it. Ahmed had been debriefed here on his arrival in the UK. He wasn't the kind of guy anyone wanted strolling straight into Thames House, after all.

It was a grand building, imposingly square with a high, pitched roof. If a child were to draw a picture of a house, it would end up being a similar shape to Maple Hall. The high walls were a faded, crumbling yellow and each side of the house had four large, tall windows. The main door had once been painted red, but the paint was now peeling off; however, the window frames seemed sound. A straight road led up to the house, with neatly trimmed lawns. You'd be able to see anyone approaching from that direction; not that you would approach from there, if you wanted to do it surreptitiously.

Country roads ran along the west and south sides of the house; the remaining sides, as well as the areas beyond the roads, were densely forested and ran uphill to the east. Along the east side – the back of the house – there was a high fence, beyond which was a footpath that led uphill into the forest and the North Downs beyond. The two SAS men – Drew had been sent back to Credenhill with a shopping list for the armourer – walked around the house and recced the surroundings.

'When he finds out where we are,' Will said, almost to himself, as they walked round the house, 'he'll come at us from the woods.'

'How do you know it'll be just him?' Kennedy asked.

'Everything we know about him points to him being a loner. He'll be by himself.'

Kennedy shrugged. *If you say so*, he seemed to say. 'He'll definitely avoid the road,' he added. 'He'll know it's too easy for us to set up surveillance and he's not to know Five have decided not to give us any support.'

'They've got their reasons,' Will told him.

'I bet they fucking have,' Kennedy replied.

Will stonewalled him. He knew that Pankhurst's decision not to set up a cordon around the house was the right one. If MI5 had a mole feeding intel to Ahmed, that would be a sure-fire way of ensuring he knew their every move. Kennedy and Drew wouldn't see it like that, however.

Kennedy looked up at the walls of the house. 'We can set up motion-sensor alarms to cover the area surrounding the house. That way we'll know as soon as he makes his approach.'

Will looked up and narrowed his eyes. 'He'll be expecting that,' he said, distractedly. 'Means he'll come at us hard and fast. If you were him, how would you enter?'

Kennedy thought for a moment. 'Depends where I thought you were located,' he said. 'On the ground floor, then through the window of whichever room you're in. Tear gas, stun grenades, the works. NV if it's after dark.' He grinned. 'Three to one's not my kind of odds – I wouldn't want to come at you unless I had some pretty heavy weaponry.'

Will nodded. 'And if we were upstairs?'

Again Kennedy thought. 'Avoid the main entrance, obviously. You'd have the advantage of height and could take me out immediately. I guess I'd try to scale up to the roof then swing in through the window again.' He looked sharply at Will. 'But that takes time and with the motion sensors we'll be ready for him.'

Again Will nodded his head, more slowly this time. They started walking to the main door of the house. 'There's no way we can fool our target into thinking that this is anything other than a set-up. If he's as good as I'm told he is, he'll know where we are and how many of us there are. He'll know we're waiting for him.' He chewed absentmindedly on his lower lip. 'We can cover all his possible entry points and try and second-guess him as much as we can, but the one thing we need to prepare for is the one thing we can't predict.'

'What's that?'

Will sniffed. 'Well, I don't know . . . The unexpected, I guess. Ahmed's only chance of success is catching us unawares. We need to make sure he doesn't do that.'

They walked up into the house and continued the recce. Inside it was in reasonable repair, but it had the atmosphere of a place that had been deserted for a long time. There was a stale smell and the high-ceilinged rooms echoed in the way only places that have not been lived in for many years ever do. There were items of furniture here and there, but Will had the impression that they had been left only because nobody had bothered to take them away, not because they were intended to add anything to the general comfort of the house.

There was a large hallway at the end of which was a sweeping flight of stairs. To the right, off the hallway, was a large kitchen with a big open fireplace and a tiny electric stove – decades old – precariously connected to the house's ancient wiring. In the corner was a door which opened on to a flight of steps leading down into the basement. Will and Kennedy examined it, but the floor of the basement was knee-deep in water, so it was no place for them to camp out.

On the other side of the hallway, opposite the kitchen, was a huge room that went the entire length of the house. There were two massive windows looking out, but aside from an old sofa and a table that had seen better days, there was nothing in there.

The stairs led up to the first floor, which was divided into four rooms, each with large windows on the outside walls. A hallway divided them down the middle. They unanimously decided that the room on the north-eastern corner would be the most advantageous position for them to set up, as they would be able to maintain surveillance on the forested areas to the north and east. Offering a vast expanse of cover, these were the directions, they decided, from where Ahmed was most likely to come at them. The room was also opposite the bathroom – surprisingly small for the size of the house – which meant they didn't have to move far.

By the time they had made their decision, Drew had arrived with a van full of equipment. They talked him through their plans and he nodded with approval. Only when they had finished did he speak. 'If I were him I'd try to disable us using gas – CS, something non-lethal if his sister is in the same room.'

'You brought gas masks?' Will asked.

Drew nodded.

'Good.' He looked out of the window. 'We've only got a few hours of daylight left. Latifa Ahmed's being delivered to us in the morning, so let's get the motion sensors set up. Everything else we can do after nightfall.'

222

Drew and Kennedy nodded and without another word they went to work.

★

The UK has been placed on its highest level of terrorism alert. The government's decision to raise the threat level to 'critical' reflects concern that a terror attack is imminent over the Christmas period. Shoppers are being warned by police to be extra vigilant and to report any suspicious packages or individuals . . .

The television was on, as it always was. He sat in front of it, his back perfectly straight, a white vest covering the dark skin and well-defined muscles of his torso.

He seldom ventured outside; the risk was too high. He needed to keep a low profile. They would be looking for him and he was determined that they wouldn't find him through his own negligence.

During the day he kept the sound down on the television. He had no interest in the foolish banalities aimed at Western housewives with nothing better to do with their time. Really it was just to remind himself that there was a world outside this basement where he spent so many hours. But come evening and the news bulletins, he would listen carefully. He was listening carefully now. Listening and doing all he could to keep his breathing steady, despite what he heard.

An Afghan woman has been arrested following anti-terror raids in London. The woman, 35-year-old Latifa Ahmed, was arrested late last night on suspicion of the commission, preparation and instigation of acts of terrorism. She is currently in custody at an undisclosed location.

He stared at the television.
He blinked, slowly.

He looked at the grainy picture of his sister that filled the screen momentarily, before the news-reader moved on to another story.

And then Faisal Ahmed's lips thinned.

Latifa. In this country. Under arrest. For a moment he could not help feeling a sense of grudging respect for his enemy. This was clever. A way to flush him out. A lie, of course, but an elegant one. A chess move worthy of a grand-master.

It was clear, of course, that the news bulletin was there for his own benefit. No doubt it would be repeated on every channel for the rest of the day. If he bought a news-paper tomorrow morning – which he seldom did – Latifa's face would be staring out of it. In this strange world of the West, where politicians send messages to their people over the airwaves, this was like a clarion call in a coded language. A language that only he could understand.

We have your sister, Faisal Ahmed, it said. *And you know what will happen to her if you do not do as we say.*

He felt a surge of love for Latifa. She alone knew the whereabouts of his hiding places. She alone in all the world could lead them to him. And yet she had not, just as he had trusted. But what horrors would they have inflicted on her to make her talk? A sudden, rampant hate burned inside him. This was not Latifa's war. She had done nothing to deserve it. How dare they? *How dare they?*

He took a deep breath. He had to remain calm if he was to do anything to help her. There would be further messages, of that he was sure. He just had to wait.

All night he sat in front of the television, without eating or sleeping. All night and all the following morning. The news didn't change; just the bare facts – if that's what you wanted to call them – of Latifa's arrest.

Only as the morning wore on was there something new.

Footage. A police van driving up to a large house. A woman being let out of the back. Her head was covered and she seemed to be having difficulty walking.

Faisal Ahmed suppressed a moment of blind rage. What had they done to her? What in the name of God had they done to her? They would pay. As Allah was his witness, they would pay for this!

He scrutinised the pictures closely. The camera followed Latifa as she was escorted to the front steps, then panned back – almost artistically in a way that would never happen for an ordinary news report – to show the place where she was being held.

He recognised it, of course. He recognised it just as they so obviously intended him to.

Here she is, they were saying. *Here she is, if you think you have the skill and the courage to rescue her.*

They knew he was planning something. They knew he would not just disappear into the night; not after what they had done. They knew he wanted revenge and they knew it would be bloody. Now they had played their best hand.

The news reporter spoke over the images.

Terror suspect Latifa Ahmed is being held under a control order while officers from Scotland Yard's anti-terror teams question her further.

The words decoded themselves in his brain even as he heard them: *Your sister is here. We have her. The only way you can save her is by coming to get her yourself.*

Instantly, Faisal Ahmed's brain started working overtime. Tactics. Scenarios. Latifa would be well guarded. Not so well guarded as to put him off a rescue attempt. But well guarded nevertheless.

They would have done their homework.

They would be waiting for him.

225

They would be sure that there was no way they could fail.

But there was a way. There had to be a way.

Faisal Ahmed's eyes narrowed. He kept perfectly calm as he considered his next move.

There was always a way.

★

The SAS team were waiting in the hallway of the house when Latifa arrived. She was walking – hobbling, really – and her hands were cuffed behind her back. A military cameraman was taking video footage of the outside of the house – obviously no real press were being allowed near – and Latifa was being accompanied by two grim-faced Met officers. The police officers handed her over, nodded a cursory greeting at Will as they gave him the keys to her handcuffs, then turned and left. Moments later the black prison van had gone, and there was nobody on the grounds other than Latifa and the three SAS men.

'Your feet are getting better,' Will observed.

Latifa didn't answer. She refused even to catch his eye.

'Can you walk up the stairs?'

She glanced in the direction of the staircase, then started walking towards it with obvious difficulty. Drew offered his arm, but she shrugged him off impatiently, so the three men simply watched helpless as, her hands still cuffed behind her back, she climbed the stairs. It took an age and was almost painful to watch.

They followed her upstairs and ushered her into the room they had prepared.

Latifa stopped at the door and looked around. 'This is to be my new prison?' she asked.

'We've tried to make it as comfortable as we could,' Will replied, gruffly, aware that he sounded ridiculous. The room looked more like a military control centre than anything else. At each of the huge windows were two tripods, one holding a set of ordinary binoculars, the other with a set of night-vision binoculars for after sunset. Leaning against one wall was a line of Heckler & Koch UMPs as well as three MP5s. The UMPs were chambered for larger cartridges with more effective stopping power; the MP5s had a longer range. Horses for courses. There were neat little piles of ammunition stacked up, as well as an array of gas masks and halogen torches. In the middle of the room was a table, on which sat a black box. A length of flex trailed from it across the floor and through a small, newly bored hole in one of the outside walls. A second length led from the box and out through another hole in the wall by the door. There was a laptop connected to a mobile phone and in one corner there was a small television set.

In another area a small gas stove and a kettle had been set up; next to these was a pile of provisions – tinned food, mainly, but also teabags, powdered milk, bars of chocolate and bottles of water. There were a couple of white, unmarked pill bottles containing ephedrine tablets – not unlike speed, regular issue in the Regiment and crucial if they found themselves getting tired during a watch.

Everything they needed while they watched and waited.

There were two beds in the room. 'That's yours,' Will told Latifa, pointing at one. Next to it was an armchair – old and threadbare, but the most comfortable one they could find. Latifa hobbled over to the chair and collapsed into it.

Will turned to Drew. 'Go and lock the front door,' he said. 'Surveillance starts now.'

Drew nodded and left the room.

'What is that?' Latifa asked. She was pointing at the black box.

Will walked to it and flicked a switch. 'An alarm,' he said. 'The house is surrounded by motion sensors. It's impossible to approach from any side without triggering them. The moment Ah –.' He paused. 'The moment your brother approaches, we'll know about it.'

'Unless he lands on the roof,' Kennedy drawled. 'But we're thinking we'll probably notice a Black Hawk hovering above us.'

Latifa looked contemptuously at him; he rolled his eyes, grabbed a UMP and took up position at one of the binoculars. Drew walked back in. 'All set,' he said.

Will turned to Latifa. 'We don't leave this room,' he told her. 'Not unless you need to use the toilet. When that happens, all three of us accompany you across the hallway to the bathroom. One of us comes in with you, the others wait outside.'

Latifa looked at him aghast. 'I refuse to—'

'I'm sorry, Latifa. We don't like it any more than you do, but there's no argument. There's a second alarm box outside the bathroom, so he won't catch us by surprise while you're –' His voice trailed off and he looked over to the second bed. 'One of us will sleep while the other two keep watch. If the buzzer sounds, you'll be held at gunpoint by one of us. We don't want to hurt you, and we don't intend to, but if your brother sees you in that kind of danger it will make him hesitate. The other two will cover the windows and the door. Speaking of which—' Will pulled a length of string from around his neck on which hung a key. He went to the door, closed it firmly, then locked it from the inside.

'Make yourself comfortable, Latifa,' he said. 'We could be here for some time.'

'I would be more comfortable,' she said, 'if you were to remove these handcuffs.'

Will shook his head. 'I'm sorry,' he replied. 'I can't do that. I'll remove them at mealtimes, but after that they go back on.' Latifa turned her head away and he could see that she was holding back tears. 'It's not for much longer, Latifa,' he said, quietly. 'Your brother will be here soon.'

He looked out of the window to the dense forest beyond. It was stupid, but he couldn't get the image out of his head of Ahmed staring back at him. There were bigger things at stake here, Will knew that; but right then he had the unerring sensation that it was him against Ahmed. Man on man. A battle of wits, as well as strength.

Will breathed deeply, then turned back to Latifa.

'Your brother will be here very soon,' he said.

FOURTEEN

Faisal Ahmed was pleased it was cold. It meant he could wear a woollen hat – and so disguise his features to an extent – without attracting attention.

What would have attracted more attention, of course, was the contents of his rucksack. An MP5 with a laser-sight attachment, NV goggles and telescope, a small pouch of explosives and various other bits of kit that he had carefully packed before leaving his safe house, no doubt never to return. He had used a couple of notes from his wallet full of cash to buy a ticket and now he was sitting by the window as the train sped towards King's Cross. His rucksack was on the shelf above him, along with the suitcases and laptop bags of the other passengers on this crowded service. Next to him, a fat man drank noisily from a beer can, despite the fact it was only noon. As the train slowed down into a station, he stood up and pulled his bag from the shelf where it had been nestled next to Ahmed's.

His rucksack looked precarious for a moment, as if it might fall. Ahmed sprang up, knocking the fat man out of the way.

'What the fuck?' the fat man spat.

Ahmed steadied the rucksack, then turned to look at him. The man seemed furious, red-faced. He pushed his great bulk against Ahmed's body, clearly spoiling for a fight. But Ahmed did not want a fight. Not here. He bowed his head. 'I apologise,' he said, meekly. 'That was extremely rude of me.'

The fat man huffed at him, but the wind had been taken

out of his sails by Ahmed's swift apology. He grabbed his bag and waddled to the door.

At King's Cross Ahmed made sure he was always in the middle of the crowd as he made his way to the underground and bought himself a ticket to Waterloo. Once there, he consulted the timetables. Of course, he would not be taking a train to the station nearest the house; he would get within a certain radius and walk the rest. Nor would he take a direct route. It needed to be circuitous, to give him a better chance of shaking off any surveillance.

He worked out his route and memorised it instantly. It was good. It would get him there at eight o'clock that evening. That meant he would be approaching under cover of night. It would take three or four hours to get there; then he would be able to work out a strategy.

Keeping his head facing down towards the ground so that he avoided the glare of any CCTV, he bought himself a ticket. The first train was already waiting on the platform, so he found the emptiest carriage, took a seat and waited for it to move away.

★

The day passed slowly.

Latifa did not speak a word and the SAS men were similarly silent. The television was on in the corner, but the sound was turned down and none of them were really paying attention to the flicker of images. The three soldiers wore their gas masks, but Latifa had refused hers and nothing they could say could persuade her otherwise. Will had taken first watch with Drew, while Kennedy slept. At lunchtime the men had eaten tins of stew heated on the stove; Latifa refused it, choosing to accept only a few sips of water. At about three o'clock, she asked to use the toilet. Will nodded, woke Drew who was by now sleeping on the bed, and the three of them – UMPs at the ready – escorted her to the bathroom. Kennedy and Drew stood guard in the hallway, while Will took her inside. He kept his back to her while she did what she needed to do. When he heard the flushing of the chain he turned around. Clearly humiliated by the circumstances, she would not meet his eye.

At 19.00 hours it was his turn to get some rest. Drew and Kennedy switched on the NV binoculars and kept watch over the encroaching gloom. As he lay on the bed, Will's mind was turning over; but he was dog tired and he soon fell asleep.

Kennedy woke him at midnight. He sat up immediately and it took a moment for him to remember where he was. Latifa was still awake, still sitting in the chair, her arms fastened tightly behind her back.

'You should try and sleep,' he told her.

'Sleep?' she asked him, one eyebrow raised. 'How could I possibly go to sleep?'

Will shrugged, grabbed a bar of chocolate, then took up his position. He had another eight hours of surveillance ahead of him and he had to keep on the ball.

★

The luminous dial of Faisal Ahmed's hand-held compass glowed dimly in the darkness. On the train he had memorised his Ordnance Survey map of the region so there was no need for him to consult it by torchlight. By his reckoning, the house would be approximately 200 metres south of here. He moved stealthily through the forest and, sure enough, a minute later he saw a bright yellow light shining through the trees.

He stopped, gently laid his rucksack on the ground and removed his NV telescope. The trees ahead of him were distinguished in the hazy green light, and the glow from the upstairs room burned too brightly for him to look at it. But that was

OK. There were other things he needed to look for first. They would have set up some kind of early-warning system. A trip-wire around the property was possible, but unlikely – too difficult to set up and too easy for wild animals to set off. No, if he were in their shoes he'd do something else.

It didn't take him long to locate the motion-sensor boxes spaced at regular intervals along the wall. No doubt they would have been set up all around the house, ready to alert the men inside the moment he approached. He moved his sights up to the roof. That was the obvious way to approach, but it was impossible.

He'd have to think of something else; but for now, he needed to keep behind the tree line.

He packed the NV telescope away and pulled out a set of ordinary binoculars. He could see one man at the window, also looking through binoculars. One very accurate shot and maybe he could kill him from here. But it was high risk and taking out just one of them would do him no good at all.

He lowered his binoculars, sat down against the trunk of a tree, closed his eyes and thought.

Gradually a strategy started to form in his head. He considered it slowly, meticulously, making a mental list of its weak points and judging whether the risks they posed were acceptable.

Eventually, he was satisfied. But he needed some equipment and that meant hiking to a nearby town.

Faisal Ahmed spent five minutes locating a hollowed-out tree trunk where he could store his rucksack; then, without hesitation, he started retracing his steps out of the forest. If he could get what he needed that morning, he would be back in situ by the afternoon.

Which meant that he could put his plan into operation as soon as it was dark again.

★

'I think perhaps you have misjudged my brother,' Latifa Ahmed said, quietly. The sun was just beginning to rise and nobody had spoken for hours.

Will turned to her. She looked desperately tired. Desperately anxious. But still she had the same fierce determination in her eyes.

'He was never going to just walk up and knock on the door, Latifa,' he replied, quietly.

She shrugged, but her attempt to look nonchalant was not successful.

'You should eat something,' Will told her. He left his post at the tripod and walked over to where the food was stashed. 'There's bread, I think. I could uncuff you for a while.'

For a moment she looked as if she was going to refuse again; but at the last minute she nodded, her wide eyes brimming once more with tears.

'Stand up,' Will told her, gently. He was glad it was Kennedy who was asleep at that moment. He could do without the sarcastic comments. Latifa did as she was told and Will undid her cuffs. She stretched out her arms in front of her, then hungrily devoured the slice of white bread Will offered, and then another.

'You really think he will come?' she asked Will.

He hesitated, aware that Drew was watching him intently. 'Do you?' he asked her.

Slowly, Latifa nodded her head. She gazed out of the window. 'He will come,' she whispered. Then she turned back to Will. 'You saved my life,' she said. 'Twice. When Faisal arrives, I will ask him not to kill you.'

Will blinked as her words sank in. Was she saying that just to reassure herself? But then why did she sound so confident?

'I need to cuff you again,' he said.

Latifa nodded, then obediently put her hands behind her back, her head bowed.

'Perhaps you should try to sleep, Latifa,' he said.

'Perhaps,' she replied quietly. 'Perhaps.'

★

He walked into the toy shop at two minutes past nine. The man behind the counter was reading a newspaper and didn't notice him until he was a metre away.

'Oh, excuse me, sir. You made me jump.' He was a jolly-looking man, elderly, with a white moustache and twinkling blue eyes.

'I'm terribly sorry,' Ahmed replied, making sure his voice betrayed no hint of an accent.

'What can I do for you, anyway?'

Ahmed smiled. He knew his face looked appealing and open when he did so. 'I would like to buy a gift for my nephew,' he said, smoothly. 'He has asked Santa for a remote-controlled car.'

The man nodded pleasantly, as if this were a request he often received and he was happy to oblige. 'There are three or four to choose from,' he said, walking out into the main area of the shop before returning with an armful of boxes. He spread them out on the counter.

Faisal Ahmed examined them. He was not interested in their size, shape or colour; he was not interested in their price. Instead, he scrutinised the technical specifications on the side of each box.

'I think my nephew will enjoy this one,' he announced brightly.

One minute later he was walking out with his new purchase.

His next stop was a builder's merchants, a large, anonymous superstore where he did not have to speak to anyone. Here he bought himself an aerosol can of insulating foam.

The final item on his shopping list would be more difficult to come by; certainly he would be unlikely to find it in a shop. Instead, he headed to an Internet café. A quick search gave him a list of names of local doctors and a few minutes later he had located their addresses on the electoral register. He checked an online map and memorised their locations immediately.

Forty-five minutes later he was outside the first address. It only took him a couple of minutes to establish that there was someone home, so he moved on to the next house on his list.

This one looked more hopeful.

There was an alleyway around the back. Checking that he wasn't being watched, he disappeared down it and moments later was climbing over a high fence into the back garden of the house. He surveyed the place from the bottom of the garden. Still no sign of life. He decided to proceed.

In his pocket was a leather pouch of metal instruments. He brought it out as he approached the back door and about thirty seconds later he had picked the lock. Once inside the kitchen, he stopped and listened.

Silence.

Then he began to search the house.

He worked quietly and neatly, not disturbing anything he came across. The jewellery was easy to find, but he left that. In the small home office there was a safe bolted to the floor. Easily opened, but it didn't interest him. This was the house of a doctor and it was a doctor's implement he required.

He found what he needed after about ten minutes, hidden away in a drawer in a spare room upstairs. It was an old stethoscope, but it still worked. It would be fine for his purposes.

Ahmed put it in the bag with the car and the builder's foam, carefully shut the drawer, then slipped downstairs. He left by the same route he had arrived and he used his metal tools to lock the kitchen door again. He felt confident that nobody would ever know he had been there.

His shopping list complete, Faisal Ahmed stealthily climbed over the garden fence and walked out into the street.

Two hours and thirty minutes later he was on the edge of the forest. There were a few houses dotted around and he knew that somewhere here he would be able to find the final thing he needed to execute his plan.

Sure enough, walking along the garden wall of a house which backed on to the forest, there was a domestic cat. It was a shaggy ginger Tom and it eyed Faisal Ahmed warily.

Ahmed stayed perfectly still.

The cat took a few steps nearer.

When Ahmed's hands flashed out to grab the animal, he did so with an uncanny speed and accuracy. The cat hissed and tried to get away, but Ahmed's grip was too firm. He held the animal under the arm that was holding his bag and with his spare hand clamped its jaws tight shut. Immediately he headed to the forest.

It took another forty-five minutes for him to reach the tree where his rucksack was being held. He would have to let the cat meow for a short time while he packed his purchases into the rucksack and hoisted it onto his back. When that was done, however, he clamped its jaws shut once more.

Then he sat and waited until nightfall.

★

The second night of surveillance. It seemed unnaturally quiet out there, as though the whole forest were holding its breath. Waiting for something to happen.

Drew was sleeping and so, finally, was Latifa. Kennedy coughed and Will turned sharply towards him. His colleague held up his hands. 'Don't shoot!' he grinned, before turning back to continue his surveillance. Will took a deep breath and went back to scanning the area for movement.

'He's out there, isn't he?' Kennedy said after a minute or so, his voice more serious now. 'He's out there somewhere.'

Will's expression remained emotionless. 'Yeah,' he said. 'He's out there somewhere.'

★

Ahmed looked at his watch. 02.00 hours. Now was the time.

He knew they were watching. Chances were they'd have NV, but even with that it would be impossible to see more than a metre or two into the forest. He would be able to get within that distance of the tree line without being detected. They were clearly relying on the motion sensors near the house to alert them to his arrival. He crept forward, his mouth firmly covering the jaws of the struggling cat. When he got as far as he dared, he started skirting round to the north, out of sight of the room with the lights on.

Any closer now and he would trigger the motion sensors.

Faisal Ahmed proceeded clinically and professionally. He removed his hand from the animal's jaws and then, swiftly, brutally, snapped the bones in two of its legs. The cat screeched pitifully, and its body went into spasm.

He had to move quickly now. He burst through the trees and, when he was a few metres from the house, he dropped the cat on the ground. The animal was in no state to move anywhere quickly: it dragged itself across the floor, but only managed to turn in a circle. Ahmed ran round to the other side of the house, past the front door. Once he was out of sight of the weakly mewing creature, he pressed his back against the wall.

Soon he would be able to get into the house.

But not yet. Not just yet.

★

The buzzer sounded.

Will had been resting, but the instant that tiny noise filled the room, he was on his feet. He grabbed his UMP and stepped towards Latifa's chair, aiming the gun towards her head. Drew and Kennedy had moved with similar speed, stepping back from the windows. Drew covered the door, Kennedy the windows. Will checked his gas mask was properly fitted.

'What is happening?' Latifa breathed, her whispered voice trembling with fright.

'He's here,' Will murmured.

The buzzer continued to sound. It meant there was still someone out there, looking for an entry, no doubt.

For a minute it sounded. Two minutes.

Will narrowed his eyes. Something wasn't right. If it was Ahmed, he wouldn't have stayed out in the open for that long – he'd have got close to the walls of the house, surely, where there was more cover. Drew and Kennedy seemed to be thinking the same thing: they were both casting him enquiring looks.

'I'm going down,' Will said, tersely. He grabbed a torch, removed the key from around his neck and unlocked the door, knowing that one of the others would lock it again after he had left.

It was dark in the hallway and he allowed himself a moment for his night vision to adjust to the change. Once that had happened, it took him a further two minutes to get down the stairs – each time he advanced he checked any new area to which he was exposed.

Now he was on the ground floor. The sound of the buzzer had faded away and all around him was silent. But then he heard something. High pitched. Like a scream, only not as loud. Carefully, he followed the sound. It took him into a room on the north side. The noise was louder here and it was coming from outside. Will crossed the room, then shone the torch through the window. The powerful beam illuminated something moving on the ground, and it was a moment before he realised what it was.

A cat, writing around but unable to move far. It had been caught in a fight, Will surmised and he had been following its desperate mews of pain.

He closed his eyes. A false alarm. He felt the curious sensation of being both disappointed and relieved at the same time.

The animal couldn't stay there. Its movements were clearly what was triggering the motion sensors. Grim-faced, Will hurried to the front door, unlocked it, stepped outside and strode around to where the cat was scratching about on the ground, clearly in great pain. He had two options: pick the animal up and throw it into the forest, well clear of the motion sensors; or put the thing out of its misery now.

The cat continued to howl and Will's decision was made for him.

It took one shot from the UMP – a weapon far too powerful for this job at such close range. The instant the shot was fired, the animal was obliterated, its flesh spattered all around. But at least it was no longer in pain; and now it could no longer trigger the motion sensors.

Will looked out into the forest. 'Where the hell are you, Ahmed?' he whispered to himself. 'Where the hell are you?'

He turned back into the house, taking care to lock the door behind him.

★

Faisal Ahmed heard the gunshot that silenced the howls of the cat with satisfaction. He remained pressed against the wall, almost entirely motionless, for an hour before he judged the time right to make his next move.

Slowly, his back still against the wall so that he remained out of the beam of the motion sensors, he edged around to the front door. For the second time that day, he made use of the metal implements from their leather pouch to

240

pick the lock. Once he was inside, he again took pains to lock the door behind him.

He was good at working silently – it was almost second nature. He crept into the kitchen and swiftly located the house's main fuse box. It opened up easily, he noted with satisfaction. That was good.

He needed a little light. He had correctly remembered the location of the door to the basement, so he went down there, shut the door behind him and drew a torch from his pocket. Out of his rucksack he pulled the receiver from the car he had bought earlier, along with a small detonating charge and a few tools. Within minutes his makeshift detonator had been created.

Stepping back into the kitchen, he fitted the charge into the fuse box, before spraying it with the builder's foam. The foam served two purposes: it held the detonator fast and when the time came it would muffle the sound.

Ahmed slung his rucksack back over his shoulders and extinguished the torch. He left the kitchen and quietly climbed the stairs at the end of the hallway.

He could see the room in which they had set up. Latifa would be in there, he realised; it was a struggle for him not to burst in, all guns blazing. But that would be foolish. Even though they would not be expecting him, they would be heavily armed and at the moment he did not know how many of them there were. No doubt he would be able to kill a number of them, but he risked being shot himself.

Patience, he told himself. Patience.

He crept across the hallway and into a room that was at the opposite corner of the house. It was very dark in here and again he allowed himself a little light from his torch. There was something he needed to locate. He found it quickly enough: a wire coming into the house just by the window. Looking through the window itself, he verified that it was indeed what he expected it to be: the wire connecting the motion sensor to whatever alarm system they had set up. It would be two-core flex. If he cut through either the live or the neutral it would disable the sensor while leaving a small snip in the flex that you would only see if you were looking for it. From his bag he removed a pair of wire cutters and in a second it was done.

Desperately slowly, as quietly as he could, Faisal Ahmed unscrewed the latch of the window on the wall opposite the door, and slid it open. He climbed outside, balanced himself precariously on the window ledge, and then slid the frame shut again.

With the motion sensor disabled, he could move freely, but it was precarious on the ledge and it took all his strength to haul himself up on to the slates of the roof. Once there, however, he worked quickly. The house was old and had not been well cared for, so the slates came off easily. He removed seven or eight, resting them in the guttering, then pulled a knife from his pocket and started scoring away at the thin layer of wood beneath. It took about ten minutes to make a hole big enough for him to squeeze through. The rucksack went first, then he gently lowered himself down, landing nimbly with his feet firmly on the sturdy joists of the attic.

It was freezing cold in the roof, but Ahmed put that from his mind. He crept to the area of the attic that covered the room in which Latifa was being held, then pulled out the doctor's stethoscope from his rucksack before lying down on his front across the joists. Gently, he pulled some of the thin layer of insulation away from the floor, laid the chestpiece against the plasterboard, then attached the earpieces to his ear.

Silence.

That was OK. It was to be expected. He'd done enough surveillance of his own to realise that it was long, silent work. But when someone spoke, he would hear. When they moved, he would know. In twenty-four hours' time, the 'false alarm' that he had engineered by breaking the cat's legs would be forgotten and he would know their routines and practices.

He would know just when to make his move.

★

The third day dawned.

'Morning campers!' Kennedy announced brightly as he shook Will awake.

Will sat up, groggily.

'Come on, shit-for-brains,' Kennedy continued. 'I need some kip.'

'All right, all right,' Will told him. He walked over to the food stash and peeled himself a couple of bananas. Latifa was drowsing in the chair, but her eyes flickered open as he looked at her.

'Daytime?' she asked.

'Daytime.'

'I would like to use the bathroom.'

Will nodded. 'You know the drill.' He turned to Drew and Kennedy. 'Come on, you two.'

Kennedy breathed out in frustration. 'What is it with me and women?' he asked no one in particular. 'As soon as I lie down, they say they need a piss. And when we get back, the moment's lost.'

★

Faisal Ahmed heard every word clearly. It had filled him with a wild surge of joy to hear his sister's voice; but it was replaced by sudden anger at the sound of that man speaking so disrespectfully in front of her.

He could not dwell on it, though. Not now.

Their conversation had told him there were four of them, including Latifa, and now his stethoscope amplified the sound

243

of them leaving the room. Swiftly, he ripped up a larger portion of the roof insulation, then took his knife and started to score into the plasterboard. He had to be delicate – the knife had to weaken the plasterboard sufficiently, but not work its way through to the other side – yet quick – if they came back before he had finished, the sound would alert them to his presence.

He worked deftly and was satisfied that the ceiling was weak enough by the time they returned to the room.

Faisal Ahmed resumed his position lying on all fours across the joists, the stethoscope firmly in his ears.

It was evening when they next went to the bathroom. His body was freezing cold and ached from lying on the joists. But that didn't matter. As soon as the room was empty, Ahmed removed the heaviest item in his rucksack – an extremely long length of thin but strong rope, one end of which he tied to the rafters of the attic. He removed his MP5, checked the laser sight was working, then fitted his NV goggles to his head – switched off for now to conserve battery. Finally he placed the remote control by his side, ready to use when the time was right, before lying down once more to listen through the ceiling at what was going on below.

The minutes ticked past.

They turned to hours.

It was perfectly dark in the attic.

He waited.

And waited.

It was gone midnight when he illuminated his watch. In the room below, he heard voices. It sounded like changeover time and with satisfaction he heard one of the men say the words he was waiting for.

'Stick the kettle on.'

Still lying on the joists, Ahmed groped for the remote control.

He flicked the switch.

No sound.

He smiled with grim satisfaction. The builder's foam had done its sound-insulating work well.

In a matter of minutes it would be over.

★

In the room, the lights suddenly failed.

'What's happening?' Drew asked, sharply.

'Wake Kennedy,' Will hissed, his voice terse as he strode over to Latifa and put his gun to her head.

'I'm awake,' Kennedy's voice came through the darkness. 'What the fuck's going on?'

'We've lost power,' Will said.

'Thanks, Einstein. Why?'

'I don't know. It's an old house. Dodgy wiring. Bit of a coincidence, though.'

'Probably the fucking kettle.' Kennedy's voice was edgy and clipped.

'Cutting the electricity's one way to disable the motion sensors,' Drew added.

'But you can't do it from outside the house,' Will said. 'We checked, remember?'

'The fuse box must have tripped, then,' Drew said. 'One of us needs to go and have a look.'

Will grabbed a torch. 'I'll go,' he said. 'Lock the door after me and one of you mark the woman. Don't let your guard down for a second.'

'Roger that,' they spoke in unison. Will could tell from the brisk, efficient sound of their voices that they had entered combat mode. It probably *was* just the kettle tripping the electrics, but you couldn't be too sure.

Will descended the stairs carefully, his weapon at the ready. As he edged slowly down to the kitchen he could feel the blood pumping in his veins. He had to get the power back on – without that, their early-warning system

245

was useless. But something wasn't right. He desperately tried to work out what he might have missed, but there was nothing. The power *couldn't* be turned off from outside and the house *couldn't* be approached without them knowing.

It was impossible. So why did he suddenly feel so nervous?

The fuse box was just ahead of him. He illuminated his torch and pointed it at the wall.

He blinked.

The door to the box was hanging open; inside was a mess of wires and foam.

No one else in the house had done that to the fuse box. It could only mean one thing.

'*Oh my God*,' he whispered to himself, a sudden, debilitating dread creeping through his limbs. '*Ahmed. He's already here.*'

And it was only then that he heard the gunshots from above.

FIFTEEN

Sixty seconds.

That was how long Faisal Ahmed gave it to allow whoever was heading down to the fuse box to get there.

He silently stood up on the ceiling joist, holding on to the top of the rope with one hand, clutching his MP5 with the other. A flick of a switch and his NV goggles powered up. Everything around him became suffused in a grainy green light. Looking down, he saw the area of the ceiling that he had scored and weakened.

And then he jumped. The ceiling plaster shattered everywhere as he crashed through into the room below. As soon as he felt the rope tighten, he started to slide down it, looking around to take in everything in the room. Latifa was in the corner, sitting in a chair: she looked around blindly in the darkness. Next to her was a man with a weapon. The gun had clearly been aimed at his sister's head, but now the man was in the process of swinging it round in Ahmed's direction.

Ahmed acted without hesitation. The laser sight illuminated its target and a single head shot was all it took to put the man to the floor.

On the other side of the room was the second man. He too seemed only to have the vaguest sense in the darkness of where Ahmed was. The second shot from the MP5 hit him in the shoulder and threw him against the wall; the third was more accurate and finished him off.

By the time Faisal Ahmed hit the floor, both of Latifa's guards lay dead.

He had to move quickly. The third man would have been alerted to his presence by the sound of gunfire and even now would be hurtling up the stairs.

'Faisal?' he heard Latifa say. Her voice was terrified.

'*Did they hurt you?*' he asked in their native Pashto.

'*No,*' she replied. '*But I cannot walk easily.*'

Still holding the rope, Ahmed strode over to her and, with one swift movement, grabbed her around the waist and slung her over his shoulders.

As he did so, there was a banging on the door. 'Drew!' a voice called. 'Kennedy! Unlock it! Let me in!'

Calmly, Ahmed aimed his MP5 at the door. The weapon was powerful enough to burst through the wood and take out his final enemy.

'*No!*' Latifa hissed. '*Do not shoot him.*'

'*What do you mean?*'

'*I owe that man my life, Faisal. Do not shoot him.*'

Faisal Ahmed had never been able to deny his sister; against his better judgement he hurried to the window. A burst of fire from the MP5 shattered the panes and a swipe of his arm cleared the fragmented glass from the edges. There was a sound of heavy gunshots from behind him as the man on the other side of the door started to shoot it through – it made Latifa gasp, but Faisal Ahmed remained coldly calm. There was plenty of rope left and they'd be out of here in seconds. He heaved himself and his sister through the window, then ignored the feel of the rope burning into his free hand as the two of them slid down to the ground.

There was nothing he could do to make the rope useless to his pursuer and he momentarily cursed himself for honouring his sister's request. But it was too late now. All he could do was run.

★

Will crashed through the door, a sick feeling running through every part of his body. The moment he was in the room he flashed the torch all around. The light fell first on Kennedy's body: the SAS man's face was an unrecognisable mess of blood and bone. 'Jesus,' Will whispered, before hunting out Drew. The third of their little unit was slumped half against the wall and even in the semi-darkness Will could see his blood still gushing from his gaping head wound.

And Latifa was nowhere to be seen.

As he stood there, his mind clamouring with shocked alarm, he became aware of the hole in the ceiling and the rope trailing from the joists and out of the window. How long had Faisal Ahmed been up there? he wondered. And then it all became clear to him, how he had fooled them. He must have been waiting for his moment for at least twenty-four hours.

The shame of being outwitted and the anger at losing Drew and Kennedy spurred him into action. Ahmed had Latifa. He couldn't move quickly with her, so Will could still make chase. Running to the window, he grabbed the rope and slipped down to the ground, then stopped to listen. Sure enough, there was a rustling up ahead, eastwards, in the forest. UMP in hand, he followed the noise.

Seconds later he was beyond the boundary of the house and standing on the path that led away from it. He heard footsteps in the distance – it sounded like someone running, and Will didn't have the impression that they were crashing through foliage. Ahmed was taking the easy escape route – he had to, if he was carrying Latifa.

Will started to run up the path. The ground was soft and

yet strangely knobbly and treacherous, thanks to the granite-like pebbles that were strewn all over the place. As Will ran, he shone the torch to the left and right, keeping an eye out for any areas where it looked as though Ahmed may have veered away from the path; then he realised he was making a target of himself, a target that no one could miss. He switched off the torch and continued in the darkness.

He moved with caution, but the nature of the terrain was such that Ahmed could have been hidden behind any of the trees that lined his route. Something told him – intuition – that he wasn't. It would have been the easiest thing in the world for the bastard to wait in the room and nail Will when he crashed through the door. But he hadn't. Will didn't know why, but he gambled that if he wasn't prepared to stop and shoot him then, he wouldn't be now. Still, he trod lightly. Every now and then he would stop and hold his breath so that the sound did not interfere with his hearing. Each time he did, he heard the steps up ahead. Was it his imagination or were they getting closer? Was he gaining on him? Will gripped his weapon a little harder and continued pushing uphill.

Suddenly he stopped.

It caught him in the eye first, the little red light. Momentarily it disappeared, but then he looked down and saw it on his chest. He knew what it meant, of course – that someone had their laser sight firmly fixed on him. And it was perfectly obvious who that someone was.

'You have ten seconds,' a voice called from somewhere in the darkness beyond, 'to discharge your weapon into the ground and throw it into the trees. Any longer and I'll shoot.'

Will hesitated. For a moment he considered a random burst of fire from the UMP, but he dismissed the notion almost as soon as it came into his head. Ahmed had already nailed Drew and Kennedy; the fact that Will was alive was a miracle.

As if in response to that thought, the voice spoke again.

'My sister asked me not to kill you,' it stated, flatly. 'That's the only reason you're still alive. But you will be dead in three seconds' time if you do not do as I say.'

Will scowled, but he knew there was no option. He lowered his weapon and discharged it fully into the ground. Then he hurled it to one side into the woods.

'Put your hands behind your back,' the voice called.

Will did as he was told.

'If I see your hands or you make any sudden move, then I shoot. Do you understand?'

Will stared straight ahead, but then became aware of the little red dot moving up to his face. 'Do you understand?'

'I understand,' he said, flatly.

There was a pause. Everything around seemed still and Will began to wonder if Ahmed had silently continued his escape. Maybe he should give chase.

But then, slowly, a figure emerged out of the darkness.

Faisal Ahmed looked different from the picture Will had seen in Lowther Pankhurst's office. Even in the midnight gloom the dark rings under his eyes were visible and his beard was less well groomed. But it was unmistakably him and Will couldn't help but stare and scowl.

When Ahmed was only a few metres away, he stopped; but he kept his gun trained on Will. 'My sister tells me you saved her life,' Ahmed said, softly. His voice was almost gentle and, unlike Latifa, he had no hint of an accent. 'For that, I thank you.'

Will's eyes narrowed. 'You just killed two of my men,' he retorted. 'Forgive me if I don't come over and shake your hand.'

'I would not recommend doing anything with your hands,' Ahmed reminded him. 'I meant what I said. As for your men, they were, presumably, instructed to shoot me on sight?'

Will felt his cheek twitch momentarily.

'I thought so,' Ahmed said, almost pensively. 'They were

soldiers too. I am sorry for their deaths, but if it wasn't them it would have been me. I'm sure they would understand.'

'I wouldn't bet on it, Ahmed,' Will said with distaste. 'They weren't the ones planning to kill thousands of people.'

'I beg your pardon?'

'Don't try and play dumb with me, Ahmed. We know the score. We *are* going to stop you.'

Ahmed raised his gun slightly. 'Stop me doing what?' he demanded. 'Tell me immediately or I shoot.'

'A terrorist hit. On the capital.'

For a moment, Ahmed's face remained emotionless; then he smiled. But it wasn't a smile of pleasure, it was a smile of understanding, as if something that had previously been unclear to him had suddenly been revealed.

'I see,' he replied quietly. 'So *that* is what they have been telling you.'

'Yeah,' Will spat. 'And it's not the only thing either.'

'That is not a surprise,' Ahmed replied, before pausing. 'My sister tells me you are a man to be trusted. Is this true, Will Jackson? *Are* you a man to be trusted?'

'That depends who you are,' Will replied, flatly.

Ahmed nodded his head and seemed to be considering something. Finally he spoke. 'It isn't true, of course,' he said. 'What they have told you. But you are an intelligent man. No doubt you suspected that already.'

'Not really,' Will told him. 'The intel seems pretty clear.'

Ahmed smiled again. 'Intelligence,' he almost purred. 'It is an interesting thing. It is amazing how often people can be made to believe a lie in the name of intelligence. Take my sister, for example. The whole of this country now believes she is a wicked Afghan terrorist, but you and I know that is not the truth. What you have been told about me is not the truth, either.'

'Enlighten me,' Will said, unable to stop himself sounding dismissive.

252

'I will,' Ahmed replied, oblivious to the contempt in Will's voice or at least hardened to it. 'You have risked your life to save my sister, it seems. You at least deserve to know why. My guess is that you have been manipulated just as I have. Sometimes we think we are knights when in fact we are merely pawns. I would guess that you are familiar with some of my history already – that I was trained by the Americans to be a mole for them within the network of al-Qaeda in Afghanistan. That I was discovered and made my way back to England.'

Will continued to look balefully at him.

Ahmed inclined his head. 'My American handlers instructed me to start working for MI5, infiltrating terrorist groups in the UK and alerting the authorities to potential strikes. I was, I should tell you, extremely successful.'

'You're not telling me anything I don't know already, Ahmed.'

'Not yet, perhaps. What I think you are unlikely to know is that my orders changed.'

'What are you talking about?'

'I was instructed by the CIA to go dark.' His face became pinched. 'They had a new policy, they told me. One that they hoped would save lives.'

Ahmed paused. Will had the impression that the Afghan was scanning his face for signs of doubt.

'My new instructions were these. To instigate a series of low-level terrorist strikes across the UK. No catastrophes, no deaths. I was to do it through my network of al-Qaeda sympathisers. The Americans believed that if the British saw that the terrorist threat on their streets was real, it would keep them on-message – more likely to do the Americans' bidding whenever they came asking for help.'

Will blinked. 'You're trying to tell me that your terrorist campaign was started by the CIA?'

'Of course,' Ahmed replied.

'That's ridiculous. I don't believe you.'

Ahmed shrugged. 'I cannot control what you believe,' he said. 'Nevertheless, it is the truth. The man who sent you to kill me, his name is Donald Priestley, is it not?'

Priestley. The image of the friendly, almost avuncular American CIA official flitted through Will's head. 'How did you know that?'

Ahmed nodded. 'It was Donald Priestley that I reported to. It was all Donald Priestley's idea. He called what we were doing Operation Firefight.' He sneered. 'Because we had to fight fire with fire. A favourite saying of his.'

Will remained silent.

'Of course, MI5's intelligence network is impressive. We always knew that they would realise I was involved in these strikes, but Priestley had the confidence of somebody high up in the British intelligence services. Every time MI5 came close to discovering my location, I was tipped off by the CIA. I did the Americans' bidding for three years and they were, I think, pleased with my success rate. Casualties were low, but the profile of my attacks was high.'

Casualties were low. The very words felt like darts being hurled into Will's body. *Not low enough, you bastard*, he felt like saying. 'If they were so pleased with you,' he managed to ask, 'why the hell would they want me to put a bullet in your head?'

'Operation Firefight was successful,' Ahmed said. 'Maybe too successful. The British became anxious. They became the Americans' poodles and that suited the US very well. Priestley wanted me to take things further. Up a level. He wanted deaths in the UK. Collateral damage, he called it. A loss of life here to save greater loss of life elsewhere. But these would be innocent civilian lives. I refused to do his bidding. The very next day my cover was blown by the CIA. The terrorist cells I was working with found out the truth about me. I had to run. Hide.'

As Faisal Ahmed spoke, Will's mind spun around in circles. He did not want to believe it; he didn't want to believe anything that came from this man's mouth. Yet Will couldn't for the life of him understand why Ahmed would feel the need for this sudden confession and he couldn't shake off the sensation that pieces of a jigsaw were fitting together.

Yet there were still anomalies. Things that didn't make sense. 'There are other sources,' Will said. 'Independent sources from abroad. They all say the same thing: that you're planning a major terrorist strike.'

Ahmed looked contemptuous. 'More intelligence?' he asked. 'Tell me, was this so-called intelligence by any chance extorted from extremist sympathisers? Were they taken to an American black camp to have information tortured out of them?'

Will didn't reply.

'It's how they work,' Ahmed continued. 'The CIA leak information to unsuspecting sympathisers; they then extract it under duress from their victim in front of their British allies. Even the source doesn't know he's misleading his interrogators – he thinks he's having the information coerced out of him. Trust me, they've been doing this for years. I know, because they taught me how to do it. And whatever you have been told about me instigating a major civilian terrorist strike is a lie. I have turned my back on it. My plan is much more simple.'

'What do you mean?'

'I intend to stop Donald Priestley and the Americans from continuing their policy of death.'

'How?'

Ahmed didn't answer.

'Where's Latifa?' Will pressed.

Ahmed shook his head. 'Latifa is no longer your concern. Nor am I. I don't expect you to take my word for every-thing, but I'm sure when you confront Priestley you will see that I am telling the truth. No doubt you have been taught, as have I, to tell when somebody is lying.' He made a flicking gesture with his gun. 'Turn around,' he said. 'And walk away.'

Will didn't move. Ahmed's face became suddenly more ruthless.

'I mean it, soldier,' he said. 'Move away or I'll shoot.'

'Not yet,' Will whispered. 'There's part of your story that you left out.'

'What are you talking about?'

'Operation Firefight, or whatever the hell you want to call it, wasn't entirely without casualties, was it? What about the bomb in Knightsbridge? Outside the department store? The one that killed a woman and her daughter?'

Ahmed's face remained stony. 'A mistake,' he said, flatly. 'An extremely unfortunate one. The device was not meant to explode in that location. It wasn't part of my plan.'

'I don't care if it was part of your plan or not, Ahmed,' Will whispered. 'The people who died that day were my wife and daughter, and *you* killed them.'

Faisal Ahmed's eyes widened slightly as some of his smug omniscience seemed to be knocked out of him.

'You might as well kill me now, Ahmed, because I swear to God I couldn't give a shit what excuses and lies you throw in my path. You murdered my family and I will not rest until I've avenged them. I will not rest until you are dead, just like them.'

'I am sorry for your loss, Will Jackson,' Ahmed said. 'Truly sorry. I know what it is to lose one's family. But you would be wise, my friend, not to follow this course. I think it has been shown that *I* am the better soldier. That *I* have the better mind. And anyway, if you kill me, another person will take my place. Is it not better to target the real criminal behind this? That is what I intend to do and you would be well advised to leave me alone to do it.'

256

He raised the laser sight to Will's head once again.

'Turn around,' he repeated, 'and walk away.'

The eyes of the two men were locked. For a moment Will considered disobedience, but a stronger instinct kicked in. Faisal Ahmed had already shot two people tonight; he wouldn't hesitate to make it a third. And if that happened, he would never pay for what he did to Will's family.

In an instant, Will drank in every feature of Ahmed's face. He wanted to be sure that he would recognise it again without even thinking. Then, slowly, he turned his back on the Afghan and started walking.

One pace.

Two paces.

Three paces.

He was several metres away when he heard Ahmed's voice again. More distant this time, but with a strange sense of urgency.

'Make no mistake about it,' Faisal Ahmed called. 'I have no quarrel with you. But if you interfere with what I have to do, it is *I* who will kill *you*.'

Will stopped, then turned. The path ahead of him disappeared into the darkness.

Faisal Ahmed was nowhere to be seen.

SIXTEEN

The sun rose upon the country house and upon the dead bodies of Mark Drew and Nathan Kennedy.

There was no way Will could ever recount the precise number of dead bodies he had seen in his life. Hundreds, certainly. Like an abattoir worker, he had become used to corpses and the sight of horrific wounds did not make him shudder as they might other people. Death had been his job for most of his adult life.

But some deaths were different. He had only been flung together with Drew and Kennedy a few days ago, but he realised, as he sat there with them, that they had formed a bond – a bond that had been shattered by Faisal Ahmed.

Deaths, he knew, were easier to take when you had someone to blame. Back in his Regiment days, blame had been an easy thing to dish out. It was them and us. Black and white. Clear cut. And someone to blame, he realised as he sat amid the devastation of the room, was what he had been seeking when he agreed to go after Faisal Ahmed in the first place. In the two years following his family's death, he had been wandering in the dark, not knowing why it had happened or whom to blame. And then he had learned about Ahmed. It was as if he had been given the final piece of a jigsaw and all he had to do was slot it in place.

Now though, things had changed. He had come face to face with his family's killer. And though he did not loathe

Ahmed any less, if what the man had told him was true the apportionment of blame was not so simple.

Who was to blame for the death of his wife and child? Faisal Ahmed and his bomb that went wrong? Or Donald Priestley and the CIA? *Sometimes you have to fight fire with fire.* Will had been in enough situations where that was true; but there were limits and Operation Firefight – if it even existed – went far beyond those limits.

And what of Drew and Kennedy? Who was to blame for their deaths? Ahmed? Priestley? Or Will himself, for bringing them into this situation, then being outwitted by the man they were intending to capture? The idea made him bang his fist against the wall in frustration. Jesus, he thought to himself. Why the hell does everyone around me seem to end up dead?

Faisal Ahmed, of course, would blame Priestley. Priestley would blame Faisal Ahmed. Nobody took responsibility for their actions. And so the memory of the dead was abused, trampled upon, forgotten.

In the last few hours, the world had grown more complicated. What was more, Will couldn't shake the feeling that the dead around him were waiting for his response.

The mobile phone attached to the laptop rang, making him jump. It could only be one person – Pankhurst. No one else knew the number. And if Will didn't reply, the DG would know something was up – this place would be crawling with spooks before he knew it. But Will needed to get his head straight, to work out his next move, and he couldn't do it here. He grabbed a sturdy bag from their stores, then filled it up with equipment. The NV binoculars, grenades, ammo and, of course, weaponry. Almost as an afterthought he grabbed the ephedrine tablets. God knows when he was going to get a chance to sleep again. He nodded, briefly, at the lifeless bodies of Drew and Kennedy, then walked out of the room. As he did so, he thought he heard Kennedy's voice. *Get the fucker for me, Jackson*, it said. *Get the fucker.*

Will headed through the forest. He moved quickly, running uphill not so much out of a sense of urgency as because he wanted to feel his body receiving a bit of punishment. It seemed only fair, after all. Soon he was at the top of the Downs. It was still too early for anyone else to be up there, and he was glad of the solitude. Looking down, he saw the sprawl of the nearest provincial town. He knew there was a railway station, so he started jogging downhill.

It was nearly eight o'clock by the time he got to the platform for the train to Waterloo. He wondered if they had found Drew and Kennedy's bodies by now; if so, they would know it was a possibility that he himself had bought it, given that he hadn't been in touch. That suited him. It gave him a bit of time.

From Waterloo he crossed London to Paddington. He stowed his bag in a left-luggage locker, then hit the streets to find some scran. Sitting in a café waiting for his food, a cup of hot, sweet coffee in front of him, he tried to get his head straight.

It seemed like an age ago that Pankhurst had interrupted Will's morning visit to Laura and little Anna. So much had happened. Will felt a surge of guilt as he remembered the random night of lust he had spent with Kate, the journalist from the pub; and he realised that, out there in the freezing wilds of Afghanistan, for the first time in two years Laura and Anna had not been the first thing on his mind. The *only* thing on his mind. He suppressed an urge to go back to Hereford, to the grave, and apologise. Apologising to the dead was useless, he thought to himself as his breakfast arrived. Anderson, Drew and Kennedy wouldn't expect an apology. They would expect him to go out there and do the right thing.

But sometimes it was difficult to know what the right thing was.

With a pang, Will felt Laura's absence more keenly than he had done in months. She was good at things like this, at seeing to the heart of the matter. At putting Will on the right track. What would she urge him to do? To hunt down Faisal Ahmed and seek revenge on her account? Or to do as the Afghan had said? Ahmed's words rang in his ears. *If you kill me, another person will take my place. Is it not better to target the real criminal behind this?*

Will shook his head. He couldn't do it. He couldn't let Ahmed walk free. And yet, if what he had told him was correct, Ahmed was not the only one to blame for Laura and Anna's deaths or for the deaths of the SAS soldiers he had led on this mission. Donald Priestley was complicit, at least as much a murderer as Faisal Ahmed.

As these thoughts chased each other in circles around Will's head, he heard Laura's voice chiming in his mind, as clearly as if she were standing there with him.

Be sure, Will, it said. *Do what you have to do, but be sure of everything before you act.*

Will blinked. In an instant, the confusion that had shrouded him since the previous night disappeared, like mist burned away by the sun. His mind was suddenly clear. The way forward was obvious.

He tucked into his food, suddenly content in the knowledge that he knew what he was going to do. Content in the knowledge that he had a plan.

All he had to do was put it into action.

★

Lowther Pankhurst looked up from his desk to see Don Priestley storm through the door.

'It's customary to knock, Don,' he said, mildly.

'It's customary not to fuck up, Lowther,' the American practically shouted, his voice loaded with sarcasm.

The call had come in several hours ago. Two of the SAS team dead, Latifa Ahmed missing and no word from Will Jackson. The surrounding area was being searched, but they were presuming that he had been taken hostage or was dead – there was no other reason for the radio silence from him. Since hearing the news, Pankhurst's day had got progressively worse and having the usually calm Don Priestley yelling at him wasn't making it any better.

'Don't you British get it? Don't you understand what this guy is capable of?'

'I think we have a pretty *good* idea what he's capable of, Don.' He handed the fuming CIA boss a sheaf of A4 photographs. 'Your boys trained him pretty well.' The pictures showed the scene of devastation at the country house, along with gruesome, bloody close-ups of the dead men. The room resembled a battlefield. Priestley examined them for a moment before looking back at Pankhurst.

'Two bodies,' the American noted. 'What about your third guy?'

'Missing,' Pankhurst replied.

It was a strange thing, but as he spoke Pankhurst couldn't help but notice a flicker of edginess pass over Priestley's face, as though what he had just said was not what he wanted to hear. 'Missing?'

'We haven't found a body yet, but Will Jackson hasn't made contact. He's either dead or taken hostage.'

Priestley nodded his head, slowly. 'Of course,' he said. 'Of course. Look, Lowther, I apologise for just now—'

'No apology required, Don,' Pankhurst replied, politely, though he could sense that there was a hint of wariness in his own voice. 'It's a stressful situation for all of us. The Prime Minister has been informed and he's called a meeting of COBRA. We're working on the assumption that when Faisal Ahmed finds out what we did to his sister it will only spur him on. The city's on high alert. We might not be able to prevent what's coming, but perhaps we can limit the casualties.'

Priestley's eyes narrowed slightly. 'You'll let me know if you find Jackson's body, Lowther?'

Pankhurst looked at his CIA counterpart. There was no doubt about it. Priestley was edgy.

'Of course I will, Don,' he replied. 'Of course I will.'

★

Will bought a change of clothes in a nearby department store, then took a tube to North London. He knew where he was going, but he had to trust to chance that she would be in. There was no one else he felt he could trust and right now he needed help more than anything else. He found he could navigate to the terraced house almost on autopilot, and at 10 a.m. he was ringing the buzzer for the upstairs flat.

No answer. 'Shit,' he muttered under his breath, and continued walking down the street.

Every hour, on the hour, he tried the doorbell. No luck. 'She'll be at work,' a neighbour told him at midday. Will nodded gruffly, put his head down and walked away.

Come nightfall, he took up position at the corner of the street. It was just after eight o'clock that a black cab pulled up in front of the door. Will waited for the familiar figure to pay the driver and let herself into the flat before he approached again and rang the bell.

'Hello?'

Kate's voice sounded confused over the intercom, as though she was not used to receiving visitors at this time of night.

'It's me. Will.'

A pause. And then, almost kitten-like, 'Hello, Will.' The door buzzed and he pushed it open. He saw Kate waiting at the top of the stairs. 'You're an international man of mystery,' she giggled as he approached and Will wondered if she'd had a couple of drinks. 'I thought you'd swanned out of my life, never to return.'

'I'm full of surprises,' he replied. Now that he was standing in front of her, he could smell alcohol on her breath. She wasn't too far gone, just mellow. She needed her wits about her if she was going to do what he intended to ask her, so that meant waiting till morning.

'Aren't you though?' She stepped aside to let him in. 'Glass of wine?'

'Thanks,' Will said. He watched as her attractive figure sashayed into the kitchen where she filled him a large glass of chilled white, then handed it to him with a look that would have been mysterious if Will hadn't seen it before. In this new world of uncertainties one thing at least was clear: he wouldn't be sleeping alone tonight. He took a sip and closed his eyes as he felt the alcohol hit his chest, then spread its relaxing tendrils through his body. For one night, at least, no one knew where he was; he could do nothing until the morning; he could try and forget about it all. He finished his glass of wine quickly and it was swiftly replenished by Kate, but he never got a chance to finish it. Only two gulps in, she was pulling him meaningfully towards her and pressing her lips against his. Will offered no resistance.

It was a serious kind of kiss and when it was over he pushed her gently on to the sofa. She fell elegantly and looked up at him with a seductive smile. 'You know what?' she breathed. 'You've really made my evening.'

'Mine too,' Will replied, feeling the almost unbearable stresses of the last few days slip momentarily away. 'Mine too.'

They made love into the small hours and after that Will slept soundly. He awoke with the daylight to find Kate sitting up, a sheet wrapped around her. She was staring intently at him, her dark hair falling appealingly over the side of her face. Will smiled up at her.

'Where've you been?' she asked.

'Here and there,' he replied, evasively.

'You're not going to tell me.'

'I can't. There's lots of reasons why.'

'OK,' she said. 'If you won't tell me that, then tell me why you left the SAS.'

Will blinked. 'How did you—?'

'I'm a journalist, Will. It's what I do.'

'And do you do background research on all your one-night stands?'

'I'm not cheap,' Kate said suddenly, earnestly. 'I don't normally—'

Before she could finish, Will had raised his hand and gently put his forefinger against her lips. 'I know,' he said.

Kate nodded and Will had the impression she was glad to have got that off her chest. 'Why have you come back?' she asked, quietly.

'To see you.'

'You're a charmer, Will. But what's the real reason?'

Will took a deep breath. She was sharp. 'I need you to do something for me.'

Kate looked at him archly. 'I did quite a lot of things for you last night.'

He smiled. 'This is a bit different. I want you to make a phone call. I'd make it myself, but the people I need to get in touch with would recognise my voice and I can't let that happen.'

She looked at him seriously. 'Why not? Who am I phoning?'

'His name is Donald Priestley. He works for the CIA in London.'

Kate narrowed her eyes. 'Is this a wind-up, Will?'

He shook his head. 'No. It's not a wind-up. It's deadly serious. I'm trying to find out if Priestley's been doing—' He searched for the words. 'Something wrong,' he concluded, a bit inadequately. 'If he finds out I suspect anything about it, I'm a dead man walking.'

He had half expected Kate to panic when he spoke those words, but she didn't. 'And if he suspects that *I* know anything about it, what then?'

'That won't happen,' Will replied, confidently. 'Because firstly, I'm not going to tell you any more; and secondly, he'll never find out. Nobody in the world knows I've ever met you and we're going to keep it that way.' He took her by the hand. 'I'm sorry, Kate. To lay this on you and everything. But I don't know who else to ask and you have to trust me. People have died because of what this man is doing and if I don't get this right, a lot more will follow. Will you help me?'

Kate thought for a moment. 'I suppose there's not even an exclusive in it for me at the end of the day,' she said a bit wistfully.

'No,' Will enunciated the word clearly. 'Kate, when this is done you have to forget all about it. Believe me, if you start snooping around, they'll kill you.'

His words seemed to echo around the room. Kate looked at him, her eyes wide and her lips pursed. 'What do I need to do?' she whispered.

'We're going to go to a public telephone,' he said. 'Somewhere well away from here. You're going to pretend to be a journalist.' He smiled. 'That's the easy bit. When you get Priestley on the phone, you're going to tell him that you know all about a thing called Operation Firefight. He'll tell you he doesn't know anything about it, but you need to be persistent. Tell him you'll be waiting for him beneath Nelson's Column tonight at seven o'clock. Then put the phone down.'

'I don't have to meet the guy, do I?'

'No,' Will replied, his face grim. 'You don't have to do anything else. I'll take it from there.'

Kate fell silent. She was thinking carefully about what Will had just explained to her. 'There's no way they'll know it's me, is there?'

266

Will shook his head. 'Trust me,' he said. 'I'm good at this sort of thing.'

She gave a weak smile. 'Not the only thing you're good at,' she replied in a half-hearted attempt to lighten the mood. 'All right.' She said it quickly, as if she wanted to get the word out before she changed her mind. 'I'll do it.'

Will closed his eyes. 'Good girl,' he said, softly. 'Thank you.'

★

They needed to make the phone call from somewhere a decent distance away from Kate's house, but that wasn't all. Priestley would have the capability to trace where the phone call came from, so the phone box they used needed to be out of the way of any CCTV cameras. That put lots of places out of bounds – shopping centres, Tube stations, even busy streets where any of the shops could have hidden cameras. The obvious solution would be to take Kate out into the countryside and find a phone box in some out of the way village, but that wouldn't do either. If Priestley knew that his anonymous caller had gone to such lengths not to be discovered, he would start to suspect that she was more than just a journalist: he'd know she was a pro.

'I need to see your wardrobe,' he told Kate. She nodded silently – numbly, almost, as though she couldn't quite believe what she had got herself into – and opened up the large, white built-in wardrobes at the end of her bedroom. Will browsed through the clothes, selecting a heavy winter coat with a high collar, a scarf and a woollen hat with flaps that covered the ears – not the sort of thing he would have expected to find in Kate's bedroom, but which he was glad of nonetheless. 'Put them on,' he said shortly.

Kate did as she was told.

'Do you have some sunglasses?'

She nodded and pulled a large pair of Jackie-O type shades from a drawer.

'Perfect,' Will said. He looked out of the window. It was still raining. 'Umbrella?' he asked.

'Two,' Kate told him, and she fetched them from the hallway.

'Take the biggest one,' he said. 'It'll give you more cover.'

'I thought you said no one was going to see me, Will.'

'I did,' he replied. 'But this is just to make sure. Come on, we need to go.'

They took the Tube down to South London. Will left the platform first, Kate following a few metres behind – he hoped that if anybody did clock them or go back and see them on CCTV, they would never think that they were together. Even if they did, Kate's features were sufficiently disguised for her to be unrecognisable.

Once they got up to street level, they started walking – Will on one side of the road, Kate on the other, a few steps behind. They had agreed that they would walk quite some distance – several Tube stops, at least, so that if anyone decided to check camera footage from the stations nearest the phone box they ended up using, they would be thrown off the scent. It didn't take long for Will to become wet through in the rain, but Kate at least had the large umbrella, which not only kept her dry but also kept her head out of sight.

After an hour walking, they came to a residential area. Terraced houses – no estates where CCTV would be all over the place. At the end of the road Will spotted a phone booth. It was just what he was looking for. He stopped and looked across the street at Kate, gave her a surreptitious nod, then watched as she walked on towards the phone box.

All he could do now was wait.

Christ, he thought to himself. He'd been doing a lot of waiting in the last few days, but for some reason this seemed more agonising than any of it. He was convinced that

Kate would be safe – that wasn't the problem. The problem was that now he was on his own. What if his little plan didn't work? What if, by the end of the day, he was as much in the dark as ever? What would he do then?

It was only ten minutes later that Kate returned, but it seemed much longer. She was walking hurriedly away from the phone box with her head down. Will let her pass, then started to follow. They walked in a random direction for at least half an hour before he caught up with her.

'Well?' he asked.

Kate looked up at him with wide eyes. 'I'm frightened,' she told him. He took her hand. It was shaking.

'Did you speak to Priestley?'

She nodded her head. 'He wouldn't speak to me at first,' she said. 'I got his secretary. But I said the words Operation Firefight and he was on the phone almost immediately.'

I'll bet he was, Will thought to himself grimly. 'What did he say?'

'Just what you thought he'd say. That he didn't know what I was talking about. So I gave him your message about meeting at Trafalgar Square tonight and—' She faltered.

'And what, Kate?'

'And then I just hung up. I'm sorry, Will. I lost my nerve. I don't think he really thought I was a journalist.' She shrugged a little sadly. 'Truth is, I'm *not* much of one.'

Will smiled. 'You did just fine, Kate,' he said. 'Just fine.' He gave her a brief hug and she clung to him. 'I have to go now,' he whispered.

'I know.' She sounded like she was fighting back tears.

'I'm going to give you my number. If you ever get worried about—'

'No,' Kate interrupted him. She released herself from his embrace and looked seriously into his eyes. 'I don't know what all this is about, Will, but if what you tell me is true, it's best that I don't know anything more about you.'

There was a pause and Will felt uneasy. She was right, of course. The less she knew, the less she could tell. But he didn't like the idea. He didn't like it at all.

She was clearly determined, though. 'I'm going to walk away now,' she said, her voice cracking slightly. She stood up on tiptoes and kissed him rather chastely on the cheek. 'Good luck, Will.'

And with that, she turned and left. Will stood and watched her go, watched until she turned a distant corner and walked out of his sight.

It was with a sense of total certainty that he realised he would never see her again.

SEVENTEEN

Will had chosen Trafalgar Square for a reason.

If Priestley was worried, if he thought Kate's call was more than just a crank, there would be surveillance here tonight – snipers for his protection and someone to photograph whoever he met. Will had decided on Trafalgar Square because he knew he could put a pretty good bet on where the surveillance would be set up. The roof of the National Gallery offered a full vista over the square and if Will had been instructed to sct up surveillance over the place, that's where he would have chosen.

He had returned to Paddington Station just after 15.00 hours to pick up his rucksack from the left-luggage locker. His plan had been to travel to the West End by underground, but when he got to the Tube station he saw that it was being patrolled by armed police – the unmistakable signs of a city on high terrorist alert. He couldn't risk trying to get into the underground with a rucksack full of weaponry on his back – chances were that he'd be stopped and searched and all hell would break loose.

Instead he hailed a black cab, which took him to Covent Garden. It was early evening by the time he arrived in the West End. He approached Trafalgar Square from the north, down Charing Cross Road and into St Martin's Place, grateful for the swarming crowds into which it was possible to melt anonymously. Approaching from this direction meant that he didn't have to cross Trafalgar Square in order to reach his destination, an advantage because he couldn't be sure how early any surveillance would be set up and it was essential that he wasn't spotted.

There was building work in progress at the church of St Martin-in-the-Fields, which meant there was scaffolding outside it, all the way up to the clock tower. He hadn't counted on that, but it was going to help. The five-thirty evensong service was in progress and the church was nearly half full. As Will slipped inside, he hoped his casual clothes and rucksack made him look like an aimless tourist there to see the sights and for a good ten minutes he stood at the back of that impressive church, listening to the monotone voice of the priest intoning a sermon. It was nearly dark outside and the huge chandeliers cast a warm yellow glow over the heavy wooden pews, illuminating the intricate patterning of the ceiling.

Will wasn't interested in the church's decorative qualities, however, nor the priest's no doubt well-meaning message. He could pray to his God for peace to all men as much as he liked, but Will knew that sometimes peace came at a greater price. That price was war and just at the moment he felt like a one-man army fighting a battle with an enemy he could never defeat through strength alone. He continued to stand at the back, looking around. Anyone who saw him would think he was just taking in the surroundings, but in fact he was searching for something quite specific.

There were two ornate balconies along the length of each side of the church and at the altar end there was a door, which he presumed led up to them. As the service came to a close and the disparate congregation rose to their collective feet and started milling about the aisle, Will edged around the side of the pews and headed for the door that he hoped would take him upwards. He opened it confidently, as if he had every right to do so and, sure enough, behind it was a flight of stone steps. He hurried up them, two at a time.

He reached the top of the stairs and looked around. There was a door leading to the balcony, but a second flight of steps headed upwards. Will was just about to climb them when he heard a voice.

'May I help you?'

He turned round to see a black-robed priest smiling blandly at him.

Will blinked. 'I was just coming up to the balcony,' he replied, instinctively. 'I just wanted somewhere quiet to sit and—'

'Reflect?' the priest completed his sentence for him. He stepped to one side and indicated the balcony door. For the first time since he had put it on, Will felt the rucksack full of military equipment digging into his back. 'You should find it more peaceful up here than downstairs on the dance floor.' The priest's smile grew broader at his own little joke.

'Thank you,' Will murmured. He stepped on to the balcony and took a seat at the end of the pew. He'd give it a couple of minutes before he made his way up the stairs again. He bowed his head in an expression of mock piety and waited.

Two minutes passed and when Will checked, the priest had left. He silently slipped up the stairs which wound upwards in a circular fashion. The sound of the congregation's hubbub down below faded away, as did the light. By the time Will had navigated his way up into the bell tower he was practically engulfed in darkness. And that suited him just fine.

The four sides of the bell tower were open to the elements and from this vantage point – beyond the scaffolding – Will had a reasonable view of Trafalgar Square and the crowds and traffic that thronged around it. But more importantly, he looked down on to the roof of the National Gallery. From here, he would be able to see everything he needed.

He glanced at his watch. Ten past six. Just under an hour until the meeting time. From his rucksack he removed the small NV binoculars he had taken from the stake-out and put them to his eye. A flick of the switch and the roof of the National Gallery was instantly illuminated in a dull green glow. He zoomed in closer and examined the area.

No one. Not yet.

Switching off the power, he sat down behind the wall of the bell tower. Out of sight, just where he needed to be.

Every fifteen minutes, he checked. He felt comfortable that no one would see him up here – they would be doing surveillance for a civilian on the ground. But at half past six there was still no one. At quarter to seven, no one. Will began to feel on edge. What if Ahmed had been stringing him a lie? What if Operation Firefight was no more than a creation of the Afghan's warped imagination?

Will looked at his watch. Five to seven. He closed his eyes, took a deep breath, then switched on his NV binoculars for another look over the rooftops.

He didn't see them at first, as they seemed somehow to blend into their surroundings. But after a few seconds of looking, a figure suddenly jumped out at him. He zoomed in closer. The man was wearing a helmet and some sort of flak jacket. But he wasn't carrying a gun, as Will might have expected. He was carrying a camera with a telescopic lens and it was pointed out towards Trafalgar Square.

And then, as soon as one of them had caught his eye, he saw the rest. There were maybe five or six in total – two of them with cameras, the others with sniper guns, trained and waiting, ready for anything suspicious.

It was all he needed to see. Confirmation. Now he could leave and implement the next part of his plan.

But then, curiosity got the better of him. He turned his

binoculars away from the surveillance team on top of the National Gallery, aiming it instead towards the throng of Trafalgar Square. There were hundreds of people there, milling around, gazing up at Nelson's Column or sitting on the vast stone lions that kept guard. Hundreds of them. But at the foot of the enormous plinth, standing still and in clear view of the surveillance team, was a man. Will had to concentrate on steadying his hands so that he could get the figure in view and as he did so he zoomed in closely on his face.

Donald Priestley stood alone, his hands plunged firmly into his pockets to ward off the cold. Even at this distance Will could see that his jaw was set, his face grim. Every now and then his eyes would flicker upwards and it was clear to Will that the CIA man was aware of the surveillance team high above him.

Will switched off the binoculars and stowed them safely in his rucksack. For some reason the sight of Priestley had both shocked and exhilarated him. The CIA man had taken the bait; all he had to do now was reel him in. However, Priestley would be on high alert and it would take all of Will's powers of deception and persuasion to implement the next stage of his plan.

But I've got you running scared now, you bastard, he thought to himself as he hurried down the stairs to the main body of the church.

I've got you running scared.

★

Donald Priestley poured himself a large whisky, downed it, replenished his glass and then took a seat on the leather sofa. The plush house on West Halkin Street in Mayfair that came with the job was warm and comfortable, yet the American felt chilled to the bone – not only from standing outside in the cold as part of this evening's wild goose chase, but also out of uneasiness. The phone call from that woman had knocked him off-kilter. Who the hell was she? Some hack trying her luck, acting on the back of a rumour? But where could she have got such a rumour? Only two people in the country knew about Operation Firefight: Priestley himself and Faisal Ahmed. His secretary knew the name, but not what it meant. And stateside it was hardly common knowledge – only the highest echelons of the CIA were in on it. Even the White House weren't aware of the policy.

But this wasn't Ahmed's style – Christ knows, Priestley had done enough work to try and get inside the man's head of late. No, something else was going on. He took another sip of his whisky, leaned back on the sofa and closed his eyes.

It scared him shitless that Faisal Ahmed was out there. He had been certain that blowing Ahmed's cover in the British terrorist organisations he had infiltrated on the CIA's behalf would have been the end of him – those bastards were animals and ruthless with it. More fool him, he supposed, for underestimating the job his countrymen had done of training the bloodthirsty Afghan in the first place. And he'd been even more of a fool for thinking that the British, with their stiff upper lips and excruciating sense of fair play, would have been able to locate Ahmed, even after his people had planted the idea in their minds that he was going to blow up half of London. How a halfwit like Lowther Pankhurst had ever made it to DG of MI5, he'd never know.

'*Shit!*' he said out loud to himself. The sooner he was called back to Langley, the better. He looked around him. At least this place was secure – guards on all the doors and high-level security at all the entrances and exits. A perk of the job and one he was glad of – he only really felt safe when he was at home.

A buzzer sounded. Priestley got to his feet and wandered

over to the heavy mahogany desk, pressing a button on the little intercom his staff used to communicate with him. 'Yeah?'

Another American voice came over the loudspeaker. 'There's a guy at the front entrance, Mr Priestley, insists on seeing you. Says his name is Will Jackson. Shall I get rid of him?'

Priestley paused and his eyes momentarily narrowed. 'Will Jackson?'

'That's right, sir.'

Again he fell silent. Will Jackson. Back from the dead — and on the very day that someone had spooked him about Operation Firefight. Coincidence? Unbidden, an old saying came into his head. *Keep your friends close, but your enemies closer.*

'Show him up,' Priestley instructed. He sat down again on the leather sofa and waited.

Moments later, Jackson was standing in the doorway to his room.

'Will,' Priestley greeted him, warily. 'Don't take this the wrong way, but I'm surprised to see you here.'

Jackson's face gave no clue to what he was thinking. 'I'm kind of lucky to *be* here, sir,' he replied.

Priestley inclined his head. 'Well, you'd better come in. What can I fix you to drink?'

'Nothing.'

'Fair enough, Will. Have a seat and tell me, does Lowther Pankhurst know you're still — ?' His voice trailed away.

'Alive?' Jackson supplied. 'Probably not. I came to you first.'

'But not immediately, Will. You've been missing for nearly forty-eight hours.'

For a moment it seemed to Priestley that Jackson wasn't going to answer; he suddenly seemed like his mind was somewhere completely different. But eventually he spoke.

'I don't suppose you'll ever know what it's like,' he said in little more than a whisper. 'To come so close to catching the man who murdered your family and to watch him get away. Don't take it personally, but I didn't really feel like a dressing-down from you and Lowther Pankhurst until I got my head in order.'

Priestley inclined his head a little. The man *sounded* sincere, at least. 'I suppose you know about your colleagues.'

Jackson nodded. 'Ahmed got the better of us. You weren't joking when you told us he was good. He managed to get me out of the way, nail Drew and Kennedy, then escape with his sister. A pretty spectacular fuck-up, all in all.'

'I won't pretend I don't agree with that, Will. Pankhurst's kind of pissed too. Hell, that's the understatement of the year.'

A pause. Priestley stood up and looked out of the ornate window and the prison-like bars beyond. 'So you didn't see or speak to Ahmed,' he said, lightly.

'Oh, I spoke to him all right.'

Priestley felt a sudden coldness in his blood. He turned slowly to look at the SAS man.

'I chased him,' Jackson continued. 'I chased him and caught up with him.'

'Why the *hell*—?' Priestley spat, before suddenly gaining control of his emotions. 'What – why the hell didn't you shoot him?'

'Because he had an MP5 with laser sights aimed at my head,' Jackson replied, 'and he made me discharge my weapon into the ground.'

Priestley's lips went thin. 'Why didn't he just kill you?' the CIA man asked. It was framed as a question, but Priestley knew it was more like wishful thinking.

'Because Latifa told him not to. Seems she was grateful to me for getting her out of the Stan and from stopping your boys from waterboarding her.'

'Maybe if "my boys" had waterboarded her a bit more,' Priestley couldn't stop himself from saying, 'we wouldn't be in this situation.'

'I don't think so,' Jackson replied, quietly.

Priestley breathed out heavily in frustration and struggled to control his temper. He looked straight into Jackson's eyes. 'What else did Ahmed say, Will?'

Jackson's face remained unreadable. 'He asked me if it was you who sent me to kill him.'

Priestley continued to breathe steadily. 'And what did you tell him, Will?'

'He had an MP5 aimed at my head. I told him the truth. He said he wasn't surprised. His exact words were, "Don Priestley knows the next bullet I have is for him."'

Jackson's words themselves were like bullets and Priestley steadied himself by holding on to the corner of the large wooden desk. 'Why did he say that, Will?'

So much rested on the SAS man's answer.

'I was hoping you might be able to tell *me* that,' Jackson replied. 'I'm afraid neither of us were in the mood for an extended chat. He made me turn around and walk away. When I looked again, he was gone.' Jackson stared at him thoughtfully. 'Why you, sir?' he asked. 'Why would Faisal Ahmed want *you* dead before anyone else?'

Priestley nodded, slowly. Was Jackson telling the truth? The CIA man had been trained to tell when someone was lying and he could see none of the telltale signifiers. But years in the job had taught Priestley to make suspicion his default position. He still hadn't forgotten about the charade in Trafalgar Square and although Jackson had said nothing to suggest he knew about Firefight, he had equally said nothing to suggest he didn't.

'Why are you here, Will?' he asked, plainly. 'Why are you reporting all this to me and not to Pankhurst? He's your handler.'

'I don't have a handler,' Jackson replied with a sudden burst of anger. 'I left the Regiment two years ago and to my knowledge I never signed up again. Pankhurst's been using me, manipulating me for his own ends. Fuck it, you both have. But all *I* want to do is kill Faisal Ahmed. Pankhurst's leads have all dried up, so it seems to me that you and I can help each other.'

Priestley blinked. 'I'm not sure I quite follow you, Will.'

'Ahmed told me straight that he's got a bullet with your name on it. Seems to me that if I want to get to him, all I have to do is hang around you.'

'Forgive me, Will, but I don't quite see what *I* get out of it.'

'A bodyguard,' Jackson replied. 'Twenty-four seven.'

Priestley smiled, but he was aware of it being a rather sickly smile – the sort of smile that only a man talking about his own potential assassination could give. 'That's very kind of you, Will,' he said. 'But my position is such that if I want a bodyguard, I really only have to say the word.'

Jackson shrugged. 'That's up to you,' he said. He stood up and now it was his turn to look through the window. He paused. 'When he comes for you,' he said, his voice subdued, 'it won't be in a dark alleyway like in the movies. It'll be when you least expect it. In a crowd, in a restaurant, when you're lying in bed – sometime when you feel safe.' He turned back to the CIA man. 'I'm the only person you can call on who's seen Ahmed in the last five years. I've looked into his eyes. I'll recognise him in an instant. Have me by your side and you might even live to see Christmas.'

Priestley fell into a terrified silence. There really wasn't much he could say to that.

'And there's one other thing,' Jackson added. 'Faisal Ahmed really wants you dead. I don't know why and I don't reckon

I'll ever find out. But this terrorist attack of yours, I think it's just a red herring.'

Priestley did his best to remain expressionless.

'But you know what? I don't care. You and Pankhurst can play your little games as much as you like. Ahmed killed my family and I want him dead. I want *him* dead even more than he wants *you* dead. If you think that's a resource you can just ignore, then fine. But it'll be your funeral, sir, so you'd better start planning it.'

Jackson's stark warning seemed to ring in the air and sent a chill all the way through Priestley's body. Perhaps this SAS man whom MI5 seemed to trust so implicitly was right. Perhaps there was something to be said for going along with his proposal.

At least for now.

The guy *really* wanted Ahmed's head on a plate, that much was beyond doubt. Why not let him do what he wanted? After all, once Ahmed was dead, Priestley could deal with Will Jackson more permanently.

He nodded his head. 'All right, Will,' he said gravely. 'You've got yourself a deal.'

★

Latifa Ahmed watched her brother as he slept.

The flat in which they were staying – fifteen floors up a vast concrete tower block on a council estate fifty miles out of London – was more like a fortress than a home. Huge bolts sealed the front entrance closed and there was weaponry and ammunition everywhere. This was not a room designed for comfort. Latifa knew that Faisal had places like this dotted all over the country. When they had arrived, however, she hadn't been able to stop herself from sounding like her mother, dead these thirty years, and asking him how he could call such a place home.

Faisal's answer had been simple. 'I would rather be alive in a prison than dead in a home.'

He lay now on a thin mattress on the floor, his ever-present gun by his side. It seemed to her that she had never seen Faisal without his weapon, not since he was a child of ten. She had never actually witnessed him killing anybody, though, not until he rescued her a couple of nights previously. He had shot those two men so unthinkingly, showing such a lack of remorse, that she could not help looking at him differently now. It had been all she could do, slung over his shoulder as they escaped that house, to beg him not to kill Will Jackson, the man who – despite everything – had done so much for her. Faisal hadn't been pleased with the idea, but she felt she had at least done something to stop the bloodshed.

He had been such an idealistic little boy; but now, looking at his chest rising and falling and at the surroundings in which they found themselves, she could not help wondering what it was he was fighting for. Maybe the fight itself was everything.

Faisal's eyes flickered open and his hand moved automatically to his weapon as he snapped himself into awareness. He smiled at Latifa when he realised she was there; but she found herself unable to return that smile.

'You have been looking at me in that way ever since we got here,' Faisal said in quiet Pashto as he stood up and walked to the sink to splash cold water on his face.

'I keep thinking of the men you shot, Faisal,' she replied. 'Does it not bother you?'

He sighed. 'I have already told you, Latifa,' he said, impatiently. 'It was them or me. Would you have preferred to see *me* lying dead on the floor?'

'Of course not,' she murmured.

'They were soldiers, Latifa. Soldiers die. They knew that when they came after me.'

Latifa tried to bite her tongue. She knew she ought not

to ask the question that was on her lips, but suddenly she couldn't help herself. 'And what of the little girl, Faisal? Will Jackson's little girl. Was she a soldier too?'

Faisal suddenly slammed his fist on the wall. 'I have explained that to you,' he shouted. 'Do not ask me about it again.'

And then Latifa was on her feet, hobbling towards her brother, who had menace in his eyes. His breath was shaking. 'Do not try to scare me like you scare them, Faisal,' she whispered. 'I am your sister. Have you forgotten what I have undergone to keep you safe?'

He lowered his eyes.

'When that man told me what you did to his family, I did not believe him. I did not *want* to believe him. I did not think you could do such a thing. But you have changed, Faisal. You have turned into something you never meant to be.'

'It was not supposed to happen,' he told her. 'It was an accident.'

'An *accident*? How can you say that? It was a little girl and her mother. How can you carry on with this way of life with such an *accident* weighing on your shoulders? Can you not see that it was only a matter of time before such a thing happened? That it will happen again?'

Faisal looked defiantly at her; but for all his fierceness she saw nothing more than the little boy she had once known. She stretched out her arms and cupped his face in her hands.

'Can you not see,' she whispered, 'that this will only end one way? The Taliban nearly killed you as they nearly killed me. We have both been given a second chance at life, Faisal. We must not squander it. What will I do if you are killed and I have no one else left in the whole world?'

Brother and sister looked deep into each other's eyes, but Faisal could not weather that stare for long. He moved her hands away from his face. 'You don't understand,' he said.

283

'For years I did the Americans' bidding. For *years*, Latifa. I was one of them. I believed I was fighting for the right side. Even when they asked me to start making phoney terrorist attacks against the British, I believed it was the right thing to do.' He turned back to look at her again. 'Believe me, Latifa. When that woman and child died, no one was more anguished than me. But then they asked me to start killing innocent civilians and I knew it was wrong.'

His brow was furrowed now and his features seemed strangely tortured. 'Can you not think what it must have been like, to realise that the people you have served all your life are not what you thought they were? Can you not understand how difficult it was to deny them? And can you not see the depth of their betrayal? After all I had risked for them, to leave me to the vultures.' Faisal's nostrils flared and he looked away from his sister.

'We can leave here,' Latifa whispered. 'Leave this country. Hide away. We don't need to have anything more to do with these people, Faisal. You cannot fight the might of the Americans, so why risk your life doing it?'

'Because I'm a soldier. All my life I have fought for someone. But now, I fight for myself.' His eyes flashed. 'Donald Priestley will pay for what he did to me, Latifa. I will not have it any other way.'

His words seemed to puncture Latifa's soul. 'And after him,' she asked. 'What then? Where will it end, Faisal? *When* will it end, all this killing? What about Will Jackson? He is a good man, but I have seen the hate in his eyes when he speaks your name.'

Faisal frowned. 'I am grateful to Will Jackson for what he did for you, Latifa, and I spared his life at your request. But I will not do so again. I do not blame him for wanting me dead – in his position I would want the same. But if he is foolish enough to come searching for me, he knows the stakes. He knows I will not hesitate to kill him.'

Latifa closed her eyes. It was impossible for her to express to her brother the deep sadness she felt at hearing his words; impossible for her to relay the dreadful sense of foreboding that seemed to permeate to her very core.

'But what,' she asked, her voice hesitant, 'if he kills you first?'

As she spoke, Faisal had his back to her. But when he heard those words, he turned his head and glanced over his shoulder. The look he gave her almost stopped Latifa's heart. In that instant, perhaps for the first time ever, she saw not the little boy she had taken care of all those years ago in a small village in Afghanistan; she saw not even the idealistic young teenager who spent his days picking off hated Russian soldiers with his well maintained AK-47; nor even the CIA-trained agent who had managed to infiltrate the highest levels of al-Qaeda for so many years.

She saw none of these things. Instead, standing before her, she seemed to see a different person. The contours of his shoulder muscles were pronounced and sinewy; his jaw was set; his lips unsmiling. But it was his eyes that shocked her most of all. They were flat. Emotionless. Murderous. The cold, unfeeling eyes of a killer.

And for the first time in her life, Latifa Ahmed felt afraid of her brother.

He did not answer her question, but that look told Latifa everything she needed to know. She bowed her head and stared out of the window while Faisal bent over, picked up his weapon and started taking it to bits, preparing to clean it.

Preparing to use it. And soon.

EIGHTEEN

CIA Headquarters, Langley, Virginia, USA.

Bradley Heller, Director of the Central Intelligence Agency, and Tyler Moore, Director of National Intelligence, sat on opposite sides of a large mahogany desk. The DCIA's office was richly appointed, with expensive art on the walls, comfortable furniture and floor-to-ceiling windows that looked out over a neatly kept lawn that nobody other than the carefully vetted groundsmen ever walked upon. It was bright, clear and cold outside; inside it was invitingly warm. Between them was a steaming pot of coffee that Heller's PA had just brought in before leaving them to their discussions.

Despite the comfortable surroundings, however, the DCIA and the DNI were troubled.

'I want to just keep you in the loop about the situation in London,' Heller told his colleague. Bradley Heller was a tall man in his mid-sixties with thinning grey hair and a deeply lined face. Tyler Moore was younger by several years, but he still seemed older than his actual age.

'Have they located Ahmed?'

Heller shook his head. 'And they've lost the sister.'

Moore gave him a look as if to say, *These goddamn British.*

'I know,' Heller replied. 'I know. One of their guys caught up with him, but Ahmed got away.' He handed Moore a thin file across the desk.

Moore opened it. 'Will Jackson,' he murmured, before

starting to read. It took him four or five minutes to absorb everything in the file. 'Quite a resumé,' he noted as he finished.

'It seems he and Faisal Ahmed had a conversation before Jackson let him get away.'

Moore's eyes narrowed. 'A conversation? Where did they meet, a gentlemen's club?'

'Hardly that,' Heller murmured.

'You think this Will Jackson knows? About Firefight, I mean?'

Heller took a sip of his coffee. 'Impossible to say,' he replied, his voice measured. 'We've got no direct evidence to suggest that Ahmed told him anything; but we'd be foolish to assume that Jackson's in the dark.'

A silence fell between the two of them as they both considered the implications of what Heller had just said.

'Of course,' the DCIA continued after a moment, 'we can make a reasonable assumption that Ahmed's sister is in the know. And now this Will Jackson. Firefight relies on its secrecy, but we suddenly seem to be springing leaks.'

Moore sniffed. 'Leaks can be plugged.'

'Of course,' Heller replied. 'But you have to find them first. We've no idea where the sister is at the moment.'

'What about Jackson?'

Heller inclined his head. 'Jackson's a bit easier.' He handed Moore an A4-sized photograph. 'You know Don Priestley, of course.'

Moore nodded, recognising Priestley's features in the photo.

'The man just behind him,' Heller continued, 'is Jackson. He claims Ahmed is planning a hit on Priestley.'

Moore looked dubious. 'Why would Ahmed admit that to Jackson?'

'My thought exactly. But Priestley seems to think Jackson's telling the truth.' He sipped at his drink once more. 'I know

Don very well,' he said. 'His instincts are good and right now he's running scared. He called me personally yesterday, requesting a transfer back to Langley.'

'Will you be granting it?'

'No,' Heller said, firmly.

'But do you think Ahmed is really—?'

'I think it's possible, yes.'

'Then we should—'

'Please, Tyler,' Heller held up a hand. 'Hear me out. Jackson has offered to bodyguard Priestley in the hope of getting a crack at Ahmed. Hardly regulation, I know, but in the circumstances it's quite neat. At the very least having Priestley on the ground gives us a chance of drawing Ahmed out into the open. And it keeps Jackson close. I've instructed Priestley to go along with Jackson. That way we can eliminate him once he's served his purpose.'

Moore raised an eyebrow.

'Look at the options,' Heller continued. 'If Jackson kills Ahmed, our problem goes away. If Ahmed kills Jackson, then at least one of our potential leaks has been plugged. And if his target is Priestley, he's going to want to take out Jackson first, wouldn't you say?'

'I guess so,' Moore replied. 'But what if he doesn't? What if he gets Priestley first? He's an American, Bradley. He's one of us.'

Heller nodded. 'I know,' he said, quietly. 'I don't like it any more than you do. But we can't get sentimental about this. If word of Firefight leaks we'll be facing an international crisis. I don't think the world needs the US and the British at each other's throats just now, do you?'

Moore took a deep breath. 'Of course not.'

'And anyway,' Heller continued. 'If Jackson gets through this, we know where he is. It won't take long for us to find out if he knows about Firefight. And if he does, well then – we'll be in a position to deal with it, won't we?'

Moore bit his lip. The longer he did this job, the more difficult it became to unwind the strands of right and wrong. In fact, he wasn't even sure that he knew what those words meant any more. He wondered if, given a few years, he would become quite as unaffected by the moral murk as Heller seemed to be. How many times do you have to make decisions like this, he asked himself, before they stop keeping you up at night?

'At what stage do we take this to the President?' Moore asked.

'We don't,' Heller said, firmly. 'We've gone to great lengths to make Operation Firefight officially deniable. Our duty to the President is very clear and that's to keep him in the dark. The moment he's informed about what has been going on, we start playing a whole new ball game.'

Tyler Moore stood up from his seat. 'Thanks for keeping me informed, Bradley,' he said, softly.

Heller inclined his head and, as Moore turned his back on him, he was sure he could feel the DCIA's eyes watching him as he made for the door. Before he could leave, Heller spoke again.

'We're at war, Tyler,' the DCIA said softly. 'It's a war on terror, but it's still a war. Wars are ugly and sacrifices have to be made.'

Moore turned and the two men stared at each other.

'I know,' the DNI replied, before leaving the room, closing the door quietly behind him.

★

'I've been meaning to ask you, Will,' Don Priestley spoke from the back of the car with an air of forced nonchalance. 'How did Ahmed get past you? How did he manage to spirit his sister away when security was so tight?'

Will steered the CIA man's car along the narrow backstreets of Belgravia. Like you don't fucking know, he thought to himself. Like you haven't been briefed by Five down to the last fucking detail. He glanced into his rear-view mirror. Priestley was sitting in the middle of the back seat – he had started doing that, Will had noticed, ever since the SAS man had insisted that they drive a car with blacked-out, bullet-proof glass. He wanted to be as far away from a bullet as he could. They were returning from a meeting in the West End and the London rush hour was in full flow. They'd be back at Priestley's place in a few minutes, however. Not that that meant any let-up for Will.

He'd been guarding Priestley for two days now and it was 24–7. The only time he managed to catnap was when the CIA man was in meetings in places Will deemed to be reasonably secure. Although he had learned to his cost that Ahmed could never be taken for granted, the chances of the Afghan assassin showing up at one of these venues were pretty slim. The US embassy was one such place. Even better was the top-secret United States communication base. It was in a secure basement behind Regent Street and Priestley would be in there for a couple of hours at a time, granting Will a block of solid sleep. The rest of the time he was surviving on ephedrine.

Priestley's home was a different matter. Having insisted that the CIA man move into a bedroom with no windows and only a single entrance, Will had to stay up all night in the adjoining room, his weapon in his hand and his mind in a state of high alert. The main entrance to the house might be guarded; the windows might be barred; but Will knew from bitter experience that Faisal Ahmed could get past almost any security.

Priestley caught sight of the fact that Will was looking at him in the mirror and his eyes flickered away.

'He created a diversion,' Will said in answer to the CIA man's question. 'We had motion sensors around the house, so as he approached he dropped a wounded animal on the perimeter.'

'What sort of animal?'

'A cat.'

'Sick bastard.'

Will grunted. 'Clever bastard, actually. Once he was in the house he got up into the loft and waited twenty-four hours. That was the really clever bit. We were on high alert after the motion sensors were triggered, so he waited for us to get back into our comfort zone before he struck. He put a small remote-controlled detonating device in the fuse box, so when the moment came he could kill the lights.' Will felt the muscles in his jaw tighten. 'It was ballsy, but I should have predicted it.'

There was a silence in the car.

'Diversionary tactics,' Priestley said after a moment.

'What?'

'Diversionary tactics,' he replied. 'Ahmed's file said he had a particular skill for them.' He looked up into the rear-view mirror and the two men locked gazes again. 'It's what he's good at, Will,' the CIA man said quietly, but with a certain emphasis. 'Putting people on the wrong track. Stringing them a lie.'

Will remained silent. This wasn't the first time he'd been at the receiving end of Priestley's subtle probing. The guy still wasn't sure how much Will knew and at this moment he was trying to plant the seeds of doubt in his mind.

'Don't worry about it,' Will replied, deliberately misinterpreting Priestley's meaning. 'I understand him now. I know how he works. He's not going to be able to pull a trick like that again.'

'I hope you're right, Will,' Priestley murmured. 'I hope you're right.'

They arrived at Priestley's place in West Halkin Street soon after that. It was a large London townhouse with a red brick façade and big white windows. To look at them, you wouldn't know that they were glazed with tough, shatterproof glass. Will parked the car in the dedicated space by the front door, then picked up the handgun that he routinely kept in the glove compartment. Stepping out of the vehicle, he glanced up and down the street, then up to the rooftops as he always did, before opening the rear passenger door and ushering Priestley quickly up to the front door. An armed police officer in a black flak jacket and helmet greeted them with a cursory nod, then opened the door and allowed them to step inside.

'Let me go first,' Will reminded Priestley. It was the way he had told the CIA man they were going to do things. Whenever they entered a house or a room, Will went first. That way he could immediately check it out. At least that was what he had told Priestley.

Priestley might have accepted Will as his bodyguard, but that wasn't the only precaution he was taking. The guy was scared. Shit-scared – anyone could tell that. Will had heard the CIA man's panicked phone calls to Langley, trying to get himself reassigned, out of the country and away from the vengeance of Faisal Ahmed. But his superiors weren't having it and each time they said no, Priestley turned a more ghostly shade of pale. They had upped his security, though. The armed policeman on the door was one thing, but anti-terrorist officers had done a sweep of the house, identifying weak security points and fixing them. Most of the house was covered by CCTV, each camera bearing a little red light that indicated at a glance that you were under surveillance. Priestley couldn't even take a shit without some guy off-site watching him doing so on a bank of video screens. Priestley didn't complain – in fact, Will could tell, it made him feel better. For everything the CIA man had said about Faisal Ahmed's training and skill, he still thought that he was well protected by the standard protocols of the security services.

Will, on the other hand, knew better.

Once they were both inside the house, Priestley closed the door behind him. The hallway was smartly appointed. It stretched almost the full depth of the house and had a black and white marble chequerboard on the floor. At one end, to the left, was a grand flight of stairs with a sweeping balustrade. There were large mirrors on the wall and art that Will would never have recognised.

Priestley removed his coat and instinctively handed it to Will.

'I'm not your butler,' Will told him, his eyes checking all the exits to the room out of habit.

Priestley looked as if he was about to say something, but clearly thought better of it. He slung his coat over the back of a chair. 'So,' he joked humourlessly. 'What shall we do tonight?'

'If you're finding this boring,' Will told him, 'say the word and I'll go out and catch a movie.'

'No,' Priestley said, his voice resigned. 'It's OK. Same routine as usual?'

'Same routine.'

Together they climbed the stairs – Priestley first, then Will, firmly gripping the holster of his handgun. The area where they spent their evenings was at the end of a thickly carpeted corridor: one large room, comfortably furnished with a large desk and an elegant chaise longue. The room had a fashionable patterned wallpaper and thick curtains – which Will insisted were kept closed at all times. A crystal chandelier hung from the middle of the ceiling. As you walked in, there was a door on the right-hand wall which led to a second room with a bathroom en suite. They walked into the main room and closed the door.

'I need to, er—' Priestley made a slightly embarrassed gesture.

Will looked at his watch. 6.30 p.m. Regular as fucking

clockwork. He nodded, then brushed past Priestley, through the bedroom and into the bathroom. The CIA man followed him and stood watching at the door, while Will checked the marble-clad bathroom. There were bars outside the window, but he peered out just in case, looking for signs of tampering. Once he was satisfied that all was as it should be, he nodded at Priestley. 'Go ahead,' he told him.

Priestley walked into the room, a rather hangdog expression on his face, while Will left. He shut the door and stood guard outside.

It had been a long forty-eight hours. Just being with Priestley, the man murkily implicated in what had happened to his family, was strain enough, let alone the constant watching. The constant waiting. Every second he expected something to happen. Every second he expected to see Faisal Ahmed coming at him.

It would happen. He knew it would. And when it did, Will just had to be ready. He had to make sure that his plan was sound.

From the bathroom, suddenly, there was a noise.

Breaking glass.

Will felt his skin tingle, then a calm descended upon him. It was always like this when you went into battle. The wait was agonising, but when the moment arrived everything kicked in. The training, the preparation – it happened without thinking. He pressed himself against the wall to one side of the door and raised the handgun.

He listened carefully: the shuffling of feet.

Any minute now, he thought to himself. Give yourself a few moments. Burst in now and he'll be expecting you; hold back for a moment and you'll have the element of surprise.

His mind was acutely clear. Crystalline.

He took a deep breath. With one foot he kicked the door open and burst into the bathroom, his gun pointing out in front of him, his finger poised on the trigger, ready to shoot.

Priestley was alone. He was standing at the sink, his trousers still unbuckled and his shirt hanging out. He looked at the handgun with horror.

Will's eyes darted around the room. Only at the last moment did he see the glass smashed on the floor.

'I – I dropped it,' Priestley stuttered, his face white. 'I – I'm sorry. I just got kind of panicky, and my hand started trembling—' He looked down at himself, at his state of semi-undress, and an expression of embarrassment crossed his face. 'Shit,' he hissed. 'Why can't they just call me back to Langley, those bastards? Why can't they just fucking airlift me out of here?'

Because they're a step ahead of you, Priestley, Will thought to himself. *They're a step ahead of you and they're hoping we might be the answer to all their problems the minute we each have Ahmed's bullets in our skulls. You think Ahmed's your enemy? Well let me tell you – you've got more enemies than you'll ever know.*

Will lowered his gun. He was breathing heavily, he realised, and he was staring at Priestley in disgust. The man looked pitiful, pathetic. How powerful he must have felt, giving the orders that put lives at risk. And now look at him. A contemptible sight. Nothing but a weak man, terrified for his life.

Unable to stand up for himself.

Unable to stand up to the consequences of his actions.

'Get dressed,' Will spat, finding him too repugnant even to look at. 'Get dressed and I'll call out for food. I'm fucking starving.'

★

Midnight.

The lights in Faisal Ahmed's flat were low and he didn't speak a word as he made his preparations. He put on nondescript clothes, then went about the time-consuming business of shaving off his beard. When it was done, he

295

turned almost defiantly to his sister. It made him look younger, Latifa thought. She had not seen him clean-shaven for many years and the sight took her back to the time when she had been like a mother to him.

She *still* felt like a mother to him, she realised, and at that moment she felt a mother's anxieties. Latifa had begged him countless times not to go and each time he had stead-fastly ignored her pleas. On the few occasions when he did speak of it, he always said the same thing. 'I'm just doing what I have to do, Latifa. You don't have to understand it – you just have to accept it.'

But she could not accept it. 'Please, Faisal. Please do not leave me. What if you come to harm? What will happen to me then?'

'I will not come to harm,' Faisal said, as he dismantled one of his many guns and placed the constituent parts into his bag.

'You don't know that, Faisal. You have given them warning that this is what you are going to do. He will be surrounded by security.'

A whisper of a smile played across Faisal's lips. '*You* were surrounded by security as well,' he noted, and to Latifa's ear his voice had the sound of a little boy gloating.

'Your pride will be your undoing, Faisal.'

For a moment he stopped what he was doing. He put down his bag, turned and walked towards his sister. She looked away from him, but he gently stretched out his hand and lifted her chin so that their eyes met again.

'Latifa,' he said, softly. 'Listen to me. The Russians killed our parents in front of us. Do you remember that day, Latifa? Do you remember it as vividly as I do?'

'How could I forget, Faisal?'

'Do you remember the way the blood seeped from their bodies and was absorbed by the earth?'

She nodded, tears welling up in her eyes.

'Every time I killed a Russian soldier, I did it for them. I did it for their memory, so they would look down on me and be proud. For all those years you gave me looks of such disapproval; and yet you never tried to stop me, because somewhere deep down you understood what I was doing.'

Latifa jutted out her chin. She refused to agree with him, yet she felt unable to disagree.

'The man I am going after now,' Faisal continued, 'he tried to do to me what the Russians did to our parents. He would not have pulled the trigger, of course. But he was responsible. And if he had been successful, he would have gone on to kill innocent people. People like our parents, Latifa. So look me in the eye now and tell me I am doing the wrong thing.'

He stared hard at her and she faltered under that gaze. There was nothing she could say to him, she saw that now. Nothing that would turn him back from the path he had chosen. 'I just don't want to lose my little brother,' she said, weakly.

Faisal lowered his hand. 'You lost your little brother many years ago, Latifa. I am not the same person. I am what the Americans made me and if that comes back to haunt them, I am a ghost of their own making.'

She looked at him again. His features were dark. Unrelenting.

'But there is one thing I swear to you, Latifa. Whatever happens, either now or in the future, I will see to it that you are safe. You have suffered enough on my account and as God is my witness I will see to it that such things do not happen again.'

She felt the tears coming to her eyes again as her reckless, impetuous brother made these promises she knew he could not keep.

'And you know that I am a man of my word, Latifa. You know that.'

Latifa shook her head. She felt somehow crushed by the power of her despair.

'Yes, Faisal,' she replied. 'You are a man of your word. I know it.'

NINETEEN

When dawn came, it brought with it streaks of red across the sky. Will Jackson stood at the window of the room adjoining the one where Priestley slept, grateful in some ways that the night had passed, but wondering what the day would bring. The red sky seemed to shout a warning at him.

Will had gone beyond tiredness now. Perhaps he would be able to grab some sleep here and there when Priestley was in meetings, but if not it didn't matter. He was surviving on raw adrenaline at the moment and he felt as if he could stay awake for days. For as long as it took to get the job done.

Priestley was an early riser and it wasn't long after dawn that Will heard him moving about in his bedroom. He knocked on the door, then opened it to see the American walking around wearing nothing but a pair of boxer shorts. He had more of a gut than Will might have expected from seeing him fully clothed and he looked over in annoyance. 'A bit of privacy would be nice.'

Will ignored him. He strode over to the bathroom, checked it out, then turned to Priestley. 'You can shower now,' he said. 'Any longer than a minute and I'm coming in.'

Priestley looked as if he were about to say something, but clearly thought better of it. He grabbed a towel and, with a scowl at Will, stomped into the bathroom.

Fifteen minutes later they were leaving the house – Will

first. There was a different armed police officer at the door, but Will recognised him from a previous shift. He greeted the officer with a brief, comradely nod, while Priestley stood in the doorway without even seeming to notice him. The car was waiting just outside. Priestley stayed at the front of the house while Will examined the undercarriage of the vehicle for anything suspicious. Once he was satisfied that all was as it should be, he returned to the house, took Priestley rather brusquely by the arm and ushered him into the back seat. Moments later they were off.

Will drove towards Thames House, where Priestley was due to meet Lowther Pankhurst. He couldn't help feeling a twinge of anxiety, not because of Ahmed – even he, Will thought to himself, would not be so foolish as to try a hit within the confines of MI5's London headquarters – but because he had had no contact with Lowther Pankhurst since that night on the North Downs. No doubt the Director General knew what Will was doing; what he thought about a former SAS man plying his trade for the CIA was another matter.

At Thames House they were swiftly ushered up to Pankhurst's office, Will leading the way. As they waited for the Director General to invite Priestley in, Will looked around. Was it really only twelve days since he was first summoned here? Only twelve days since he first heard the name of Faisal Ahmed? As the two of them waited in silence in the comfortable anteroom, it seemed to Will as if Faisal Ahmed had been in his mind far longer than that. The idea of catching up with him had become an obsession.

The idea of *killing* him.

A door opened and Pankhurst appeared. The Director General smiled tersely at Priestley, then looked over at Will and gave him a meaningful look. 'Do come in, Don,' he said, politely. 'If you can be spared, that is.'

Priestley looked over at Will, who nodded, and the CIA

man disappeared into Pankhurst's office. Will took a seat and rested his head against the wall. He should sleep, he thought to himself, now he was somewhere safe. He shut his eyes and tried to relax, but for some reason sleep wouldn't come. A secretary appeared and offered him coffee, which he accepted gratefully.

A large window faced out on to the street below and Will clutched his hot mug of coffee as he looked down. Despite the early hour it was already crowded with busy commuters making their way to work. Will had barely been near a television in the past few days, but on the one occasion he had seen the news it had been filled with the jowly features of the Commissioner of the Met, warning Londoners to be on high alert. How many of these people would be getting on the Tube, he wondered, with a sense of apprehension? Would they feel comforted by the sight of heavily armed police officers in the street? For a second, he felt a twinge of doubt. Perhaps he was going about this the wrong way. Perhaps he was letting his own vendetta compromise the safety of other people. The Director General of MI5 was just in the next room. Will had access; he knew he'd be heard out. Maybe he should just walk in there and tell Pankhurst everything Ahmed had said. About Operation Firefight. About what the CIA were up to.

He took a gulp of his coffee and allowed the hot liquid to burn his throat. No. It would be too high-risk. Operation Firefight was easily deniable – Will would never be believed by the British. God knows he'd racked his brains trying to think of ways to prove what he knew, people he could go to. But, ultimately, it would be foolish. If it leaked out to the CIA that he knew what they'd been doing, he felt sure that at some point in the none too distant future, he himself would be meeting with a mysterious accident.

Will turned aside from the window and the bustling commuters. He was going to do this *his* way.

The door opened and Priestley walked out. Pankhurst was there too. 'I wonder, Don,' he addressed the CIA man, 'if I might have a private word with Will.'

A look of nervousness crossed Priestley's face and Will opened his mouth to object. But before he did so, Pankhurst interrupted. 'Come now, gentlemen,' he said, quietly. 'I hardly think we're at risk within the confines of Thames House, do you?'

Will sniffed. 'All right,' he told Pankhurst, before turning to the American. 'Don't leave this room,' he instructed. 'And stay away from the window.'

Priestley looked over at the window in alarm, then made his way to the far side of the room. Will strode past Pankhurst into his office. The Director General closed the door behind him and took a seat at his desk.

'Sit down, Will.'

'I'll stand.'

'Whatever suits,' Pankhurst murmured. He took a deep breath, collecting his thoughts. 'I was a little taken aback that you decided to debrief yourself to Donald Priestley and not to me after the little debacle on the North Downs.'

'I don't work for you,' Will replied flatly.

'Agreed,' Pankhurst replied. 'But I did rather think you were working *with* me.' He stared at Will for a moment. 'I'm not sure if you're aware,' he continued, 'but they're burying Mark Drew and Nathan Kennedy this afternoon. Three o'clock.'

Will felt his jaw clenching. He hadn't known that, as it happened. And frankly, just at that moment, he could do without the image of his unit being lowered into the ground, their families weeping at the side of the grave. He could do without the thought of the Regiment gossip and disapproval at his absence. He knew how easily it could have been him.

'I know that there's an army myth, Will, that people like me don't care when people like you get killed on active service. But it's not true. We're the guys that send you into battle and, when things go wrong, we might not feel it in the gut as much as the soldiers, but we do feel it, Will. We feel it. Mark Drew and Nathan Kennedy should be spending Christmas with their families. My job is to make sure that their deaths *mean* something.'

He continued to stare at Will for a long, uncomfortable time.

'So would you care to tell me,' he asked plainly, 'what the hell is going on?'

Will took a deep breath. For some reason it filled him with anger to hear Pankhurst talking about Drew and Kennedy in that way; yet there was no doubting the simple sincerity in the DG's voice. Still, Will had made his decision. He knew how he was going to play this.

'I'm sure Priestley filled you in,' he said.

Pankhurst leaned back in his chair, his fingers pressed lightly together. 'Don Priestley has told me a lot of things,' he said. 'Not many of them make a great deal of sense.'

Will remained tight-lipped.

'All right, Will,' Pankhurst continued, his voice oozing patience. 'If you're not going to put your cards on the table, perhaps you'll allow me to tell you what *I've* been thinking.'

'Go ahead,' Will replied, unemotionally.

'I understand why you're sticking to Priestley like a limpet: you think Faisal Ahmed is going to make an assassination attempt. But why? What has Priestley done, personally, to warrant that? You're a clever man, Will. I don't believe you haven't asked yourself that question. Or maybe you already know the answer.'

Will didn't reply, leaving the Director General's accusation hanging in the air.

Pankhurst shrugged. 'Have it your way, Will,' he said. 'But

at least tell me one thing. London is on high terror alert. It costs us millions to do this and I can't help thinking we're barking up the wrong tree. *Are* we barking up the wrong tree, Will?'

Will blinked. Pankhurst was perceptive – he had to grudgingly admit that. But he couldn't answer the question, not without giving the game away. 'I'm not your security adviser, sir,' he said quietly.

Pankhurst breathed out deeply. 'Very well, Will,' he said, passing his hand over his eyes. 'You'd better get back to him. He's acting like a frightened schoolgirl.'

Will nodded, then turned towards the door. But before he could open it, Pankhurst spoke again.

'Will?' he said. There was something in his voice. It was less official. Friendly almost.

He turned. 'Sir?'

Pankhurst was looking at him with intense concentration. 'Good luck, Will,' he said. 'Whatever it is you're doing.'

Will inclined his head slightly. 'Thank you, sir,' he replied, before leaving the DG's office and closing the door behind him.

★

It was gone six in the evening by the time Will parked outside Priestley's Belgravia residence once more and the strains of their enforced proximity were becoming even more evident. As soon as the car came to a halt, Priestley made to open his door.

'Don't move!' Will shouted at him and the American froze.

'What is it?' he asked, breathlessly.

'For Christ's sake,' Will told him. 'You know the drill by now.' He opened his own door, handgun at the ready, checked up and down the street and did a visual sweep of the rooftops. Only when he was satisfied that he had the all-clear did he open Priestley's door and hustle him up past the armed police officer. Will entered the house first, then gave Priestley the sign that he could come in.

Priestley strode impatiently down the chequerboard hallway, slung his coat over the banister of the stairs and started making his way up. 'Don't take this the wrong way, Will,' he drawled, his voice grumpy, 'but I'm starting to wonder if a bullet in the head isn't preferable to another evening of us sitting upstairs scowling at each other.'

'Your call,' Will murmured.

Priestley stopped halfway up the stairs and looked back at Will. His face had morphed into an unpleasant sneer – halfway between fear and contempt, Will thought. 'Come on,' he spat, before turning and climbing the rest of the stairs.

Will stared balefully at him from the ground floor as he disappeared round the corner. The sooner this was over, he thought to himself, the bett—

He stopped.

Something wasn't right.

At the top of the stairs was a CCTV camera which covered the landing leading to the rooms they were using. Normally a small red light indicated that it was in use, but as he stared at it Will could see that the light was off. He felt his heart in his mouth as he looked over his shoulder at the camera covering the hallway.

No light.

Will knew immediately what it meant. The CCTV had been disabled and there could only be one reason for that. How Faisal Ahmed had got into the house, he didn't know. How he had disabled the CCTV without anyone being alerted, he didn't know. But of one thing he was sure.

Ahmed was here. *Now.*

Will looked back towards the front door. It was shut and there was no indication that the police officer outside knew what was going on.

The next minute was crucial. Everything he had been preparing for up to this point rested on what happened now.

Ahmed would have been watching them. No doubt about it. Ahmed would know that the first person to enter any room was Will. He would know which rooms they were camping out in. His eyes flickered up. There was no sign of Priestley. He would be approaching the room right now.

Will bounded up the stairs, quickly but lightly. As he moved, his brain worked as speedily as his feet. Timing was everything now. Critical. He had to play it just right. The first shot had to be his.

He stopped, as an idea crystallised in his mind.

Ahmed had respect for his abilities as a soldier; somehow he knew that. He would suspect that Will had seen the cameras were disabled. And he would assume that a good SAS man would follow standard operating procedure in a situation like this and enter the room first. He'd be ready and waiting.

Something the Afghan had said when they last met flicked through his brain. *Sometimes we think we are knights, when in fact we are merely pawns.*

Today they were neither. Today they were both kings, each trying to outwit the other, both one step away from checkmate.

And it was Will's move.

At the top of the stairs he saw Priestley waiting obediently by the door of the room. Will walked silently down the corridor, doing his best to look nonchalant. When he was three metres from the door he raised his right hand and flicked it, as if to indicate to Priestley that he should just go in.

Priestley's brow furrowed. He looked momentarily surprised, then shrugged his shoulders and opened the door.

Instinctively, Will's hand reached for his gun. In the next five seconds, he knew, he would either hear the sound of gunshot or Ahmed would have been momentarily wrong-footed by the incorrect person entering the room.

He stepped towards the door. No gunshot, just a sound of shuffling. He held his gun out and entered.

Ahmed had his back to him and was in the process of throwing Priestley towards the centre of the room. He, too, had his gun arm outstretched, towards the CIA man, and he was just turning round to check his back.

He never got the chance.

When you hold a gun for long enough, it becomes part of you, like an extra limb. That was how Will's handgun felt now – an extension of his body, under his control, ready to do his bidding, to respond to his split-second decision. In that moment, as a deadly calm descended on him, it was as though there were only three people in the whole world: himself, Faisal Ahmed and Donald Priestley. Will Jackson and his enemies, and everything was about to come full circle.

All he had to do was pull the trigger now and it would be over.

But killing Ahmed would not be enough. The Afghan was not the only person responsible for his family's death. There was someone else, too, and that person was in the room with them.

Will stepped forward and put the barrel of his gun gently against the back of Faisal Ahmed's head. He sensed Ahmed's body twitch in surprise, but then the Afghan stayed perfectly still.

'Any sudden move, Ahmed,' he whispered, 'and I swear I'll kill you without a second's hesitation.'

A hush descended on the room. Ahmed kept his gun trained on Priestley, who crawled backwards up against the wall.

'Clever,' the Afghan said, softly. 'Very clever.' The mere sound of his voice made Will tingle with hate.

Another silence. Ahmed, after an initial moment of shock, had instantly regained his composure. He stood like a statue, his gun still aimed at the American. Priestley himself, previously paralysed by abject terror, seemed to relax slightly at the sight of Will holding his gun to Ahmed's head. His body became less tense and stooped. He drew himself up to his full height, a flicker of contempt playing on his lips, his eyes gleaming with a newfound triumph.

'Well done, Will,' he whispered, his voice little more than a hiss. Will noticed, though, that his eyes still flickered towards Ahmed's gun. 'My man seems to have got the better of you, Faisal,' he continued. 'Time to put the weapon down. It's all over.'

'No,' Ahmed replied, quietly. 'I do not think so.' Will detected a tone of resignation in his voice.

Priestley's face twitched and he nodded his head sharply at Will. That nod was easily interpreted: *Do it.*

But Will did nothing. He just kept the gun to Ahmed's head.

The Afghan spoke again. 'If you wanted me dead, Will Jackson,' he said quietly, but clearly, 'you would have killed me already.'

'Oh, I want you dead, Ahmed. You needn't make any mistake about that.'

'And yet,' Ahmed replied, 'here I am. You have been clever, Will. Cleverer than I have given you credit for.' There was something about the way Ahmed addressed him in so familiar a fashion that made Will feel very uncomfortable. 'Could it be that there is something you want me to do for you first, Will? Something you cannot do yourself?'

'You've got the idea, Ahmed,' Will replied. 'So go ahead. In your own time.'

'What the hell are you both talking about?' Priestley demanded, his voice urgent. 'Jackson, *do it!*' He took a step forward. '*Kill him!*'

'If you make another move,' Will hissed at him, 'I'll kill you myself.'

Priestley stopped still and his eyes widened as a sudden realisation hit him. 'What do you mean?' he whispered.

'I would have thought it was clear,' Ahmed replied. 'He wants revenge. He is, after all, only human. But it is not just me he blames for his family's death, Don. It is you, too, and rightly so. Am I right, Will?'

'Get on with it, Ahmed.'

'You see, Don, he cannot shoot you with impunity, so he is gambling that I will do it for him. He is gambling that I want you dead so badly that I am willing to make it the last thing I do before he takes his revenge on me. That is correct, is it not, Will?'

'Got it in one, Ahmed,' Will growled.

Priestley's eyes flickered, terrified, from one man to the other, and then towards the open door.

'You needn't worry,' Ahmed spoke, softly, 'that anyone is coming to save you. The cameras have been disabled and a loop of footage recorded earlier today is being transmitted out of here. An old CIA trick, Don – I'm a little surprised you didn't predict it.'

'This is madness—!' Priestley choked, but his outburst was cut short. Because as he spoke, Ahmed fired – not into his head, as Will had expected – but directly into his thigh. Ahmed's suppressed weapon let out a faint whistling thud and instantly the CIA man crumpled to the ground. Blood oozed on to the floor, but he didn't scream. Instead, he started shaking violently. Shock, Will told himself in a detached fashion. He'd seen the symptoms enough times to recognise them.

And then Ahmed spoke again. He still sounded calm

and in control – it was not the voice of a man whose life was on the line. Will found himself wishing that he could see his face rather than just the back of his head, wishing that he could look into the man's eyes before he killed him.

'It seems,' Ahmed intoned, 'that I have been out-manoeuvred. My sister tried to warn me of this. She had more faith in your abilities than I did.'

Will remained silent. For some reason the mention of Latifa made him feel uneasy. Her devotion to her brother was complete and he could only imagine the feelings of hate she would harbour towards him when she found out that he had killed Ahmed.

At the side of the room, Priestley continued to tremble, little more than a frightened, wounded animal. The image of Laura and Anna lying dead on the ground flashed through Will's head.

'Your gamble has paid off,' Ahmed continued. 'I came here to assassinate Donald Priestley and I will not leave until that is done. If that means you're going to kill me, then so be it. In many ways it will be a release. But there is something I want you to do for me.'

Will blinked. 'You're not in a position to be asking me for favours, Ahmed.'

'It is not for me,' he whispered. 'But for my sister.'

Will paused. His target seemed unnaturally still. Unnaturally calm. It put Will even more on his guard. 'Go on.'

'When I am dead, there will be no one to look after her. She knows about Operation Firefight. The Americans will see her as a risk. They will try to eliminate her.'

For the first time, Will detected a sense of tension in Ahmed. His breathing was shallow and measured, but it trembled slightly.

'Operation Firefight has claimed enough victims, Will,' the Afghan continued. 'Your family to start with and now me.

Latifa does not deserve to be next on that list. I do not blame you for killing me – in your position I would do the same. But if Latifa is right about you, then I think you will understand and I think you will do the right thing by her.'

Will found his hand trembling. He steadied it. 'Where is she?'

'In hiding. In a safe house. I have a mobile telephone in my pocket. You will find a number for her there. When you see her, tell her—' Ahmed's voice suddenly cracked with emotion, but he instantly conquered it. 'Tell her she was right. And tell her I am sorry.'

From the floor, Priestley whimpered – the first sound he had made since the bullet had entered his leg. His breathing was heavy and he seemed to be sweating.

'And I am truly sorry for you, too, Will,' Ahmed continued. 'It is no consolation, I know, but I understand what it is to lose your family. Your wife and daughter were not meant to die. No one was meant to die. It has haunted me ever since.'

Will gritted his teeth. 'Just do it, Ahmed,' he said.

Another whimper escaped Priestley's mouth, a sound of such horror that for an instant Will felt a twinge of sympathy.

And then the American spoke, the dreadful effort sounding clearly in the tone of his voice. '*It was Ahmed who killed your family, Will,*' he wheedled. '*Ahmed. Not me. You should kill him. Kill him now, Will.*'

As Priestley spoke, all Will's sympathy was stripped away as he revealed himself for the sickening coward that he was. 'Shut up, Priestley!' he burst out. 'Just shut the fuck up! It's just a fucking game of soldiers to you, isn't it? Who cares if people die? My daughter was six years old. *Six years old.* How do you live with that, Priestley? How do you fucking live with that?'

311

Priestley's body was juddering now; his blood loss was copious. 'Will,' he breathed. 'You're angry —'

'Damn right I'm angry,' Will retorted, all his fury suddenly spilling out of him. 'I'm angry about Anderson, dead in some shit hole in the Stan. I'm angry about Drew and Kennedy, pushing up the fucking daisies thanks to this arsehole. I don't suppose you stopped to think about them, did you? A few dead soldiers don't mean much in the bigger picture, do they?'

'Will, please. I—'

'Save it, Priestley. I don't want to hear your justifications. I don't want to hear your excuses. Save it for the Pearly fucking Gates.' He nudged Ahmed in the back of his head with the gun. 'Do it,' he said.

Donald Priestley opened his mouth to save his life, but the words never left him. Faisal Ahmed's aim was perfect. The bullet entered Priestley's head directly between the eyes, ripping a hole in his forehead and creating a small, silent explosion of bone and soft brain matter. The CIA man fell dead to the floor.

An unholy quiet descended upon the room.

Will felt his finger twitch on the trigger of his gun, the weapon's barrel still pressed hard against Faisal Ahmed's skull. The Afghan lowered his gun. 'If you are going to kill me, Will, I would ask that you do it quickly.'

He took a deep breath. Now was the moment. The moment when the demons that had plagued him for the past two years could be laid, finally, to rest.

And yet, something was stopping him. Something was stopping him from pulling that trigger. He didn't know what it was — maybe he just didn't want to shoot a man from behind.

'Throw the gun to the ground,' he said.

Ahmed did as he was told. The weapon landed only inches from Priestley's body.

'Take two steps forward.'

Ahmed walked.

'Now put your hands on your head.'

Will watched as Ahmed slowly followed his instructions.

'Another three paces, then turn around.'

'It does not feel as I thought it would,' Ahmed said as he turned around. The sight of his face made Will catch his breath. His beard had been shaved off and he looked much younger than he had when they first met several nights ago. His eyes were piercing and clear and the only thing that suggested he felt any fear about what was about to happen was a thin trickle of sweat down the side of his face.

'What doesn't?' Will asked.

Ahmed's eyes flickered down to the sight of Priestley's body on the ground. 'Revenge,' he said simply. 'I thought it would feel different to this. Better.' He turned his gaze back to Will. 'You will find this out soon enough.' The Afghan closed his eyes and waited for the inevitable.

He's manipulating you, a voice spoke in Will's head. *Don't listen to him. Do what you have to do.*

But still something stopped him. A sudden doubt that this was the right thing to do. Surely the real criminal had been dealt with. The man who had been ultimately responsible for his family's death lay dead at his feet. The general had been killed; only the foot soldier remained. And as Ahmed stood there, resolutely waiting for death, Will couldn't help a creeping feeling of respect.

But respect wasn't enough to save Ahmed now.

'Open your eyes,' Will growled.

Ahmed's eyelids flickered open and he stared at Will, his face impossible to read.

'How did you get in here?'

A faint smile flickered across Ahmed's face. 'You don't really expect me to give away *all* my secrets, do you, Will?'

They stood there in silence, Ahmed's hands still firmly on his head, Will's arm outstretched, the handgun pointing straight at his enemy. He took a deep breath and prepared to fire.

To end it all.

Now.

It happened so quickly. At lightning speed, Ahmed's right arm delved into his coat and reappeared holding another weapon.

A sudden surge of adrenaline rushed through Will's body. He squeezed the trigger. But it was too late.

Ahmed's bullets were almost noiseless as they exploded from the suppressed firearm, but they slammed into Will's left shoulder with a thumping ferocity. He was knocked back against the wall and, as if in slow motion, he saw a hole explode in the wall where his own stray bullets made contact; then he saw Ahmed repositioning his gun, aiming it at his head.

Will Jackson knew he only had one chance to save his life.

He fired three times in quick succession. The shots cracked loudly.

The first bullet hit Ahmed in the chest, knocking him back half a metre and ensuring that the Afghan's next shot fell wide of its mark.

The second bullet found his throat. Ahmed dropped his gun and moved his hands up to where the blood was suddenly spurting from him like some grotesque fountain.

It was the third bullet that killed him as it thudded directly into the upper region of his head.

The Afghan crumpled to the ground. Motionless. Dead. Will's training demanded that he walk over to his target and despatch a head shot to ensure that the guy had been finished off. But there was no need. No one took that kind of punishment and lived. Not even Faisal Ahmed.

There is nothing more silent than death and in the stillness that followed, Will almost forgot that he'd been hit. He staggered towards Ahmed's body and looked down at him. The man's face was unrecognisable. A bloodied mess. And as Will stared at the sight he had longed for, he felt curiously numb.

Ahmed had been right, the thought flashed through his head. Revenge wasn't sweet. Revenge wasn't what he thought it would be at all.

And then, with a sudden, agonising stab, the pain hit him – a cold, sinister pain spreading from his wound. He felt his legs going weak and, looking down, he saw he was losing blood quickly. He needed help, but there was one thing he had to do first. Will bent down and felt in between the folds of the dead man's clothes. Sure enough there was a mobile phone.

He pocketed it, then staggered back to the door. Taking one look back at the room – it looked like a fucking slaughterhouse – he stumbled along the landing and down the hall, leaving a trail of blood. He started to feel light-headed and as he went down the stairs he stumbled, smearing blood over the banister as he fell against it.

At the foot of the stairs he tumbled again. Jesus, the blood was pouring out of him now. He needed help. Quickly. It took all his strength to push himself up to his feet and he slipped slightly in his own blood as he launched himself across the hallway towards the front door.

The room was spinning. He gritted his teeth and banged weakly on the door. Then collapsed to the ground.

The door opened and the armed policeman towered above Will. It took him a moment to take in what was happening. 'Fucking hell!' he muttered as he saw the blood flowing out of Will's gunshot wound.

When Will spoke his voice sounded alarmingly weak, even to him. 'Get me a medic,' he croaked, hoarsely. '*Now!*'

And then, like a black wave crashing over his mind, darkness engulfed him as he passed out.

TWENTY

Will awoke gradually. The first thing he noticed was the pain.

His left shoulder throbbed and pulsated; the rest of his body ached and his head had the woolly stuffiness that instantly told him he had been sedated. There was something on his face and as he forced his bleary eyes open he realised it was an oxygen mask. It was uncomfortable and water vapour from his breath had condensed on the inside. Fumbling to take it off, he noticed a dressing on his shoulder, fresh and white and taped down on to his skin with sticking plaster. Each of his hands had intravenous tubes injected into the skin and on either side of his bed there were clear bags of colourless liquid being drip-fed into his system.

The curtains in his room were closed and he noticed in his half-awake state that there was carpet on the floor. That meant it was a private room. A private hospital. But where? With difficulty he pushed himself up on to his elbows, but he soon collapsed heavily back down on to the bed and closed his eyes again.

'How are you feeling, Will?' a voice asked.

Will forced his eyes open again. He hadn't noticed anyone else in the room and he didn't like the surprise. The voice was familiar, but for the moment his mind was too muddled for him to be able to place it. 'Who's that?' he breathed with difficulty.

A pause, and then he became aware of a figure standing

over his bedside. He opened his eyes and squinted them into focus. A face appeared – thick black hair and square glasses.

'Pankhurst,' Will said, weakly. 'Where the hell am I?

'Hospital,' Pankhurst stated, before repeating his question. 'How do you feel?'

'Like shit.'

'Then you feel better than you look. It's been touch and go for you. Priestley's house looked like a bloodbath, Will, and our guys seemed to think that a lot of the blood was yours.'

'Ahmed hit me.'

'Obviously. But you hit him better. Assuming, that is, that the chap with half a face was indeed Faisal Ahmed.'

'Yeah,' Will replied. 'That was him.' He groaned as a wave of pain passed through his wound.

'Then congratulations,' Pankhurst replied, blandly. 'You got what you wanted. Does that make you feel a bit better?'

For some reason it wasn't a question Will felt inclined to answer. His face screwed up again as another wave of pain hit him.

'You have a self-administered morphine drip attached to you,' Pankhurst pointed out. He fumbled by Will's bedside and showed him the handheld pump. 'I wouldn't recommend using it, though.' He placed the pump just out of Will's reach.

Will looked up at the DG's blurry face. 'Why the hell not?' he asked, suddenly desperate for the morphine now he knew it was there.

Pankhurst took a couple of steps backwards.

'Because you need to get out of here as quickly as possible. We managed to scrape you up from Priestley's house without the CIA knowing where we were taking you, but we're not going to be able to keep them in the dark for long. They'll track you down any moment and I can promise you that they're going to want some answers.'

'About what?' Will asked. His throat was desperately dry and his mouth had an unpleasant taste in it.

'About Priestley, Will,' Pankhurst replied, like a patient teacher explaining something to a child. 'About how he died.'

'Ahmed shot him,' Will said.

'We know that, Will. And you shot Ahmed. But things don't stack up at the scene. For example, why did Ahmed have two guns – one in his hand and one on the floor?'

'I—' Will hesitated as he desperately tried to kick his slow-moving brain into gear.

But Pankhurst interrupted him. 'Be quiet, Will, and listen to me. You've got what you wanted. You've played it out as far as it can go. But the game stops here. I don't have to be Sherlock Holmes to know that there's more to Priestley's death than meets the eye. Nor do the Americans. They've just lost one of their top men and they're going to want to get to the bottom of it. That means coming after you. I can help you, Will, but not until you tell me what the hell this is all about.'

Will breathed in sharply through his teeth. The pain in his shoulder was agonising, but he tried to put it from his mind. Pankhurst was right. If the Americans suspected something, they'd be coming after him. He didn't know if he could trust the DG of MI5, but right now he was the lesser of two evils.

'Have you ever heard of Operation Firefight?' he asked.

Pankhurst stared at him blankly.

'Then you'd better listen carefully.'

And then he told him.

Pankhurst's face was expressionless as the extent of Priestley's deceit unfolded. He said nothing, simply letting Will explain, in detail, what he knew. When he had finished, Pankhurst remained silent for a while. He stepped over to the window of the room, pulled back the curtain an inch or two and glanced outside.

319

When he turned around again he had the air of a man who had made a decision.

'A lot of things suddenly make more sense than they did ten minutes ago,' he said, quietly.

'I'm glad *you* think so,' Will commented.

'Trouble is, with Faisal dead, there's no way you can prove what you just told me.'

'For fuck's sake,' Will whispered. 'Why would I make it up?'

'Oh, don't worry, Will. *I* believe you – for what it's worth. But you've got to see that this is too politically sensitive to go any further up the chain. You understand that, don't you?'

Will said nothing.

'Everyone's going to deny it, Will. Everyone's going to pretend it never happened. You're going to be the wild card, though. You're going to be the one they'll want to silence. And they're going to come to me, Will, sooner than you think – put pressure on me to hand you over. If they do that, I'm not going to be able to say no. Not if you're still around. You need to get out of here. You need to disappear. And soon.'

There was a silence as Pankhurst's words sunk in.

'How long have I been out?'

'Forty-eight hours.'

'And where are we?'

'Just off Great Portland Street. We kept you out of the public hospitals as a safety measure. I have to go now, Will. They can't know you've tipped me off. I'll keep them off your tracks for as long as I can, but they won't be relying on me in order to learn your location.' He approached the bed again and looked down at Will, whose eyesight was clearing now. The DG's face appeared sharper. 'You've done a good job, Will, but now you're on your own. If the Americans think I'm involved in what went on there it could have repercussions that nobody wants, so I can't have any more face-to-face contact with you. I hope you understand. But if you need anything – any help from Five – get in touch discreetly and we'll see what we can do.'

Will nodded his head, weakly. 'Thank you, sir.'

'Thank *you*, Will,' the DG said quietly. Will watched as he turned and swiftly left the room.

Will lay in silence for a few minutes, trying to make sense of what Pankhurst had just said. He knew nobody could nail Priestley's death on him, but Pankhurst was right – the Americans would put two and two together about him killing Priestley and they'd want some answers. Answers he didn't want to give. He pushed himself on to his elbows once more, this time managing to stay up, even though it felt as though it took up all his energy. Slowly he heaved his legs over the side of the bed, then sat still for a moment while he allowed a moment of nausea to pass.

The intravenous needles were taped on to his skin. He fumbled at the sticking plaster and managed to pull it off before pulling out the needles as slowly as his shaking hands could manage. A small amount of blood seeped from the punctures in his flesh, but he barely noticed it against the altogether more overwhelming pain of the bullet wound. Will pushed himself up on to his feet and took a couple of shaky steps before being forced to stop and hold on tight to the foot of the bed, his legs like jelly.

As he stood there, the door opened and a nurse walked in. She was young, with pretty blonde hair and grey-blue eyes that looked aghast at Will when she saw him out of bed. 'What are you doing?' she gasped, stepping forward and putting her small hands against Will's naked arms. They felt warm on his skin. 'You have to get back into bed,' she urged him. 'You're not well enough to be up and about.'

Will gritted his teeth against the pain, then brushed her aside. 'I'm discharging myself,' he growled. Looking around, he saw some clothes draped over a chair. He staggered towards it and started to dress, wincing painfully as he pulled a shirt over his wound.

'But the doctors—'

'Fuck the doctors,' Will growled, impatiently, before immediately regretting it. The poor girl was only doing her job. He turned round to look at her and saw an expression of thin-lipped disapproval on her attractive face.

'I'm going to find one,' she stated, sternly. 'You need a clean dressing. Now *stay there.*' She spun on her heel and left the room.

Will continued to dress, the adrenaline surge created by the sudden urgency doing a great deal to clear his head.

Once he was dressed, he looked around. By his bedside there was a clear plastic bag with his personal belongings – a wallet, a watch and Faisal Ahmed's mobile phone. It was the sight of the phone that brought everything flooding back to him. Ahmed's final minutes. His plea to Will to take care of his sister. His last, reckless moment of madness. Will had expected to feel elated that Ahmed was dead, but he didn't. He didn't really feel anything. Just a pain in the shoulder and an urgent need to get the hell out of there before anyone else caught up with him.

He opened the door and looked both ways down the corridor. There was a glass-fronted nurse's station opposite, but it was empty, and about halfway down the corridor was a trolley full of clean linen. To Will's relief there were no people. He didn't know which way was the exit, so at random he turned right into the corridor and followed his nose. He hadn't got far, however, when he heard voices approaching, so he opened the nearest door and hid.

The room in which he found himself was a medical store

cupboard, neatly packed with hundreds of small boxes and bottles of medicine. It had a clean, antiseptic smell – the smell of fresh bandages – and Will thanked his good luck. He found a stash of sterilised swabs and antiseptic lotion; then he scanned through the drugs until he located the one thing he was sure he was going to need. Orally administered morphine would make it possible to cope with the pain when he was out of there. Finally, he found a set of freshly laundered doctor's overalls. Putting them on was painful and difficult, but they meant that he would have a better chance of walking along the hospital's corridors unchallenged.

He remained in the store cupboard for several minutes before quietly pushing the door open a few inches. He listened carefully. Nothing, so he slipped out.

Minutes later he was walking past the reception. It took every ounce of energy he had to walk normally, but it paid off. Ignoring the excruciating pain in his shoulder, he walked out into the street.

Nobody even raised an eyebrow.

★

Zack Levinson looked around his new London office – bland, featureless shit hole that it was – with bleary eyes.

Levinson was tired. Damned tired. He'd caught the red-eye from Washington just the night before and the DCIA was already on his case. Donald Priestley's body had barely been cold when Levinson had been drafted in to replace him and for a few blissful hours he thought he was on to a soft option – an extended vacation in London. He'd soon been disabused of that stupid idea.

The DCIA was in a panic – that much was clear. Levinson didn't know why he wanted former SAS soldier Will Jackson, but he *really* wanted him, and the full force of the CIA's London resources were given over to finding the guy.

Levinson's mobile rang and he answered it immediately. 'Give me good news,' he said.

'We think we've found him.'

'Alle-fuckin'-luia. Where?'

'Central London. Private hospital. We're going in now.'

Levinson breathed a sigh of relief. 'OK,' he said. 'Go get him and bring him straight to me.'

He hung up and leaned back in his chair. Zack Levinson's day had just taken a turn for the better.

★

The moment he walked out of the hospital, Will hailed a taxi. He slumped heavily into the back seat. 'Holiday Inn,' he told the driver. 'Nearest one.'

'You all right, mate?' the driver asked, genuinely worried.

'Fine,' Will breathed. 'Just drive.'

The taxi slid away.

Half an hour later he was in a reassuringly bland room of the hotel, having checked in under an assumed name. He sat on the side of the bed, swallowed a couple of morphine tablets, and then set about attending to his wound. He winced as the dressing peeled away from the skin, the flimsy gauze sticking slightly to the still wet blood around the stitched-up entry point. He staggered to the bathroom, splashed cold water over the sticky wound, then dabbed it dry with a clean, white hotel towel which immediately became stained with patches of scarlet. Back in the bedroom he unwrapped the packaging of the fresh dressing with shaking fingers, pressed it to the wound and stuck it to his skin with sticking plaster. It looked a lot less professional than the previous job, but at least it was clean.

Minutes later, to his overwhelming relief, the morphine started to kick in. Will stood up and looked at himself in a mirror. Jesus, he thought. You look like death warmed up. His skin was pallid, his eyes bloodshot and tired. He wished, more than anything, that he could just lie down and sleep – for days, if necessary. But that wasn't going to be possible. His mind was suddenly ablaze with plans, with things he had to do. Pankhurst's warning had been stark, and for the first time ever Will felt an absolute confidence that the DG of Five was on his side. And Pankhurst was right. Will might have done enough to stop the law coming after him, but the CIA would be slightly more tenacious, especially if they suspected that he knew anything about Operation Firefight.

He had to make arrangements. Set things in motion. He cursed the debilitating wound in his shoulder, but he couldn't let it get in his way. Will could only stay anonymous for so long; the Americans would catch up with him eventually. Unless . . .

Unless . . .

He sat again on the side of his bed, a slideshow of images flickering through his brain. He saw Latifa Ahmed, brutalised and only days from death in the hut in Afghanistan. He saw the bodies of his fellow SAS men, dead and cold. He saw the flat, emotionless eyes of Faisal Ahmed as they stood together by Priestley's bleeding corpse. And he saw his family's grave, silent and still.

So much violence.

So much death.

And it seemed to Will Jackson as he sat in that bland hotel room that there was only one way to put an end to it. He looked out of the window as a strategy began to form in his head.

By his side was the clear bag of his personal possessions he had taken from the hospital. He opened it up and pulled out the phone he had removed from Ahmed's body. There were still bloodstains on it, though who the blood belonged to he couldn't tell. He flicked through the memory until he found what he was looking for.

Then, with a deep breath, he shuffled up the bed towards the hotel phone. First he called directory enquiries; then, when he had the number he needed, he dialled it.

The phone rang twice before it was answered. 'Good morning, Thames House.'

'Put me through to the Director General,' he said. 'Tell him it's Will Jackson on the line.'

★

Lowther Pankhurst put the phone down, then pressed his fingertips together and closed his eyes. Jackson was asking a lot. An awful lot. It could cost Pankhurst his job if it ever came out.

But by God, if anyone had earned a break it was Jackson. He thought back to the interrogation Latifa Ahmed had undergone. Nasty. He and Jackson might have had their differences, but the guy didn't deserve anything like that. In an official capacity, Pankhurst had to keep his nose clean; as a man, he owed Will Jackson a helping hand.

He buzzed through to his secretary. 'Get Ashley Jones up here, would you?' he requested.

Minutes later, Jones was being ushered into the DG's office. He was a good man. Unassuming, with his mousy brown hair and short stature, but reliable. Discreet. He stood respectfully on the other side of the desk and for a moment Pankhurst couldn't help noticing the difference in attitude between Jones and Jackson. A rueful smile flickered over his face, but he quickly checked it.

'What I'm about to tell you goes no further than the two of us,' he said.

'No, sir.'

'I need you to arrange two passports, then deliver them

326

to a contact in forty-eight hours. 11.30 a.m., Friday. St Pancras Station.'

'The contact's name, sir?'

'You don't need to know that. He'll find you.'

Jones nodded, without asking any further questions.

'You have a pen and paper?' Pankhurst continued. 'Good. Take this down. These are the details you'll need . . .'

★

It was a busy forty-eight hours, but slow, and it passed in a haze of morphine. Will travelled twice out of London – both of them difficult, traumatic trips, but necessary. When he wasn't travelling, he stayed in his hotel room – out of sight, recuperating as best he could, and hoping that Five would come through for him.

As he lay alone in the room, he had time to reflect. He didn't need any more regrets in his life, that was for sure. Killing people had been his job for a long time, after all. But while he was unable to mourn the passing of Donald Priestley, in his moments of honesty he had started to feel a grudging respect for the man who had killed his wife, his daughter and his military colleagues.

Maybe that was why he was doing what he was doing.

Friday morning arrived and Will was up at eight o'clock. It was a bright, clear day, not a cloud in the sky. The wound was still painful, but bearable now and he felt he could face the day without any morphine, avoiding the lethargy that it brought on. He still cleaned the wound well, however, and applied a new dressing before putting on the same clothes he had been wearing for the past few days, which were now beginning to smell.

He looked at his watch. Ten to nine. The meet was at 11.30. He'd stay in the room till eleven before making his move. He lay down on the bed and switched the television on in the hope that it would distract him. It didn't.

There was a knock at the door. Will cursed. He'd put the DO NOT DISTURB sign on the handle when he first arrived, but the cleaners seemed to ignore it. 'No thanks!' he shouted grumpily.

A pause, then another knock. Firmer this time. 'Will Jackson?' an American voice called.

Will's heart stopped. His fingers instinctively felt for a gun, but he didn't have one. He glanced towards the window, but the room was five flights up. There was only one way out and that was through the door. He pulled himself to his feet. 'Who is it?' he called, warily.

Another knock. Three solid, determined raps. Then the voice again. 'Open the door, Jackson. We don't want to break it down.'

His eyes flickered around the room. There was almost nothing he could use as a weapon. The lamps were fastened to the surfaces and there was nothing else of any weight that would serve as a bludgeon. But on the floor there was a dressing gown. Will picked it up and pulled the cord from out of the loops, then pulled it tight from each end. It was strong enough, should it come to that. Will held it firmly in his right hand, then gingerly opened the door, keeping the dressing-gown cord out of sight.

There were two men there, about Will's age, maybe a little younger. They were dressed in casual clothes – jeans, trainers and warm padded overcoats. One of them had his hands in his pockets, and Will's practised eye immediately noticed that there was more of a bulge in one of them than there should have been. He was being held at gunpoint.

There were no introductions, no pleasantries. 'We'd like you to come with us,' the man with the gun said, almost politely.

Will sniffed. 'How did you find me?' he asked.

The man inclined his head slightly, but didn't answer. 'There's two ways to do this,' he said. 'Our way or the other way. Our way is easier and will hurt less.'

'I bet it will,' Will murmured. 'I need to get my things together.'

The American nodded, then they both followed him into the room. 'Drop the cord,' the man said as soon as he saw it in Will's hand and Will had no option but to do as he said. When he was ready, he turned back to the Americans.

'This is what we're going to do,' he was told. 'We walk on either side of you. I don't need to tell you what will happen if you do anything that makes us even slightly nervous. Don't try and check out – your room bill has already been paid. There's a red Laguna waiting outside. You get straight in it, using the back door on the sidewalk side. We've got men in the lobby and men outside. We know who you are and we're aware of your training. I hope you'll believe us when we say that we've got every exit covered.'

'Yeah,' Will said flatly. 'I believe you.' Inside he was cursing. How the *hell* had they caught up with him? Nobody knew he was here. *Nobody.* If he missed his meet, everything would go tits up. But these guys were clearly CIA, they weren't going to let him get away and he was in no fit state for heroics.

'Good. Let's go.'

It seemed to take forever as they walked silently down the deserted hotel corridor to the lift and no one said a word as they descended to the ground floor. Once they were in the lobby, Will couldn't help his eyes glancing around to see if he could spot the plain-clothes agents. He couldn't. They were good.

His mind turned somersaults, desperately trying to think of a way out of this. The clock was ticking and he couldn't risk being late, but the CIA guys flanked him tightly and there was no getting away. As soon as they were all in the

329

Laguna, the central-locking system shut down and the car slipped into the traffic.

'Where are we going?' Will asked.

No answer.

They headed up towards the West End.

It took them ten minutes to reach their destination – plush, gentrified Brook Street in Mayfair. They stopped and Will was hustled out of the car. The building to which he was led looked just the same as all the other houses, giving no indication as to what went on there. Will did notice, however, two guys hanging around in plain clothes, one a few metres from the door, the other on the opposite side of the road. No doubt there would be others. They approached the door and one of the men pressed a buzzer by a small entry camera; a few moments later they were buzzed in.

The inside of the building was a lot less gentrified than the outside. A bland, empty corridor gave on to a number of closed doors and there was the antiseptic smell of whatever bleach had been used to clean the shiny, vinyl floor. 'Care to tell me who I'm meeting with?' Will asked as they crossed the threshold.

Neither man spoke, but one of them knocked on the nearest door. It was swiftly opened and Will's two guards stepped aside to let him in.

The man waiting for him was a good deal older than Will – mid-sixties, perhaps. He had a thick head of greying hair and a ruddy complexion. There was a broad, friendly smile on his face. 'Good morning,' he greeted Will as the door was closed behind them, leaving the two of them alone in the room.

Will nodded. 'Who are you?'

'Zack Levinson.' The man held out his hand. 'Don Priestley's successor. I hope our boys weren't too rough with you. It's the way they're trained, but I guess you know all about that.'

Will felt his eyes narrowing and cautiously shook Levinson's hand. 'Take a seat, please,' the American smiled at him.

He sat in the armchair that Levinson indicated.

'Damn shame about Priestley,' the American said. 'He was a good guy. I came up through the ranks with him. *Damn* good guy.' Will noticed that Levinson stared straight at him as he spoke, as if gauging his minutest reaction.

'I didn't know him that well,' he replied.

'No,' Levinson muttered. 'No, of course. Look, I'm sorry about the two heavies bringing you in like that. Langley are pretty keen for me to speak to you, find out exactly what happened. Five are being a bit shifty about the whole thing. Not that I blame them – always a bit of an embarrassment to have a foreign agent killed on your own turf.'

'Faisal Ahmed was CIA trained,' Will reminded him.

Levinson held up his hands. 'Sure,' he said, mollifyingly. 'Sure. Don't get me wrong, Will. We're grateful to you for bringing Ahmed down. When a guy like that goes haywire there's no telling how it'll end. But it's always difficult to lose one of your own.'

You don't have to tell *me* that, Will thought.

'There was just one thing, Will, that I wanted to ask you. Our sources say that there were two guns at the scene – one that killed Priestley, the other that shot you.' Levinson smiled, blandly. 'I'm sure there's an obvious explanation for that – why Ahmed felt the need to put one of his guns down, I mean.' His eyes remained locked on Will's.

Inside, Will's stomach was doing somersaults, but he did his best to maintain a calm exterior. 'I disarmed him and tried to take him alive,' he said. 'But he pulled another pistol on me.'

'I see,' he replied. His smile grew a little broader. 'Forgive me,' he said, 'but our reports from Don Priestley suggest that your intention was always to shoot to kill.'

'I don't kill people when I don't have to,' Will replied, quietly.

'No,' Levinson shook his head. 'No, of course not. What I'm wondering, Will, is if you can throw any light on why Ahmed targeted Priestley.'

'I'm afraid we didn't really get a chance to chat, Zack. Awkward social situation and all that.'

Levinson nodded his head, slowly. He stood up and walked to the window. 'Let me level with you, Will. We're worried about Ahmed's sister. From what we've heard she was roughed up pretty bad by the Taliban. The American government would like to offer her sanctuary – a place to live, a small pension. My superiors feel it's the least we can do.' He turned to look at Will again. 'But we've no idea where she is. Tell me, Will, do you think it's likely that she might get in contact with you?'

'Not really.'

'We think otherwise, Will. You've done a lot for the woman. Saved her life on more than one occasion. As far as we can tell, she doesn't know anyone else in the country. If I were a betting man, Will, I'd put a few dollars on you hearing from her sometime pretty soon.'

'I killed her brother,' Will said, flatly.

'She doesn't know that,' the CIA man retorted. 'She doesn't even know he's dead. This has all been kept on the q.t.'

Will shrugged.

'So if she gets in contact with you, Will, you'll let us know. Bring her to us. It'll be in her own best interest.'

'Sure,' Will replied. 'Anything else?'

Levinson shook his head. 'No. Not for now. You're free to go.'

Will stood up.

'Oh, and Will?'

'Yeah?'

'Thank you. You did a brave thing going after Faisal Ahmed. The world's a far better place without him.'

Will nodded curtly and left the room.

★

Zack Levinson watched Jackson leave. The moment the door was shut he picked up the phone and dialled through to Langley. 'It's Zack Levinson in London,' he told the switchboard. 'The DCIA's expecting my call.'

'Hold please,' a polite American voice told him.

Bradley Heller came on to the line immediately. 'You get him?'

'We got him.'

'And?'

'He's a pretty cold fish.'

'Did you get the impression he knew why Ahmed was after Priestley?'

'I asked him outright. Says he has no idea. Of course, it would help, sir, if *I* knew what was going on.'

'That's a headache above your pay grade, Zack,' the DCIA replied, evasively. 'Is Jackson being trailed?'

Levinson's eyes flickered through the window. 'Yeah, he's being trailed.'

'Good. Give him forty-eight hours. If he makes contact with the woman, bring them both in. If not, apprehend him and we'll deal with her later. Then I want Jackson on the first US military transport out of the country.'

'Am I allowed to know where to, sir?'

A pause. 'You have your instructions, Zack. This is a big gig for you. Don't let me down.'

Levinson's jaw clenched momentarily. 'I won't let you down, sir. You have my word.'

★

Alarm bells had started to sound in Will's head the moment Zack Levinson had started to question him. They knew Priestley's killing didn't stack up. They couldn't prove anything, but they knew. And what was that bullshit about offering Latifa Ahmed sanctuary? Days ago they had been waterboarding her, now they wanted to set her up in a cosy little condo with an income for life. He didn't think so. Zack Levinson had been perfectly transparent: Will knew that he and Latifa were in danger. Immediate danger.

He stepped out into the street. The guys he had clocked on each side of the road were still standing around nonchalantly, but as he continued walking he kept one eye on the side mirrors of the cars parked at the edge of the road. Sure enough there they were, following him at a distance. Two trails, and they were just the ones he could see. No doubt there would be more. As casually as possible he looked over his shoulder. A black cab was edging slowly up the street, its FOR HIRE light extinguished. He looked ahead again – suddenly everyone he saw was a potential trail. Guys on bikes, mums with prams. He knew he was being followed and any of them could be involved.

He had to lose his trail. He had to lose them quickly.

Will looked at his watch: 10.45. He had three quarters of an hour and he couldn't afford to be late. It took a supreme effort for him not to keep looking around – if he alerted them to the fact he knew they were there, it would make losing them all the more difficult. So he slowed his pace and headed to the centre of town.

It took him ten minutes to reach Selfridges. He strode in confidently, fully aware of the fact that while he was in there all the main exits were likely to be watched. He headed across the ground floor, breathing in the heady smell of the perfume department, until he reached a line of elevators. He pressed the up button, then waited. It took a minute or so for the lift to come and in that time maybe seven or eight other customers congregated around him. The lift doors hissed open and they all politely entered. Just as the doors were starting to close, however, Will twisted his body sideways on and slipped out. To his relief, no one was quick enough to follow him. He rushed to the escalator and made his way up to menswear.

Once there, he found himself a large heavy overcoat and a brightly coloured woollen hat. He took them into a changing cubicle and, having checked that there was no CCTV, he ripped the security tabs off the items, then put on the overcoat and shoved the hat in his pocket. He walked brashly out, knowing that confidence alone was likely to avoid any harassed shop assistants from stopping him – they were too busy with the swarms of last-minute Christmas shoppers in any case.

A change of clothes, he thought to himself as he left the department store by a different exit, won't be enough to fool the best surveillance teams, but if he threw every trick he knew at them, then he had a chance. And Will had plenty more tricks up his sleeve.

His next destination was Hamleys on Regent Street. As Will had calculated, it was full of parents and their excited children. Will pushed his way in and negotiated his way through the crowds until he reached the far side of the ground floor. It took him a short while to find what he was looking for – a small, red fire alarm on the wall. He shuffled up against it, his back to the wall, then jabbed it sharply with an elbow. The glass shattered and immediately a high-pitched wail filled the air.

For a brief moment everyone stopped. And then, as one, the crowd dissolved into a state of blind panic. Everyone headed for the exit doors, which became blocked with a scrambling sea of people.

Will joined the throng. As he did so, he took the woollen hat from his pocket and put it firmly on, then bowed his head towards the floor. If he kept in the middle of the crowd, he would be unrecognisable.

It took several minutes to leave the shop, but that suited Will just fine. Once he was out in the cold air, the pavement was still crowded. He headed south down Regent Street towards Piccadilly Circus, quickly ducking down into the underground station.

The Tube concourse was circular, exits heading off at regular intervals, and Will decided to use this to his advantage. If anyone was still following him, they would expect him to get on a train to try and shake them off; he was going to do something different. If he walked quickly enough and put sufficient distance between himself and any trails, the circular concourse would mean that he could get out of their line of sight and take one of the exits before they noticed he had gone.

Like everywhere else, the station was crowded and Will thanked his luck as he hurried down the south-eastern exit and into Lower Regent Street. As soon as he was above ground again, he hailed a black cab. 'St Pancras!' he hollered at the driver as he climbed in and moments later he was heading north again. From the windows of the cab he kept track of any car coming up behind them. By the time they were in Cambridge Circus, Will was convinced that he had lost his trail.

He looked at his watch: 11.20. Ten minutes to go. He was going to make it.

Will asked the cab driver to stop just short of the station. He paid him, then stood on the pavement for a couple of minutes looking out for any other possible surveillance. There was none, so he headed up into the station.

It was only a couple of days until Christmas, but the station was still busy. That suited Will as he walked speedily but unobtrusively through St Pancras. Up ahead he saw what he was looking for: the huge black statue of a couple embracing. The most romantic meeting place in Europe, he seemed to remember someone calling it and in another life maybe it would have been. But romance was a long way from Will's mind. He realised his heart was thumping nervously. This morning had underlined that he was right to be doing this; but he just hoped there weren't any more surprises.

A number of people were milling around, waiting for loved ones or looking impatiently at their watches. Will ignored almost all of them. There was only one person he was looking for right now and he realised his heart was in his throat at the prospect of that person not having made it. He scanned the crowds around the statue, but there were no familiar faces.

A Tannoy announcement echoed around the station and a few people moved away from the statue. Will checked his watch: 11.30. *Shit.* She should be here by now.

11.31.

He'd told her not to be late.

11.32.

She knew the risks. He couldn't stay here for long.

And then he saw her.

Latifa Ahmed seemed to appear from nowhere, walking out of the crowd with a slight limp, but with a steady determination in her gait. She wore a heavy coat against the cold and a headscarf that covered her hair. As she grew near, Will saw that she had applied a little make-up to her face. It disguised her well; but it also, he noticed, enhanced the natural prettiness that he had never noticed in her before.

'I thought you weren't coming,' Will said, abruptly.

'I almost didn't,' she replied. Her voice was sad.

'You don't trust me?'

'I don't trust anyone. But coming with you is better than sitting and waiting for the Americans to—' Her voice trailed off.

Will nodded. He knew what she was trying to say. They were both in the same boat.

Now Latifa was here, he started looking around again. He knew what he was after: a man by himself, probably not in a suit, so as to stand out to anyone who knew what they were looking for. There was such a guy on the other side of the statue. Just standing there. Waiting.

'Don't move,' Will told Latifa and he sauntered around to where the man was standing.

Their eyes met, and the man seemed entirely comfortable with a stranger staring at him. Will sidled up to him. 'You got something from Pankhurst?' he asked.

The man said nothing; he just nodded and handed Will a white, padded envelope. Will glanced inside. Two passports, just as he'd asked for; and a thick wad of euros, which he hadn't requested but was pleased to see. He looked back up at the man. 'I'll watch you leave,' he said.

The man didn't respond. He just walked away, out into the crowds of St Pancras, and didn't look back.

Will returned to Latifa, who was just standing there, expressionless. 'Is it time?' she asked.

He nodded.

'And we will be safe, once we have left the country?'

He shrugged. 'Safer. The world's a big place. There are lots of places to hide. You could even go back to Afghanistan, if you wanted.'

Latifa shook her head. 'No,' she said. 'I do not think I will do that. There are too many memories for me there.' A vacant look passed across her face.

'You can't escape your memories, Latifa. They travel with you.'

She looked straight into his eyes. 'You are right,' she said, sadly. 'Thank you for doing this, Will. I know I do not deserve it, after what my brother did.'

Will took a deep breath. He knew how much it took for Latifa to say that. 'You're not your brother, Latifa,' he replied. 'You're not your brother.'

She inclined her head. 'You are leaving a lot behind, Will. Are you sure this is what you want?'

'You're wrong,' Will replied. 'I don't have anything to stay for.' He smiled. 'Only memories. And like I say, memories –'

'– travel with you.'

'Exactly.' He took her lightly by the arm. 'The train for Paris leaves in ten minutes. We need to be on it. Are you ready?'

That distant look crossed her face again and for a moment she didn't speak. But when she did it was clearly and firmly, with a confidence that Will didn't expect.

'I'm ready.'

Will nodded and together they walked away from the statue into the teeming crowds of St Pancras.

And into whatever the uncertain future held.

EPILOGUE

Christmas Eve
Snow had fallen.

Father Jack Butler had a tradition. Every Christmas Eve he would walk around the cemetery of the Hereford church-yard, spending a few seconds at each of the many graves. He was not a young man and each year it took him a little longer to pay his silent respects to the dead. Today it chilled him just to look at the thick snow, but it was a tradition and a worthwhile one at that, he thought. He braced himself against the cold and started his annual round, shuffling through the white powder with creaky joints.

They were like old friends, some of these tombstones. Constant. Ever-present. They grew increasingly elderly with him, each year a little more marked and decrepit. But he drew a kind of comfort from the knowledge that these blocks of stone, these memorials to life – each of them holding their own secrets and stories – would outlive any of the visitors that came here for moments of quietness and reflection.

He found it more difficult to be so philosophical around the newer graves, however. This was a sadder part of the churchyard and seemed even more so today, covered with the silent blanket of snow. His eyes were caught by the fresh mounds covering the graves of the two men he had buried in the past week. Soldiers, both of them – it would be a good six months before their stone memorials were erected.

341

Addressing their families had been difficult. No one had been informed of the circumstances of their death and Father Jack Butler had been the incumbent of a Hereford church for long enough to know what *that* meant. He nodded respectfully at the two mounds of earth before turning back towards the church.

His route through the snow took him past that bit of the churchyard that always saddened him most. A single grave, but home to two bodies: a mother and daughter. They had been buried here for a couple of years now and each time he passed this stone he felt his very faith being questioned. He remembered their deaths; he remembered the horror of it. From time to time, after the funeral, he had seen, from a distance, a man at their graveside. The priest had watched him, watched how he stood, immobile and hunched, for such long periods of time. Such terribly long periods of time. Now and then he had considered approaching and talking to him. But when you have been a priest for as long as he had, you developed a kind of sixth sense, an intuition that tells you whether words of Christian comfort are likely to be of help to certain people.

Father Jack Butler's intuition had told him he would be of no help at all to that man.

As he passed the grave, he noticed something. Propped up against the tombstone, covered with a delicate dusting of snow, was a flower. A single flower. For some reason it caught the priest's heart and he walked a few steps nearer. He bent down to take a closer look and picked the flower up with his pale, shaking hands.

Tied to the rose with a piece of gold ribbon was a card. It was damp from the snow and he held it lightly, not wanting to damage the paper. In the corner of the card was a small, florid illustration, but it was not this that caught his eye. It was the writing in the middle. The blue ink was slightly smudged, but he could still tell that the handwriting was firm yet spidery – not like his own flowing copper-plate. It crossed the priest's mind that it was written by someone not used to holding a pen.

A single word. A simple word.

Goodbye.

Father Jack Butler blinked and he wondered what on earth it could mean. What story could possibly lie behind this plain, poignant message?

For a long while he stared at the card, but finally the cold got to him and he realised his hand was shaking more than usual. He gently replaced the flower, stood up and nodded respectfully at the tombstone that always reminded him of the violence there was in the world. Then he turned and slowly trudged back towards the church.

It was Christmas. A time for peace. There was a family service that afternoon, and he had much to do.